LUMBERJANES™

CAMPFIRE SONGS

BOOM!
BOX™

BOOM! BOX™ **LUMBERJANES CAMPFIRE SONGS, April 2020.** Published by BOOM! Box, a division of Boom Entertainment, Inc. Lumberjanes is ™ & © 2020 Shannon Watters, Grace Ellis, Noelle Stevenson & Brooklyn Allen. Originally published in single magazine form as BOOM! BOX'S SOME EN-HAUNTED EVENING 2017, LUMBERJANES: A MIDSUMMER NIGHT'S SCHEME No. 1, LUMBERJANES #50, LUMBERJANES: SOMEWHERE THAT'S GREEN No. 1 ™ & © 2017, 2018, 2019 Shannon Watters, Grace Ellis, Noelle Stevenson & Brooklyn Allen. All rights reserved. BOOM! Box™ and the BOOM! Box logo are trademarks of Boom Entertainment, Inc., registered in various countries and categories. All characters, events, and institutions depicted herein are fictional. Any similarity between any of the names, characters, persons, events, and/or institutions in this publication to actual names, characters, and persons, whether living or dead, events, and/or institutions is unintended and purely coincidental. BOOM! Box does not read or accept unsolicited submissions of ideas, stories, or artwork.

For information regarding the CPSIA on this printed material, call: (203) 595-3636 and provide reference #RICH – 883296.

BOOM! Studios, 5670 Wilshire Boulevard, Suite 400, Los Angeles, CA 90036-5679. Printed in USA. First Printing.

ISBN: 978-1-68415-567-5 eISBN: 978-1-64144-733-1

THIS LUMBERJANES FIELD MANUAL BELONGS TO:

NAME:_____

TROOP:_____

DATE INVESTED:_____

FIELD MANUAL TABLE OF CONTENTS

LUMBERJANES FIELD MANUAL

For the Intermediate Program

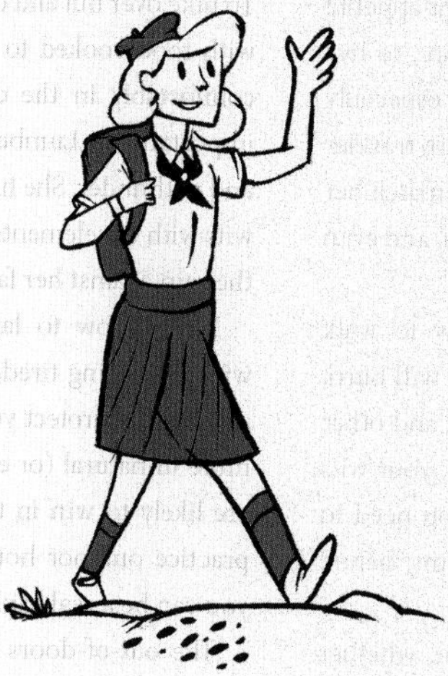

Prepared for the

Miss Qiunzella Thiskwin Penniquiqul Thistle Crumpet's

CAMP FOR [redacted] HARDCORE LADY-TYPES

"Friendship to the Max!"

A MESSAGE FROM THE LUMBERJANES HIGH COUNCIL

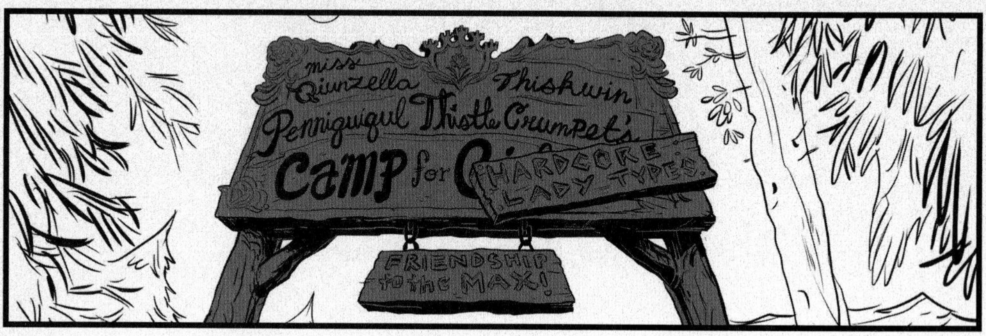
miss
Quinzella Thiskwin
Penniquiqul Thistle Crumpet's
Camp for
HARDCORE LADY TYPES
FRIENDSHIP to the MAX!

Wherever you go, there will be friends to make—companions to laugh with, sisters to find, bonds to forge and promises to keep. Some friends will become the people you carry with you in your heart wherever you go, for as long as you live. They will become the people you remember, whose words stay with you even long after you've forgotten the context in which they were spoken. The love you felt as an eleven, twelve, or thirteen-year-old will stay with you and grow alongside you, an ecosystem of its own, even when you are far away—in distance or in years—from the friends who inspired it.

It is also important to remember that the friendships of your childhood and teen years are not the only ones you will ever have, and that there are no deadlines on making bosom friends, or finding true connections. Our relationships are constantly changing—constantly breaking apart and forming anew. The pattern is always shifting, but always beautiful, even in those uncomfortable moments of transition or loneliness, when your next step feels wobbly and uncertain. There is value to be found in all sorts of relationships, even when that value can be hard to see at first, and we hope that you will make the effort. Let your friendships grow and change. Let them develop organically, growing towards the sun. Trust in your friends, and trust in your heart. They may lead you in directions you wouldn't expect, but you'll make wonderful discoveries along those paths.

THE LUMBERJANES PLEDGE

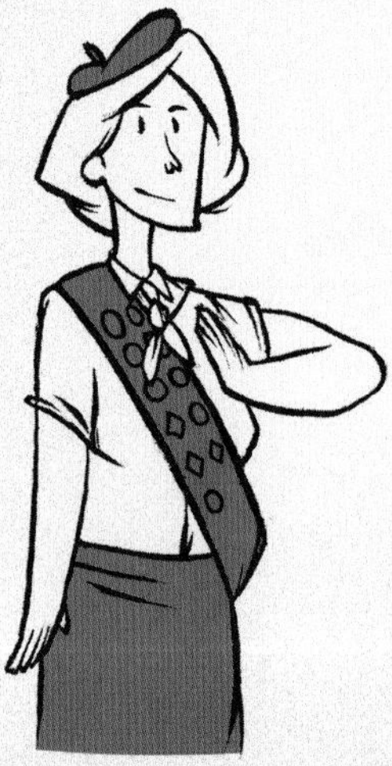

I solemnly swear to do my best
Every day, and in all that I do,
To be brave and strong,
To be truthful and compassionate,
To be interesting and interested,
To pay attention and question
The world around me,
To think of others first,
To always help and protect my friends,
[redacted]
And to make the world a better place
For Lumberjane scouts
And for everyone else.

THEN THERE'S A LINE ABOUT GOD, OR WHATEVER

LUMBERJANES™
CAMPFIRE SONGS

Created by **Shannon Watters, Grace Ellis, Noelle Stevenson & Brooklyn Allen**

A Midsummer Night's Scheme

Written by
Nicole Andelfinger

Illustrated by
Maddi Gonzalez

A Pondering Mystery

Written & Illustrated by
Brittney Williams

Somewhere That's Green

Written by
Seanan McGuire

Illustrated by
Alexa Bosy

Weather Woes

Written & Illustrated by
Mari Costa

Lettered by **Ariana Maher**

Some En-Haunted Evening

Written by
Liz Prince

Illustrated by
Kat Leyh

Colored by
Sarah Stern

Lettered by
Jim Campbell

COADY AND THE CREEPIES
created by **Liz Prince** & **Amanda Kirk**

GIANT DAYS
created by **John Allison**

GOLDIE VANCE
created by **Hope Larson** & **Brittney Williams**

HEAVY VINYL
created by **Carly Usdin**

MISFIT CITY
created by **Kirsten "Kiwi" Smith** & **Kurt Lustgarten**

SLAM!
created by **Pamela Ribon** & **Veronica Fish**

A Memory

Written by
Shannon Watters

Illustrated by
Brooklyn Allen

Colored by
Maarta Laiho

Lettered by
Aubrey Aiese

Cover by
Kris Anka

Pin Designs
Marie Krupina
Grace Park

Designer
Marie Krupina

Series Editors
Dafna Pleban
Sophie Philips-Roberts

Collection Editors
Jeanine Schaefer
Sophie Philips-Roberts

*Special thanks to **Kelsey Pate** for giving the Lumberjanes their name.*

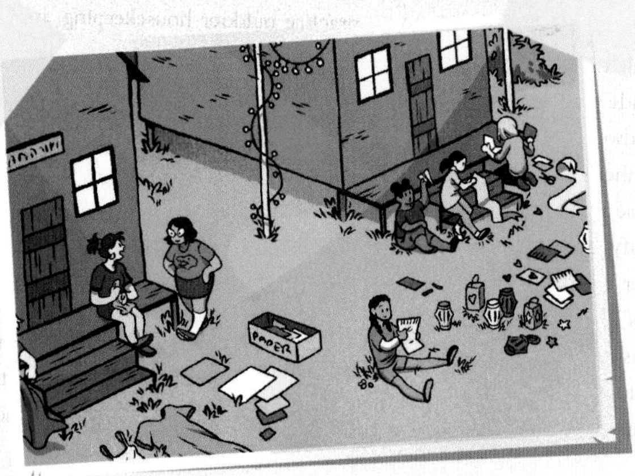
PAPER

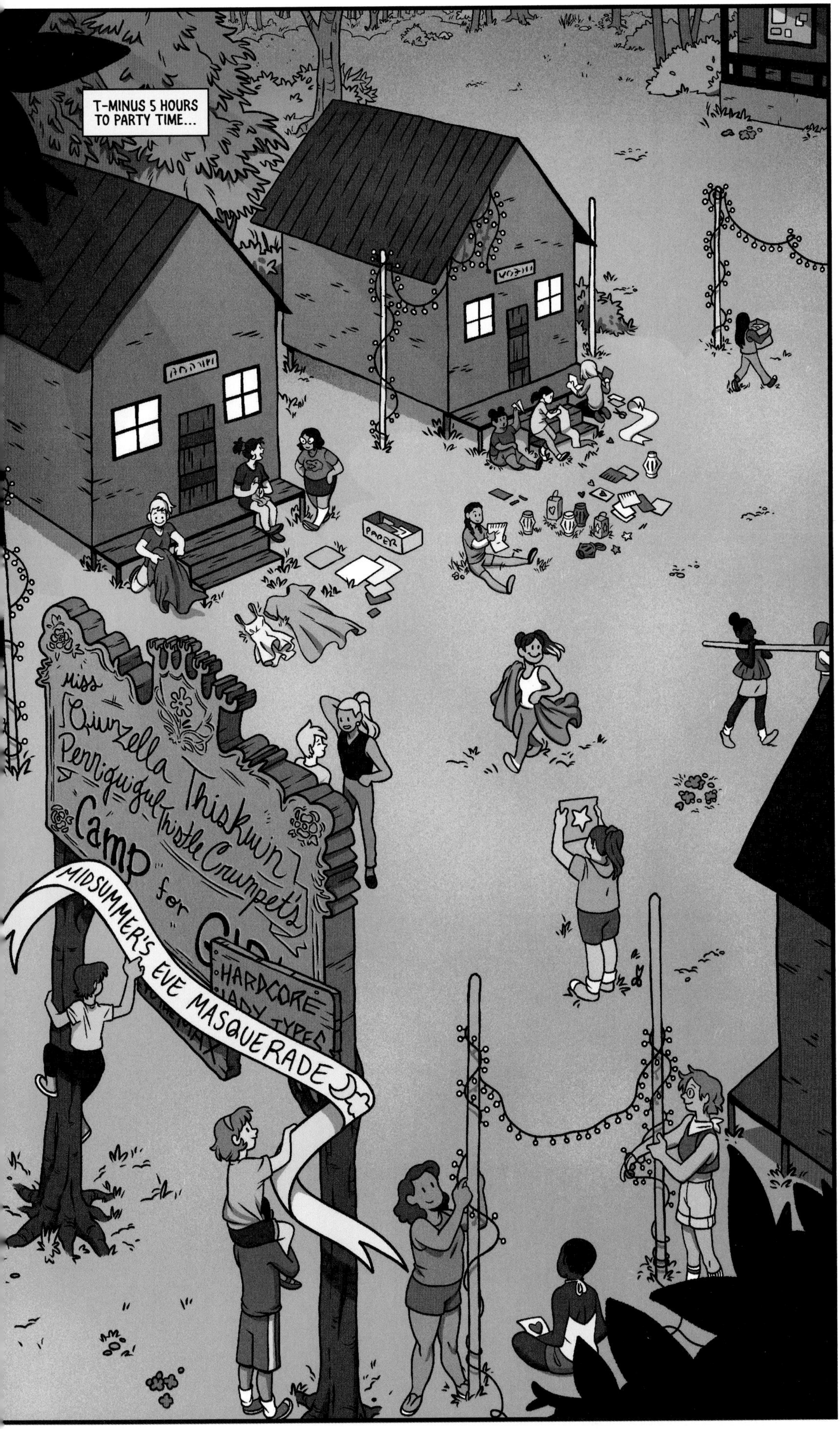
T-MINUS 5 HOURS TO PARTY TIME...
Miss Qiunzella Thiskwin Penniquiqul Thistle Crumpet's
Camp for
HARDCORE
MIDSUMMER'S EVE MASQUERADE
PAPER

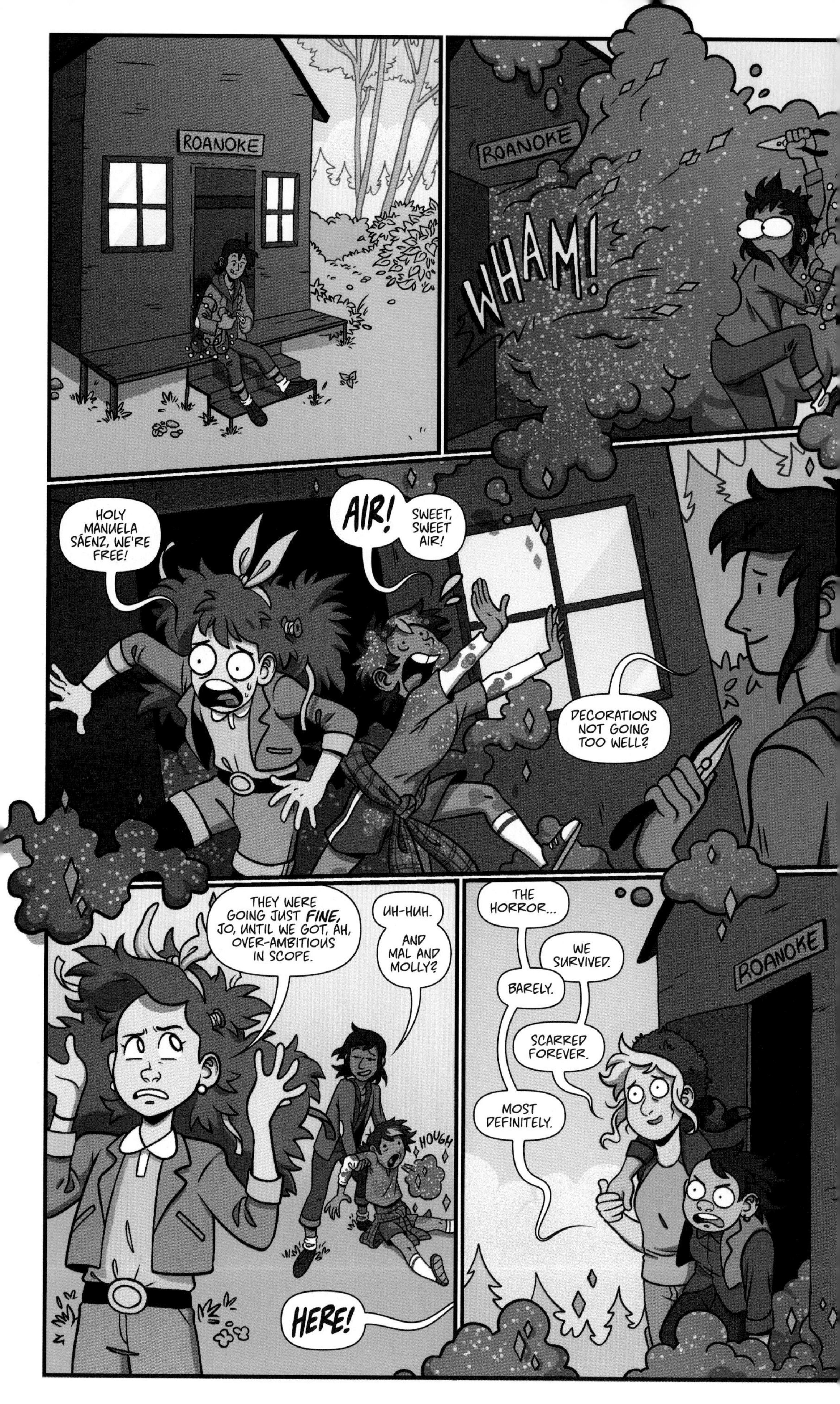
ROANOKE
ROANOKE
WHAM!
HOLY MANUELA SÁENZ, WE'RE FREE!
AIR!
SWEET, SWEET AIR!
DECORATIONS NOT GOING TOO WELL?
THEY WERE GOING JUST FINE, JO, UNTIL WE GOT, AH, OVER-AMBITIOUS IN SCOPE.
UH-HUH.
AND MAL AND MOLLY?
HOUGH
HERE!
THE HORROR...
WE SURVIVED.
BARELY.
SCARRED FOREVER.
MOST DEFINITELY.
ROANOKE

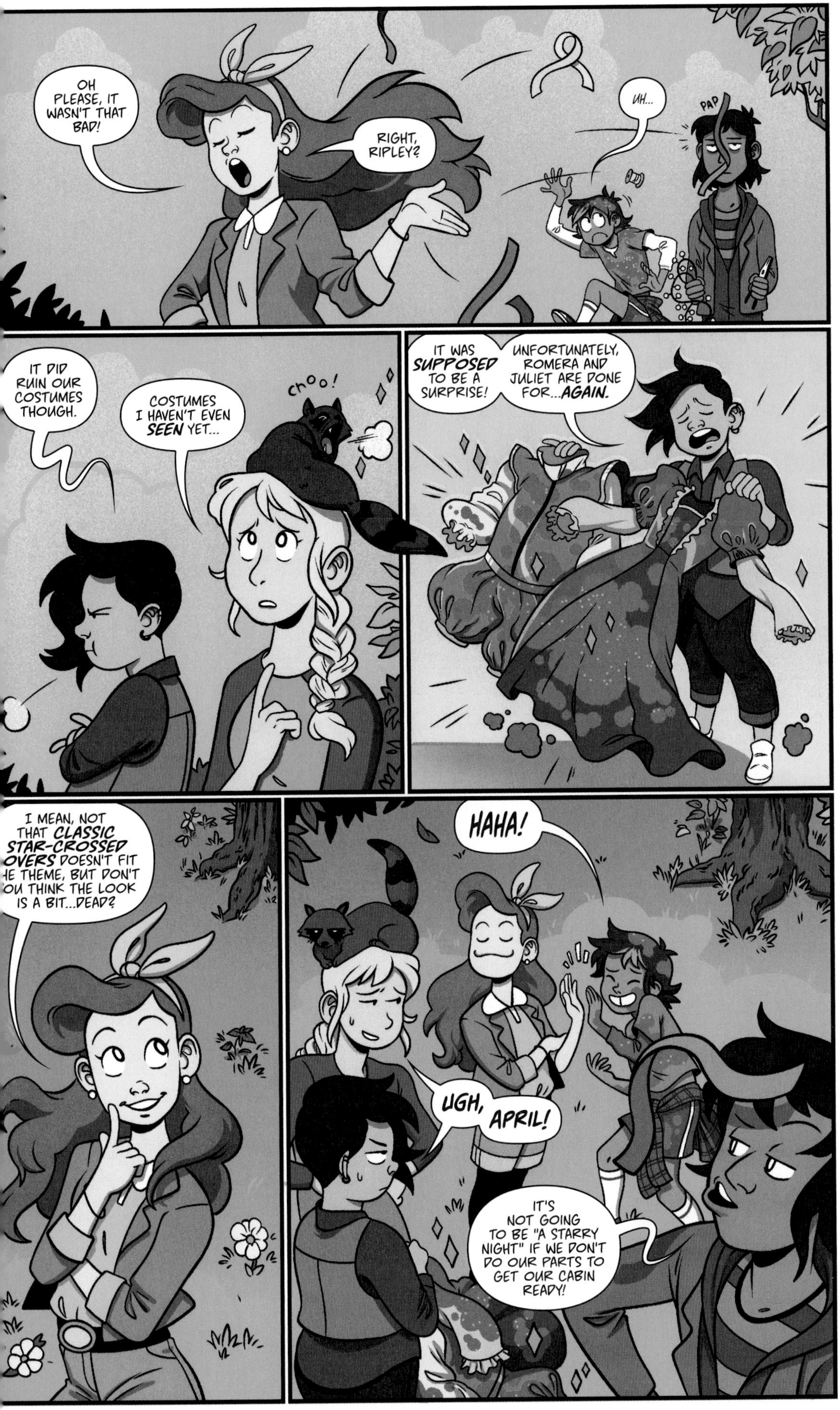
OH PLEASE, IT WASN'T THAT BAD!
RIGHT, RIPLEY?
UH...
PAP
IT DID RUIN OUR COSTUMES THOUGH.
COSTUMES I HAVEN'T EVEN SEEN YET...
choo!
IT WAS SUPPOSED TO BE A SURPRISE!
UNFORTUNATELY, ROMERA AND JULIET ARE DONE FOR...AGAIN.
I MEAN, NOT THAT CLASSIC STAR-CROSSED OVERS DOESN'T FIT HE THEME, BUT DON'T OU THINK THE LOOK IS A BIT...DEAD?
HAHA!
UGH, APRIL!
IT'S NOT GOING TO BE "A STARRY NIGHT" IF WE DON'T DO OUR PARTS TO GET OUR CABIN READY!

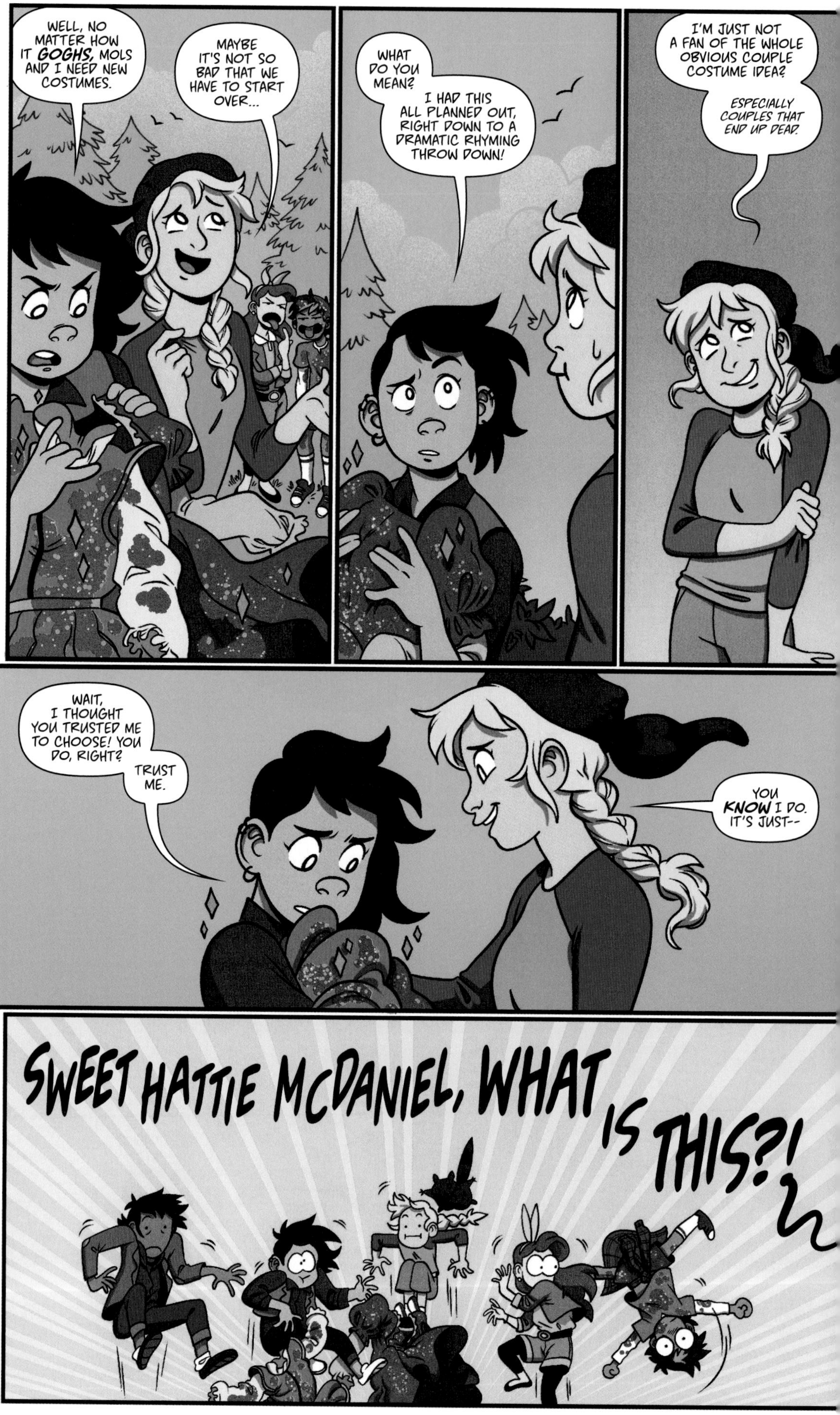
WELL, NO MATTER HOW IT GOGHS, MOLS AND I NEED NEW COSTUMES.
MAYBE IT'S NOT SO BAD THAT WE HAVE TO START OVER...
WHAT DO YOU MEAN?
I HAD THIS ALL PLANNED OUT, RIGHT DOWN TO A DRAMATIC RHYMING THROW DOWN!
I'M JUST NOT A FAN OF THE WHOLE OBVIOUS COUPLE COSTUME IDEA?
ESPECIALLY COUPLES THAT END UP DEAD.
WAIT, I THOUGHT YOU TRUSTED ME TO CHOOSE! YOU DO, RIGHT?
TRUST ME.
YOU KNOW I DO. IT'S JUST--
SWEET HATTIE McDANIEL, WHAT IS THIS?!

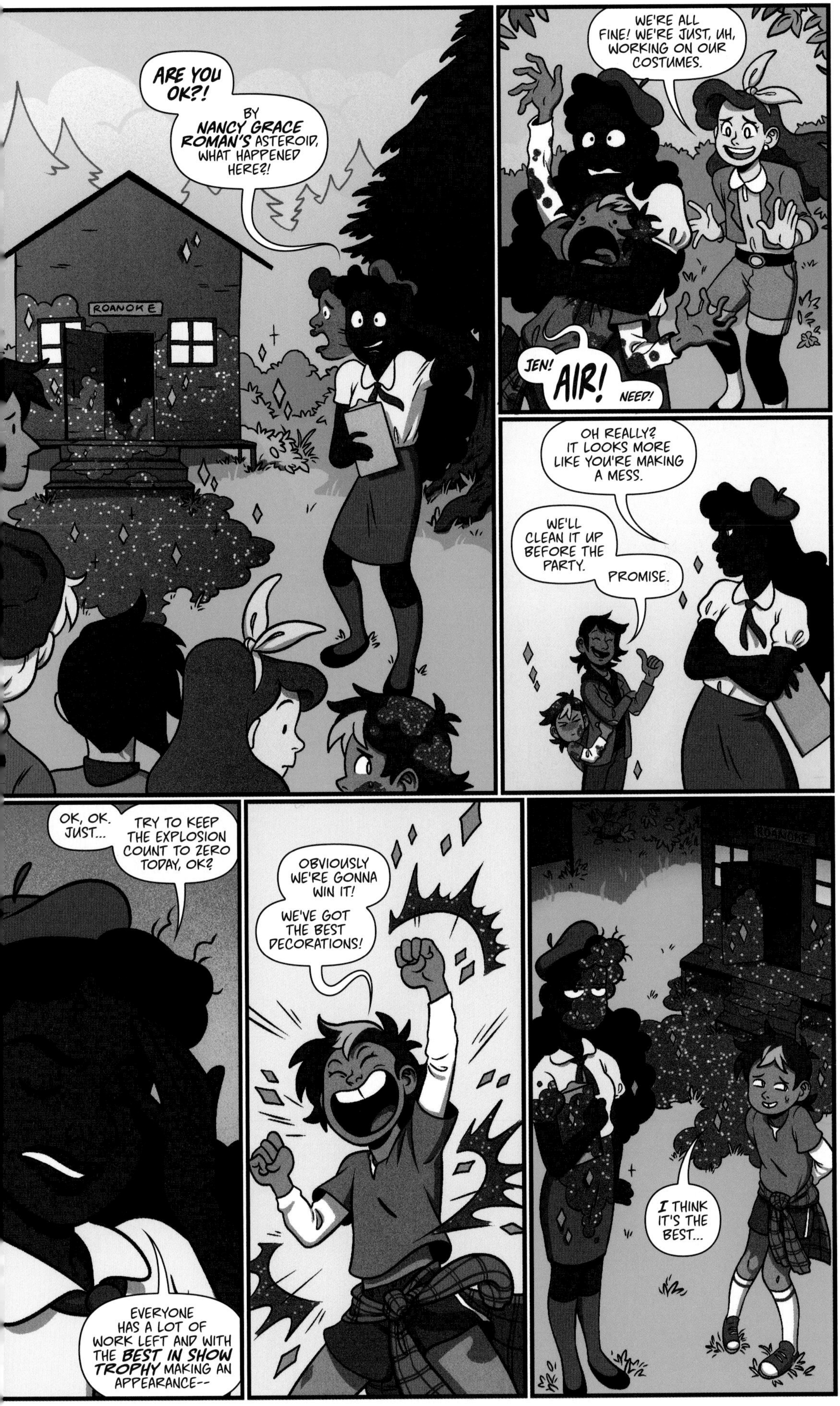
ARE YOU OK?!
BY NANCY GRACE ROMAN'S ASTEROID, WHAT HAPPENED HERE?!
ROANOKE
WE'RE ALL FINE! WE'RE JUST, UH, WORKING ON OUR COSTUMES.
JEN! AIR! NEED!
OH REALLY? IT LOOKS MORE LIKE YOU'RE MAKING A MESS.
WE'LL CLEAN IT UP BEFORE THE PARTY.
PROMISE.
OK, OK. JUST...
TRY TO KEEP THE EXPLOSION COUNT TO ZERO TODAY, OK?
EVERYONE HAS A LOT OF WORK LEFT AND WITH THE BEST IN SHOW TROPHY MAKING AN APPEARANCE--
OBVIOUSLY WE'RE GONNA WIN IT!
WE'VE GOT THE BEST DECORATIONS!
ROANOKE
I THINK IT'S THE BEST...

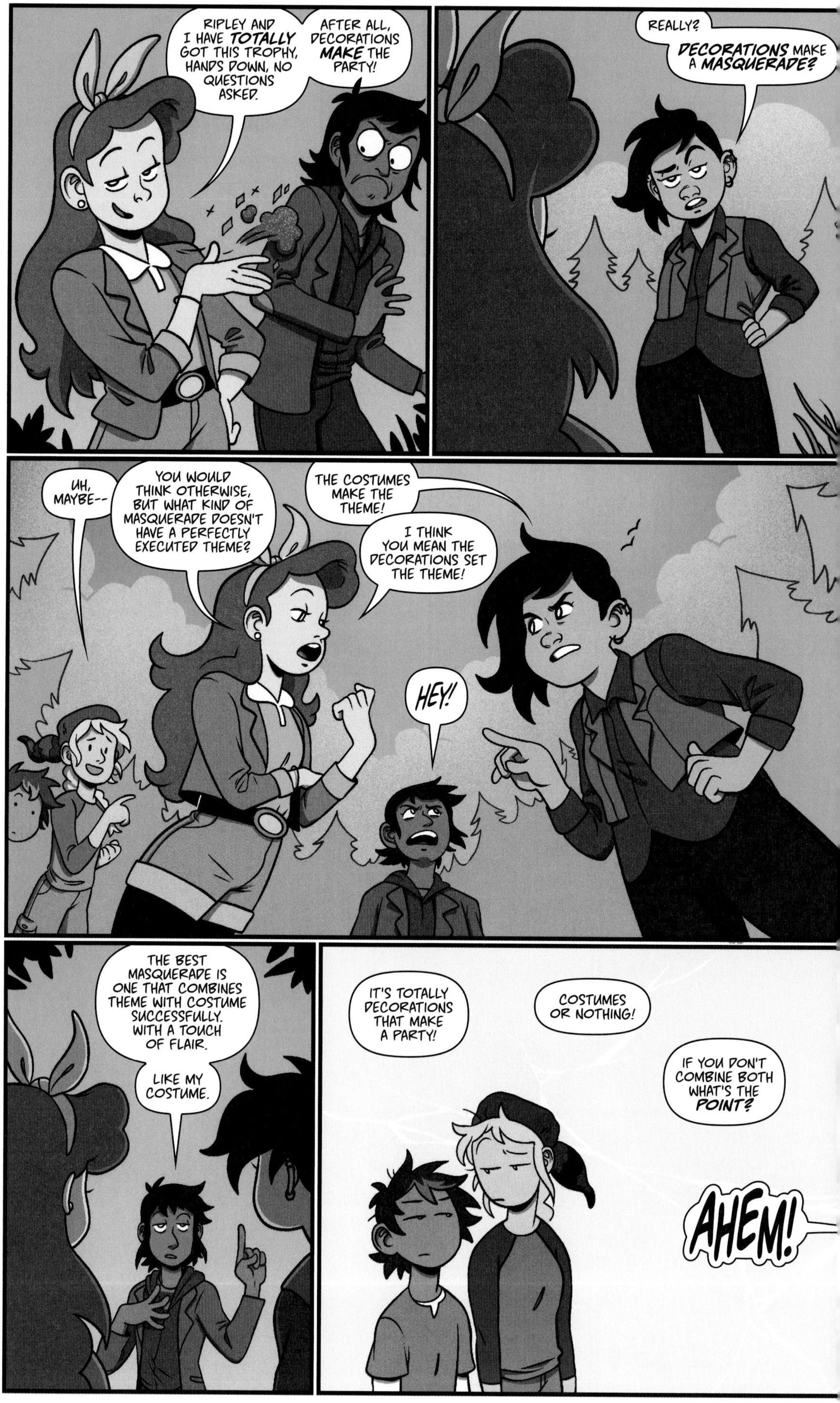
RIPLEY AND I HAVE TOTALLY GOT THIS TROPHY, HANDS DOWN, NO QUESTIONS ASKED.
AFTER ALL, DECORATIONS MAKE THE PARTY!
REALLY?
DECORATIONS MAKE A MASQUERADE?
UH, MAYBE--
YOU WOULD THINK OTHERWISE, BUT WHAT KIND OF MASQUERADE DOESN'T HAVE A PERFECTLY EXECUTED THEME?
THE COSTUMES MAKE THE THEME!
I THINK YOU MEAN THE DECORATIONS SET THE THEME!
HEY!
THE BEST MASQUERADE IS ONE THAT COMBINES THEME WITH COSTUME SUCCESSFULLY. WITH A TOUCH OF FLAIR.
LIKE MY COSTUME.
IT'S TOTALLY DECORATIONS THAT MAKE A PARTY!
COSTUMES OR NOTHING!
IF YOU DON'T COMBINE BOTH WHAT'S THE POINT?
AHEM!

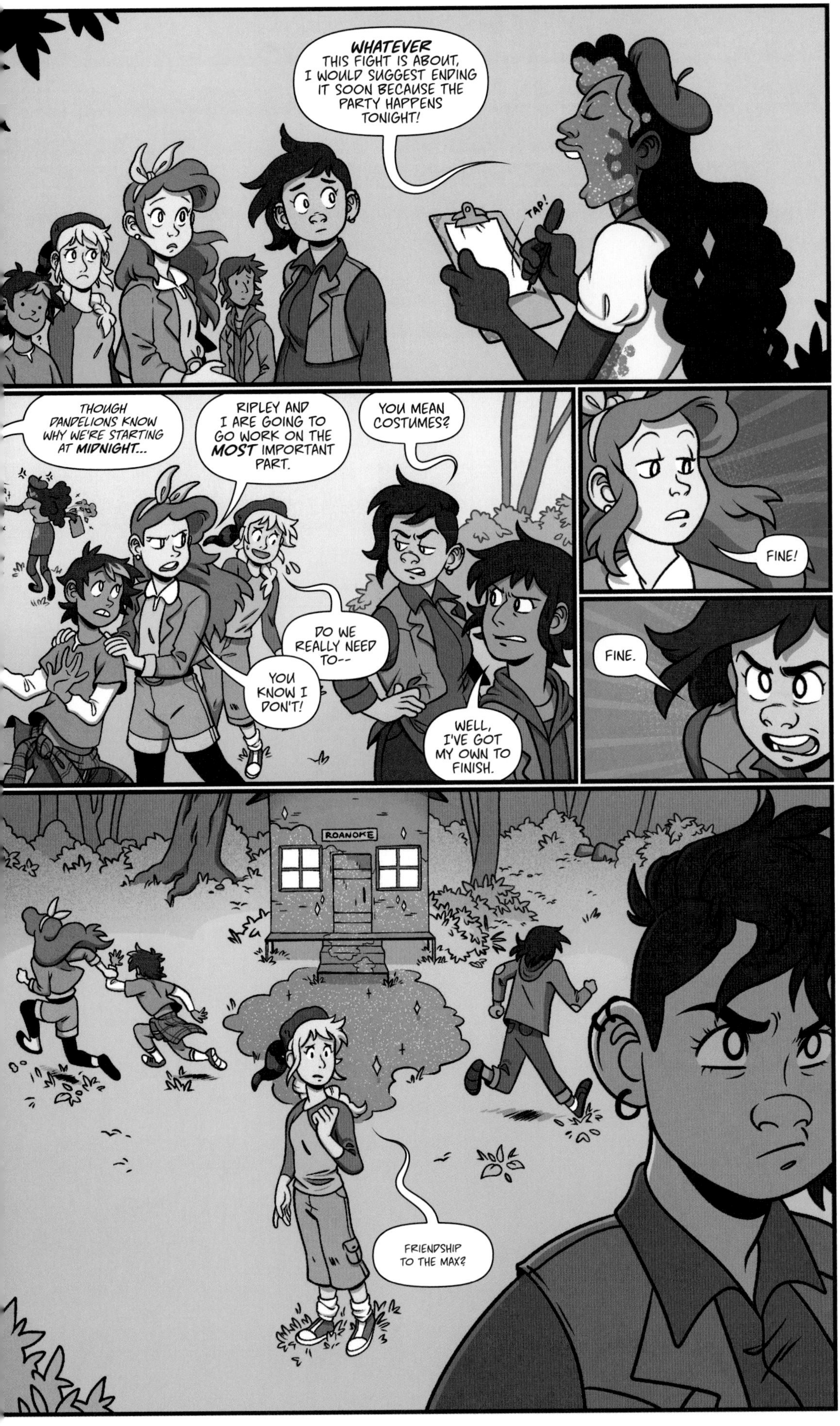
WHATEVER THIS FIGHT IS ABOUT, I WOULD SUGGEST ENDING IT SOON BECAUSE THE PARTY HAPPENS TONIGHT!
TAP!
THOUGH DANDELIONS KNOW WHY WE'RE STARTING AT MIDNIGHT...
RIPLEY AND I ARE GOING TO GO WORK ON THE MOST IMPORTANT PART.
YOU MEAN COSTUMES?
DO WE REALLY NEED TO--
YOU KNOW I DON'T!
WELL, I'VE GOT MY OWN TO FINISH.
FINE!
FINE.
ROANOKE
FRIENDSHIP TO THE MAX?

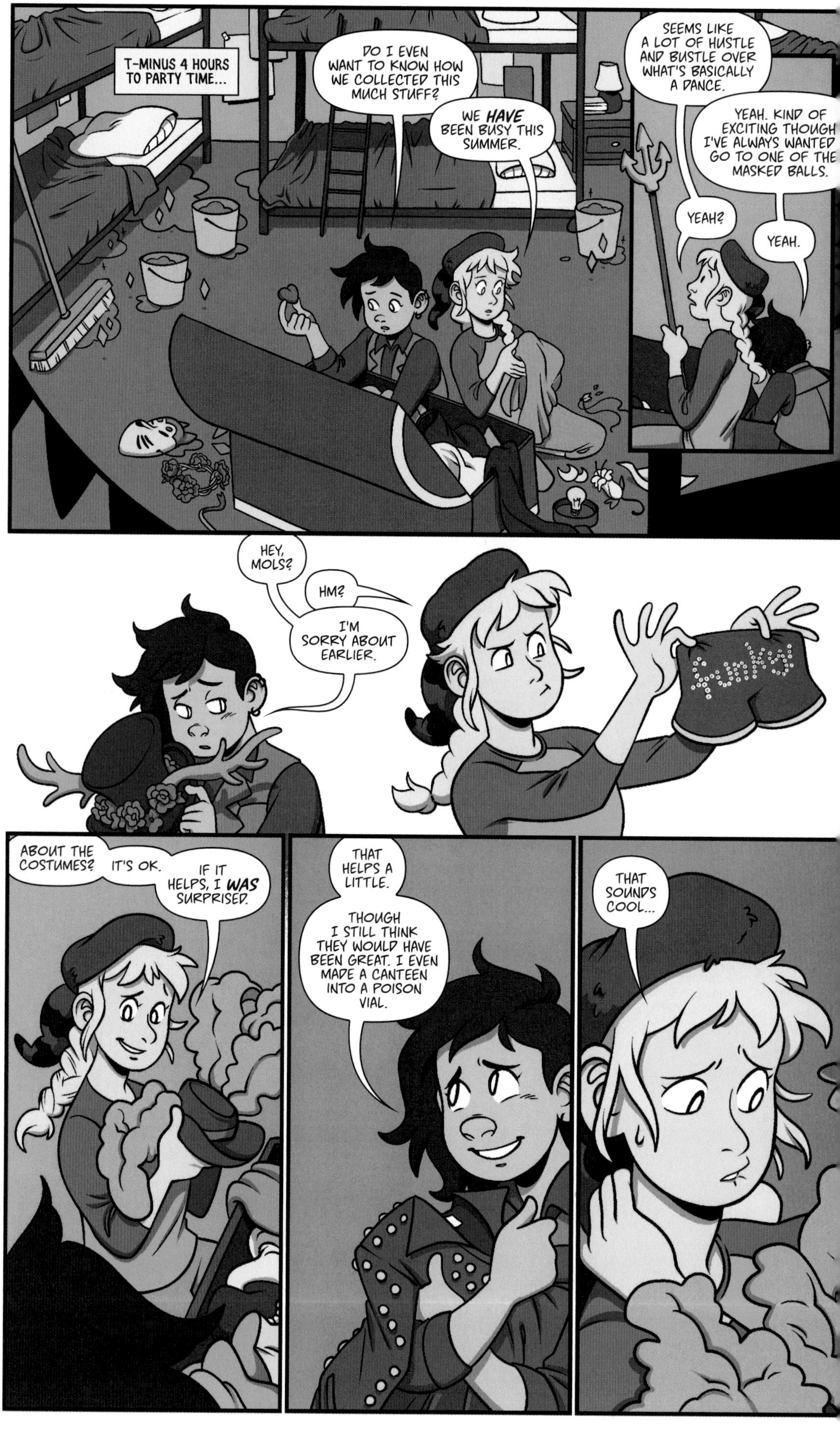
T-MINUS 4 HOURS TO PARTY TIME...
DO I EVEN WANT TO KNOW HOW WE COLLECTED THIS MUCH STUFF?
WE HAVE BEEN BUSY THIS SUMMER.
SEEMS LIKE A LOT OF HUSTLE AND BUSTLE OVER WHAT'S BASICALLY A DANCE.
YEAH?
YEAH. KIND OF EXCITING THOUGH. I'VE ALWAYS WANTED TO GO TO ONE OF THE MASKED BALLS.
YEAH.
HEY, MOLS?
HM?
I'M SORRY ABOUT EARLIER.
ABOUT THE COSTUMES?
IT'S OK.
IF IT HELPS, I WAS SURPRISED.
THAT HELPS A LITTLE.
THOUGH I STILL THINK THEY WOULD HAVE BEEN GREAT. I EVEN MADE A CANTEEN INTO A POISON VIAL.
THAT SOUNDS COOL...

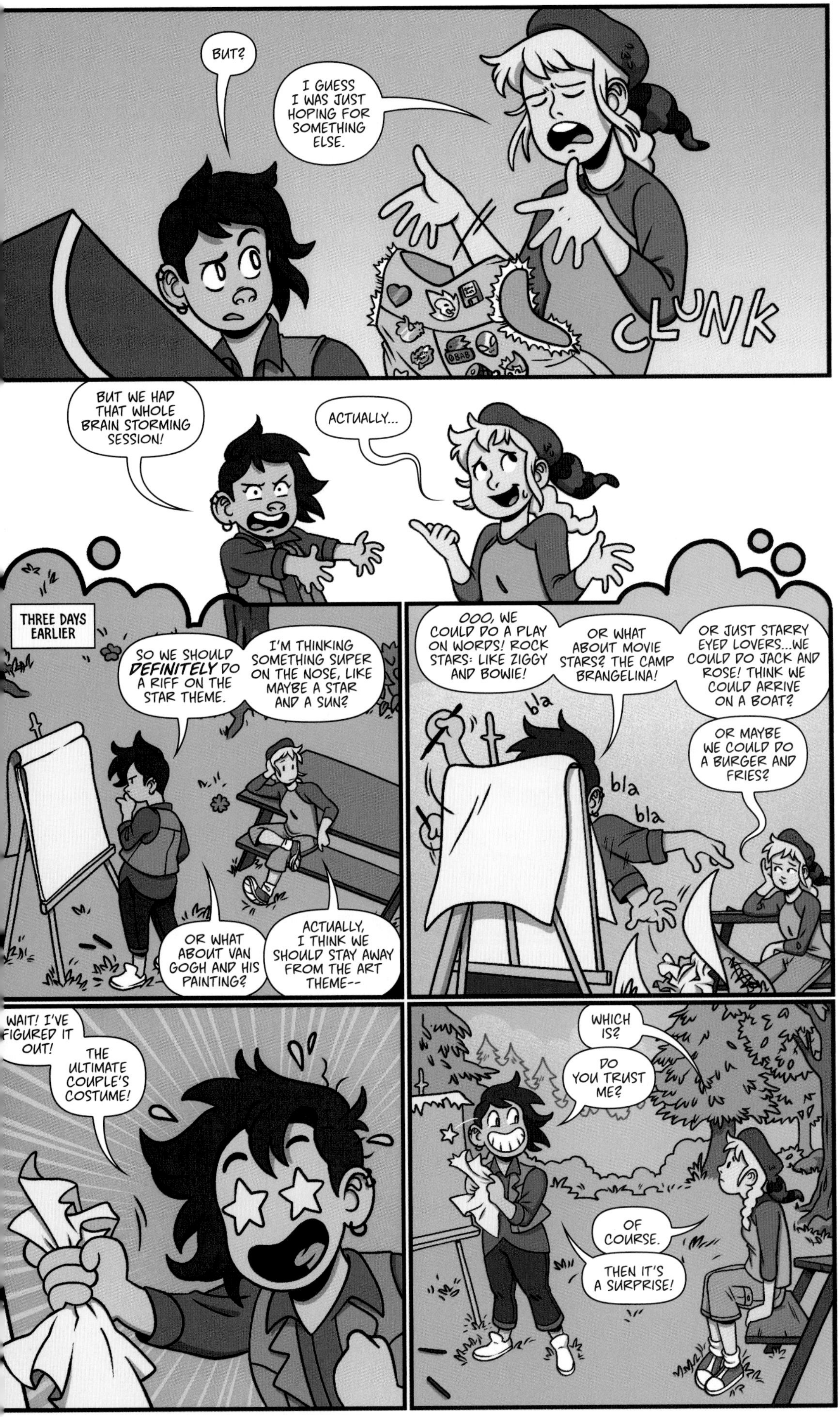
BUT?
I GUESS I WAS JUST HOPING FOR SOMETHING ELSE.
CLUNK
BUT WE HAD THAT WHOLE BRAIN STORMING SESSION!
ACTUALLY...
THREE DAYS EARLIER
SO WE SHOULD DEFINITELY DO A RIFF ON THE STAR THEME.
I'M THINKING SOMETHING SUPER ON THE NOSE, LIKE MAYBE A STAR AND A SUN?
OR WHAT ABOUT VAN GOGH AND HIS PAINTING?
ACTUALLY, I THINK WE SHOULD STAY AWAY FROM THE ART THEME--
OOO, WE COULD DO A PLAY ON WORDS! ROCK STARS: LIKE ZIGGY AND BOWIE!
OR WHAT ABOUT MOVIE STARS? THE CAMP BRANGELINA!
OR JUST STARRY EYED LOVERS...WE COULD DO JACK AND ROSE! THINK WE COULD ARRIVE ON A BOAT?
bla
bla
bla
OR MAYBE WE COULD DO A BURGER AND FRIES?
WAIT! I'VE FIGURED IT OUT!
THE ULTIMATE COUPLE'S COSTUME!
WHICH IS?
DO YOU TRUST ME?
OF COURSE.
THEN IT'S A SURPRISE!

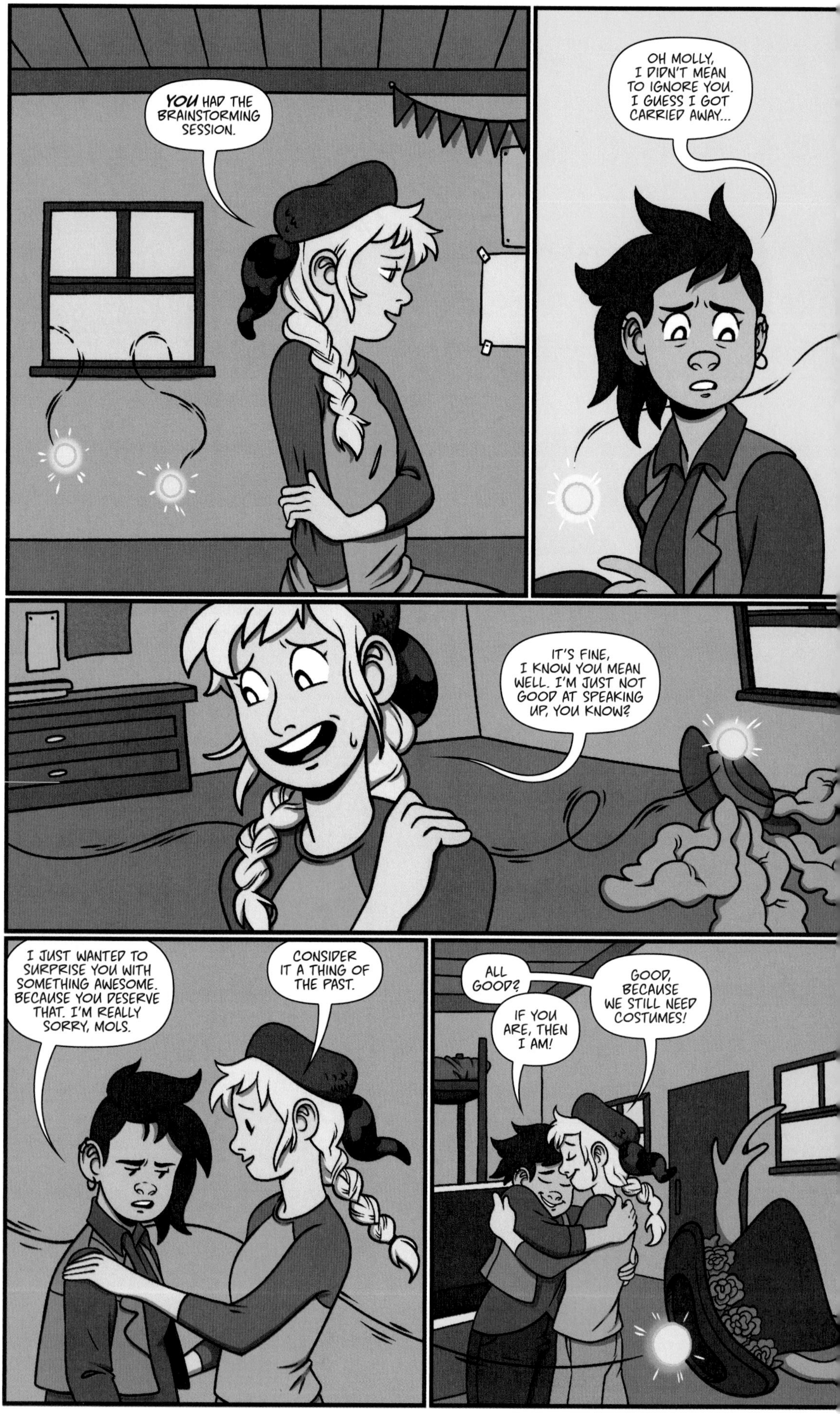
YOU HAD THE BRAINSTORMING SESSION.
OH MOLLY, I DIDN'T MEAN TO IGNORE YOU. I GUESS I GOT CARRIED AWAY...
IT'S FINE, I KNOW YOU MEAN WELL. I'M JUST NOT GOOD AT SPEAKING UP, YOU KNOW?
I JUST WANTED TO SURPRISE YOU WITH SOMETHING AWESOME. BECAUSE YOU DESERVE THAT. I'M REALLY SORRY, MOLS.
CONSIDER IT A THING OF THE PAST.
ALL GOOD?
IF YOU ARE, THEN I AM!
GOOD, BECAUSE WE STILL NEED COSTUMES!

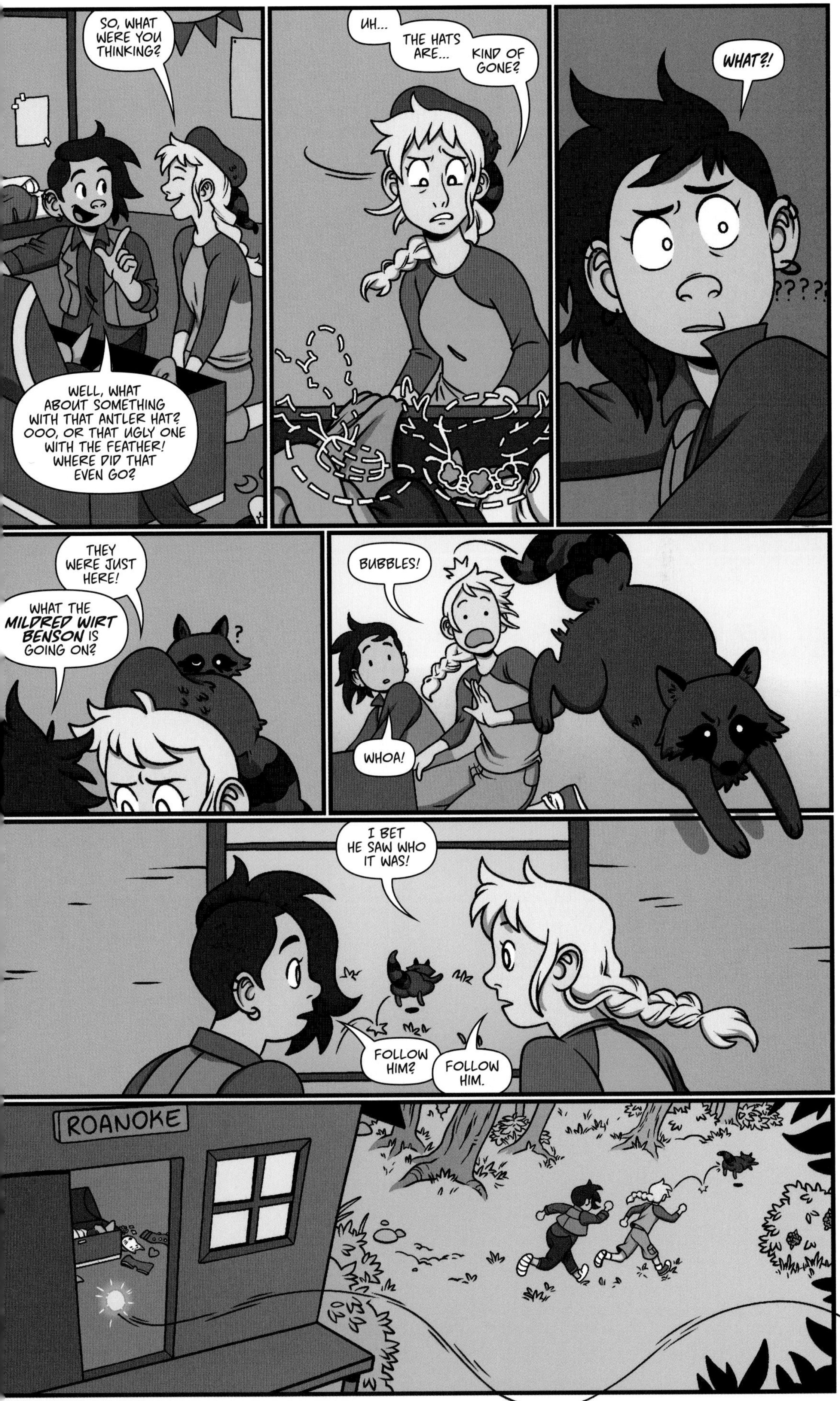
SO, WHAT WERE YOU THINKING?
WELL, WHAT ABOUT SOMETHING WITH THAT ANTLER HAT? OOO, OR THAT UGLY ONE WITH THE FEATHER! WHERE DID THAT EVEN GO?
UH...
THE HATS ARE...
KIND OF GONE?
WHAT?!
????
THEY WERE JUST HERE!
WHAT THE MILDRED WIRT BENSON IS GOING ON?
?
BUBBLES!
WHOA!
I BET HE SAW WHO IT WAS!
FOLLOW HIM?
FOLLOW HIM.
ROANOKE

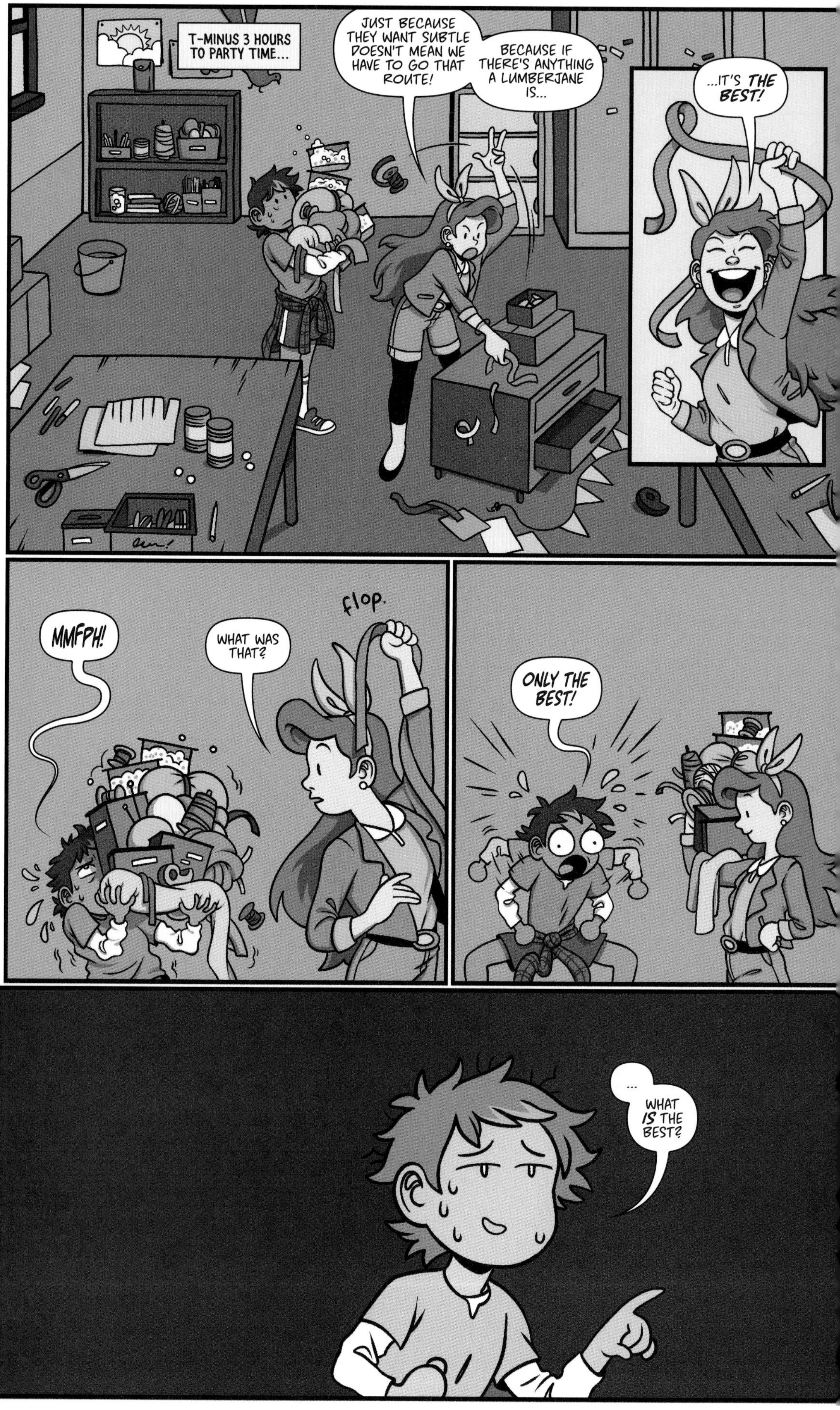
T-MINUS 3 HOURS TO PARTY TIME...
JUST BECAUSE THEY WANT SUBTLE DOESN'T MEAN WE HAVE TO GO THAT ROUTE!
BECAUSE IF THERE'S ANYTHING A LUMBERJANE IS...
...IT'S THE BEST!
MMFPH!
WHAT WAS THAT?
flop.
ONLY THE BEST!
... WHAT IS THE BEST?

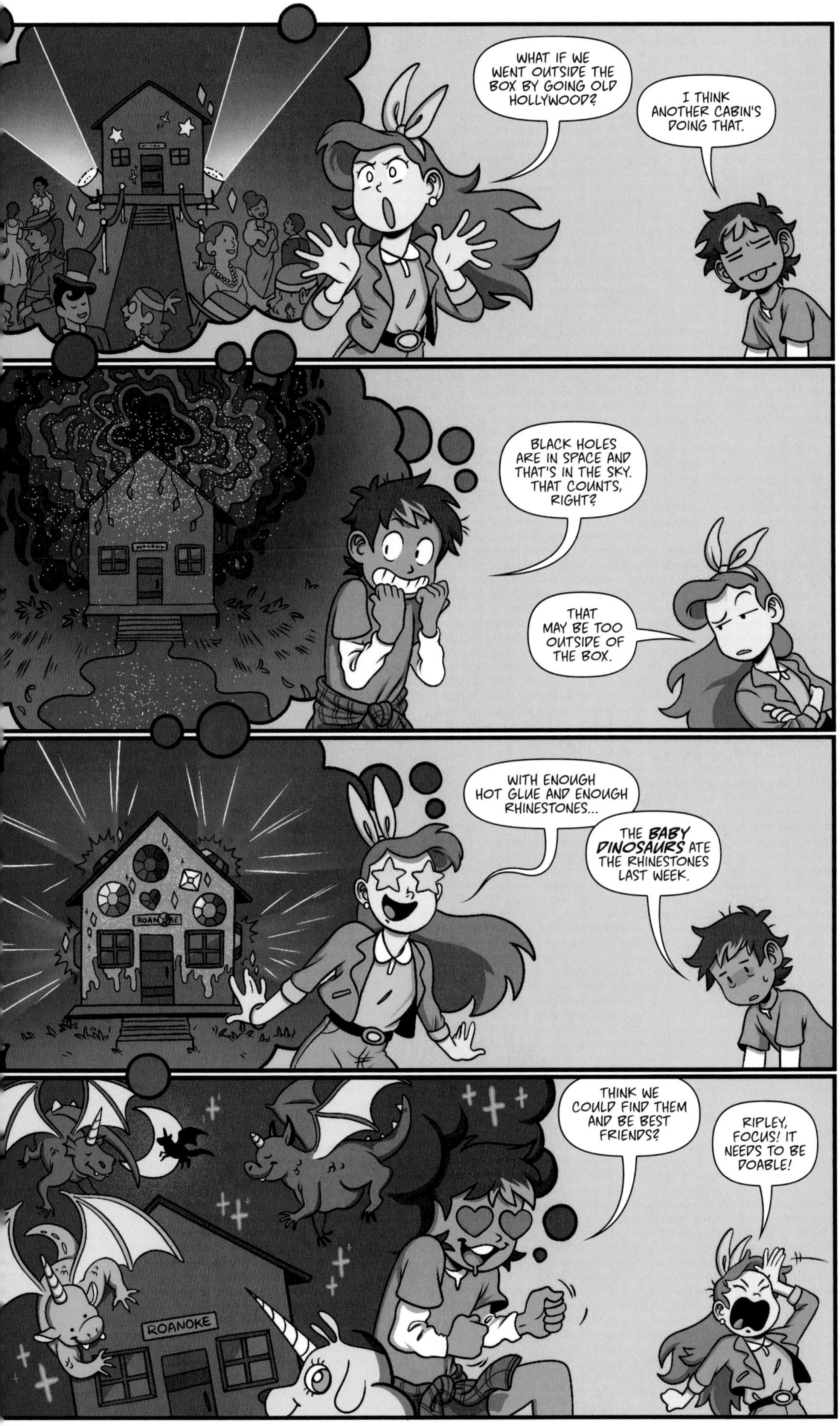
WHAT IF WE WENT OUTSIDE THE BOX BY GOING OLD HOLLYWOOD?
I THINK ANOTHER CABIN'S DOING THAT.
BLACK HOLES ARE IN SPACE AND THAT'S IN THE SKY. THAT COUNTS, RIGHT?
THAT MAY BE TOO OUTSIDE OF THE BOX.
WITH ENOUGH HOT GLUE AND ENOUGH RHINESTONES...
THE ***BABY DINOSAURS*** ATE THE RHINESTONES LAST WEEK.
THINK WE COULD FIND THEM AND BE BEST FRIENDS?
RIPLEY, FOCUS! IT NEEDS TO BE DOABLE!
ROANOKE

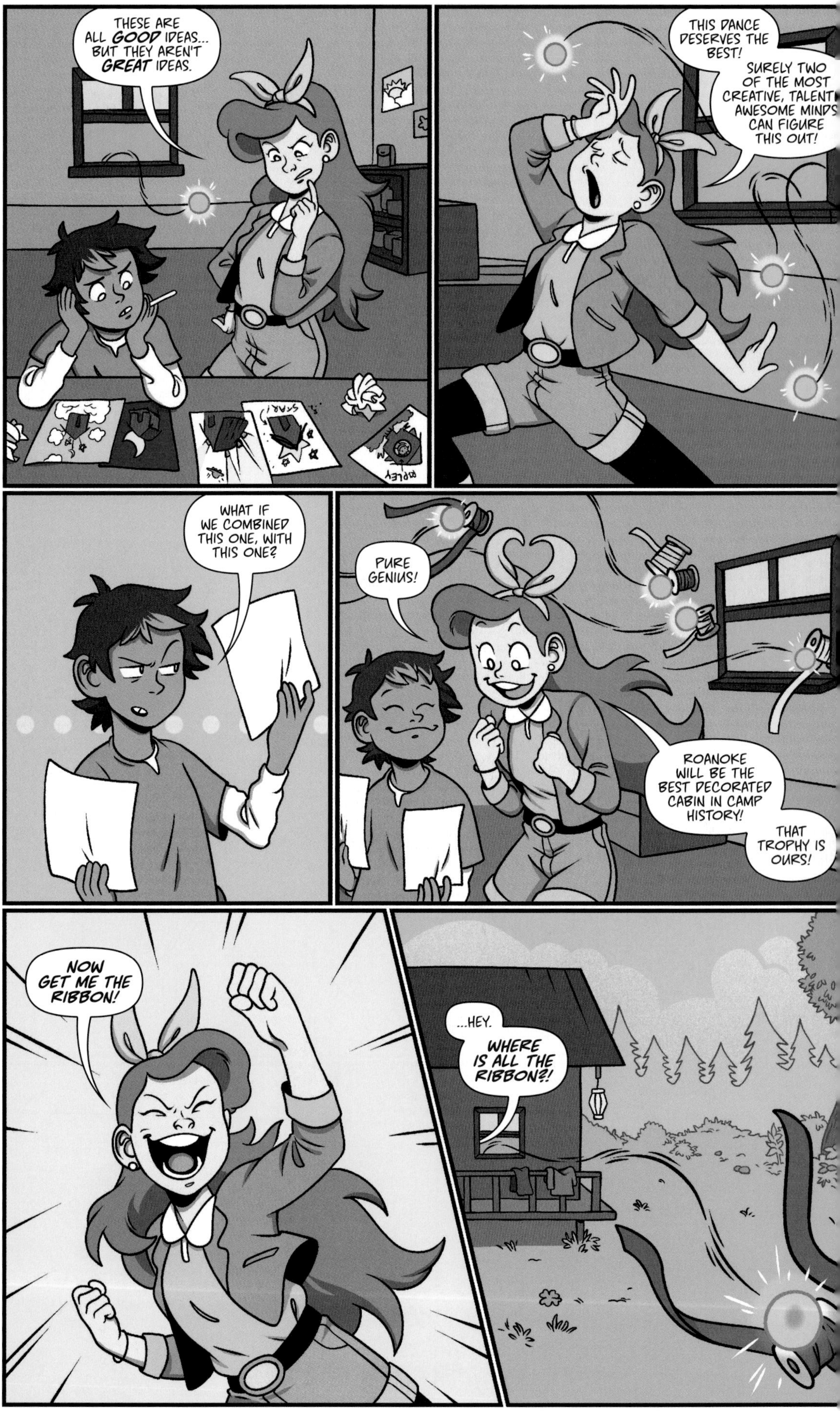
THESE ARE ALL GOOD IDEAS... BUT THEY AREN'T GREAT IDEAS.
THIS DANCE DESERVES THE BEST!
SURELY TWO OF THE MOST CREATIVE, TALENT AWESOME MINDS CAN FIGURE THIS OUT!
WHAT IF WE COMBINED THIS ONE, WITH THIS ONE?
PURE GENIUS!
ROANOKE WILL BE THE BEST DECORATED CABIN IN CAMP HISTORY!
THAT TROPHY IS OURS!
NOW GET ME THE RIBBON!
...HEY.
WHERE IS ALL THE RIBBON?!

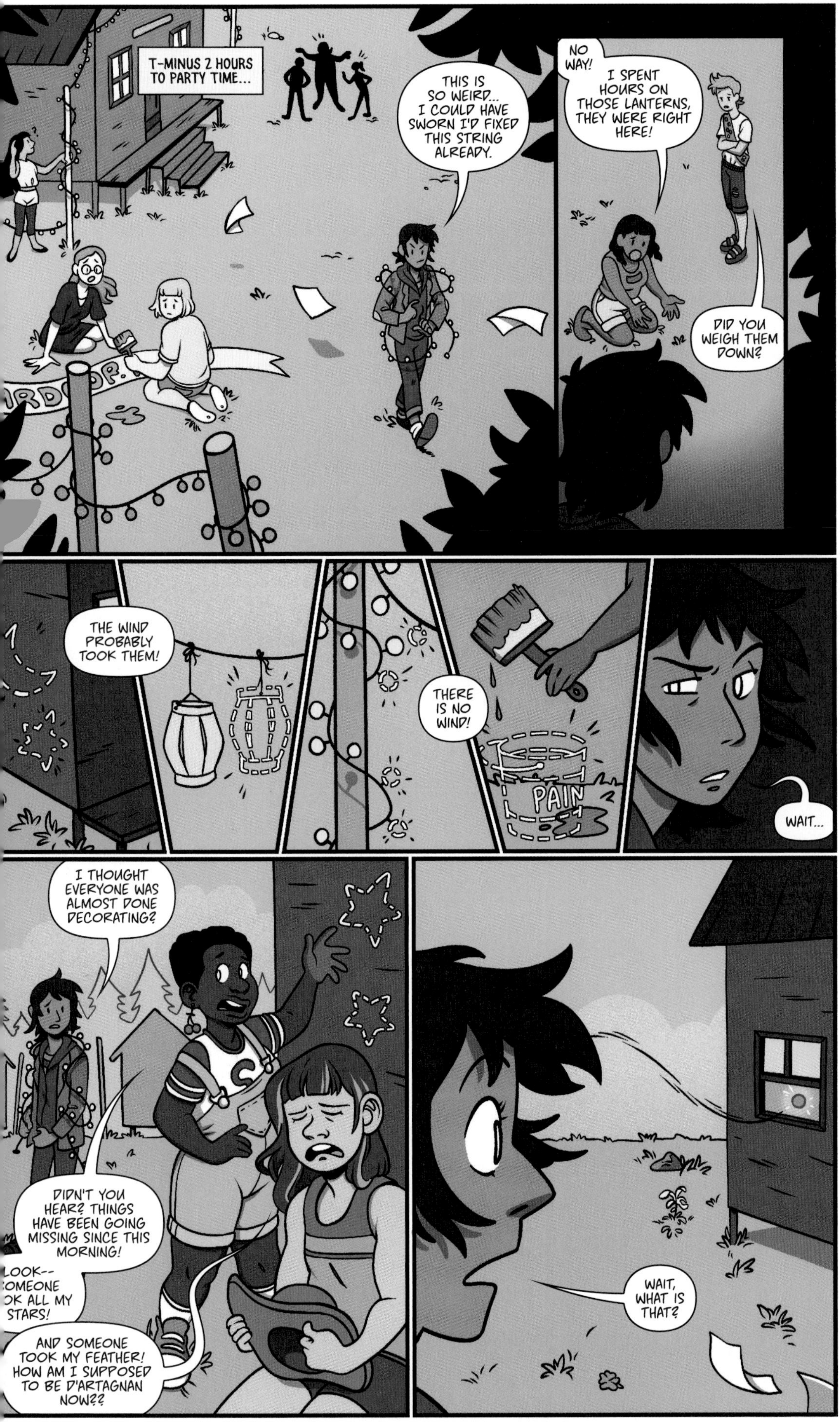
T-MINUS 2 HOURS TO PARTY TIME...
THIS IS SO WEIRD... I COULD HAVE SWORN I'D FIXED THIS STRING ALREADY.
NO WAY!
I SPENT HOURS ON THOSE LANTERNS, THEY WERE RIGHT HERE!
DID YOU WEIGH THEM DOWN?
THE WIND PROBABLY TOOK THEM!
THERE IS NO WIND!
PAIN
WAIT...
I THOUGHT EVERYONE WAS ALMOST DONE DECORATING?
DIDN'T YOU HEAR? THINGS HAVE BEEN GOING MISSING SINCE THIS MORNING!
LOOK-- SOMEONE OK ALL MY STARS!
AND SOMEONE TOOK MY FEATHER! HOW AM I SUPPOSED TO BE D'ARTAGNAN NOW??
WAIT, WHAT IS THAT?

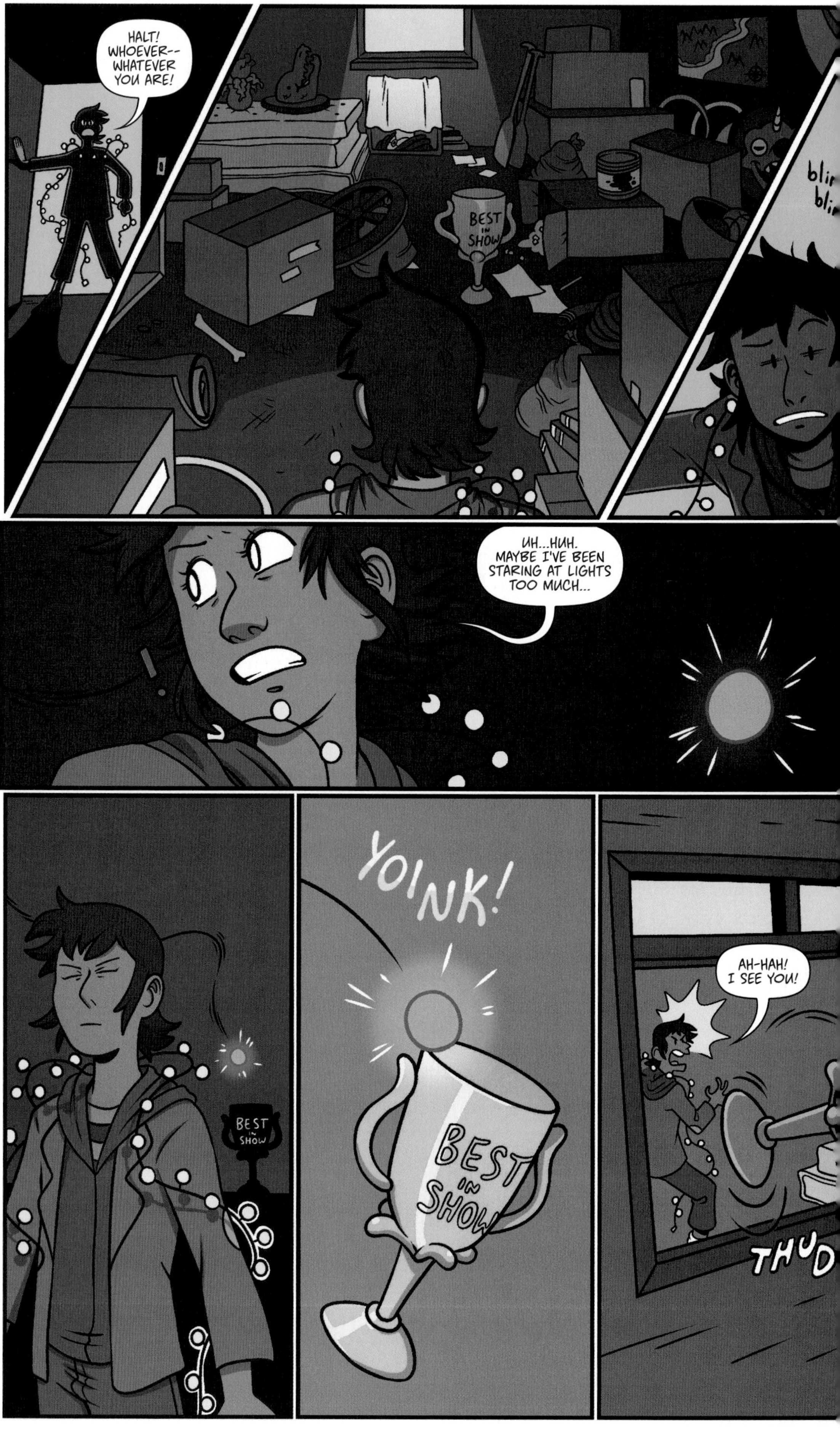
HALT! WHOEVER-- WHATEVER YOU ARE!
BEST IN SHOW
blir
blir
UH...HUH. MAYBE I'VE BEEN STARING AT LIGHTS TOO MUCH...
BEST IN SHOW
YOINK!
BEST IN SHOW
AH-HAH! I SEE YOU!
THUD

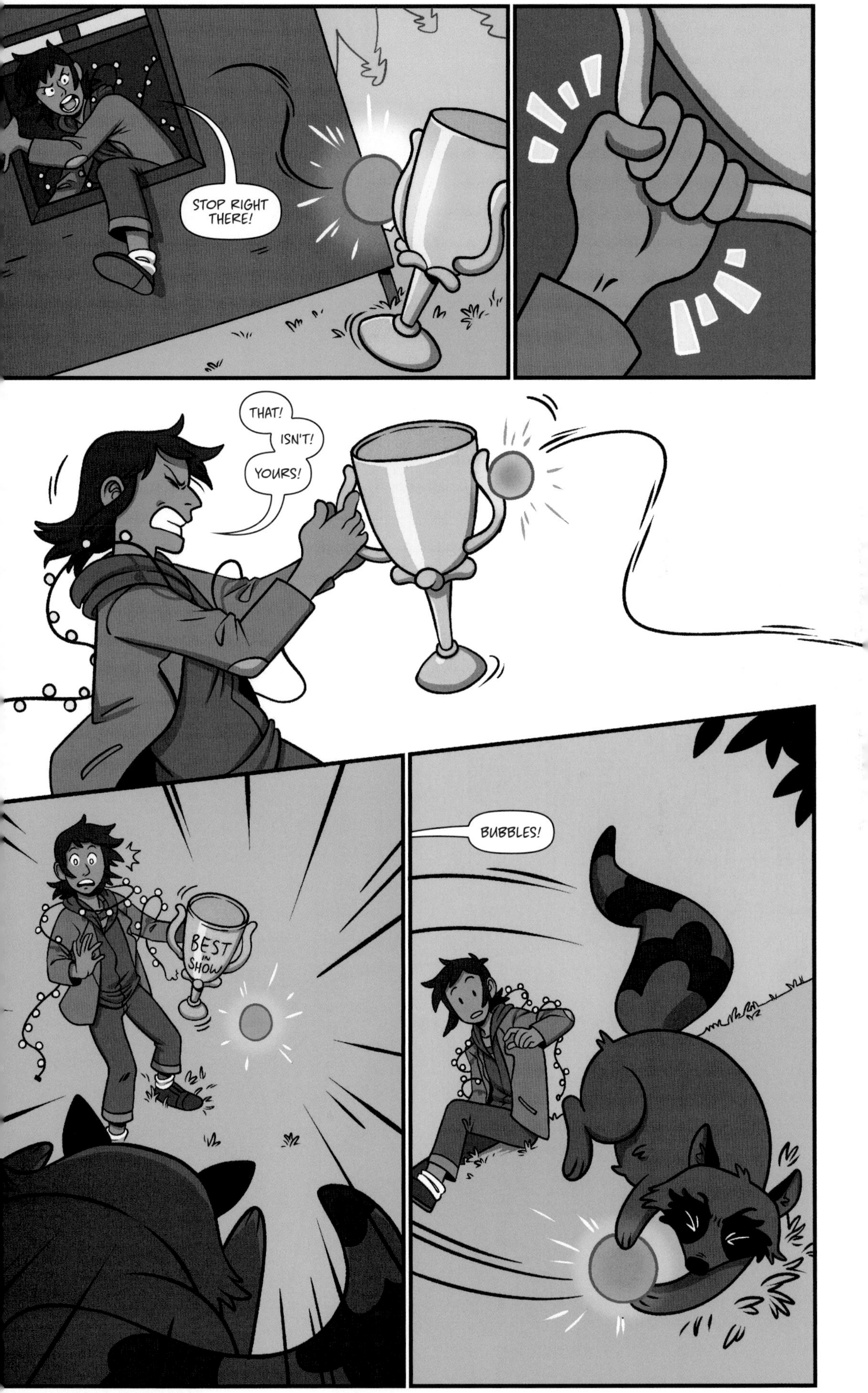
STOP RIGHT THERE!
THAT!
ISN'T!
YOURS!
BEST IN SHOW
BUBBLES!

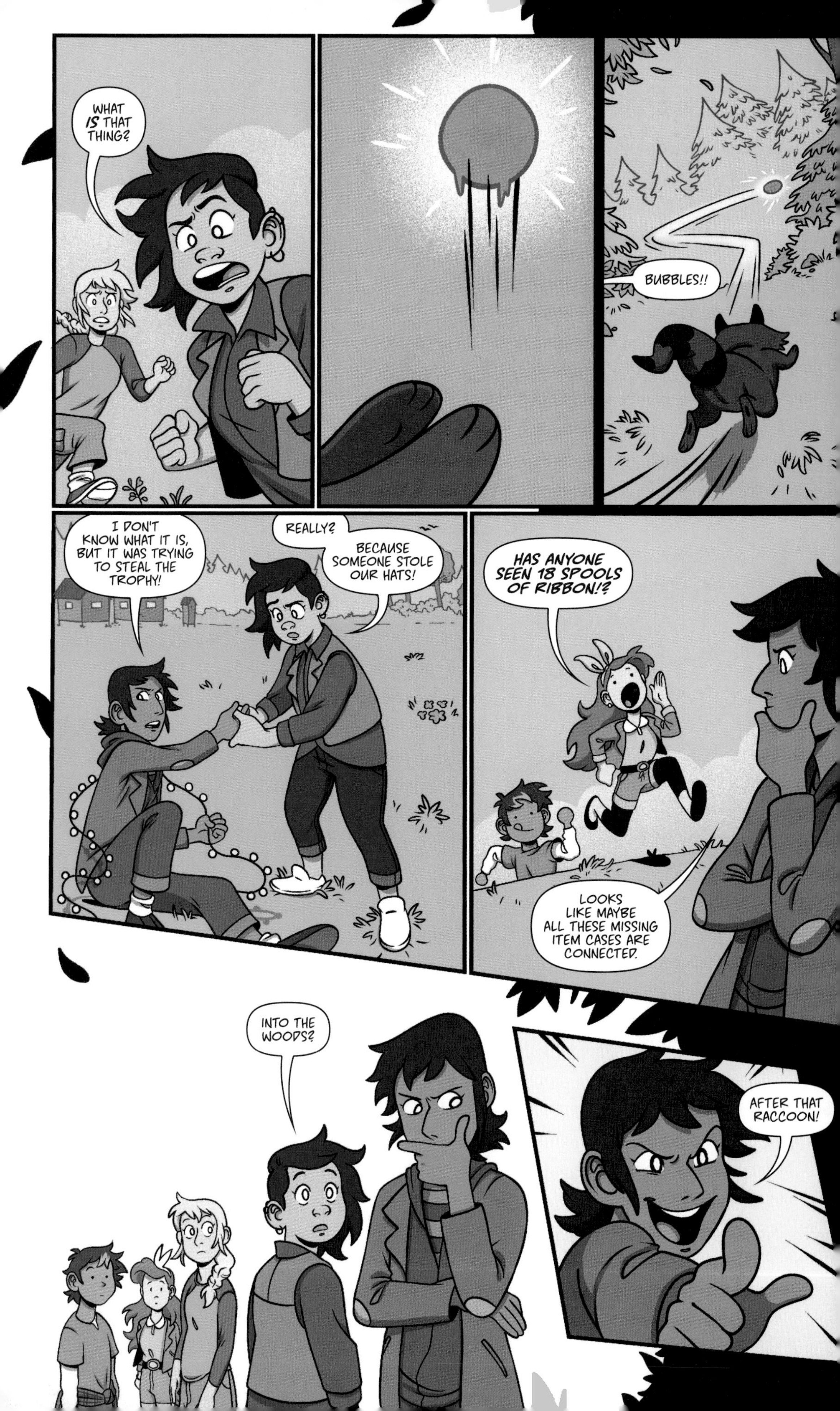
WHAT IS THAT THING?
BUBBLES!!
I DON'T KNOW WHAT IT IS, BUT IT WAS TRYING TO STEAL THE TROPHY!
REALLY?
BECAUSE SOMEONE STOLE OUR HATS!
HAS ANYONE SEEN 18 SPOOLS OF RIBBON!?
LOOKS LIKE MAYBE ALL THESE MISSING ITEM CASES ARE CONNECTED.
INTO THE WOODS?
AFTER THAT RACCOON!

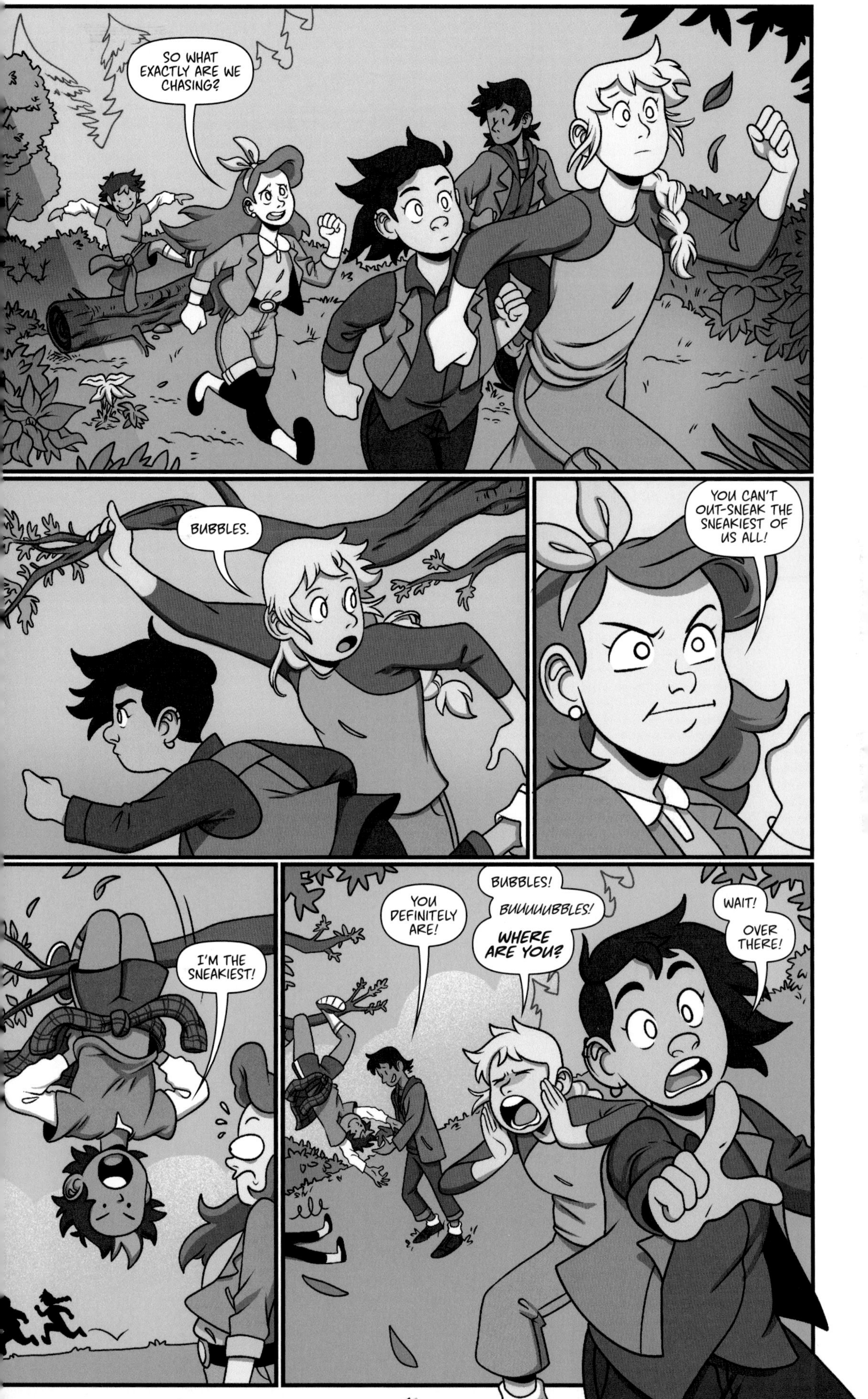
SO WHAT EXACTLY ARE WE CHASING?
BUBBLES.
YOU CAN'T OUT-SNEAK THE SNEAKIEST OF US ALL!
I'M THE SNEAKIEST!
YOU DEFINITELY ARE!
BUBBLES!
BUUUUUBBLES!
WHERE ARE YOU?
WAIT!
OVER THERE!

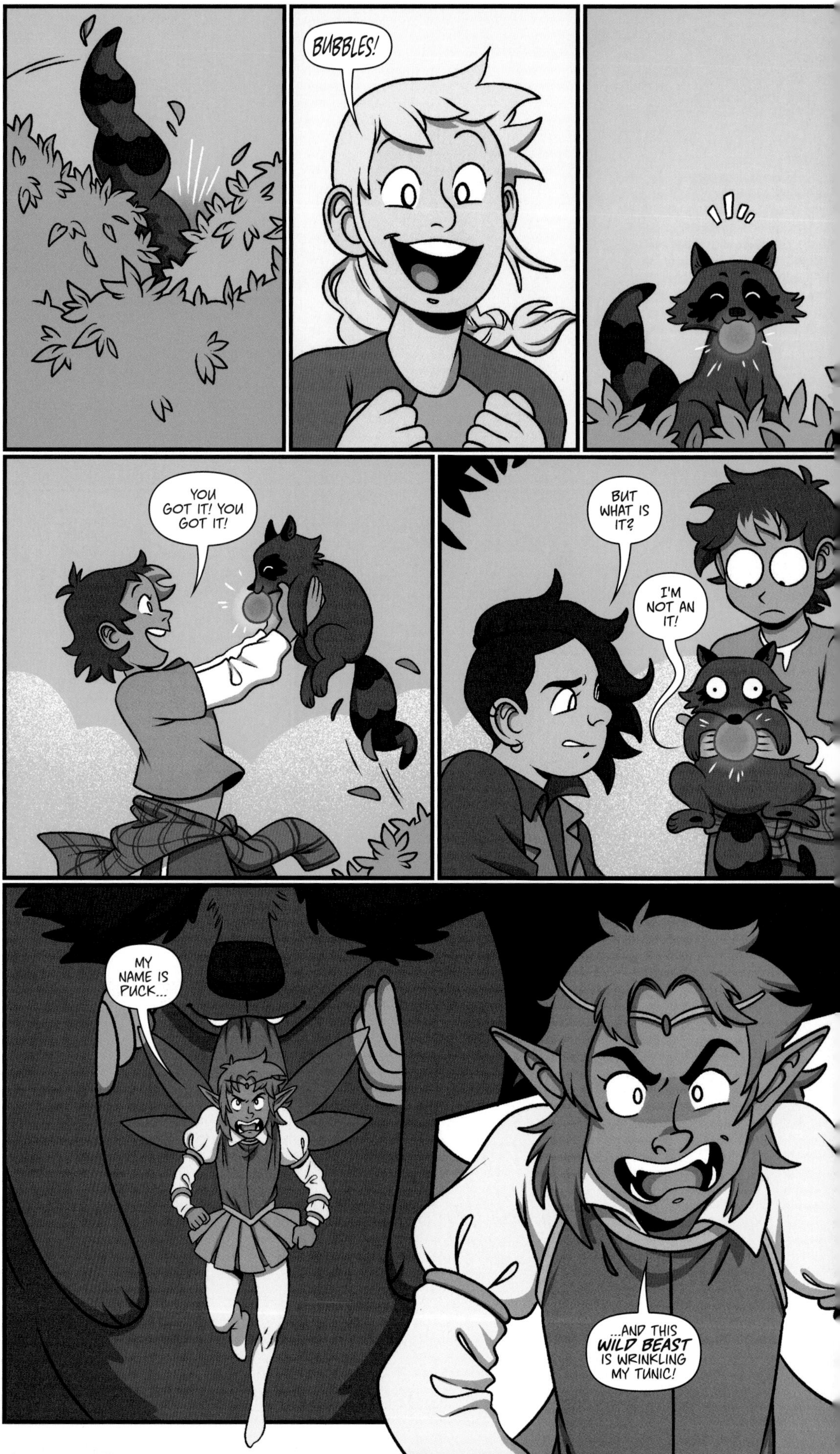
BUBBLES!
YOU GOT IT! YOU GOT IT!
BUT WHAT IS IT?
I'M NOT AN IT!
MY NAME IS PUCK...
...AND THIS WILD BEAST IS WRINKLING MY TUNIC!

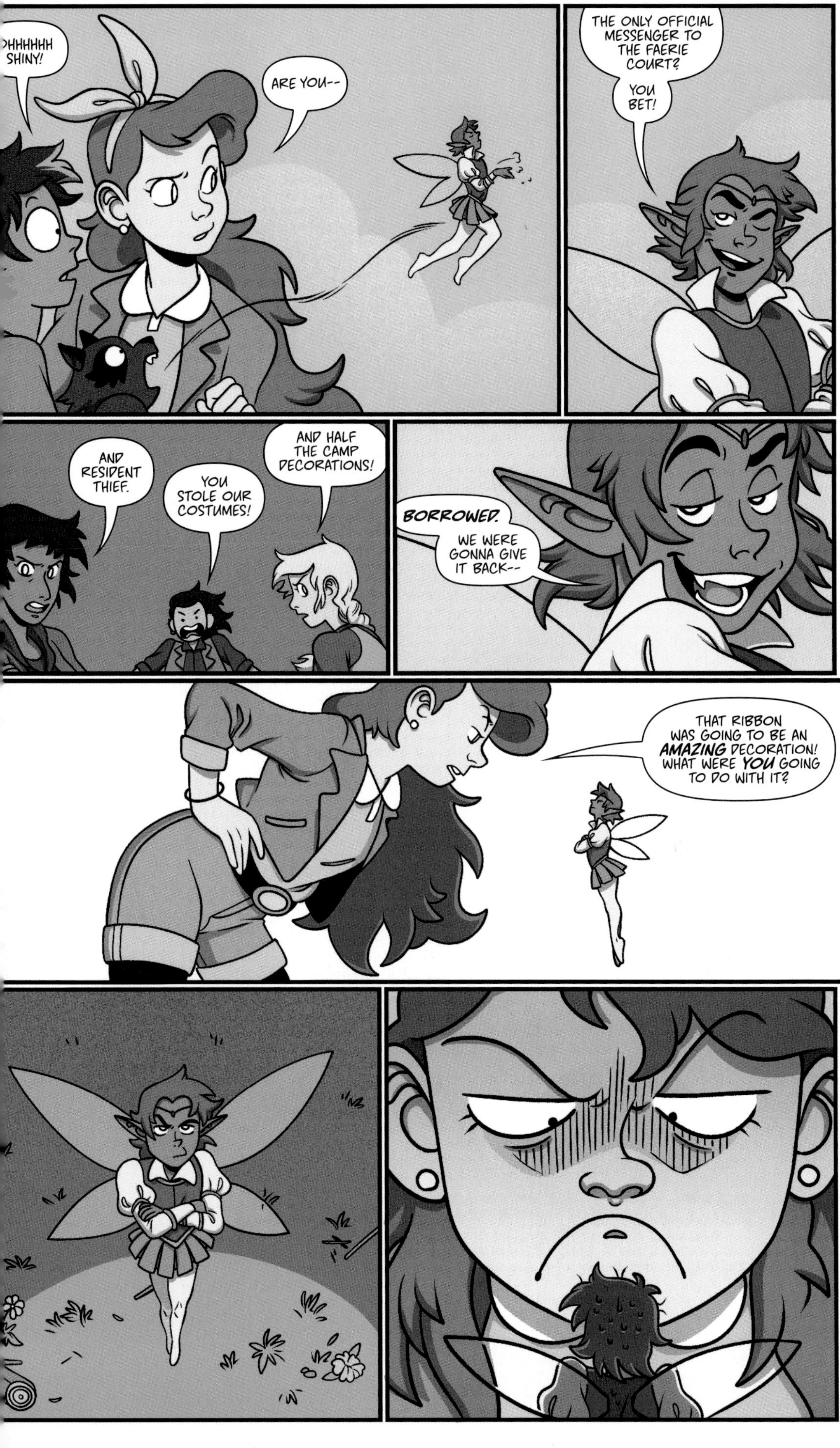
OHHHHHH SHINY!
ARE YOU--
THE ONLY OFFICIAL MESSENGER TO THE FAERIE COURT?
YOU BET!
AND RESIDENT THIEF.
YOU STOLE OUR COSTUMES!
AND HALF THE CAMP DECORATIONS!
BORROWED.
WE WERE GONNA GIVE IT BACK--
THAT RIBBON WAS GOING TO BE AN AMAZING DECORATION! WHAT WERE YOU GOING TO DO WITH IT?

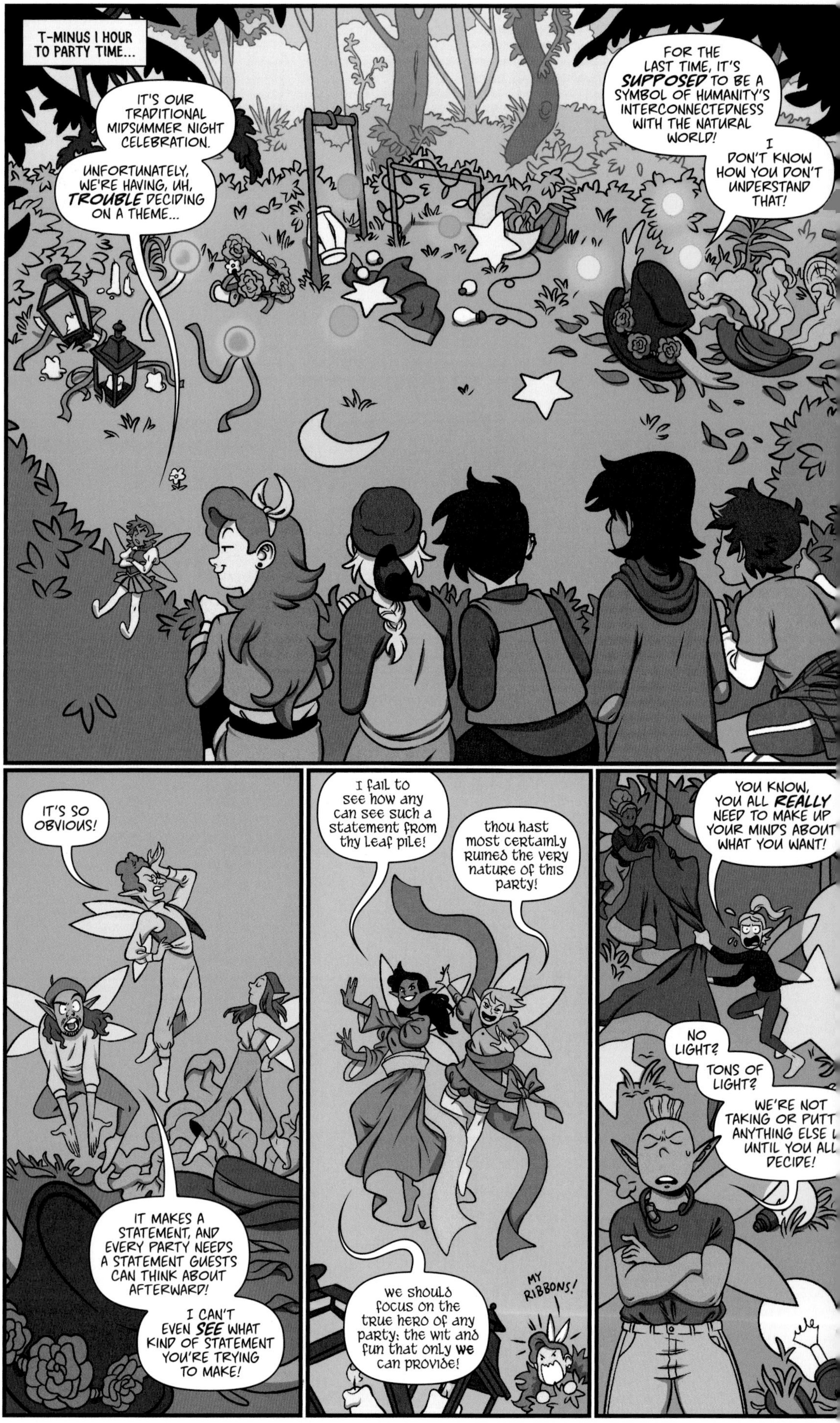
T-MINUS 1 HOUR TO PARTY TIME...
IT'S OUR TRADITIONAL MIDSUMMER NIGHT CELEBRATION.
UNFORTUNATELY, WE'RE HAVING, UH, TROUBLE DECIDING ON A THEME...
FOR THE LAST TIME, IT'S SUPPOSED TO BE A SYMBOL OF HUMANITY'S INTERCONNECTEDNESS WITH THE NATURAL WORLD!
I DON'T KNOW HOW YOU DON'T UNDERSTAND THAT!
IT'S SO OBVIOUS!
IT MAKES A STATEMENT, AND EVERY PARTY NEEDS A STATEMENT GUESTS CAN THINK ABOUT AFTERWARD!
I CAN'T EVEN SEE WHAT KIND OF STATEMENT YOU'RE TRYING TO MAKE!
I fail to see how any can see such a statement from thy leaf pile!
thou hast most certainly ruined the very nature of this party!
we should focus on the true hero of any party: the wit and fun that only we can provide!
MY RIBBONS!
YOU KNOW, YOU ALL REALLY NEED TO MAKE UP YOUR MINDS ABOUT WHAT YOU WANT!
NO LIGHT?
TONS OF LIGHT?
WE'RE NOT TAKING OR PUTT ANYTHING ELSE U UNTIL YOU ALL DECIDE!

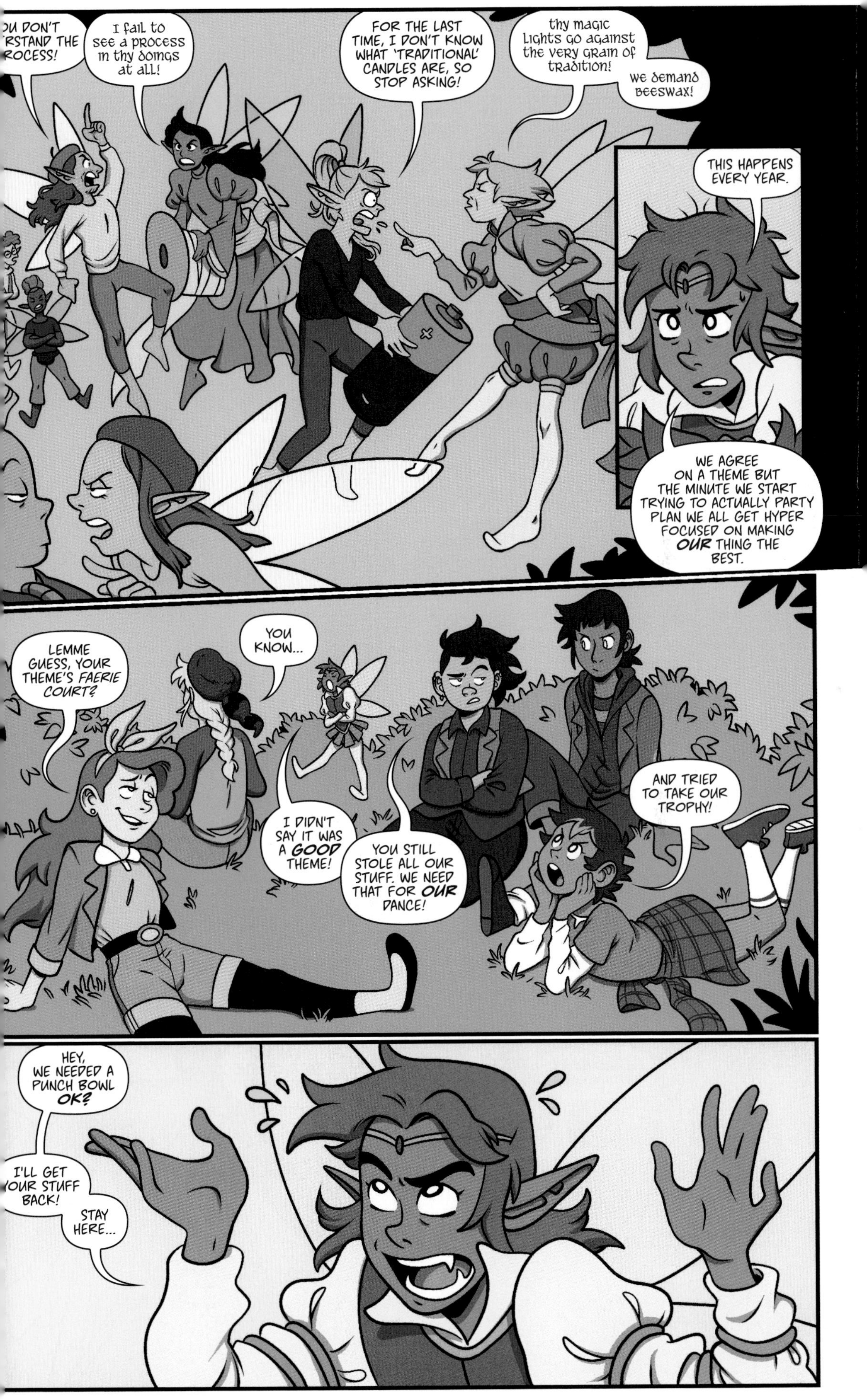

OU DON'T RSTAND THE ROCESS!
I fail to see a process in thy doings at all!
FOR THE LAST TIME, I DON'T KNOW WHAT 'TRADITIONAL' CANDLES ARE, SO STOP ASKING!
thy magic lights go against the very grain of tradition!
we demand beeswax!
THIS HAPPENS EVERY YEAR.
WE AGREE ON A THEME BUT THE MINUTE WE START TRYING TO ACTUALLY PARTY PLAN WE ALL GET HYPER FOCUSED ON MAKING **OUR** THING THE BEST.
LEMME GUESS, YOUR THEME'S *FAERIE COURT*?
YOU KNOW...
I DIDN'T SAY IT WAS A ***GOOD*** THEME!
YOU STILL STOLE ALL OUR STUFF. WE NEED THAT FOR ***OUR*** DANCE!
AND TRIED TO TAKE OUR TROPHY!
HEY, WE NEEDED A PUNCH BOWL ***OK?***
I'LL GET OUR STUFF BACK!
STAY HERE...

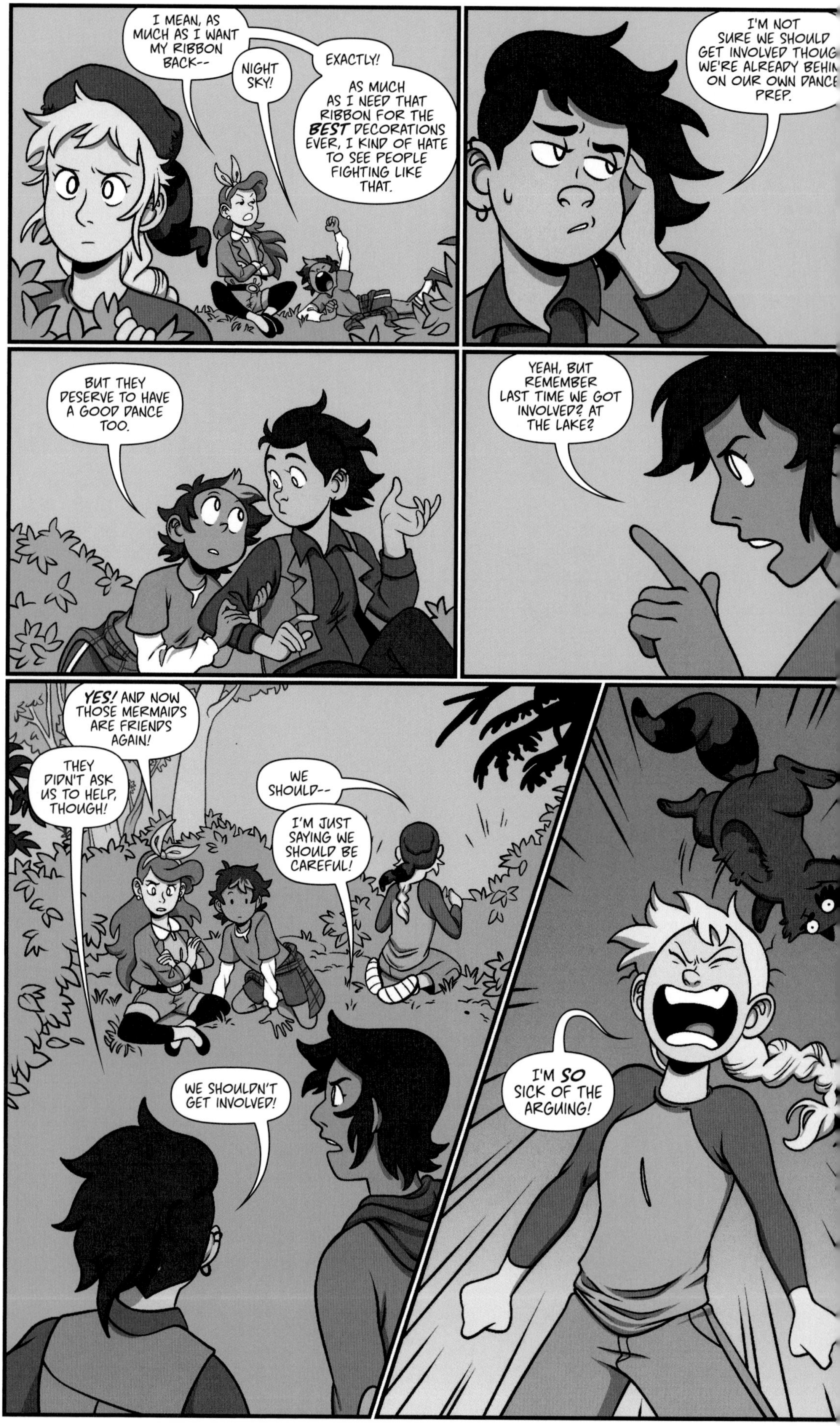
I MEAN, AS MUCH AS I WANT MY RIBBON BACK--
NIGHT SKY!
EXACTLY!
AS MUCH AS I NEED THAT RIBBON FOR THE BEST DECORATIONS EVER, I KIND OF HATE TO SEE PEOPLE FIGHTING LIKE THAT.
I'M NOT SURE WE SHOULD GET INVOLVED THOUG WE'RE ALREADY BEHIN ON OUR OWN DANCE PREP.
BUT THEY DESERVE TO HAVE A GOOD DANCE TOO.
YEAH, BUT REMEMBER LAST TIME WE GOT INVOLVED? AT THE LAKE?
YES! AND NOW THOSE MERMAIDS ARE FRIENDS AGAIN!
THEY DIDN'T ASK US TO HELP, THOUGH!
WE SHOULD--
I'M JUST SAYING WE SHOULD BE CAREFUL!
WE SHOULDN'T GET INVOLVED!
I'M SO SICK OF THE ARGUING!

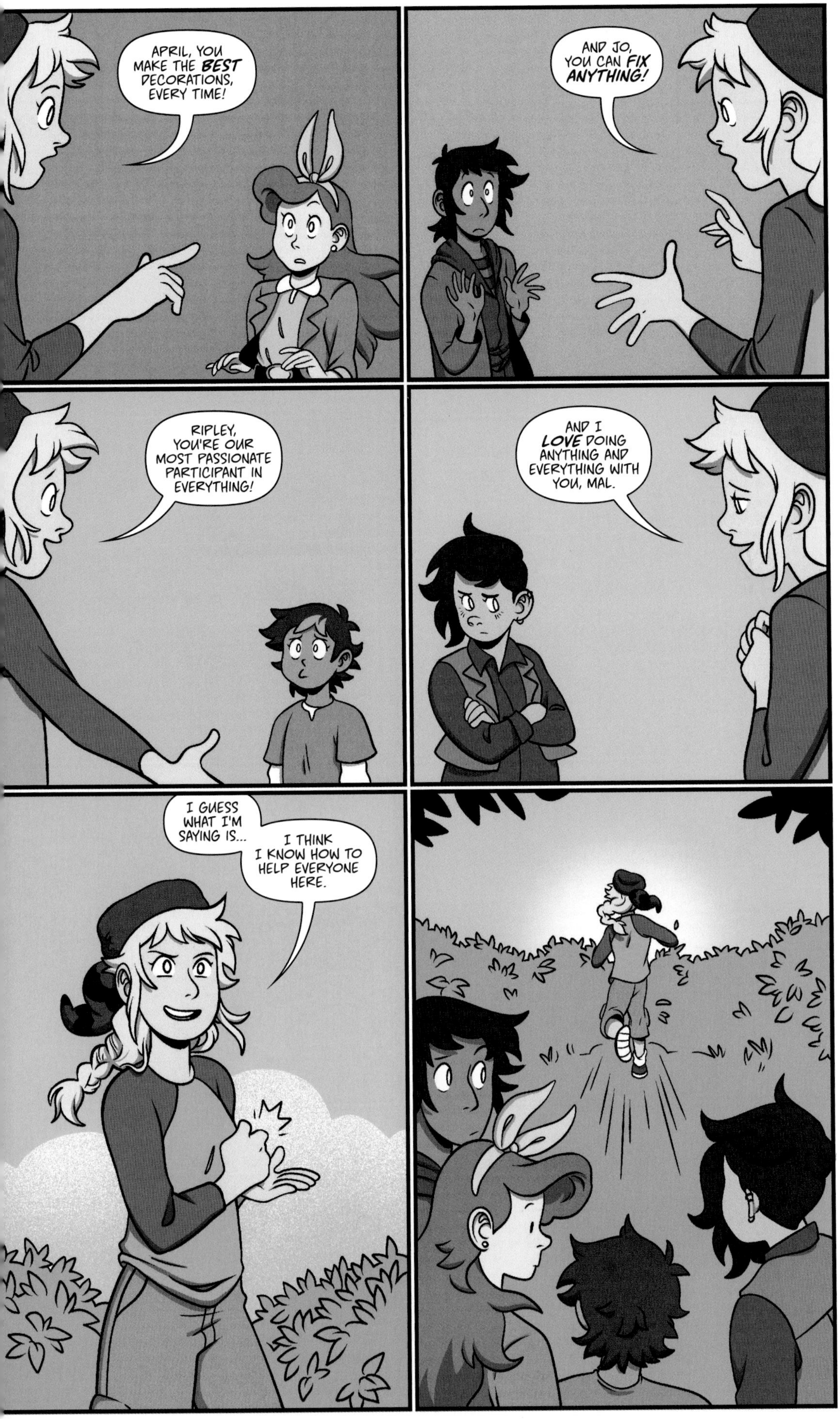
APRIL, YOU MAKE THE BEST DECORATIONS, EVERY TIME!
AND JO, YOU CAN FIX ANYTHING!
RIPLEY, YOU'RE OUR MOST PASSIONATE PARTICIPANT IN EVERYTHING!
AND I LOVE DOING ANYTHING AND EVERYTHING WITH YOU, MAL.
I GUESS WHAT I'M SAYING IS...
I THINK I KNOW HOW TO HELP EVERYONE HERE.

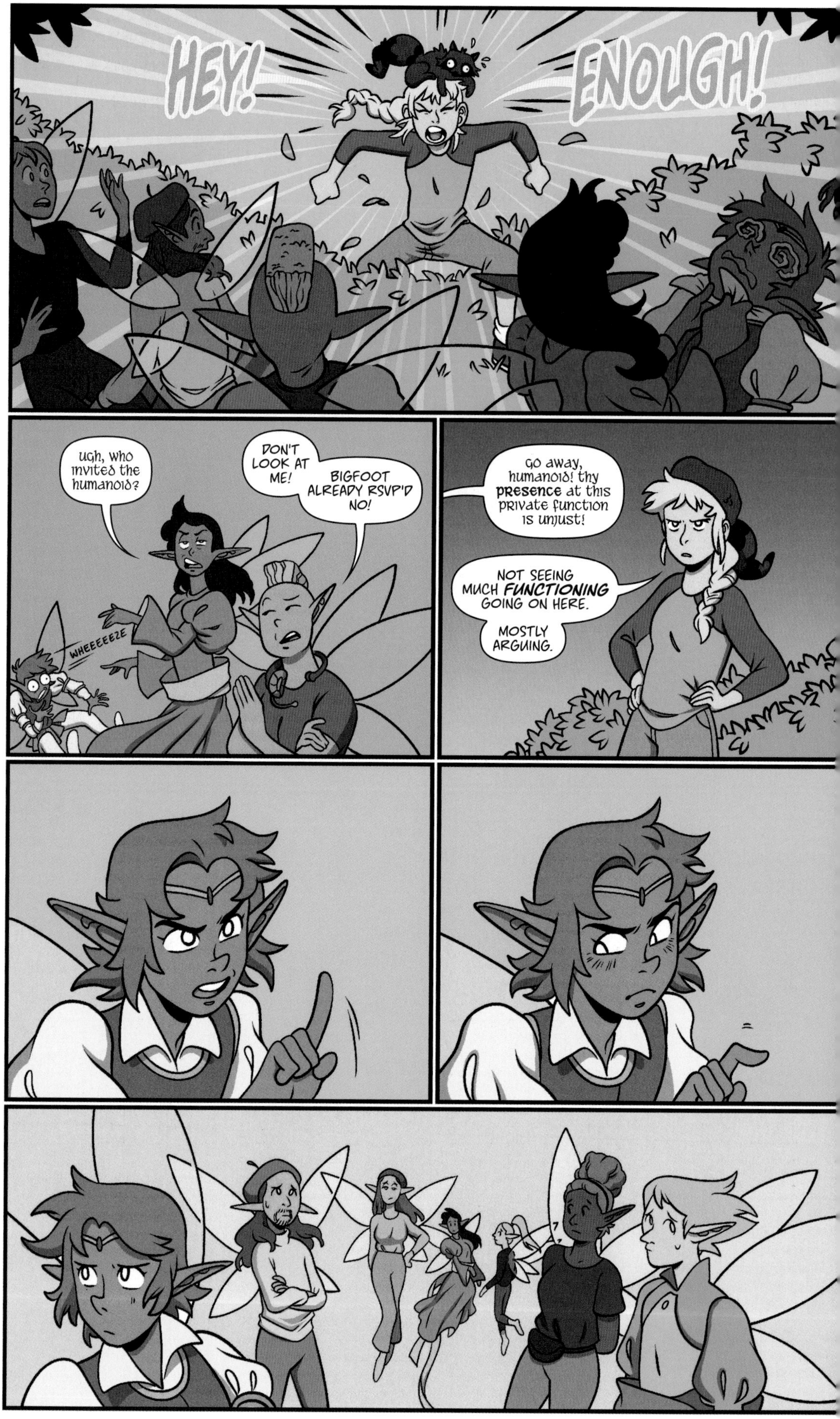
HEY!
ENOUGH!
ugh, who invited the humanoid?
DON'T LOOK AT ME!
BIGFOOT ALREADY RSVP'D NO!
WHEEEEEZE
go away, humanoid! thy presence at this private function is unjust!
NOT SEEING MUCH FUNCTIONING GOING ON HERE.
MOSTLY ARGUING.

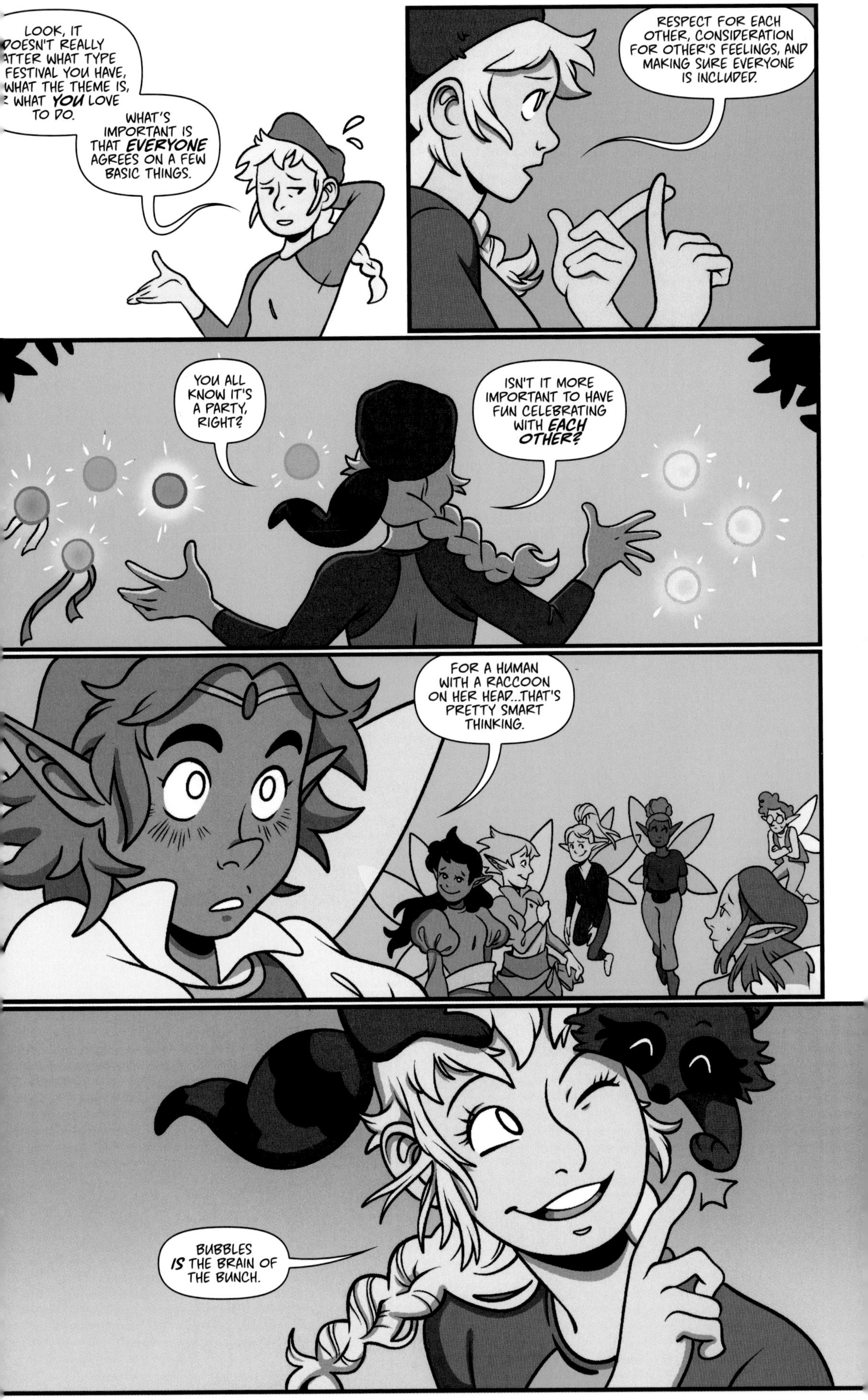
LOOK, IT DOESN'T REALLY ATTER WHAT TYPE FESTIVAL YOU HAVE, WHAT THE THEME IS, WHAT *YOU* LOVE TO DO.
WHAT'S IMPORTANT IS THAT *EVERYONE* AGREES ON A FEW BASIC THINGS.
RESPECT FOR EACH OTHER, CONSIDERATION FOR OTHER'S FEELINGS, AND MAKING SURE EVERYONE IS INCLUDED.
YOU ALL KNOW IT'S A PARTY, RIGHT?
ISN'T IT MORE IMPORTANT TO HAVE FUN CELEBRATING WITH *EACH OTHER?*
FOR A HUMAN WITH A RACCOON ON HER HEAD...THAT'S PRETTY SMART THINKING.
BUBBLES *IS* THE BRAIN OF THE BUNCH.

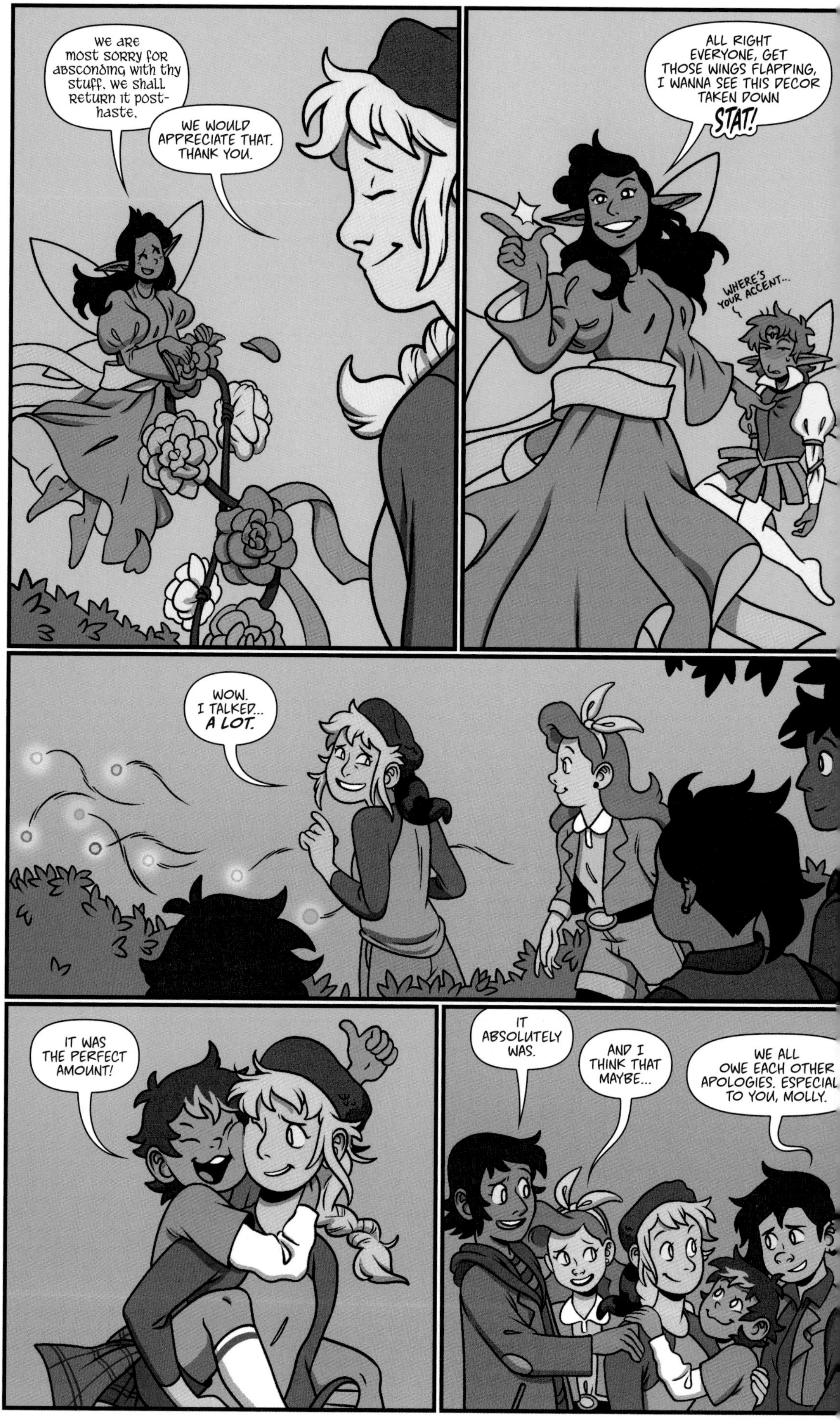
We are most sorry for absconding with thy stuff. We shall return it post-haste.
WE WOULD APPRECIATE THAT. THANK YOU.
ALL RIGHT EVERYONE, GET THOSE WINGS FLAPPING, I WANNA SEE THIS DECOR TAKEN DOWN STAT!
WHERE'S YOUR ACCENT...
WOW. I TALKED... A LOT.
IT WAS THE PERFECT AMOUNT!
IT ABSOLUTELY WAS.
AND I THINK THAT MAYBE...
WE ALL OWE EACH OTHER APOLOGIES. ESPECIAL TO YOU, MOLLY.

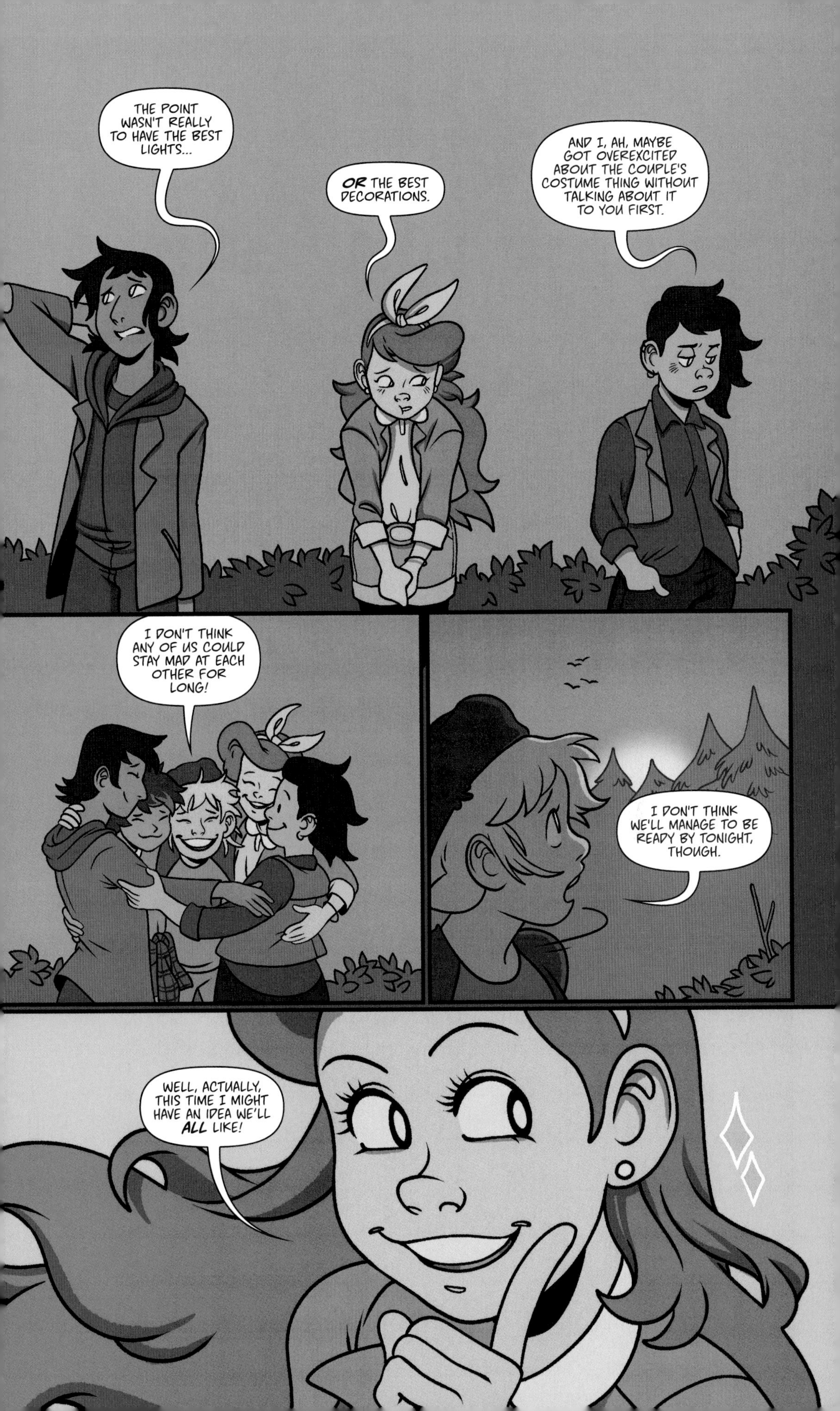
THE POINT WASN'T REALLY TO HAVE THE BEST LIGHTS...
OR THE BEST DECORATIONS.
AND I, AH, MAYBE GOT OVEREXCITED ABOUT THE COUPLE'S COSTUME THING WITHOUT TALKING ABOUT IT TO YOU FIRST.
I DON'T THINK ANY OF US COULD STAY MAD AT EACH OTHER FOR LONG!
I DON'T THINK WE'LL MANAGE TO BE READY BY TONIGHT, THOUGH.
WELL, ACTUALLY, THIS TIME I MIGHT HAVE AN IDEA WE'LL **ALL** LIKE!

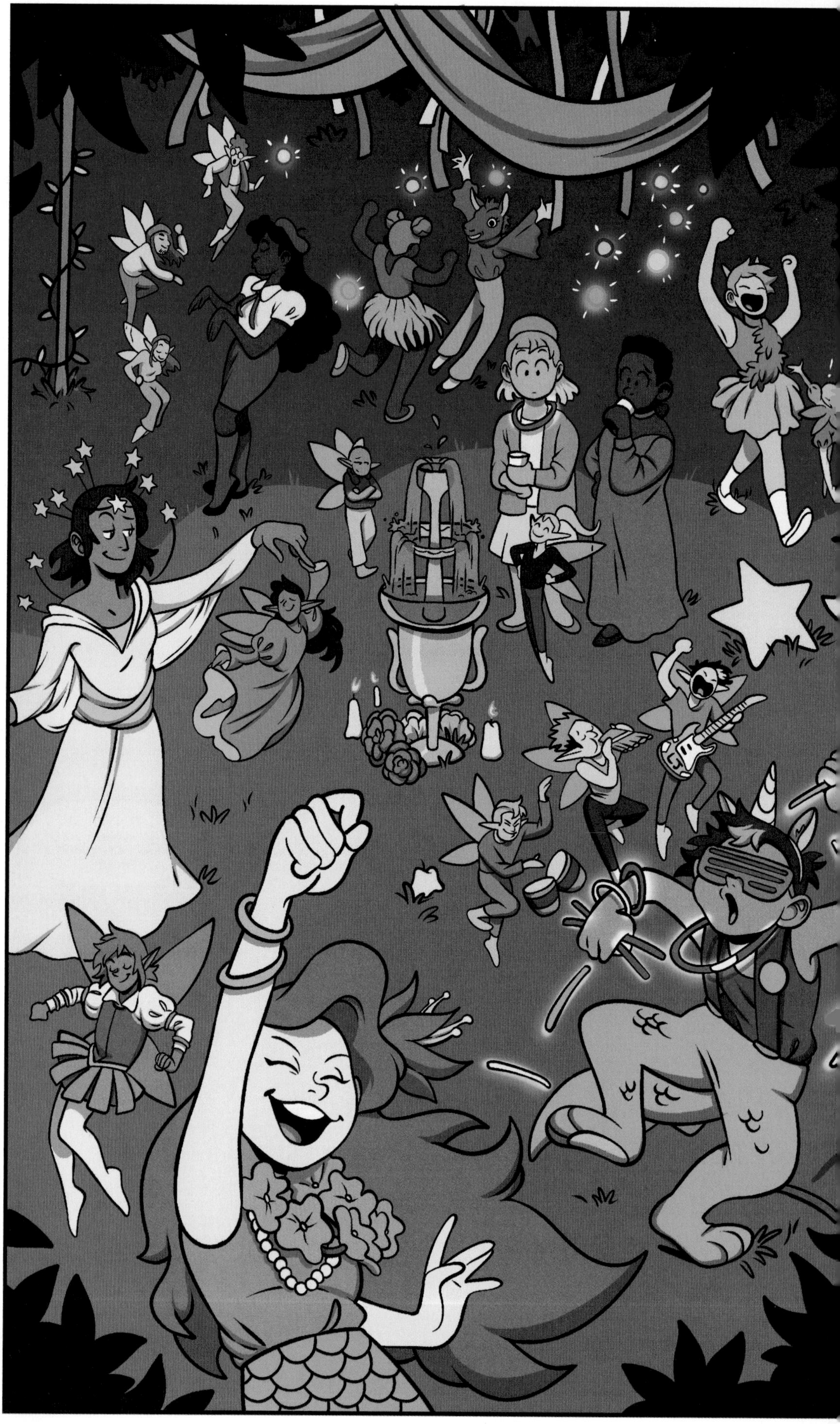

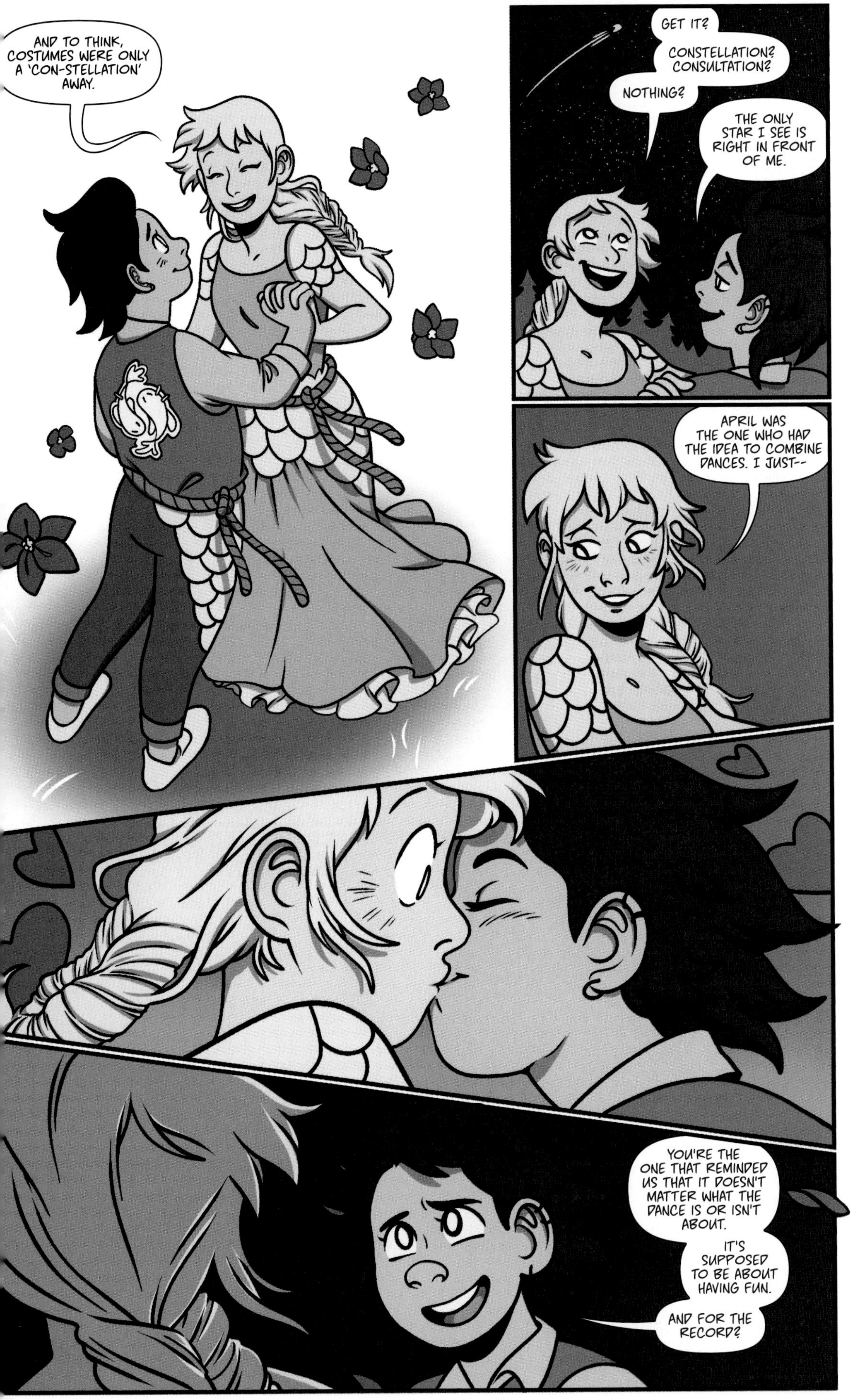
AND TO THINK, COSTUMES WERE ONLY A 'CON-STELLATION' AWAY.
GET IT?
CONSTELLATION? CONSULTATION?
NOTHING?
THE ONLY STAR I SEE IS RIGHT IN FRONT OF ME.
APRIL WAS THE ONE WHO HAD THE IDEA TO COMBINE DANCES. I JUST--
YOU'RE THE ONE THAT REMINDED US THAT IT DOESN'T MATTER WHAT THE DANCE IS OR ISN'T ABOUT.
IT'S SUPPOSED TO BE ABOUT HAVING FUN.
AND FOR THE RECORD?

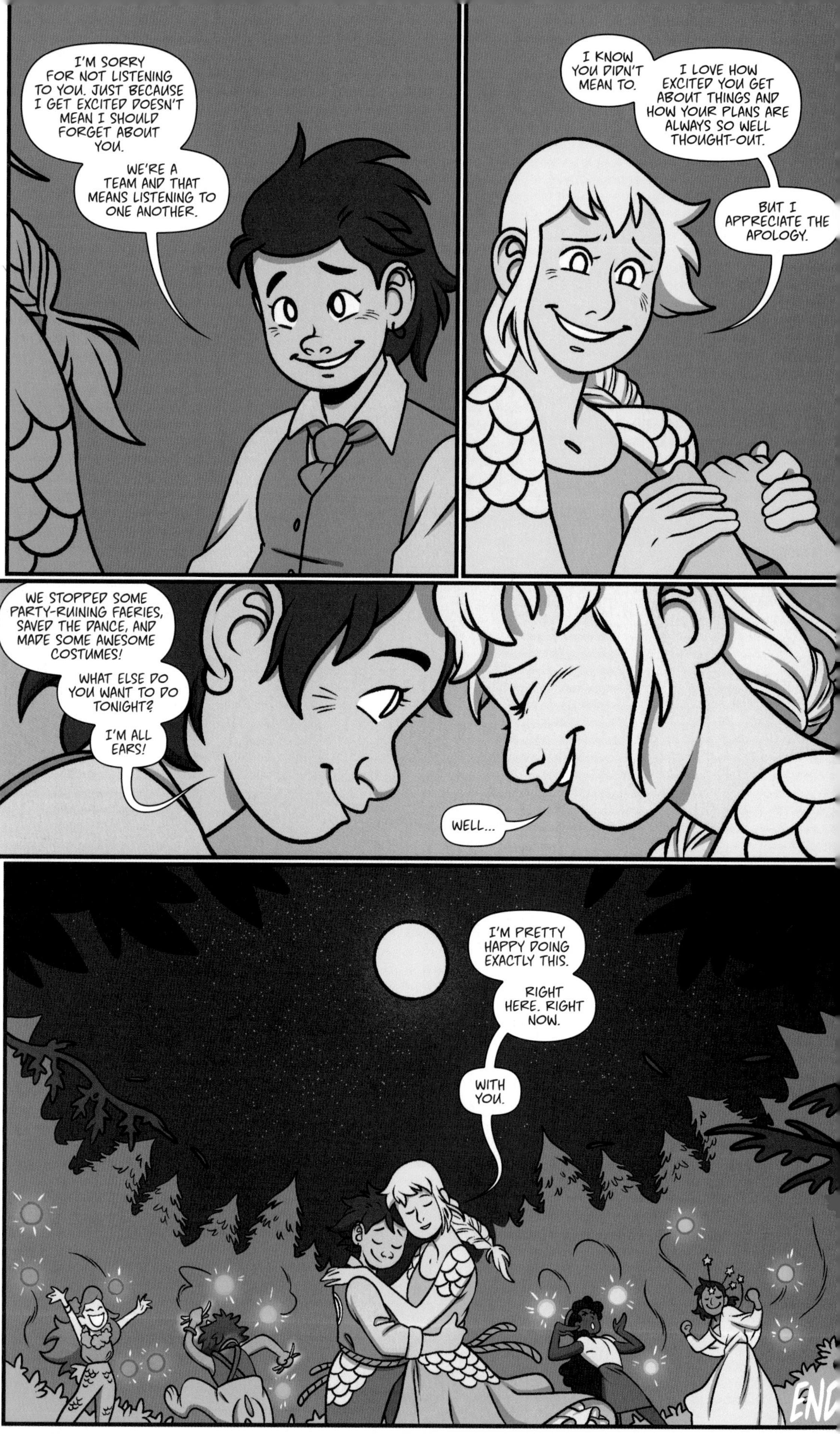
I'M SORRY FOR NOT LISTENING TO YOU. JUST BECAUSE I GET EXCITED DOESN'T MEAN I SHOULD FORGET ABOUT YOU.
WE'RE A TEAM AND THAT MEANS LISTENING TO ONE ANOTHER.
I KNOW YOU DIDN'T MEAN TO.
I LOVE HOW EXCITED YOU GET ABOUT THINGS AND HOW YOUR PLANS ARE ALWAYS SO WELL THOUGHT-OUT.
BUT I APPRECIATE THE APOLOGY.
WE STOPPED SOME PARTY-RUINING FAERIES, SAVED THE DANCE, AND MADE SOME AWESOME COSTUMES!
WHAT ELSE DO YOU WANT TO DO TONIGHT?
I'M ALL EARS!
WELL...
I'M PRETTY HAPPY DOING EXACTLY THIS.
RIGHT HERE. RIGHT NOW.
WITH YOU.

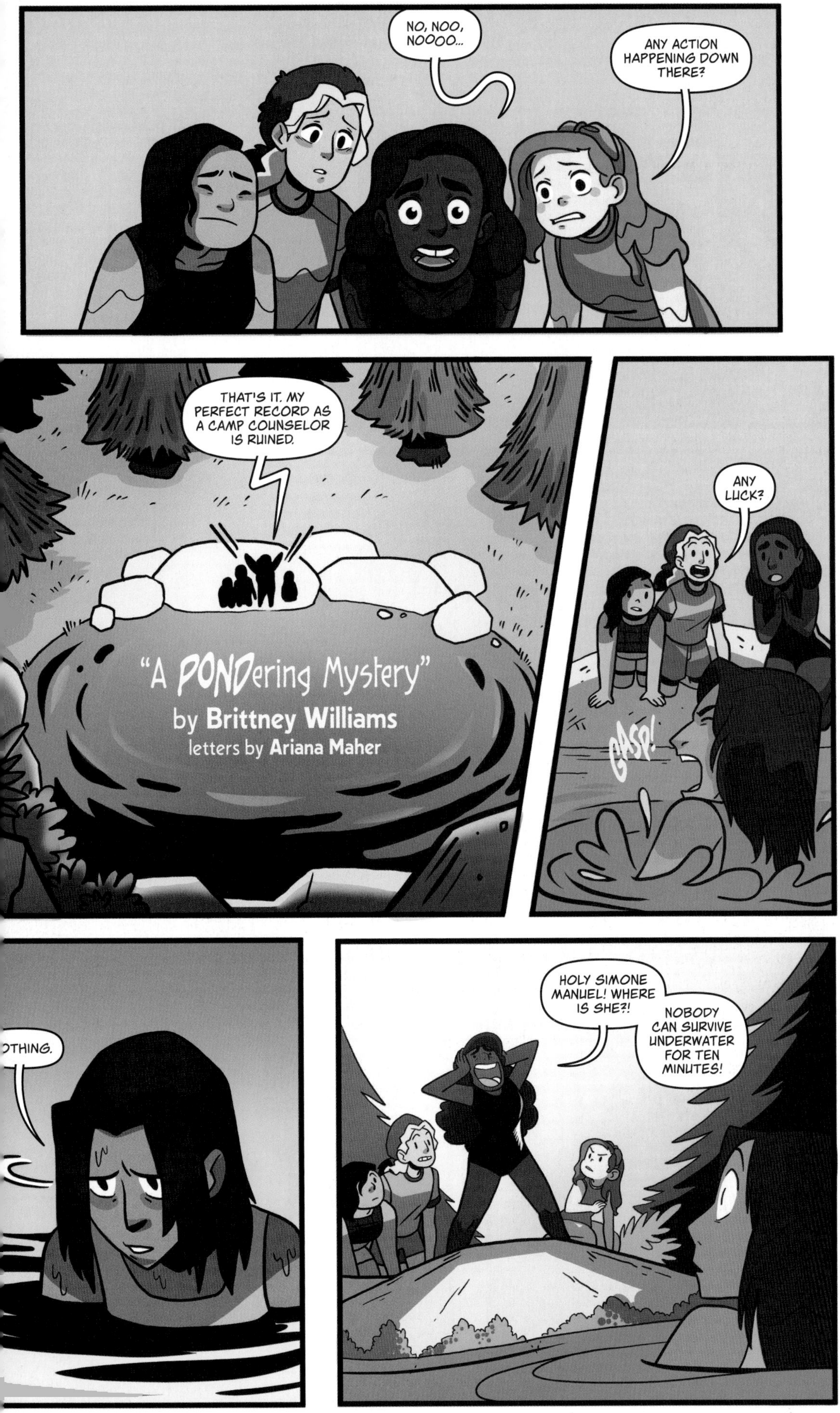
NO, NOO, NOOOO...
ANY ACTION HAPPENING DOWN THERE?
THAT'S IT. MY PERFECT RECORD AS A CAMP COUNSELOR IS RUINED.
"A PONDering Mystery"
by Brittney Williams
letters by Ariana Maher
ANY LUCK?
GASP!
OTHING.
HOLY SIMONE MANUEL! WHERE IS SHE?!
NOBODY CAN SURVIVE UNDERWATER FOR TEN MINUTES!

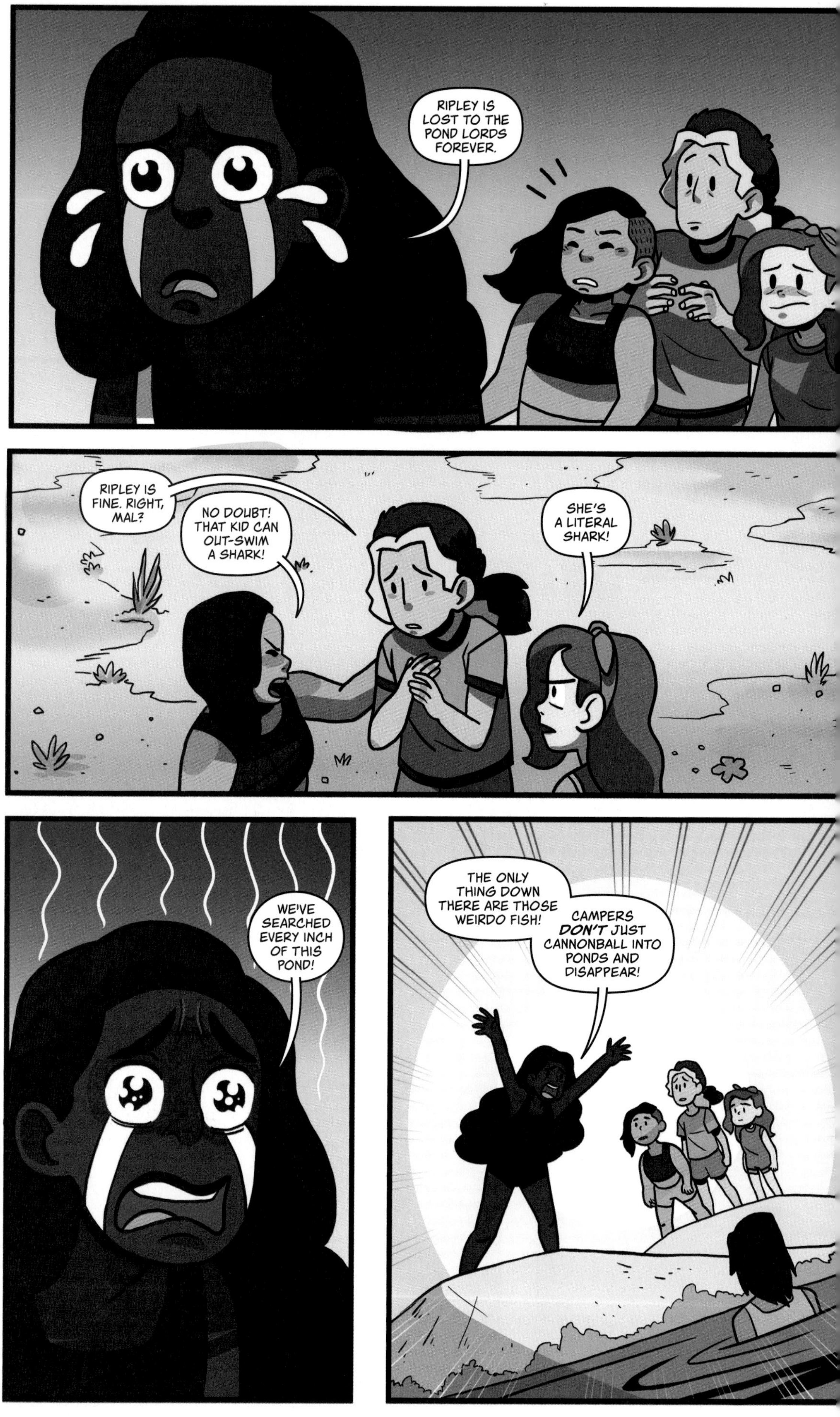
RIPLEY IS LOST TO THE POND LORDS FOREVER.
RIPLEY IS FINE. RIGHT, MAL?
NO DOUBT! THAT KID CAN OUT-SWIM A SHARK!
SHE'S A LITERAL SHARK!
WE'VE SEARCHED EVERY INCH OF THIS POND!
THE ONLY THING DOWN THERE ARE THOSE WEIRDO FISH!
CAMPERS DON'T JUST CANNONBALL INTO PONDS AND DISAPPEAR!

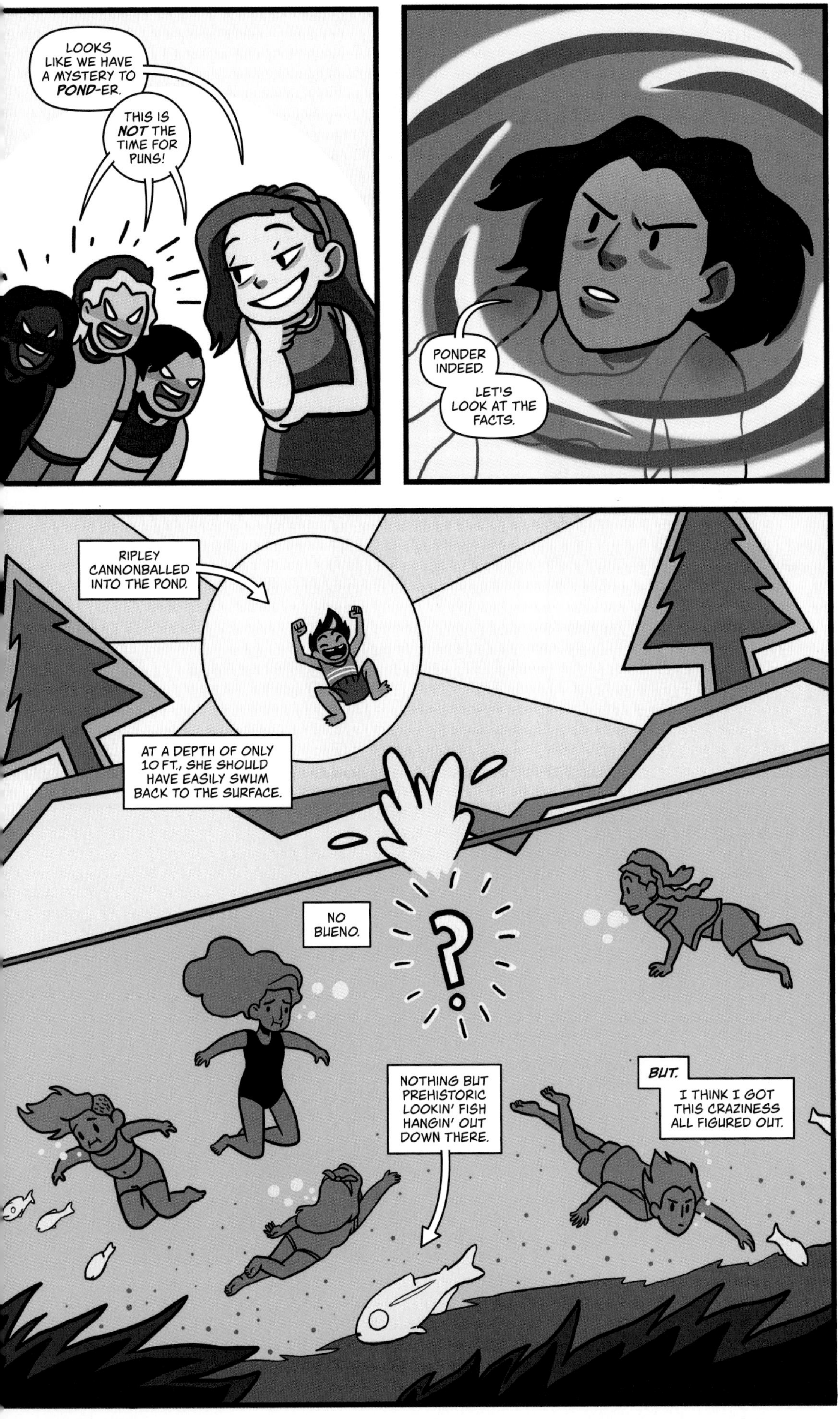
LOOKS LIKE WE HAVE A MYSTERY TO ***POND***-ER.
THIS IS ***NOT*** THE TIME FOR PUNS!
PONDER INDEED.
LET'S LOOK AT THE FACTS.
RIPLEY CANNONBALLED INTO THE POND.
AT A DEPTH OF ONLY 10 FT., SHE SHOULD HAVE EASILY SWUM BACK TO THE SURFACE.
NO BUENO.
?
NOTHING BUT PREHISTORIC LOOKIN' FISH HANGIN' OUT DOWN THERE.
BUT.
I THINK I GOT THIS CRAZINESS ALL FIGURED OUT.

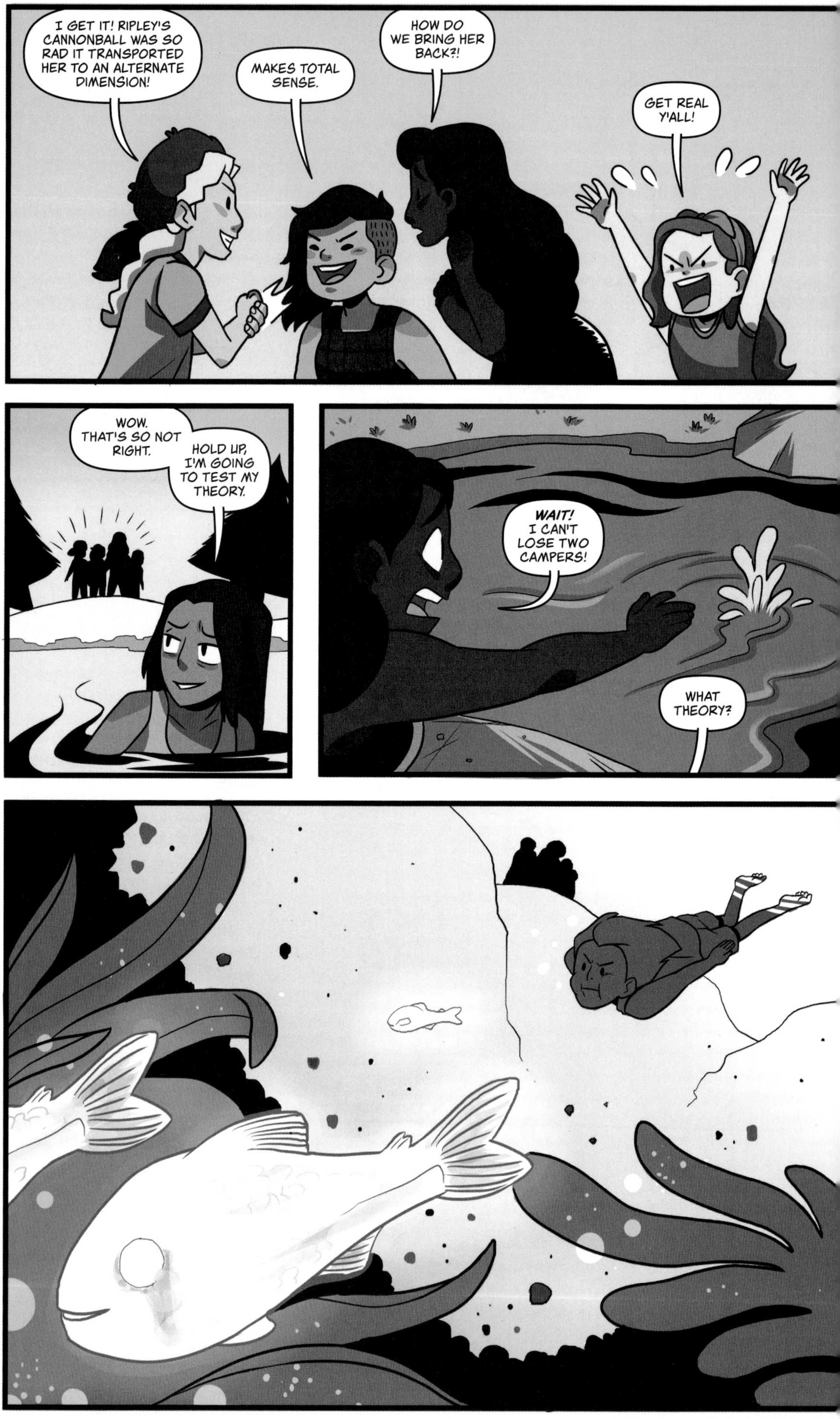
I GET IT! RIPLEY'S CANNONBALL WAS SO RAD IT TRANSPORTED HER TO AN ALTERNATE DIMENSION!
MAKES TOTAL SENSE.
HOW DO WE BRING HER BACK?!
GET REAL Y'ALL!
WOW. THAT'S SO NOT RIGHT.
HOLD UP, I'M GOING TO TEST MY THEORY.
WAIT! I CAN'T LOSE TWO CAMPERS!
WHAT THEORY?

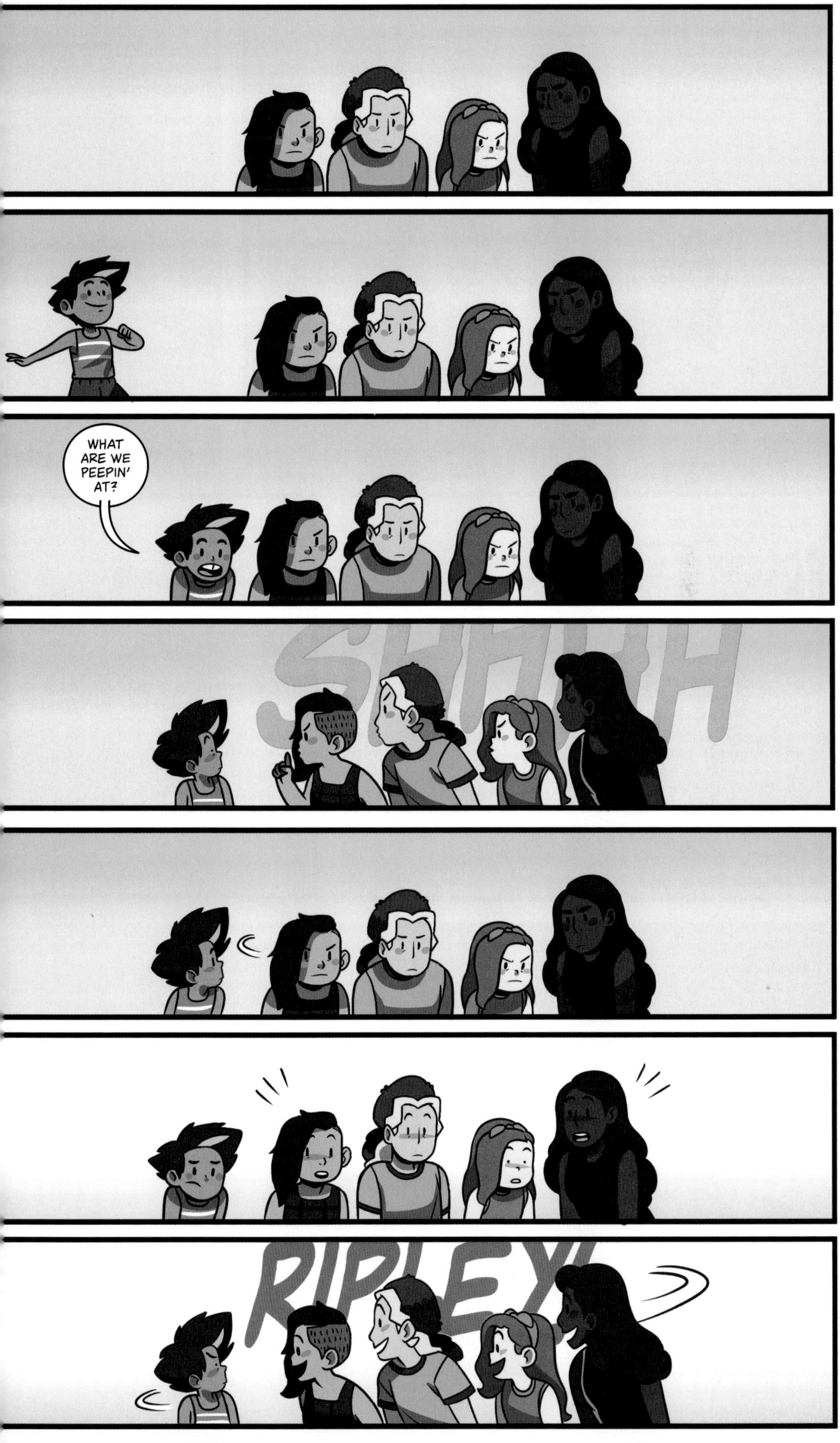
WHAT ARE WE PEEPIN' AT?
SHHHH
RIPLEY!

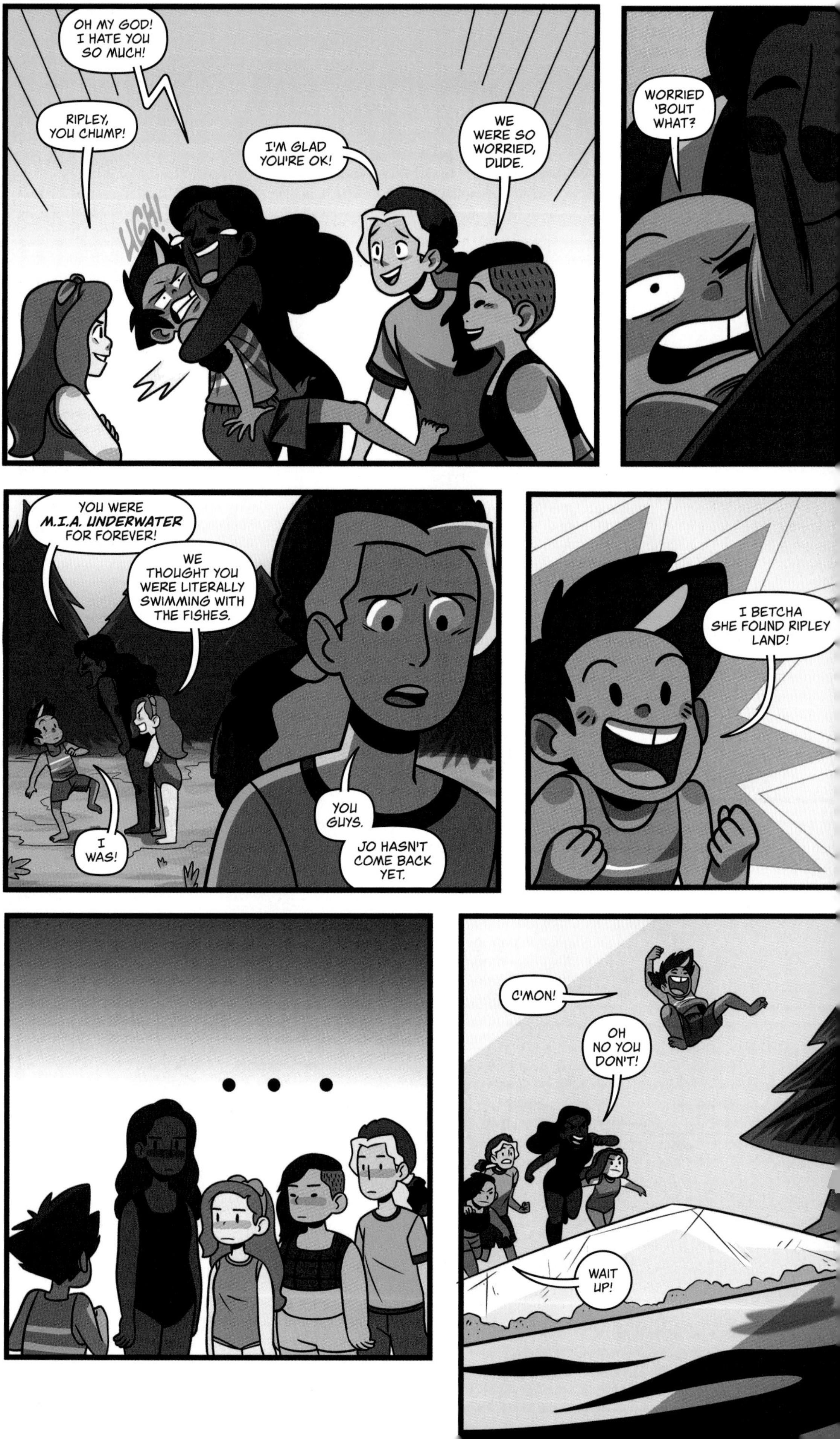
OH MY GOD! I HATE YOU SO MUCH!
RIPLEY, YOU CHUMP!
UGH!
I'M GLAD YOU'RE OK!
WE WERE SO WORRIED, DUDE.
WORRIED 'BOUT WHAT?
YOU WERE *M.I.A. UNDERWATER* FOR FOREVER!
WE THOUGHT YOU WERE LITERALLY SWIMMING WITH THE FISHES.
I WAS!
YOU GUYS.
JO HASN'T COME BACK YET.
I BETCHA SHE FOUND RIPLEY LAND!
...
C'MON!
OH NO YOU DON'T!
WAIT UP!

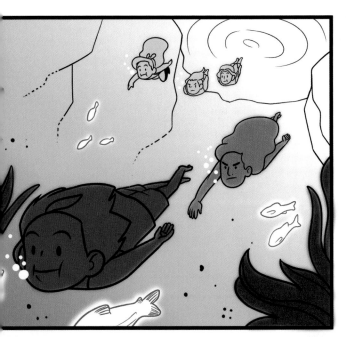

GASP!

WHOA!

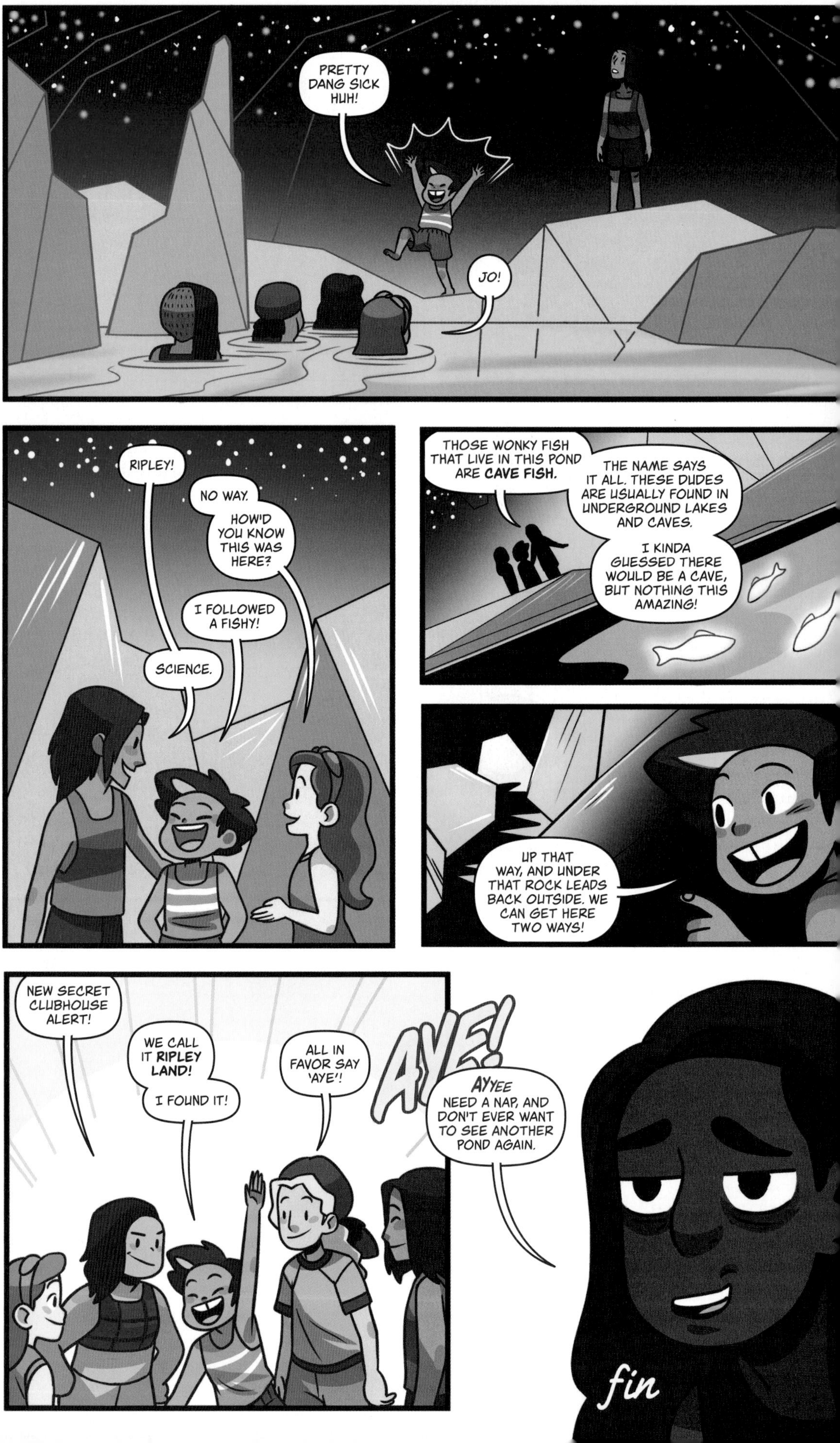

PRETTY DANG SICK HUH!
JO!
RIPLEY!
NO WAY.
HOW'D YOU KNOW THIS WAS HERE?
I FOLLOWED A FISHY!
SCIENCE.
THOSE WONKY FISH THAT LIVE IN THIS POND ARE **CAVE FISH.**
THE NAME SAYS IT ALL. THESE DUDES ARE USUALLY FOUND IN UNDERGROUND LAKES AND CAVES.
I KINDA GUESSED THERE WOULD BE A CAVE, BUT NOTHING THIS AMAZING!
UP THAT WAY, AND UNDER THAT ROCK LEADS BACK OUTSIDE. WE CAN GET HERE TWO WAYS!
NEW SECRET CLUBHOUSE ALERT!
WE CALL IT **RIPLEY LAND!**
I FOUND IT!
ALL IN FAVOR SAY 'AYE'!
AYE!
AYyee NEED A NAP, AND DON'T EVER WANT TO SEE ANOTHER POND AGAIN.
fin

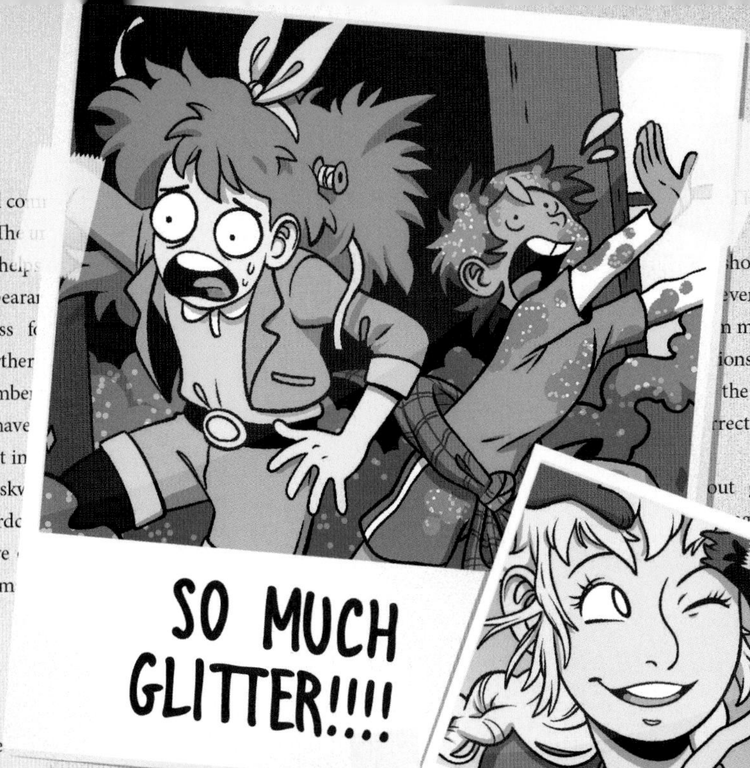
SO MUCH GLITTER!!!!

will co…
The u…
It helps…
appeara…
dress f…
Further…
Lumbe…
to have…
part in…
Thiskw…
Hardc…
have …
them…

…THE UNIFORM

…should be worn at camp …events when Lumberjanes …n may also be worn at other …ions. It should be worn as a … the uniform dress with …rrect shoes, and stocking or …

…out grows her uniform or …ther Lumberjane. …a she has …n her …f her

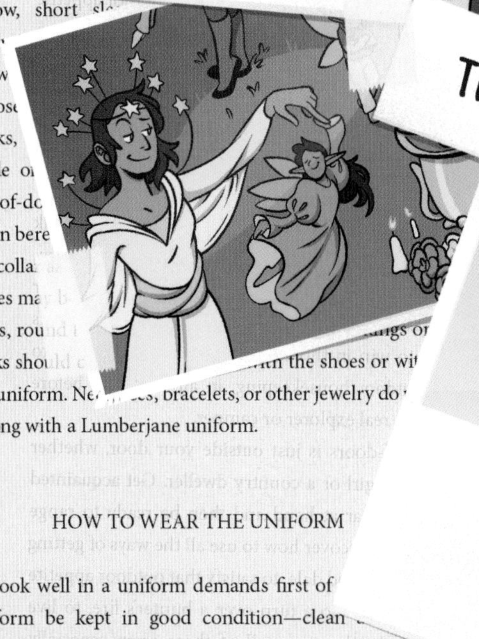

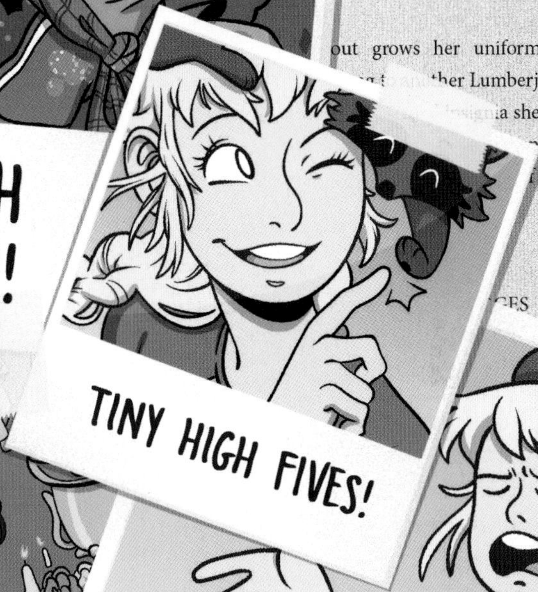
TINY HIGH FIVES!

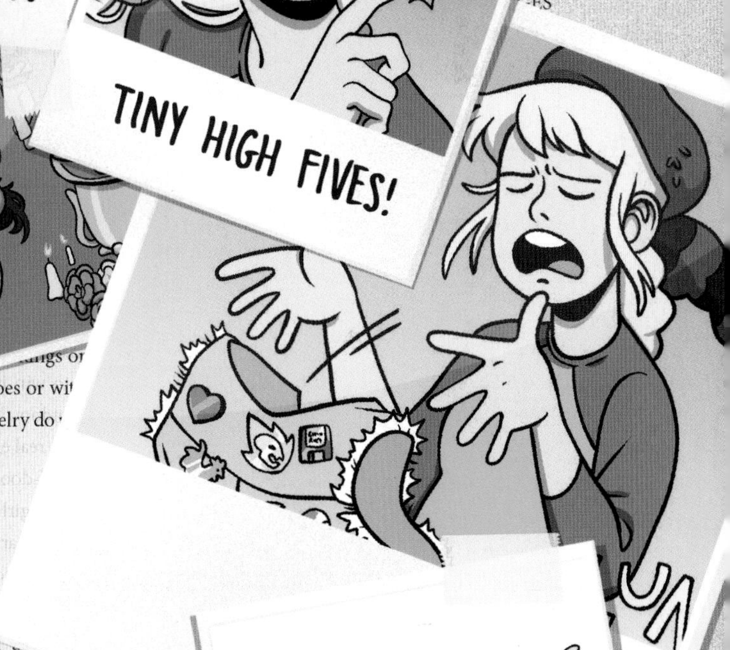

The …
yellow, short sl…
emb…
the w…
choose…
slacks, …
made o…
out-of-do…
green bere…
the colla…
Shoes ma…
heels, rou… …ngs or
socks shou… …with the shoes or wi…
the uniform. Ne… bracelets, or other jewelry do…
belong with a Lumberjane uniform.

…GES

HOW TO WEAR THE UNIFORM

To look well in a uniform demands first of … uniform be kept in good condition—clean … pressed. See that the skirt is the right length for your own height and build, that the belt is adjusted to your waist, that your shoes and stockings are in keeping with the uniform, that you watch your posture and carry yourself with dignity and grace. If the beret is removed indoors, be sure that your hair is neat and kept in place with an inconspicuous clip or ribbon. When you wear a Lumberjane uniform you are identified as a member of this organization and you should be doubly careful to conduct yourself in a way that will show everyone that courtesy and thoughtfulness are part of being a Lumberjane. People are likely to judge a whole nation by the selfishness of a few individuals, to criticize a whole family because of the misconduct of one member, and to feel unkindly toward an organization because of the

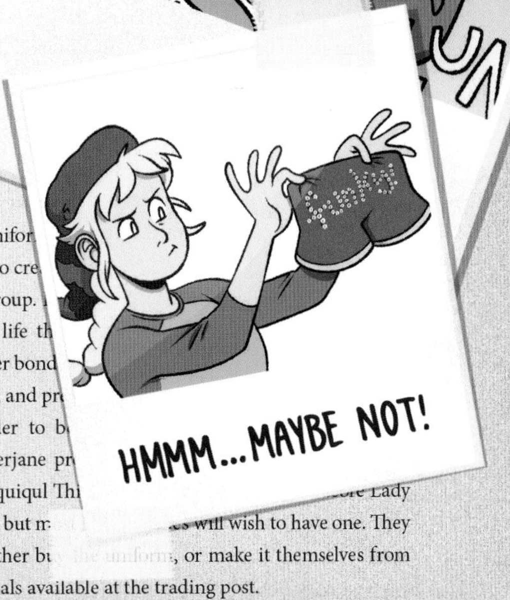
HMMM...MAYBE NOT!

The unifor…
helps to cre…
in a group. …
active life th…
another bond…
future, and pr…
in order to b…
Lumberjane pr…
Penniquiqul Thi… …Lady
Types, but m… …will wish to have one. They can either bu… uniform, or make it themselves from materials available at the trading post.

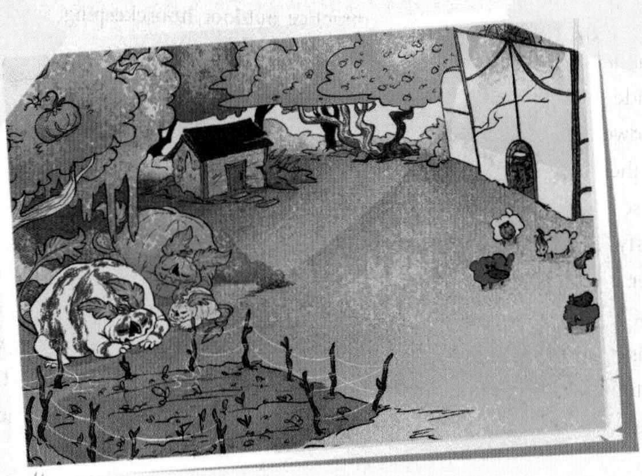

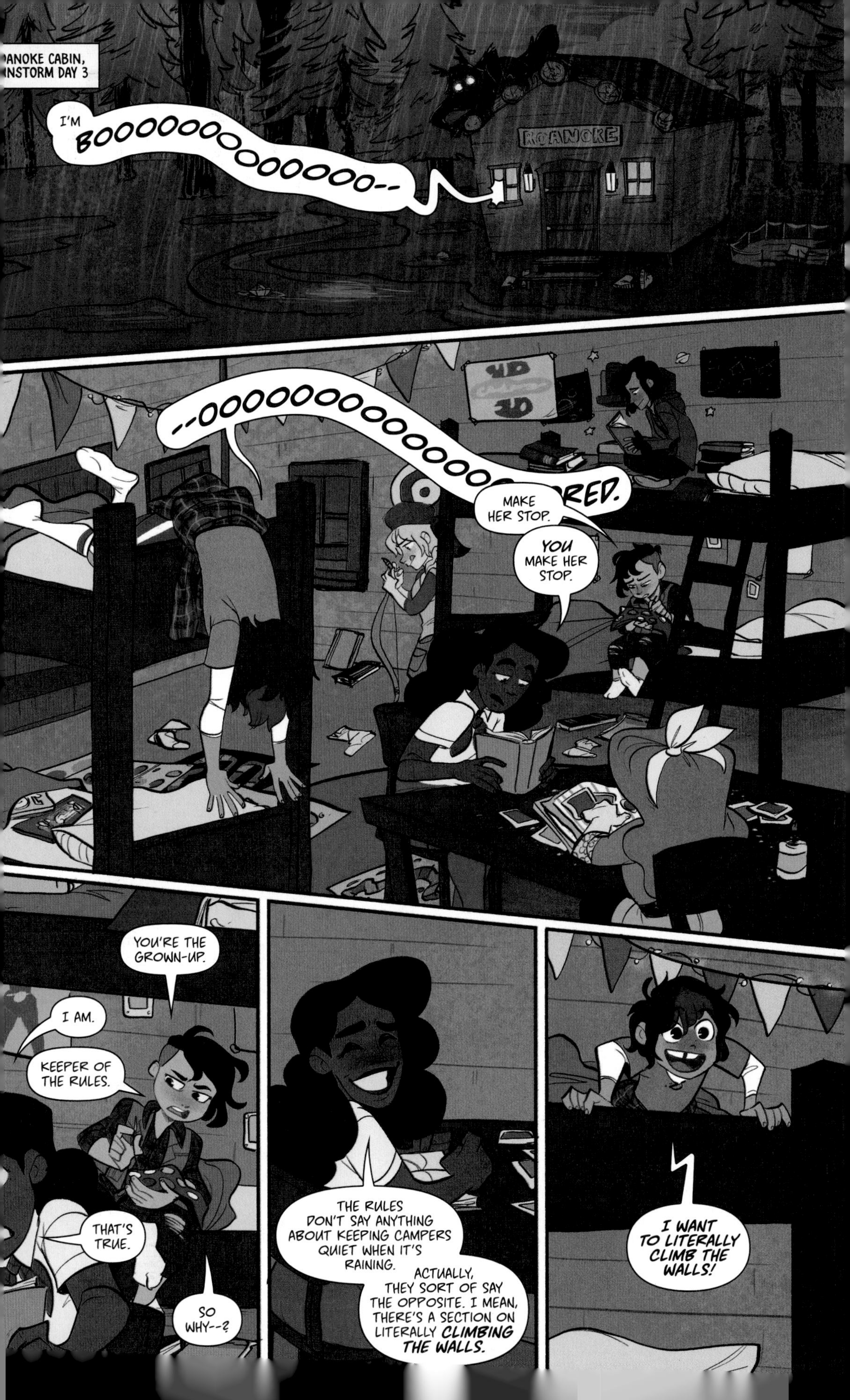

ANOKE CABIN,
NSTORM DAY 3
I'M BOOOOOOOOOOOOOO--
--OOOOOOOOOOOOOOOOORED.
MAKE HER STOP.
YOU MAKE HER STOP.
YOU'RE THE GROWN-UP.
I AM.
KEEPER OF THE RULES.
THAT'S TRUE.
SO WHY--?
THE RULES DON'T SAY ANYTHING ABOUT KEEPING CAMPERS QUIET WHEN IT'S RAINING.
ACTUALLY, THEY SORT OF SAY THE OPPOSITE. I MEAN, THERE'S A SECTION ON LITERALLY CLIMBING THE WALLS.
I WANT TO LITERALLY CLIMB THE WALLS!

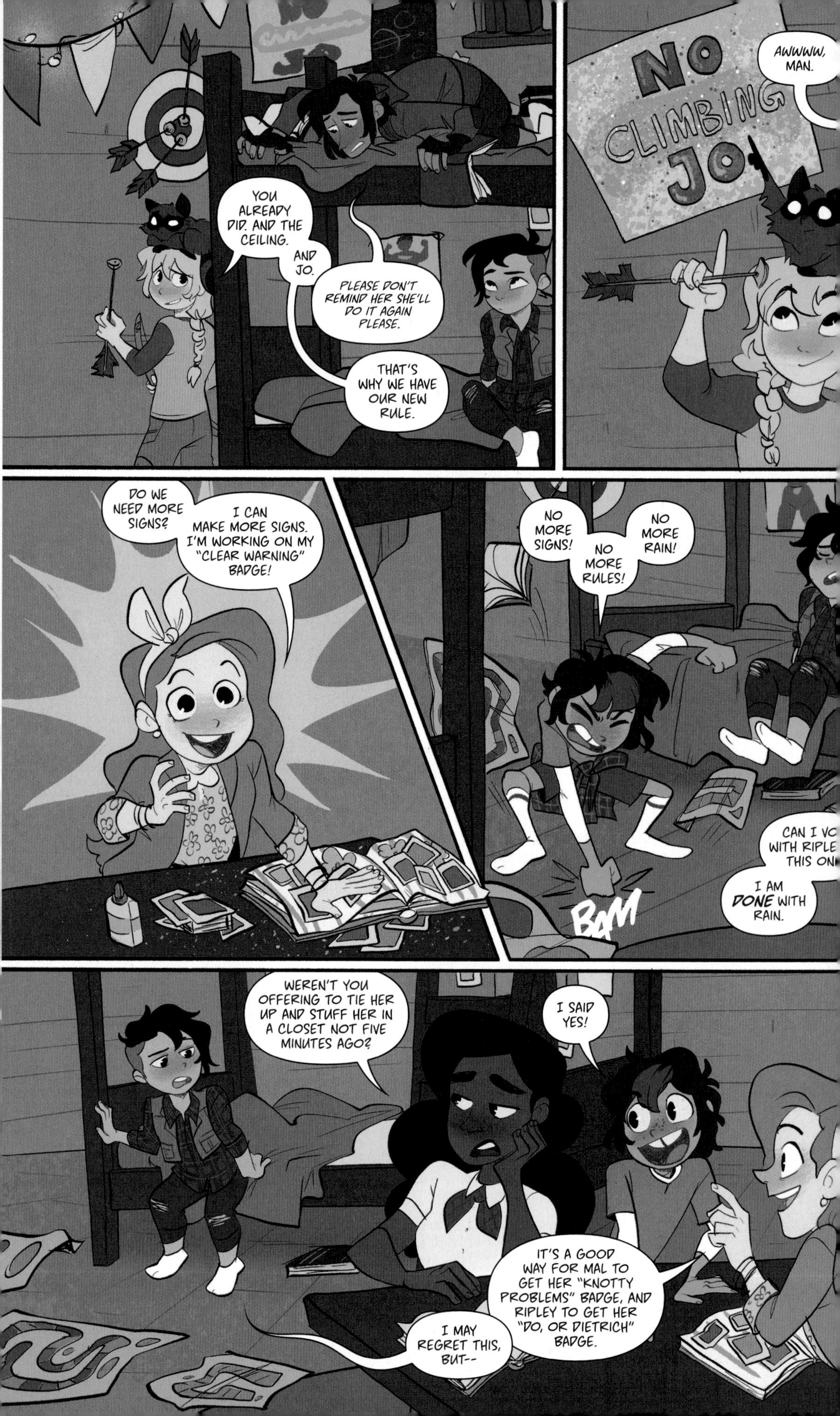
YOU ALREADY DID. AND THE CEILING.
AND JO.
PLEASE DON'T REMIND HER SHE'LL DO IT AGAIN PLEASE.
THAT'S WHY WE HAVE OUR NEW RULE.
NO CLIMBING JO
AWWWW, MAN.
DO WE NEED MORE SIGNS?
I CAN MAKE MORE SIGNS. I'M WORKING ON MY "CLEAR WARNING" BADGE!
NO MORE SIGNS!
NO MORE RULES!
NO MORE RAIN!
BAM
CAN I VO WITH RIPLE THIS ON
I AM DONE WITH RAIN.
WEREN'T YOU OFFERING TO TIE HER UP AND STUFF HER IN A CLOSET NOT FIVE MINUTES AGO?
I SAID YES!
IT'S A GOOD WAY FOR MAL TO GET HER "KNOTTY PROBLEMS" BADGE, AND RIPLEY TO GET HER "DO, OR DIETRICH" BADGE.
I MAY REGRET THIS, BUT--

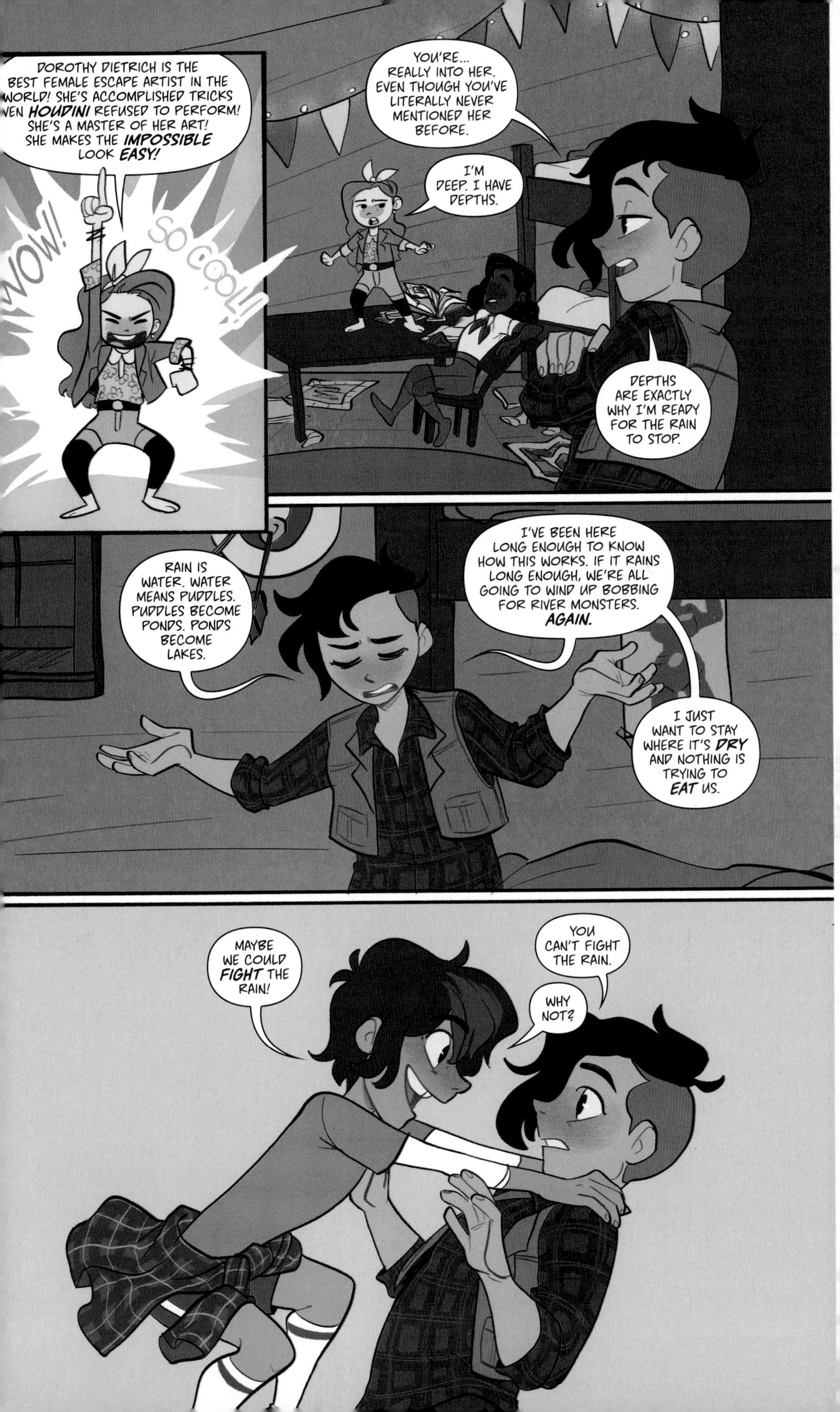

DOROTHY DIETRICH IS THE BEST FEMALE ESCAPE ARTIST IN THE WORLD! SHE'S ACCOMPLISHED TRICKS EVEN HOUDINI REFUSED TO PERFORM! SHE'S A MASTER OF HER ART! SHE MAKES THE IMPOSSIBLE LOOK EASY!
WOW!
SO COOL!
YOU'RE... REALLY INTO HER. EVEN THOUGH YOU'VE LITERALLY NEVER MENTIONED HER BEFORE.
I'M DEEP. I HAVE DEPTHS.
DEPTHS ARE EXACTLY WHY I'M READY FOR THE RAIN TO STOP.
RAIN IS WATER. WATER MEANS PUDDLES. PUDDLES BECOME PONDS. PONDS BECOME LAKES.
I'VE BEEN HERE LONG ENOUGH TO KNOW HOW THIS WORKS. IF IT RAINS LONG ENOUGH, WE'RE ALL GOING TO WIND UP BOBBING FOR RIVER MONSTERS. AGAIN.
I JUST WANT TO STAY WHERE IT'S DRY AND NOTHING IS TRYING TO EAT US.
MAYBE WE COULD FIGHT THE RAIN!
YOU CAN'T FIGHT THE RAIN.
WHY NOT?

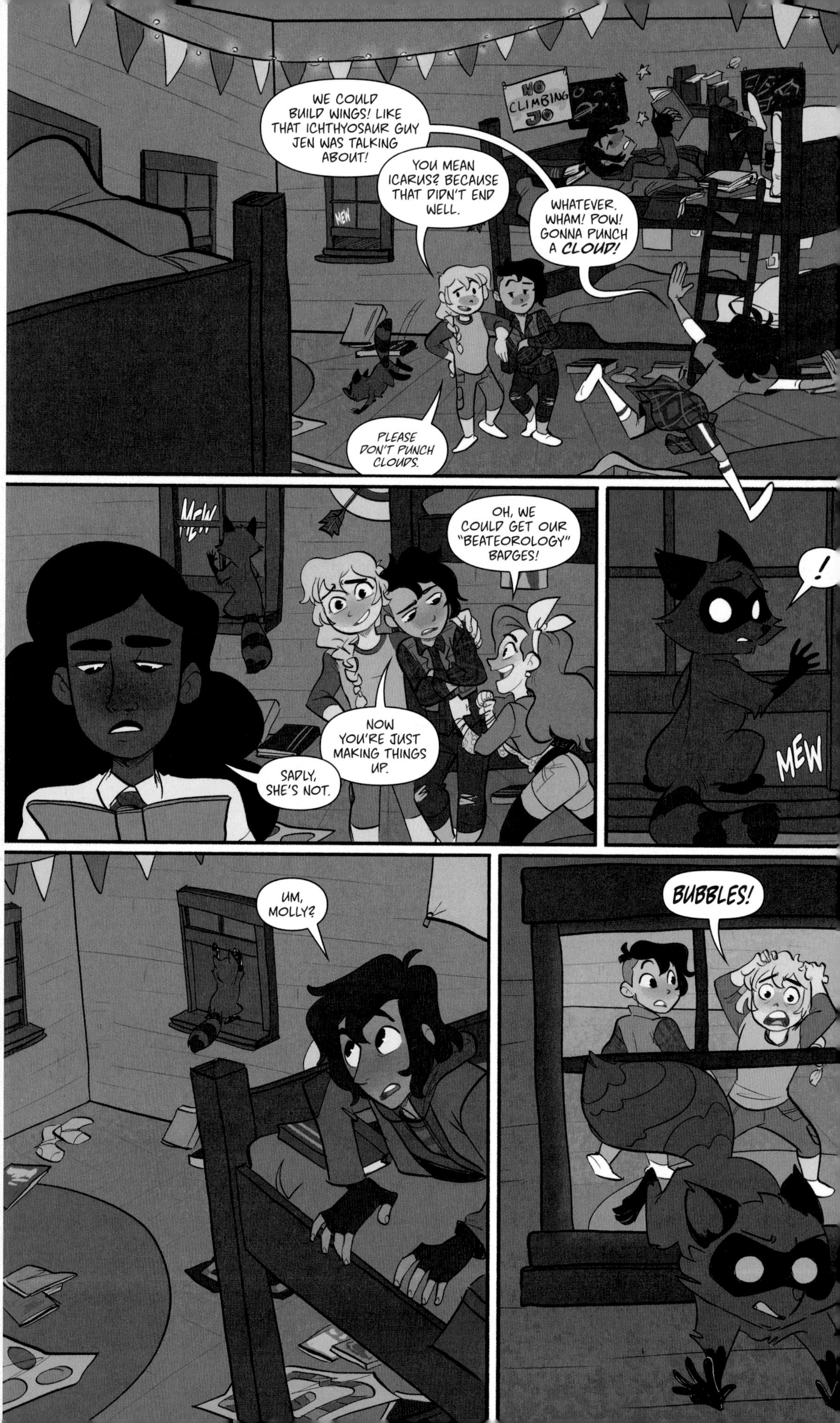
NO CLIMBING JO
WE COULD BUILD WINGS! LIKE THAT ICHTHYOSAUR GUY JEN WAS TALKING ABOUT!
YOU MEAN ICARUS? BECAUSE THAT DIDN'T END WELL.
WHATEVER. WHAM! POW! GONNA PUNCH A CLOUD!
MEW
PLEASE DON'T PUNCH CLOUDS.
MEW
OH, WE COULD GET OUR "BEATEOROLOGY" BADGES!
NOW YOU'RE JUST MAKING THINGS UP.
SADLY, SHE'S NOT.
!
MEW
UM, MOLLY?
BUBBLES!

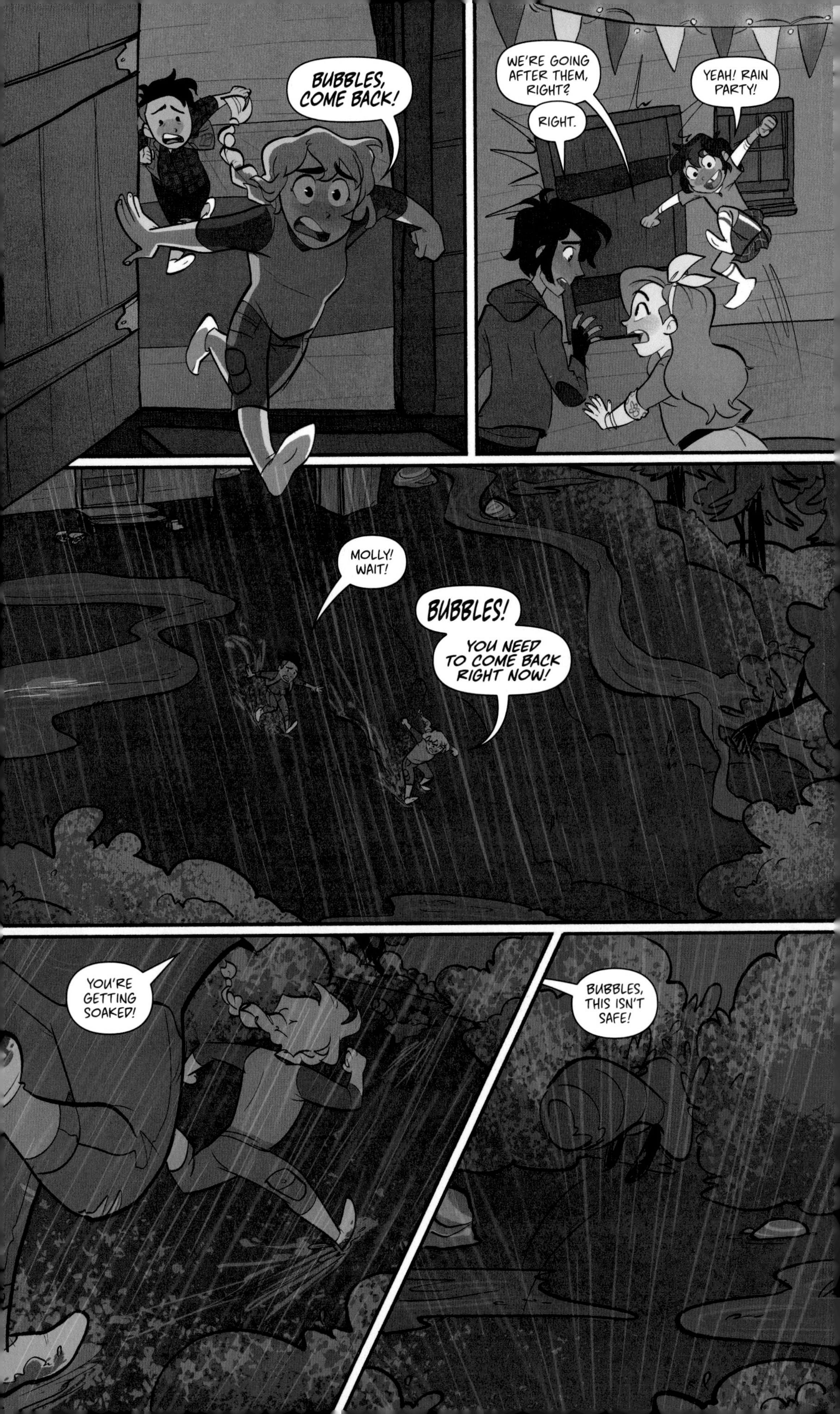
BUBBLES, COME BACK!
WE'RE GOING AFTER THEM, RIGHT?
RIGHT.
YEAH! RAIN PARTY!
MOLLY! WAIT!
BUBBLES!
YOU NEED TO COME BACK RIGHT NOW!
YOU'RE GETTING SOAKED!
BUBBLES, THIS ISN'T SAFE!

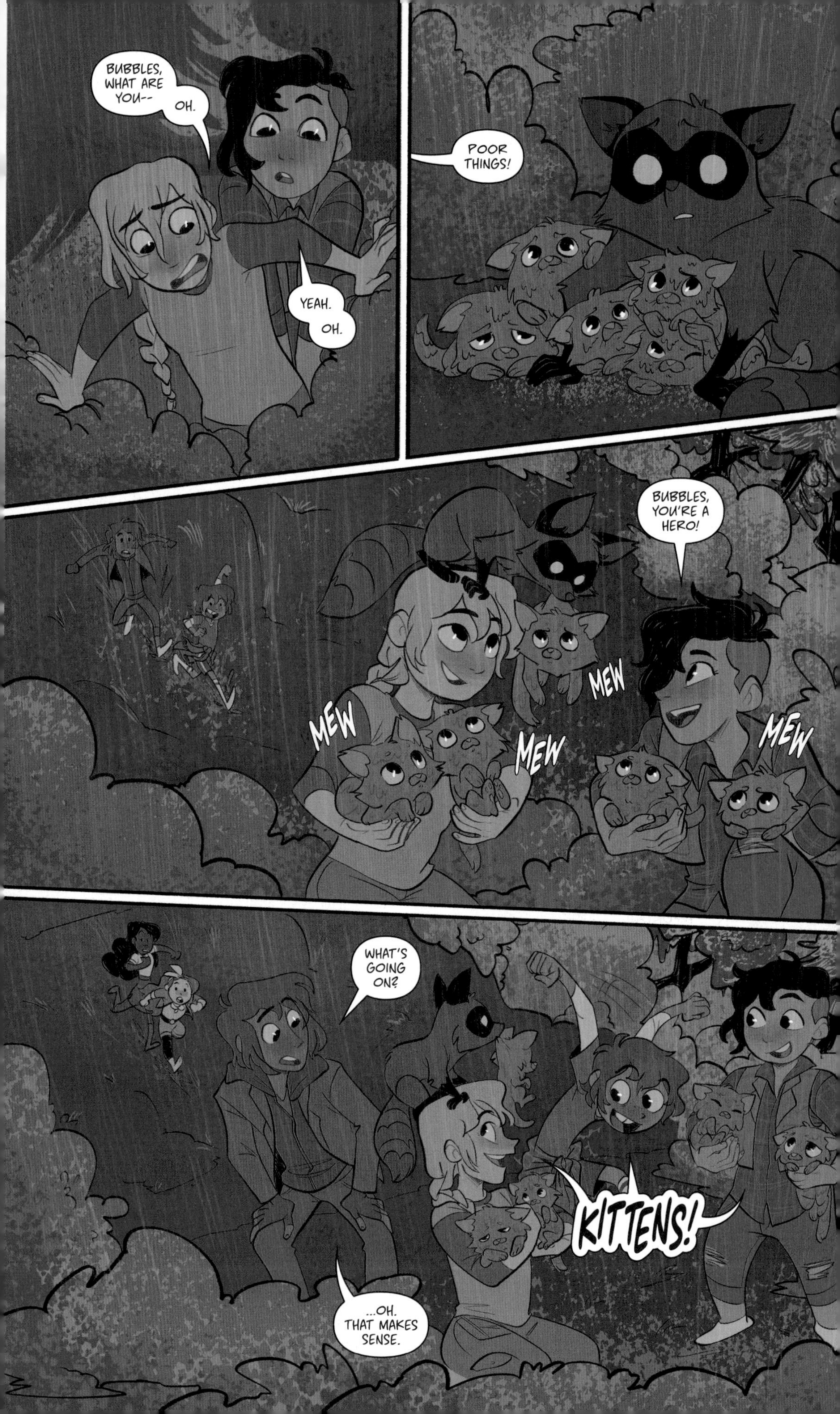
BUBBLES, WHAT ARE YOU--
OH.
YEAH.
OH.
POOR THINGS!
BUBBLES, YOU'RE A HERO!
MEW
MEW
MEW
MEW
WHAT'S GOING ON?
KITTENS!
...OH. THAT MAKES SENSE.

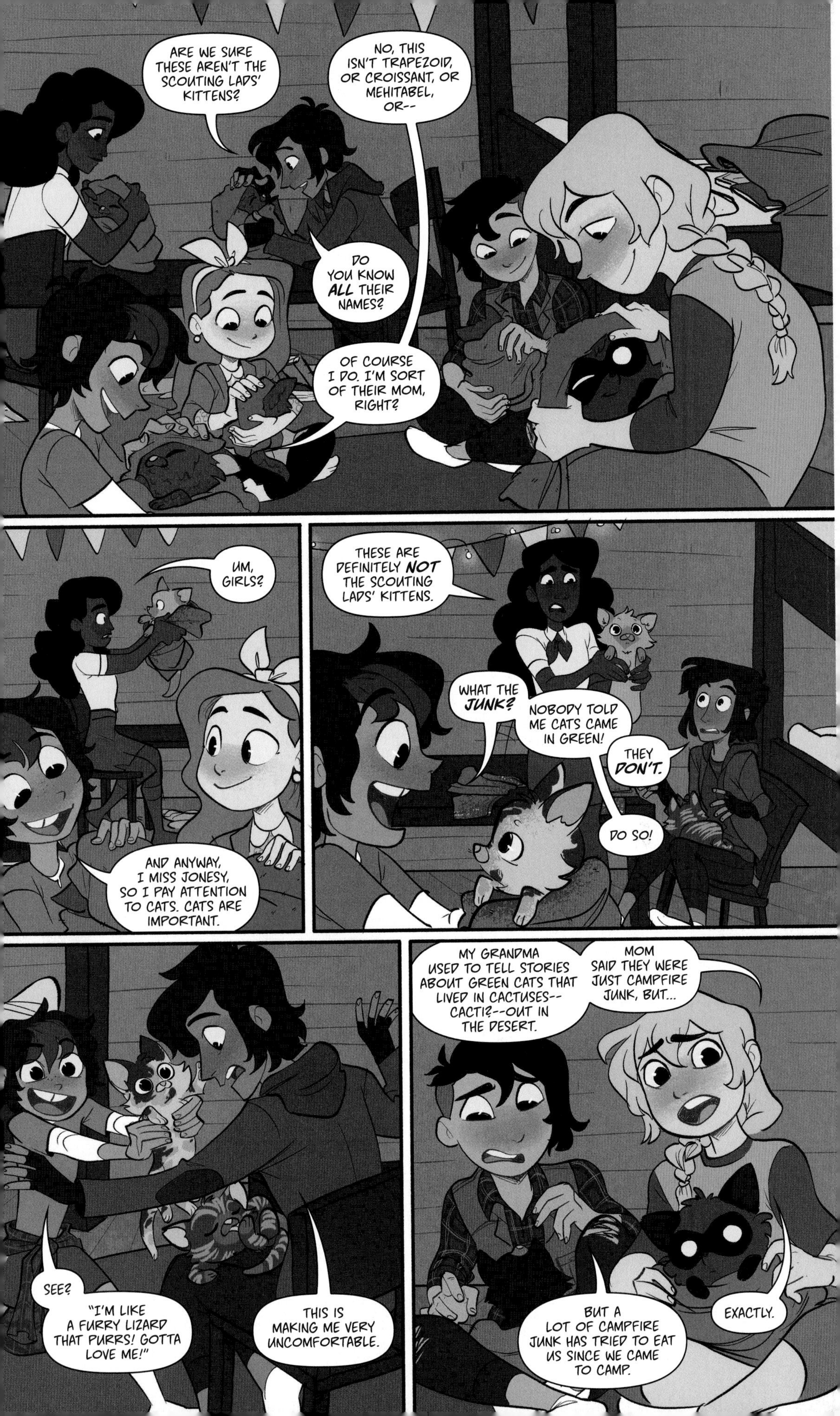
ARE WE SURE THESE AREN'T THE SCOUTING LADS' KITTENS?
NO, THIS ISN'T TRAPEZOID, OR CROISSANT, OR MEHITABEL, OR--
DO YOU KNOW ALL THEIR NAMES?
OF COURSE I DO. I'M SORT OF THEIR MOM, RIGHT?
UM, GIRLS?
AND ANYWAY, I MISS JONESY, SO I PAY ATTENTION TO CATS. CATS ARE IMPORTANT.
THESE ARE DEFINITELY NOT THE SCOUTING LADS' KITTENS.
WHAT THE JUNK?
NOBODY TOLD ME CATS CAME IN GREEN!
THEY DON'T.
DO SO!
SEE?
"I'M LIKE A FURRY LIZARD THAT PURRS! GOTTA LOVE ME!"
THIS IS MAKING ME VERY UNCOMFORTABLE.
MY GRANDMA USED TO TELL STORIES ABOUT GREEN CATS THAT LIVED IN CACTUSES--CACTI?--OUT IN THE DESERT.
MOM SAID THEY WERE JUST CAMPFIRE JUNK, BUT...
BUT A LOT OF CAMPFIRE JUNK HAS TRIED TO EAT US SINCE WE CAME TO CAMP.
EXACTLY.

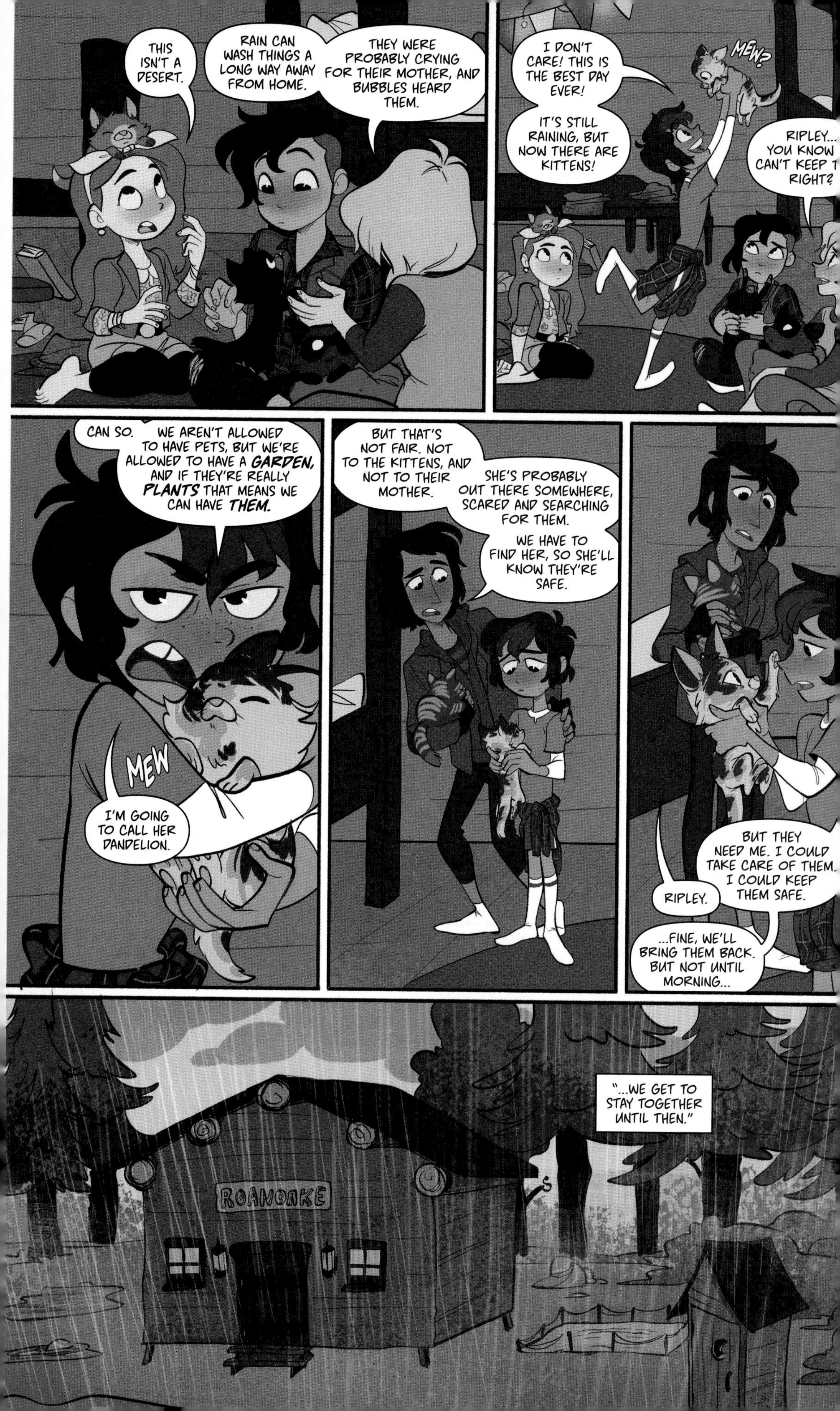

THIS ISN'T A DESERT.
RAIN CAN WASH THINGS A LONG WAY AWAY FROM HOME.
THEY WERE PROBABLY CRYING FOR THEIR MOTHER, AND BUBBLES HEARD THEM.
MEW?
I DON'T CARE! THIS IS THE BEST DAY EVER!
IT'S STILL RAINING, BUT NOW THERE ARE KITTENS!
RIPLEY... YOU KNOW
CAN SO.
WE AREN'T ALLOWED TO HAVE PETS, BUT WE'RE ALLOWED TO HAVE A GARDEN, AND IF THEY'RE REALLY PLANTS THAT MEANS WE CAN HAVE THEM.
MEW
I'M GOING TO CALL HER DANDELION.
BUT THAT'S NOT FAIR. NOT TO THE KITTENS, AND NOT TO THEIR MOTHER.
SHE'S PROBABLY OUT THERE SOMEWHERE, SCARED AND SEARCHING FOR THEM.
WE HAVE TO FIND HER, SO SHE'LL KNOW THEY'RE SAFE.
BUT THEY NEED ME. I COULD TAKE CARE OF THEM. I COULD KEEP THEM SAFE.
RIPLEY.
...FINE, WE'LL BRING THEM BACK. BUT NOT UNTIL MORNING...
"...WE GET TO STAY TOGETHER UNTIL THEN."
ROANOKE

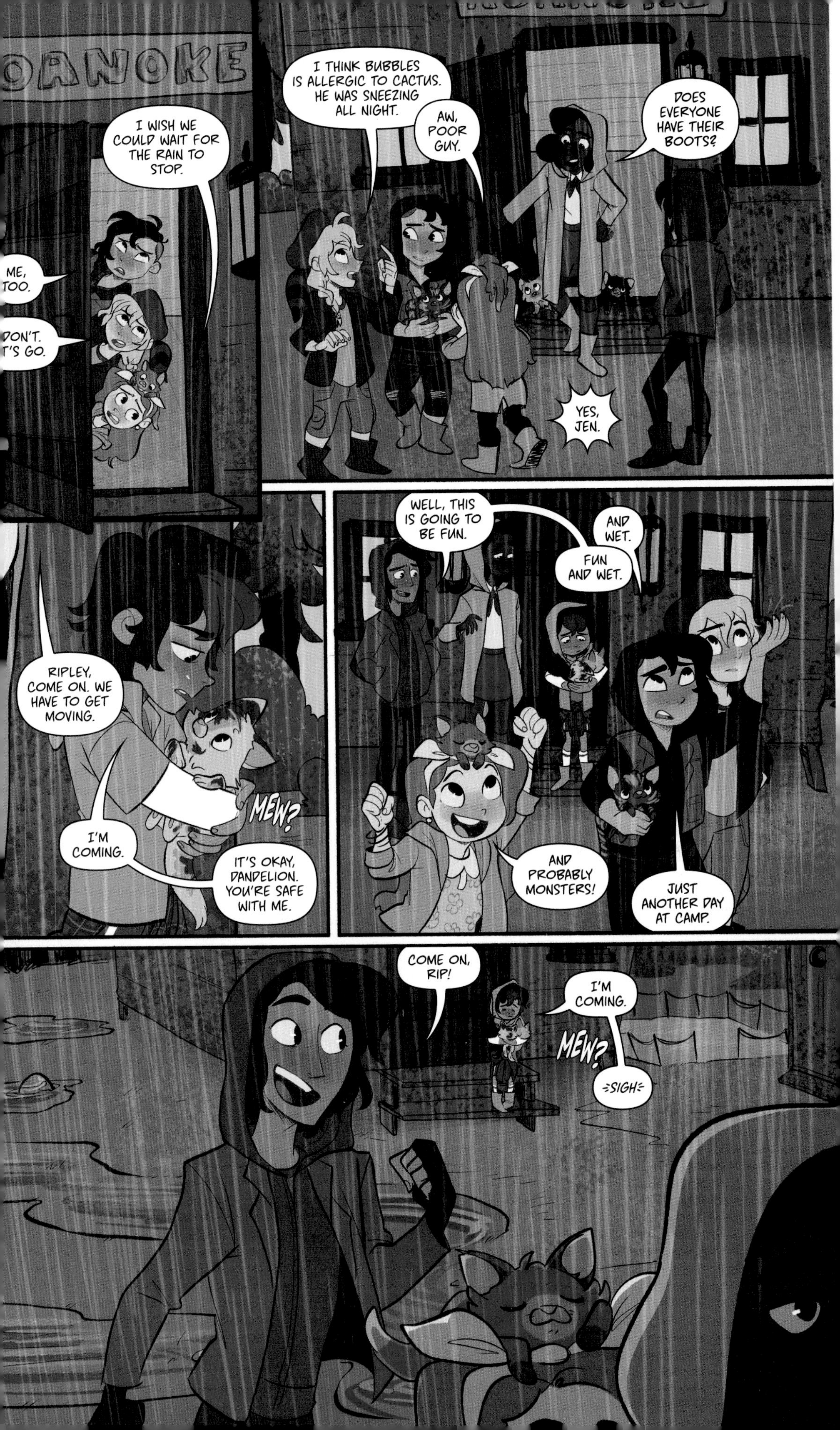

OANOKE
I WISH WE COULD WAIT FOR THE RAIN TO STOP.
ME, TOO.
DON'T. 'T'S GO.
I THINK BUBBLES IS ALLERGIC TO CACTUS. HE WAS SNEEZING ALL NIGHT.
AW, POOR GUY.
DOES EVERYONE HAVE THEIR BOOTS?
YES, JEN.
RIPLEY, COME ON. WE HAVE TO GET MOVING.
MEW?
I'M COMING.
IT'S OKAY, DANDELION. YOU'RE SAFE WITH ME.
WELL, THIS IS GOING TO BE FUN.
AND WET.
FUN AND WET.
AND PROBABLY MONSTERS!
JUST ANOTHER DAY AT CAMP.
COME ON, RIP!
I'M COMING.
MEW?
SIGH

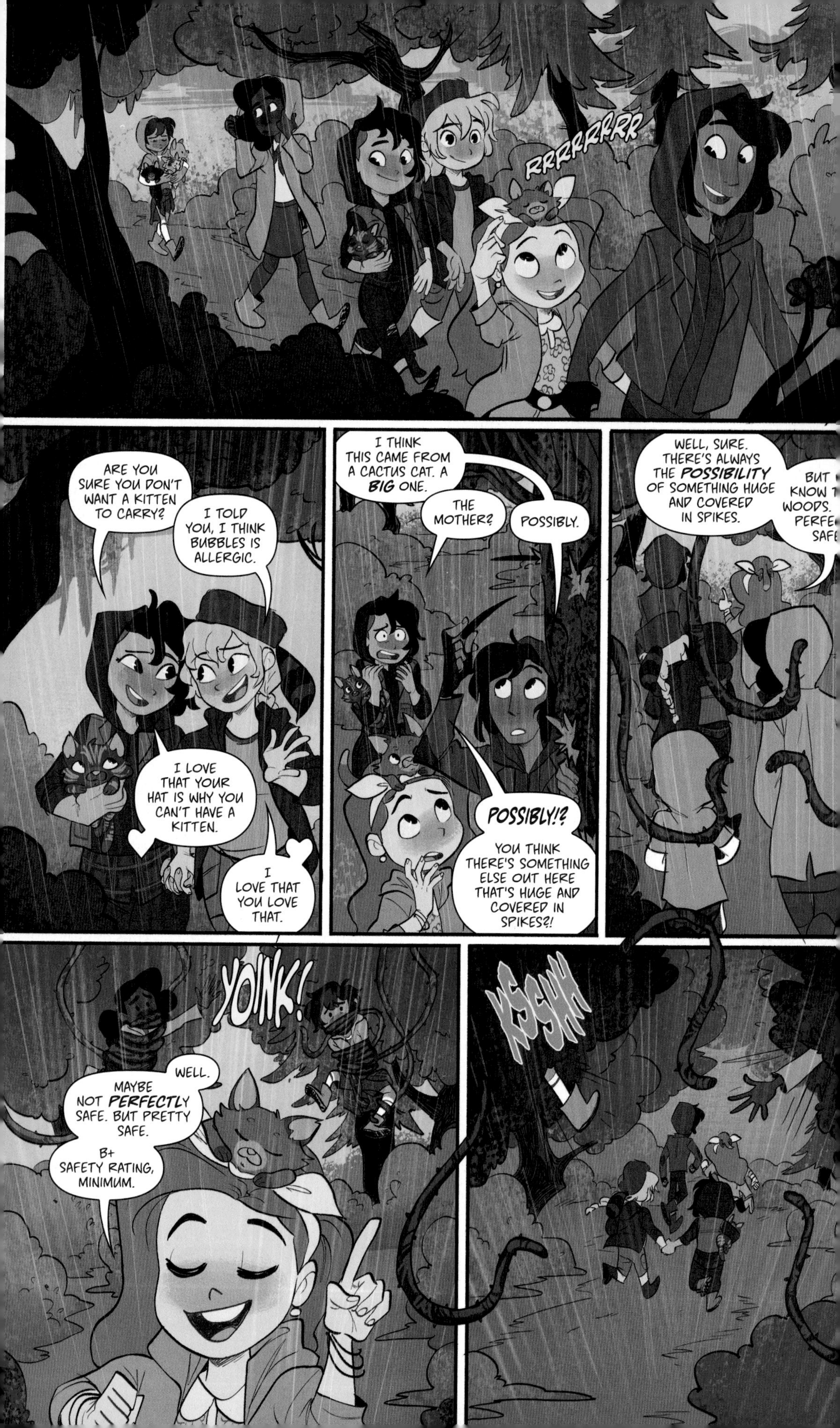
RRRRRRRRR
ARE YOU SURE YOU DON'T WANT A KITTEN TO CARRY?
I TOLD YOU, I THINK BUBBLES IS ALLERGIC.
I LOVE THAT YOUR HAT IS WHY YOU CAN'T HAVE A KITTEN.
I LOVE THAT YOU LOVE THAT.
I THINK THIS CAME FROM A CACTUS CAT. A **BIG** ONE.
THE MOTHER?
POSSIBLY.
POSSIBLY!?
YOU THINK THERE'S SOMETHING ELSE OUT HERE THAT'S HUGE AND COVERED IN SPIKES?!
WELL, SURE. THERE'S ALWAYS THE ***POSSIBILITY*** OF SOMETHING HUGE AND COVERED IN SPIKES.
YOINK!
WELL.
MAYBE NOT ***PERFECT***LY SAFE. BUT PRETTY SAFE.
B+ SAFETY RATING, MINIMUM.
KSSH

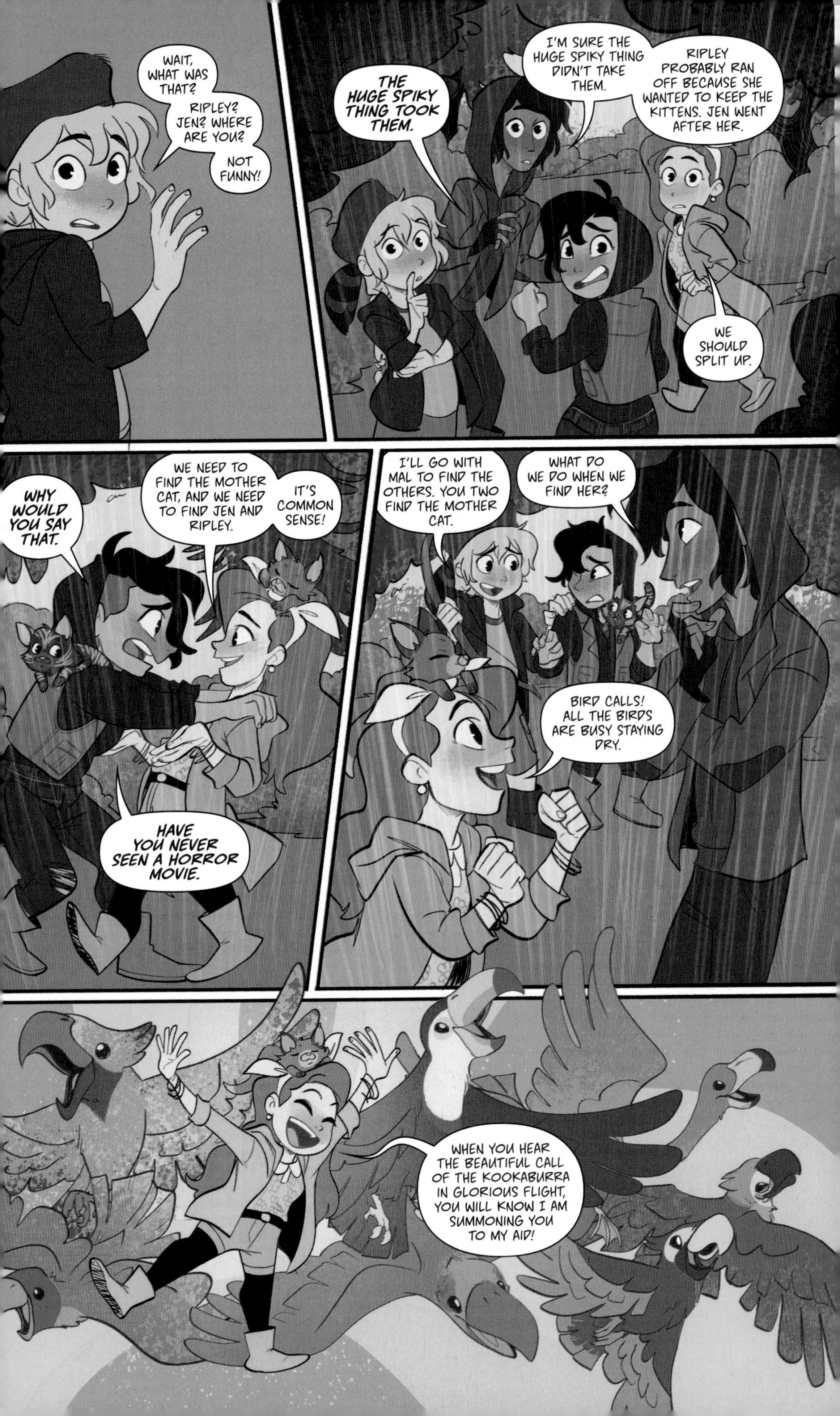
WAIT, WHAT WAS THAT?
RIPLEY? JEN? WHERE ARE YOU?
NOT FUNNY!
THE HUGE SPIKY THING TOOK THEM.
I'M SURE THE HUGE SPIKY THING DIDN'T TAKE THEM.
RIPLEY PROBABLY RAN OFF BECAUSE SHE WANTED TO KEEP THE KITTENS. JEN WENT AFTER HER.
WE SHOULD SPLIT UP.
WHY WOULD YOU SAY THAT.
HAVE YOU NEVER SEEN A HORROR MOVIE.
WE NEED TO FIND THE MOTHER CAT, AND WE NEED TO FIND JEN AND RIPLEY.
IT'S COMMON SENSE!
I'LL GO WITH MAL TO FIND THE OTHERS. YOU TWO FIND THE MOTHER CAT.
WHAT DO WE DO WHEN WE FIND HER?
BIRD CALLS! ALL THE BIRDS ARE BUSY STAYING DRY.
WHEN YOU HEAR THE BEAUTIFUL CALL OF THE KOOKABURRA IN GLORIOUS FLIGHT, YOU WILL KNOW I AM SUMMONING YOU TO MY AID!

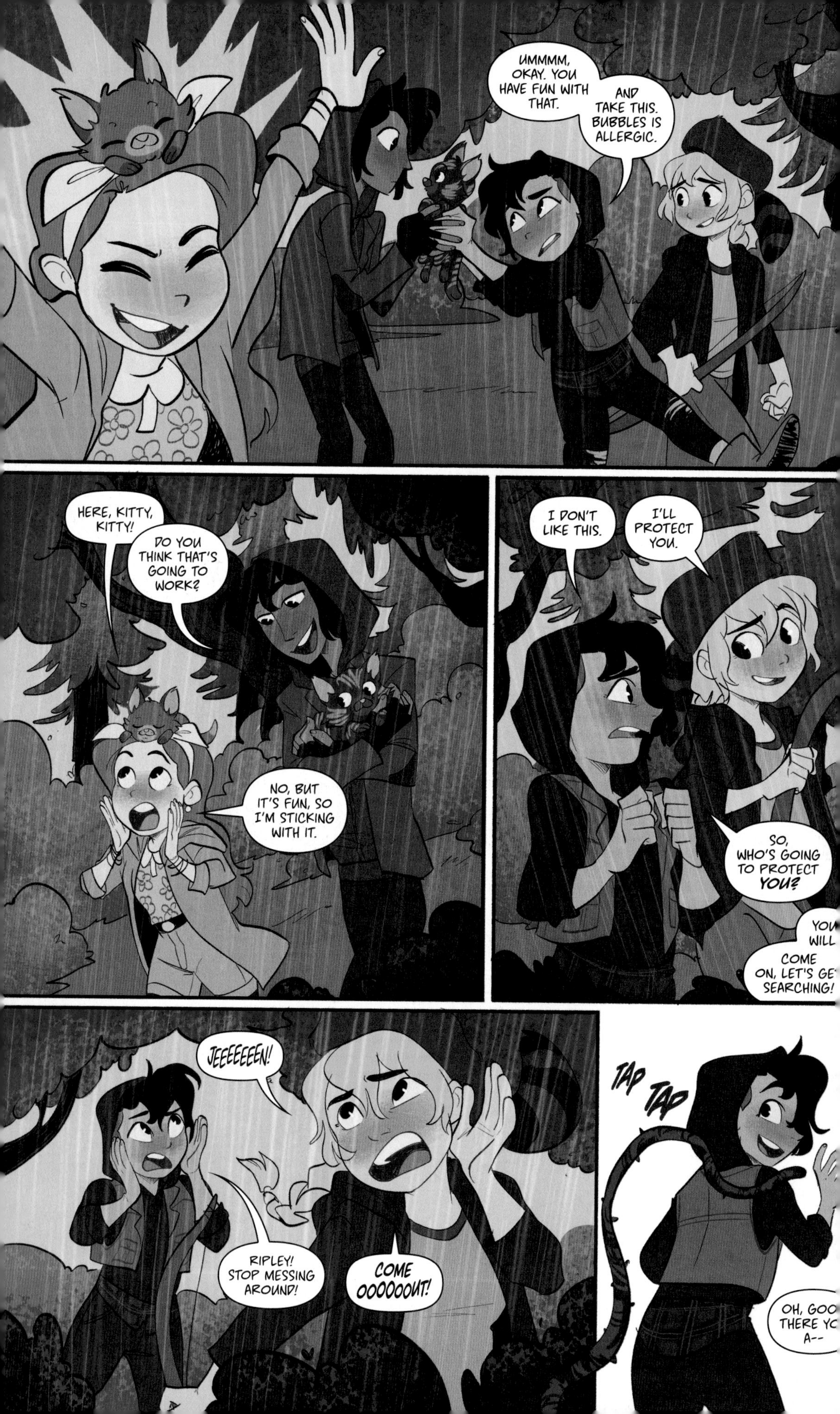
UMMMM, OKAY. YOU HAVE FUN WITH THAT.
AND TAKE THIS. BUBBLES IS ALLERGIC.
HERE, KITTY, KITTY!
DO YOU THINK THAT'S GOING TO WORK?
NO, BUT IT'S FUN, SO I'M STICKING WITH IT.
I DON'T LIKE THIS.
I'LL PROTECT YOU.
SO, WHO'S GOING TO PROTECT YOU?
YOU WILL
COME ON, LET'S GE SEARCHING!
JEEEEEEEN!
RIPLEY! STOP MESSING AROUND!
COME OOOOOOUT!
TAP TAP
OH, GOO THERE YO A--

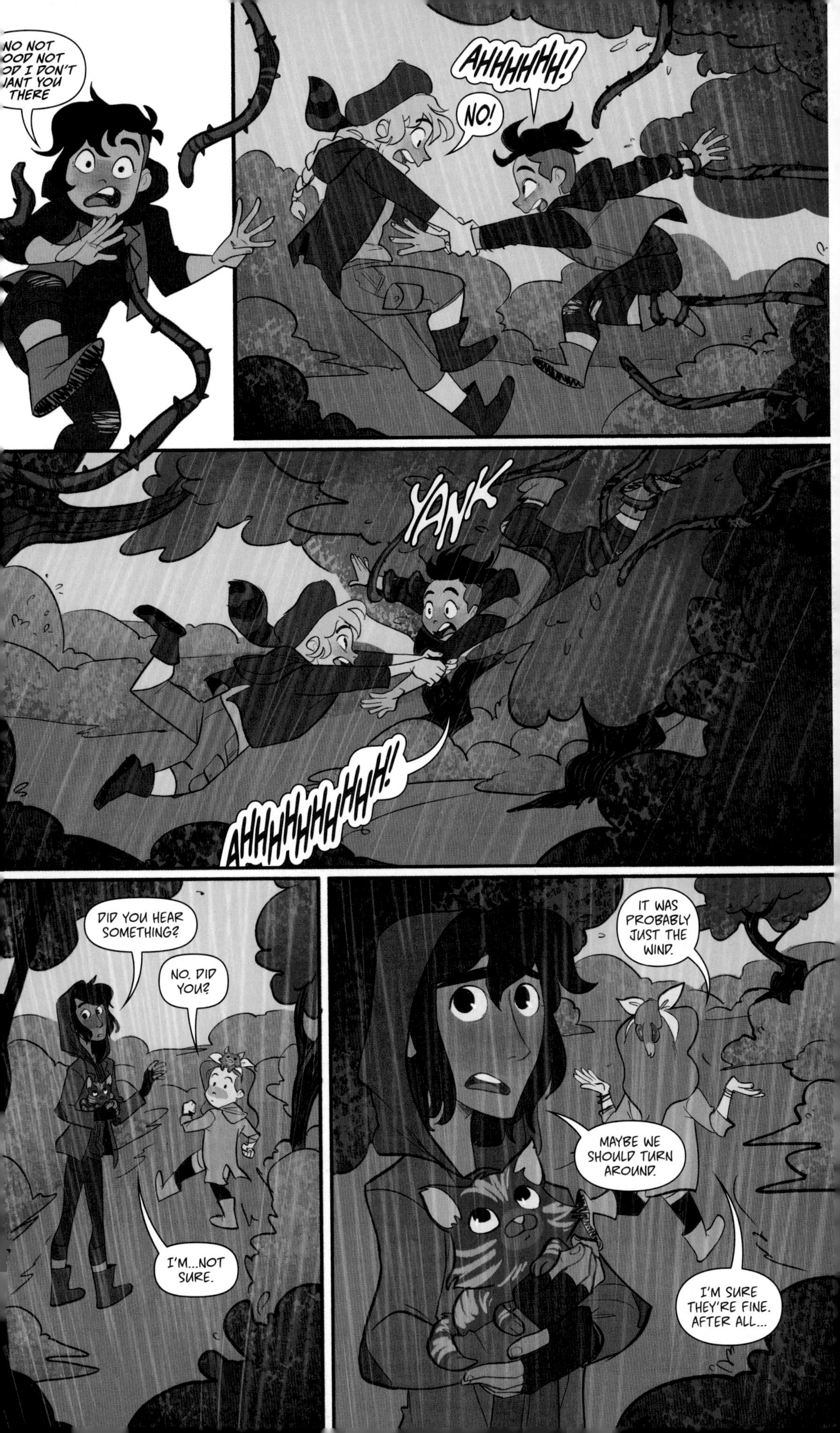

NO NOT OOD NOT OD I DON'T ANT YOU THERE
AHHHHHH!
NO!
YANK
AHHHHHHHHHHH!
DID YOU HEAR SOMETHING?
NO. DID YOU?
I'M...NOT SURE.
IT WAS PROBABLY JUST THE WIND.
MAYBE WE SHOULD TURN AROUND.
I'M SURE THEY'RE FINE. AFTER ALL...

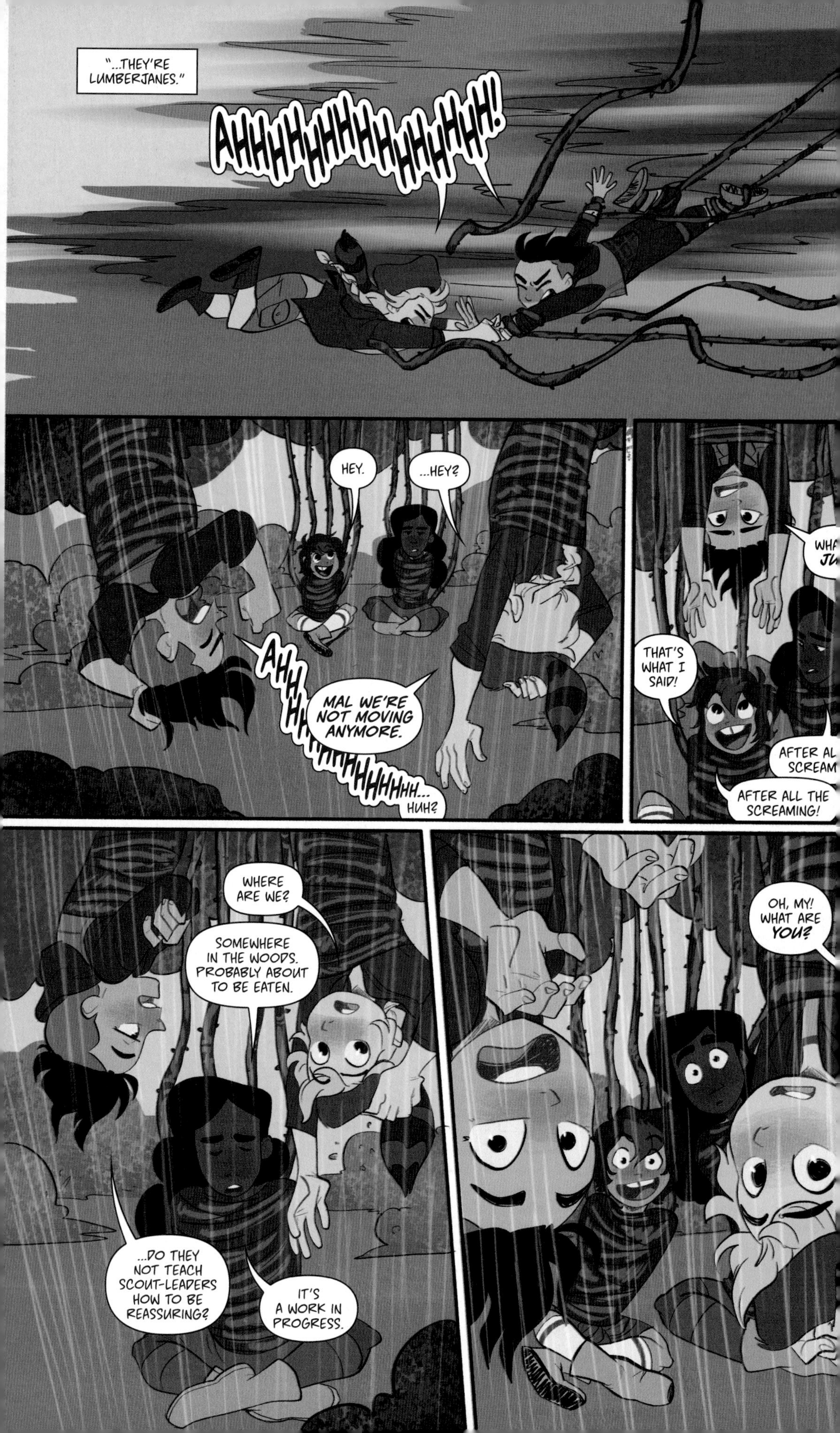
"...THEY'RE LUMBERJANES."
AHHHHHHHHHHHHHHHH!
HEY.
...HEY?
AHHHHHHHHHHHHHHH... HUH?
MAL WE'RE NOT MOVING ANYMORE.
THAT'S WHAT I SAID!
AFTER ALL THE SCREAMING!
WHERE ARE WE?
SOMEWHERE IN THE WOODS. PROBABLY ABOUT TO BE EATEN.
...DO THEY NOT TEACH SCOUT-LEADERS HOW TO BE REASSURING?
IT'S A WORK IN PROGRESS.
OH, MY! WHAT ARE YOU?

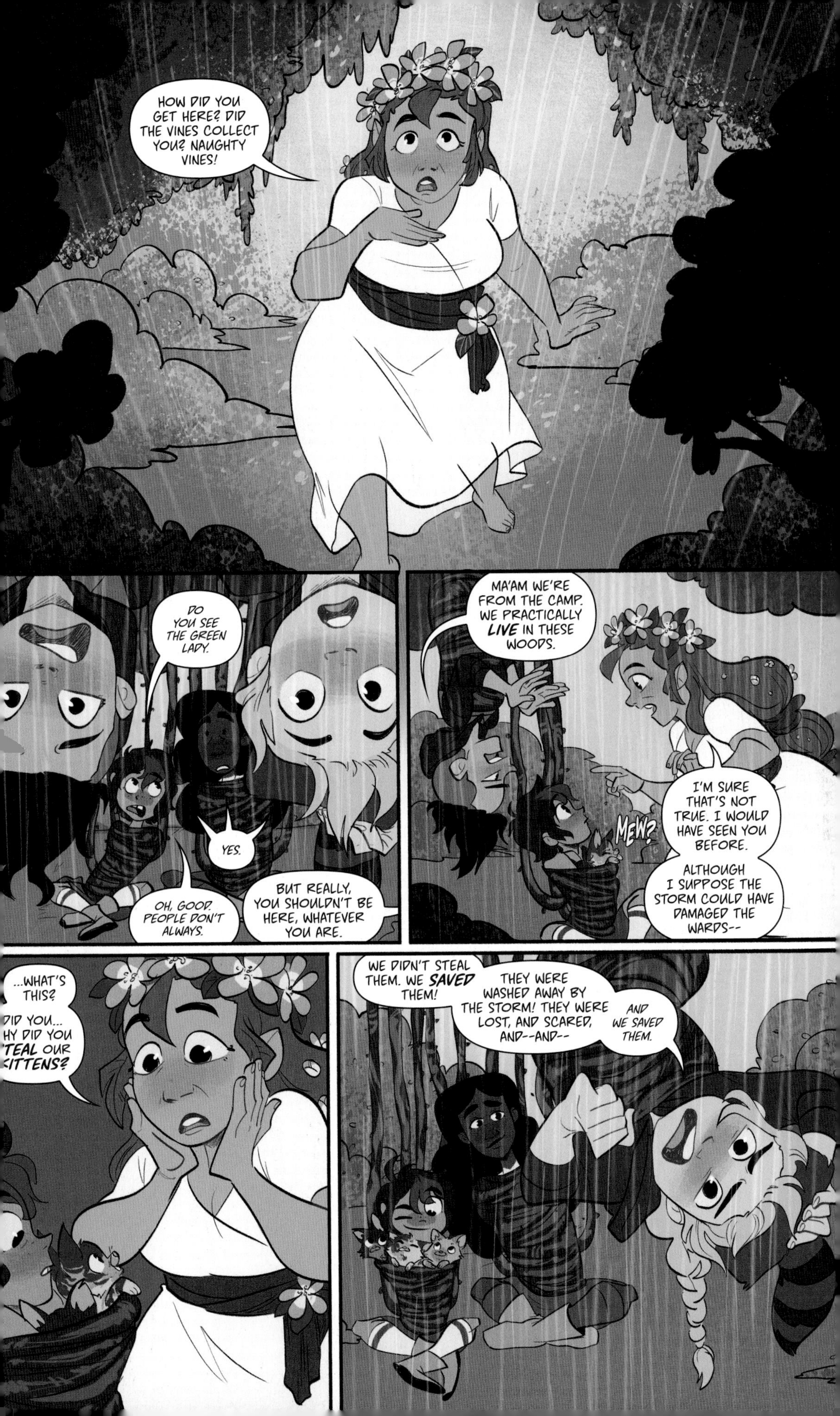
HOW DID YOU GET HERE? DID THE VINES COLLECT YOU? NAUGHTY VINES!
DO YOU SEE THE GREEN LADY.
YES.
OH, GOOD. PEOPLE DON'T ALWAYS.
BUT REALLY, YOU SHOULDN'T BE HERE, WHATEVER YOU ARE.
MA'AM WE'RE FROM THE CAMP. WE PRACTICALLY LIVE IN THESE WOODS.
I'M SURE THAT'S NOT TRUE. I WOULD HAVE SEEN YOU BEFORE.
ALTHOUGH I SUPPOSE THE STORM COULD HAVE DAMAGED THE WARDS--
MEW?
...WHAT'S THIS?
DID YOU... WHY DID YOU STEAL OUR KITTENS?
WE DIDN'T STEAL THEM. WE SAVED THEM!
THEY WERE WASHED AWAY BY THE STORM! THEY WERE LOST, AND SCARED, AND--AND--
AND WE SAVED THEM.

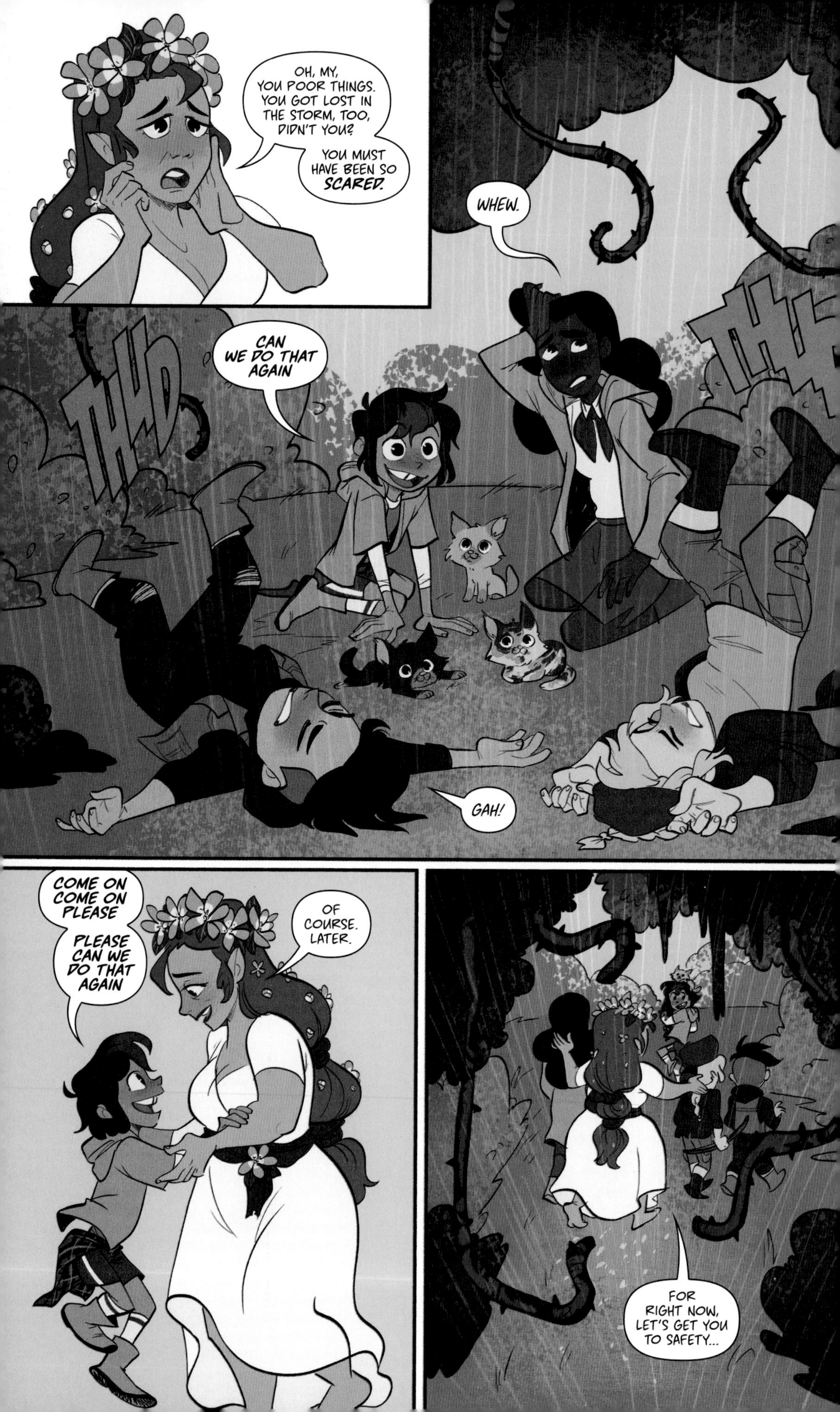

OH, MY, YOU POOR THINGS. YOU GOT LOST IN THE STORM, TOO, DIDN'T YOU?
YOU MUST HAVE BEEN SO SCARED.
WHEW.
THUD
THUD
CAN WE DO THAT AGAIN
GAH!
COME ON COME ON PLEASE
PLEASE CAN WE DO THAT AGAIN
OF COURSE. LATER.
FOR RIGHT NOW, LET'S GET YOU TO SAFETY...

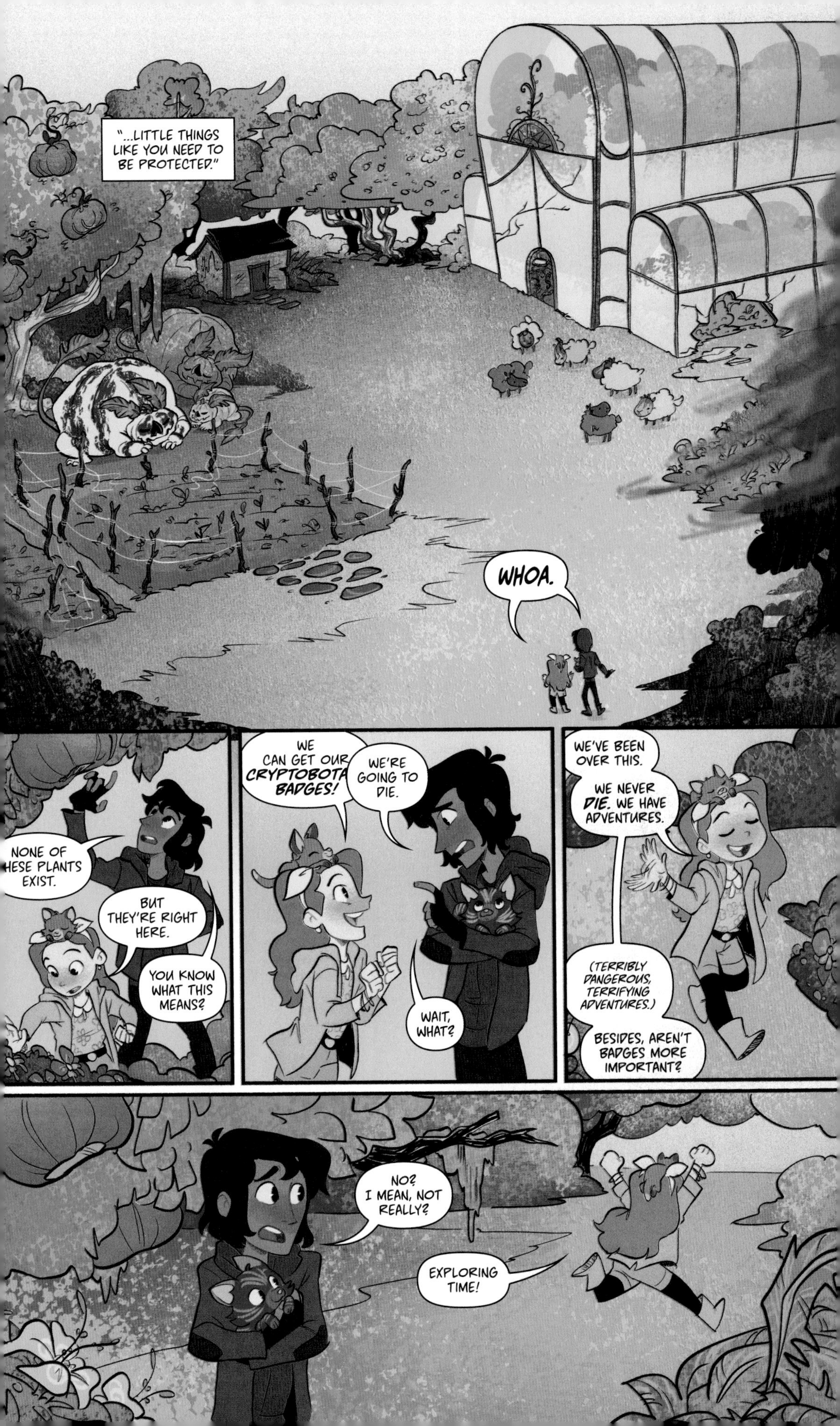
"...LITTLE THINGS LIKE YOU NEED TO BE PROTECTED."
WHOA.
NONE OF HESE PLANTS EXIST.
BUT THEY'RE RIGHT HERE.
YOU KNOW WHAT THIS MEANS?
WE CAN GET OUR CRYPTOBOTA BADGES!
WE'RE GOING TO DIE.
WAIT, WHAT?
WE'VE BEEN OVER THIS.
WE NEVER DIE. WE HAVE ADVENTURES.
(TERRIBLY DANGEROUS, TERRIFYING ADVENTURES.)
BESIDES, AREN'T BADGES MORE IMPORTANT?
NO? I MEAN, NOT REALLY?
EXPLORING TIME!

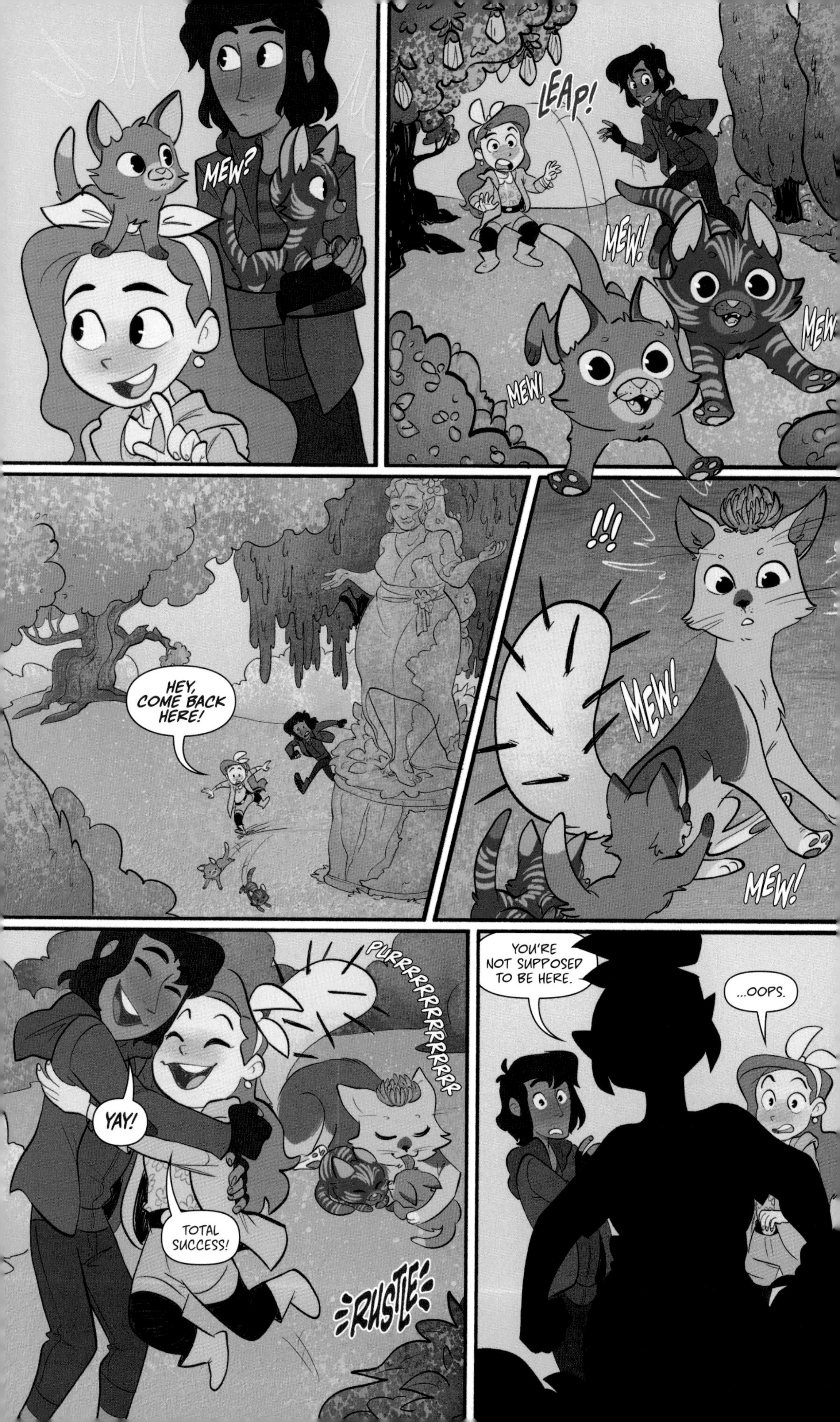
MEW?
LEAP!
MEW!
MEW!
MEW
HEY, COME BACK HERE!
!!!
MEW!
MEW!
YAY!
TOTAL SUCCESS!
PURRRRRRRRRRRRR
RUSTLE
YOU'RE NOT SUPPOSED TO BE HERE.
...OOPS.

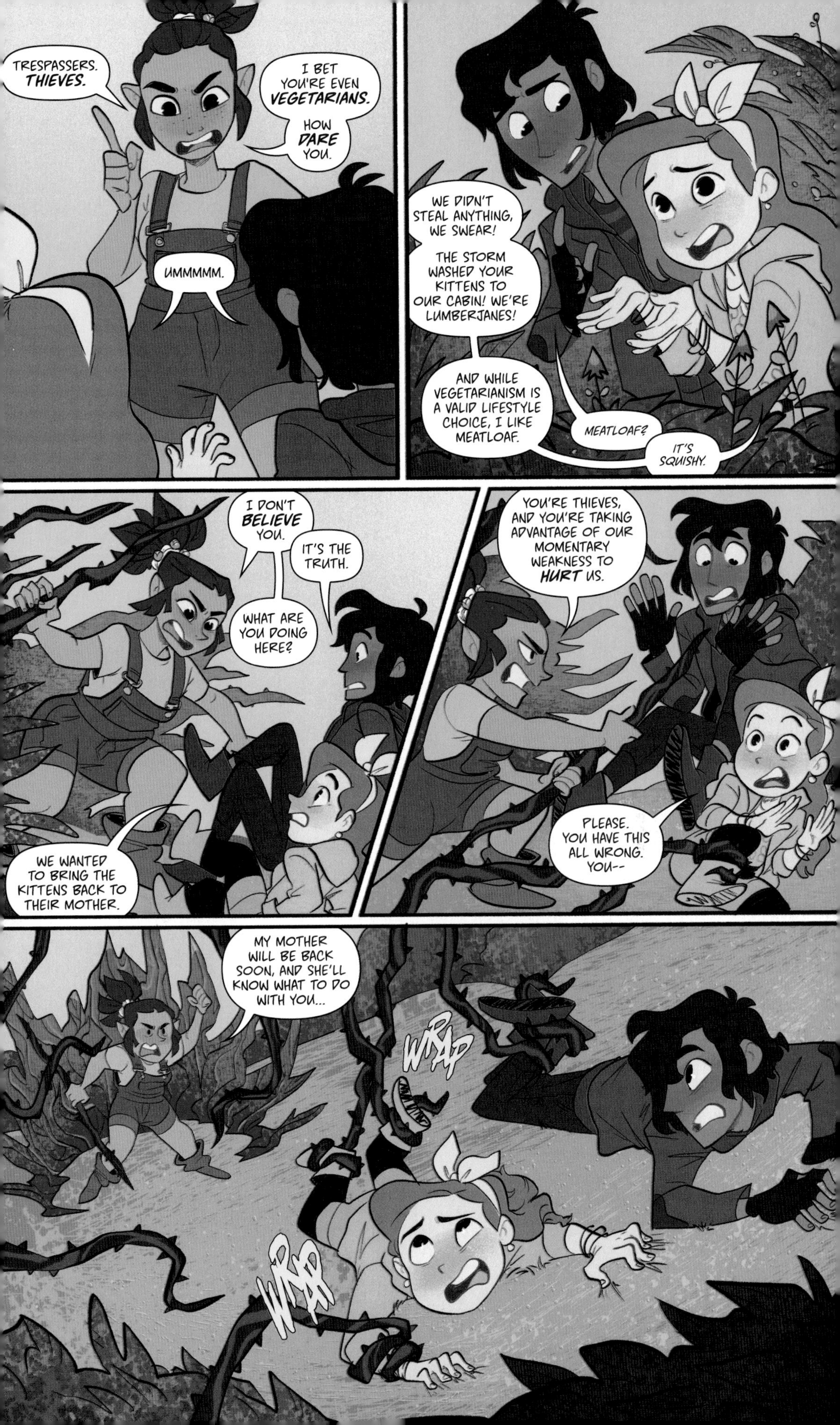

TRESPASSERS. THIEVES.
I BET YOU'RE EVEN VEGETARIANS.
HOW DARE YOU.
UMMMMM.
WE DIDN'T STEAL ANYTHING, WE SWEAR!
THE STORM WASHED YOUR KITTENS TO OUR CABIN! WE'RE LUMBERJANES!
AND WHILE VEGETARIANISM IS A VALID LIFESTYLE CHOICE, I LIKE MEATLOAF.
MEATLOAF?
IT'S SQUISHY.
I DON'T BELIEVE YOU.
IT'S THE TRUTH.
WHAT ARE YOU DOING HERE?
WE WANTED TO BRING THE KITTENS BACK TO THEIR MOTHER.
YOU'RE THIEVES, AND YOU'RE TAKING ADVANTAGE OF OUR MOMENTARY WEAKNESS TO HURT US.
PLEASE. YOU HAVE THIS ALL WRONG. YOU--
MY MOTHER WILL BE BACK SOON, AND SHE'LL KNOW WHAT TO DO WITH YOU...
WRAP
WRAP

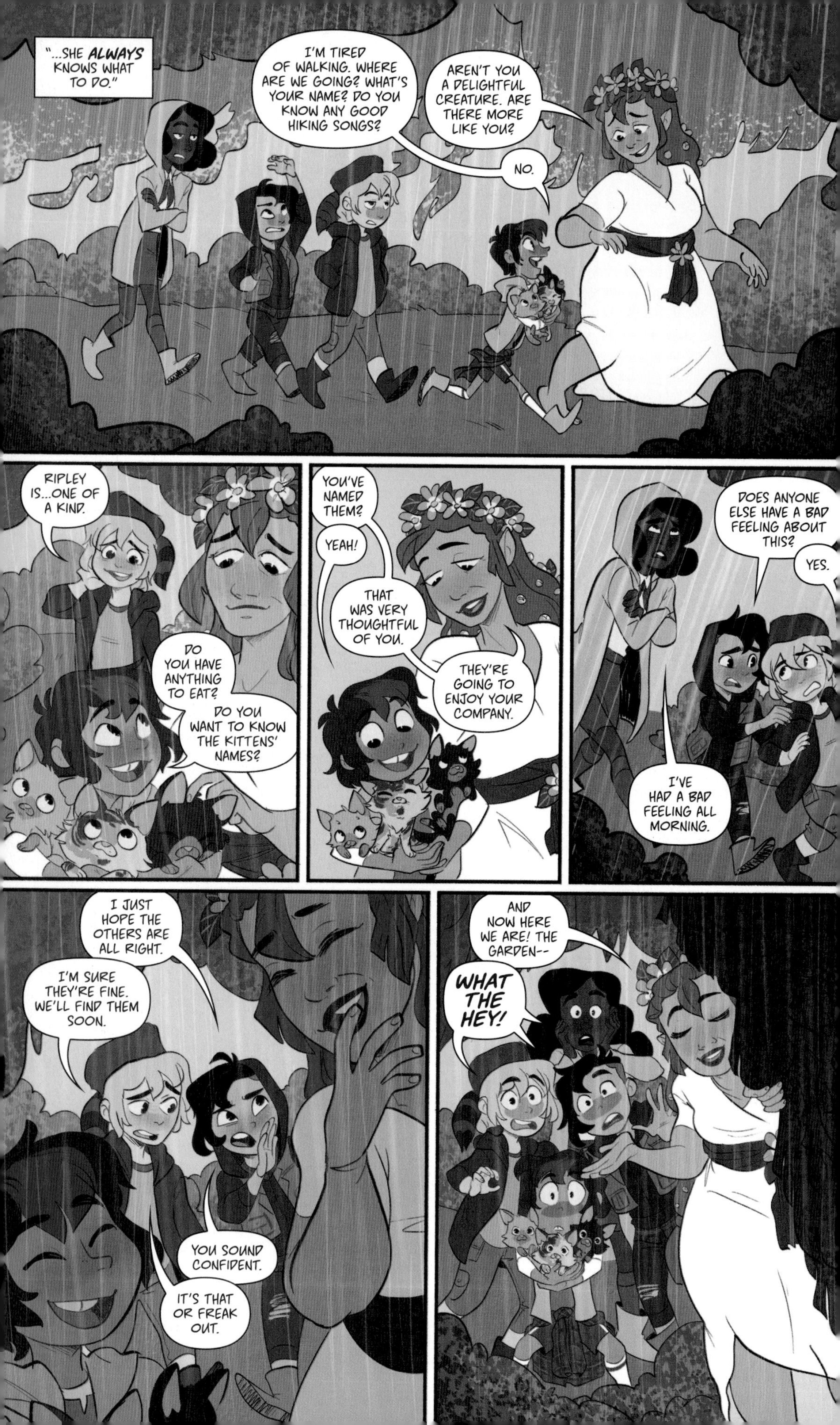

"...SHE **ALWAYS** KNOWS WHAT TO DO."
I'M TIRED OF WALKING. WHERE ARE WE GOING? WHAT'S YOUR NAME? DO YOU KNOW ANY GOOD HIKING SONGS?
AREN'T YOU A DELIGHTFUL CREATURE. ARE THERE MORE LIKE YOU?
NO.
RIPLEY IS...ONE OF A KIND.
DO YOU HAVE ANYTHING TO EAT?
DO YOU WANT TO KNOW THE KITTENS' NAMES?
YOU'VE NAMED THEM?
YEAH!
THAT WAS VERY THOUGHTFUL OF YOU.
THEY'RE GOING TO ENJOY YOUR COMPANY.
DOES ANYONE ELSE HAVE A BAD FEELING ABOUT THIS?
YES.
I'VE HAD A BAD FEELING ALL MORNING.
I JUST HOPE THE OTHERS ARE ALL RIGHT.
I'M SURE THEY'RE FINE. WE'LL FIND THEM SOON.
YOU SOUND CONFIDENT.
IT'S THAT OR FREAK OUT.
AND NOW HERE WE ARE! THE GARDEN--
WHAT THE HEY!

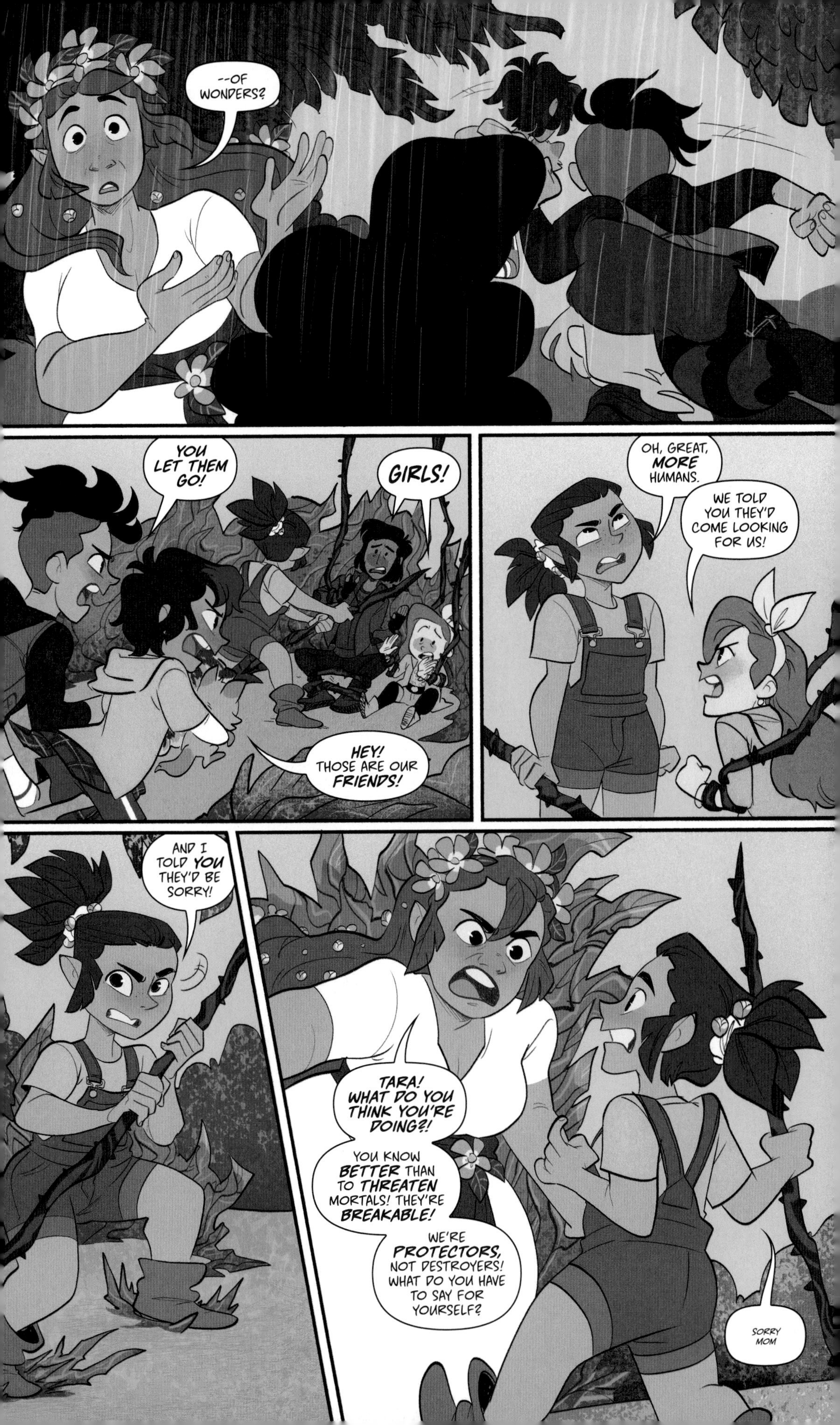
--OF WONDERS?
YOU LET THEM GO!
GIRLS!
HEY! THOSE ARE OUR FRIENDS!
OH, GREAT, MORE HUMANS.
WE TOLD YOU THEY'D COME LOOKING FOR US!
AND I TOLD YOU THEY'D BE SORRY!
TARA! WHAT DO YOU THINK YOU'RE DOING?!
YOU KNOW BETTER THAN TO THREATEN MORTALS! THEY'RE BREAKABLE!
WE'RE PROTECTORS, NOT DESTROYERS! WHAT DO YOU HAVE TO SAY FOR YOURSELF?
SORRY MOM

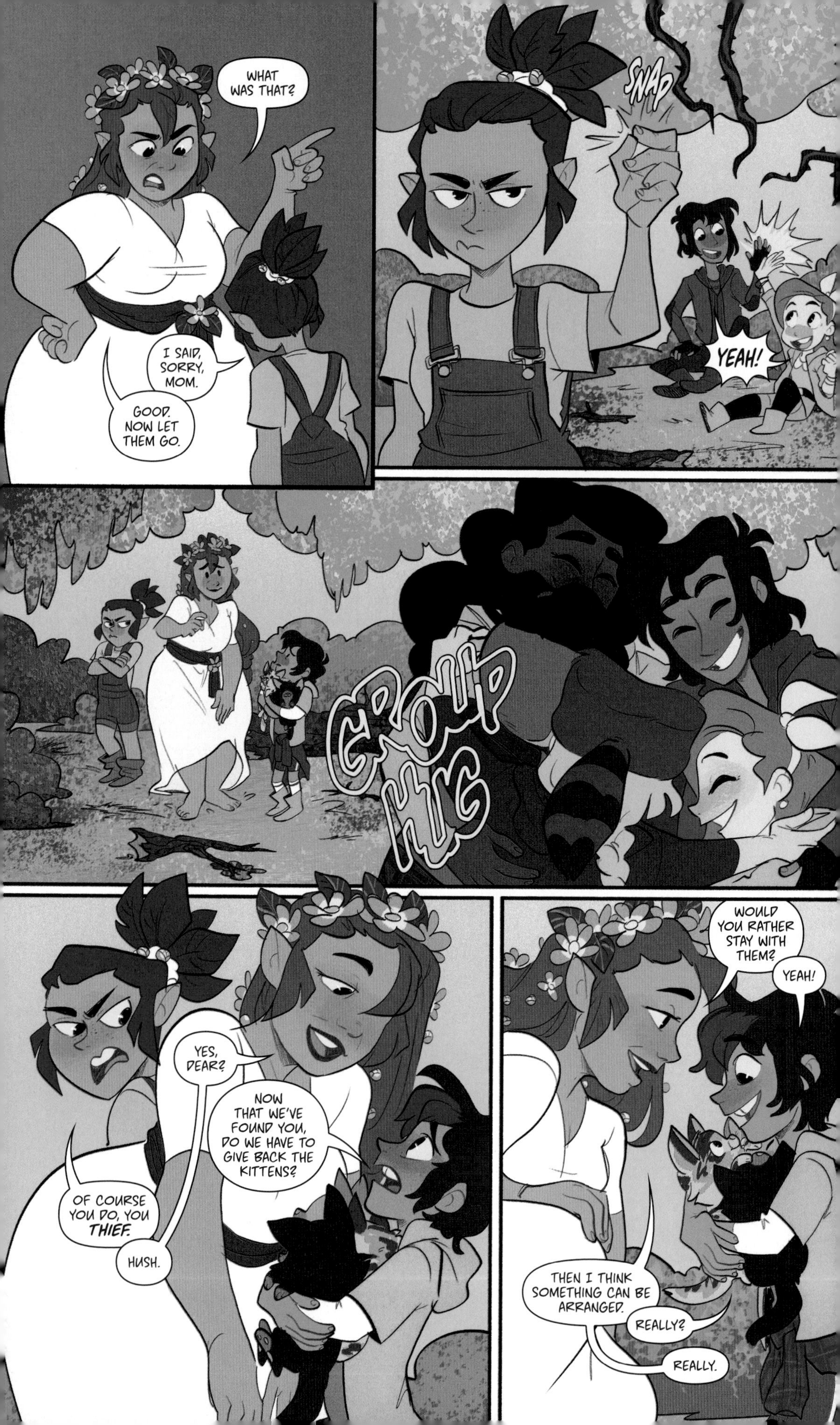
WHAT WAS THAT?
I SAID, SORRY, MOM.
GOOD. NOW LET THEM GO.
SNAP
YEAH!
GROUP HUG
YES, DEAR?
NOW THAT WE'VE FOUND YOU, DO WE HAVE TO GIVE BACK THE KITTENS?
OF COURSE YOU DO, YOU THIEF.
HUSH.
WOULD YOU RATHER STAY WITH THEM?
YEAH!
THEN I THINK SOMETHING CAN BE ARRANGED.
REALLY?
REALLY.

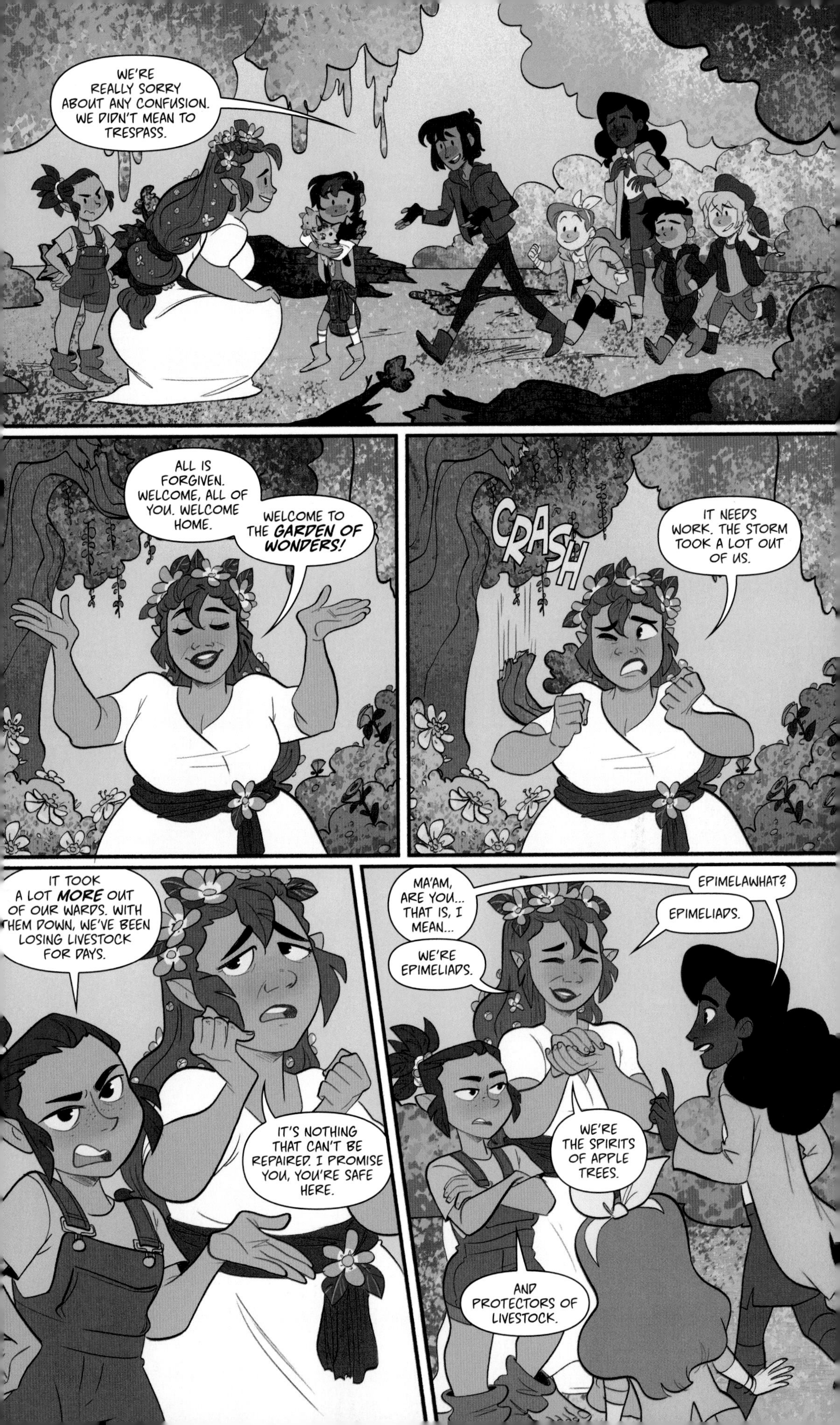

WE'RE REALLY SORRY ABOUT ANY CONFUSION. WE DIDN'T MEAN TO TRESPASS.
ALL IS FORGIVEN. WELCOME, ALL OF YOU. WELCOME HOME.
WELCOME TO THE GARDEN OF WONDERS!
CRASH
IT NEEDS WORK. THE STORM TOOK A LOT OUT OF US.
IT TOOK A LOT MORE OUT OF OUR WARDS. WITH THEM DOWN, WE'VE BEEN LOSING LIVESTOCK FOR DAYS.
IT'S NOTHING THAT CAN'T BE REPAIRED. I PROMISE YOU, YOU'RE SAFE HERE.
MA'AM, ARE YOU... THAT IS, I MEAN...
WE'RE EPIMELIADS.
EPIMELAWHAT?
EPIMELIADS.
WE'RE THE SPIRITS OF APPLE TREES.
AND PROTECTORS OF LIVESTOCK.

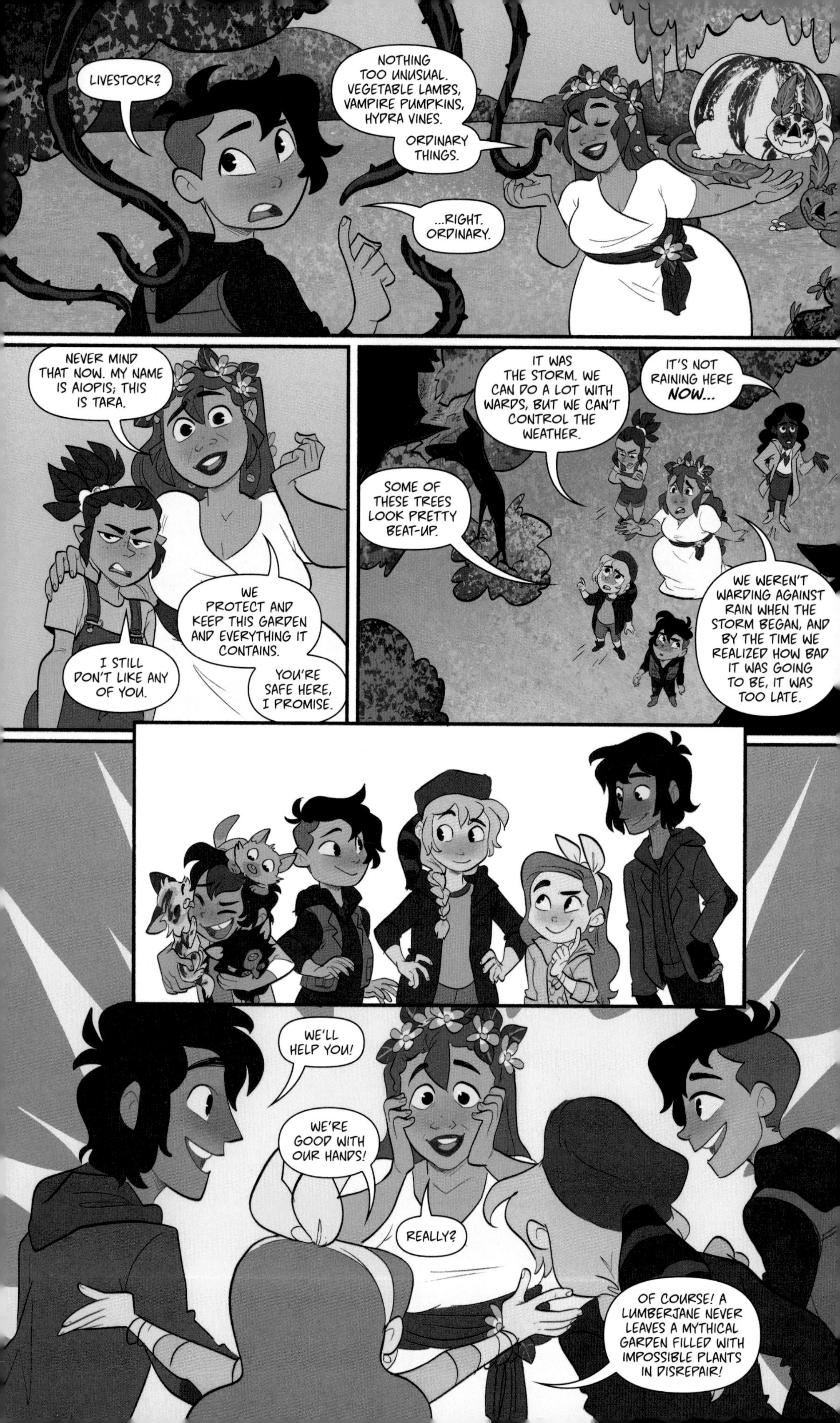
LIVESTOCK?
NOTHING TOO UNUSUAL. VEGETABLE LAMBS, VAMPIRE PUMPKINS, HYDRA VINES.
ORDINARY THINGS.
...RIGHT. ORDINARY.
NEVER MIND THAT NOW. MY NAME IS AIOPIS; THIS IS TARA.
WE PROTECT AND KEEP THIS GARDEN AND EVERYTHING IT CONTAINS.
I STILL DON'T LIKE ANY OF YOU.
YOU'RE SAFE HERE, I PROMISE.
SOME OF THESE TREES LOOK PRETTY BEAT-UP.
IT WAS THE STORM. WE CAN DO A LOT WITH WARDS, BUT WE CAN'T CONTROL THE WEATHER.
IT'S NOT RAINING HERE **NOW...**
WE WEREN'T WARDING AGAINST RAIN WHEN THE STORM BEGAN, AND BY THE TIME WE REALIZED HOW BAD IT WAS GOING TO BE, IT WAS TOO LATE.
WE'LL HELP YOU!
WE'RE GOOD WITH OUR HANDS!
REALLY?
OF COURSE! A LUMBERJANE NEVER LEAVES A MYTHICAL GARDEN FILLED WITH IMPOSSIBLE PLANTS IN DISREPAIR!

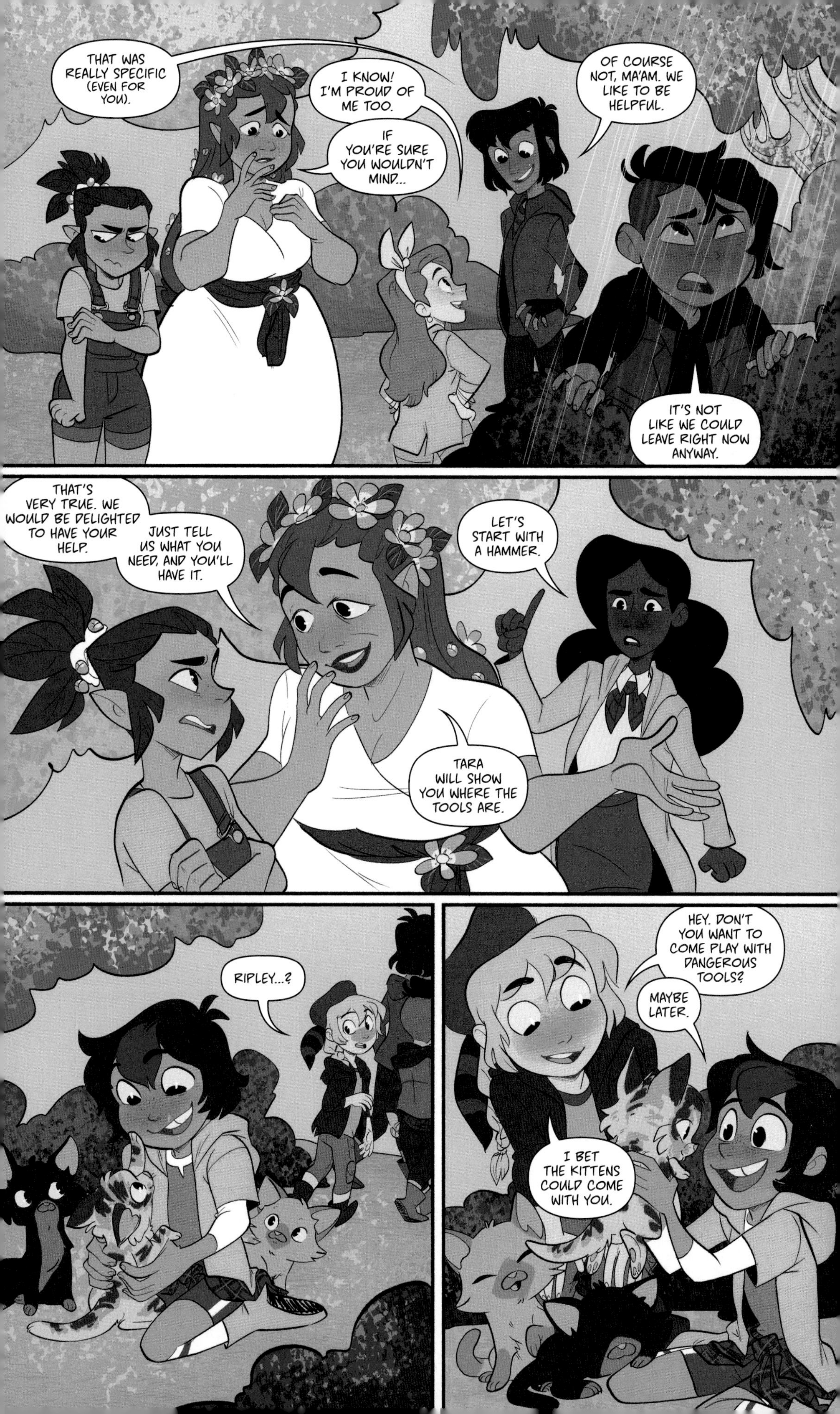
THAT WAS REALLY SPECIFIC (EVEN FOR YOU).
I KNOW! I'M PROUD OF ME TOO.
IF YOU'RE SURE YOU WOULDN'T MIND...
OF COURSE NOT, MA'AM. WE LIKE TO BE HELPFUL.
IT'S NOT LIKE WE COULD LEAVE RIGHT NOW ANYWAY.
THAT'S VERY TRUE. WE WOULD BE DELIGHTED TO HAVE YOUR HELP.
JUST TELL US WHAT YOU NEED, AND YOU'LL HAVE IT.
LET'S START WITH A HAMMER.
TARA WILL SHOW YOU WHERE THE TOOLS ARE.
RIPLEY...?
HEY. DON'T YOU WANT TO COME PLAY WITH DANGEROUS TOOLS?
MAYBE LATER.
I BET THE KITTENS COULD COME WITH YOU.

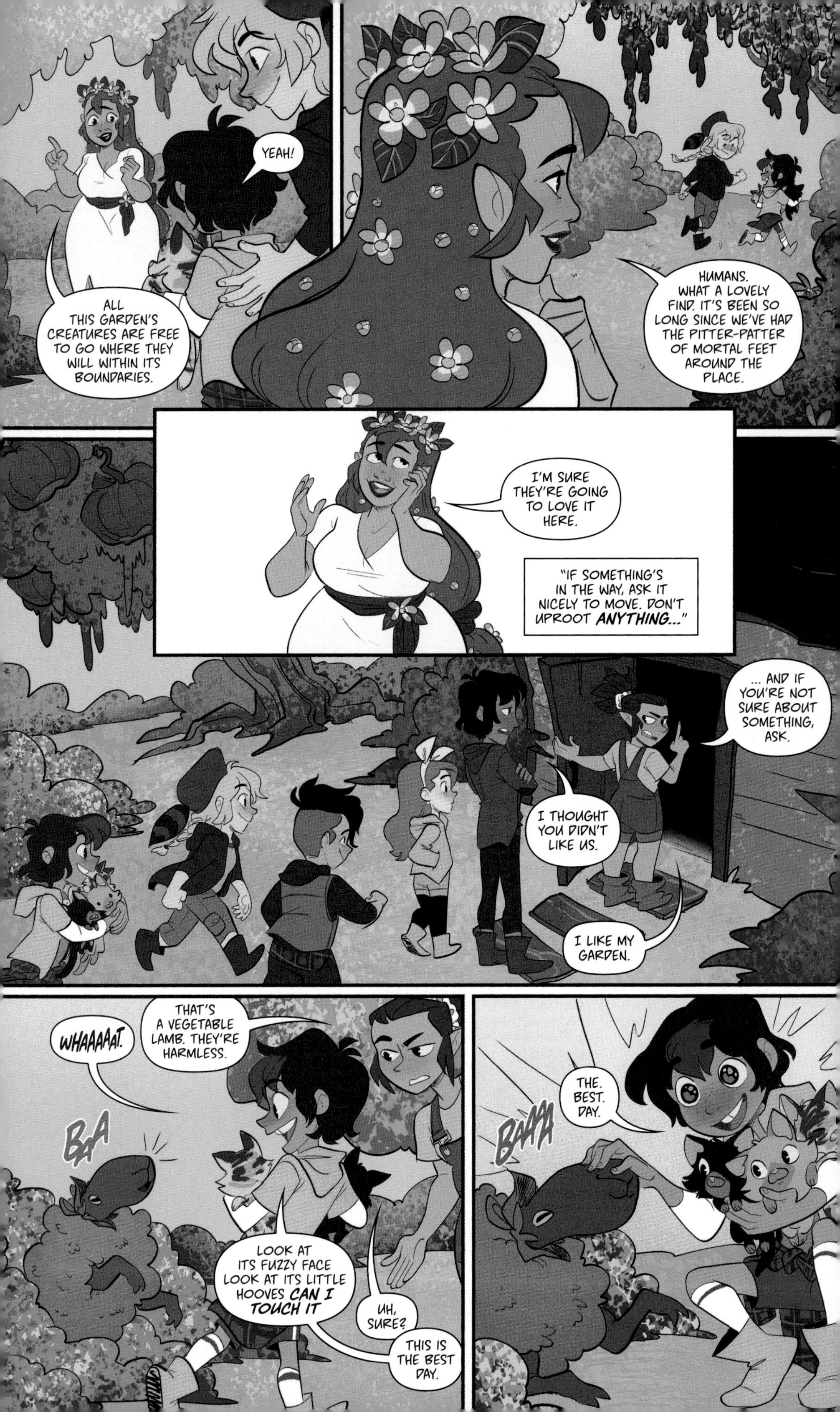
YEAH!
ALL THIS GARDEN'S CREATURES ARE FREE TO GO WHERE THEY WILL WITHIN ITS BOUNDARIES.
HUMANS. WHAT A LOVELY FIND. IT'S BEEN SO LONG SINCE WE'VE HAD THE PITTER-PATTER OF MORTAL FEET AROUND THE PLACE.
I'M SURE THEY'RE GOING TO LOVE IT HERE.
"IF SOMETHING'S IN THE WAY, ASK IT NICELY TO MOVE. DON'T UPROOT ANYTHING..."
... AND IF YOU'RE NOT SURE ABOUT SOMETHING, ASK.
I THOUGHT YOU DIDN'T LIKE US.
I LIKE MY GARDEN.
WHAAAAAT.
THAT'S A VEGETABLE LAMB. THEY'RE HARMLESS.
BAA
LOOK AT ITS FUZZY FACE LOOK AT ITS LITTLE HOOVES CAN I TOUCH IT
UH, SURE?
THIS IS THE BEST DAY.
THE. BEST. DAY.
BAAA

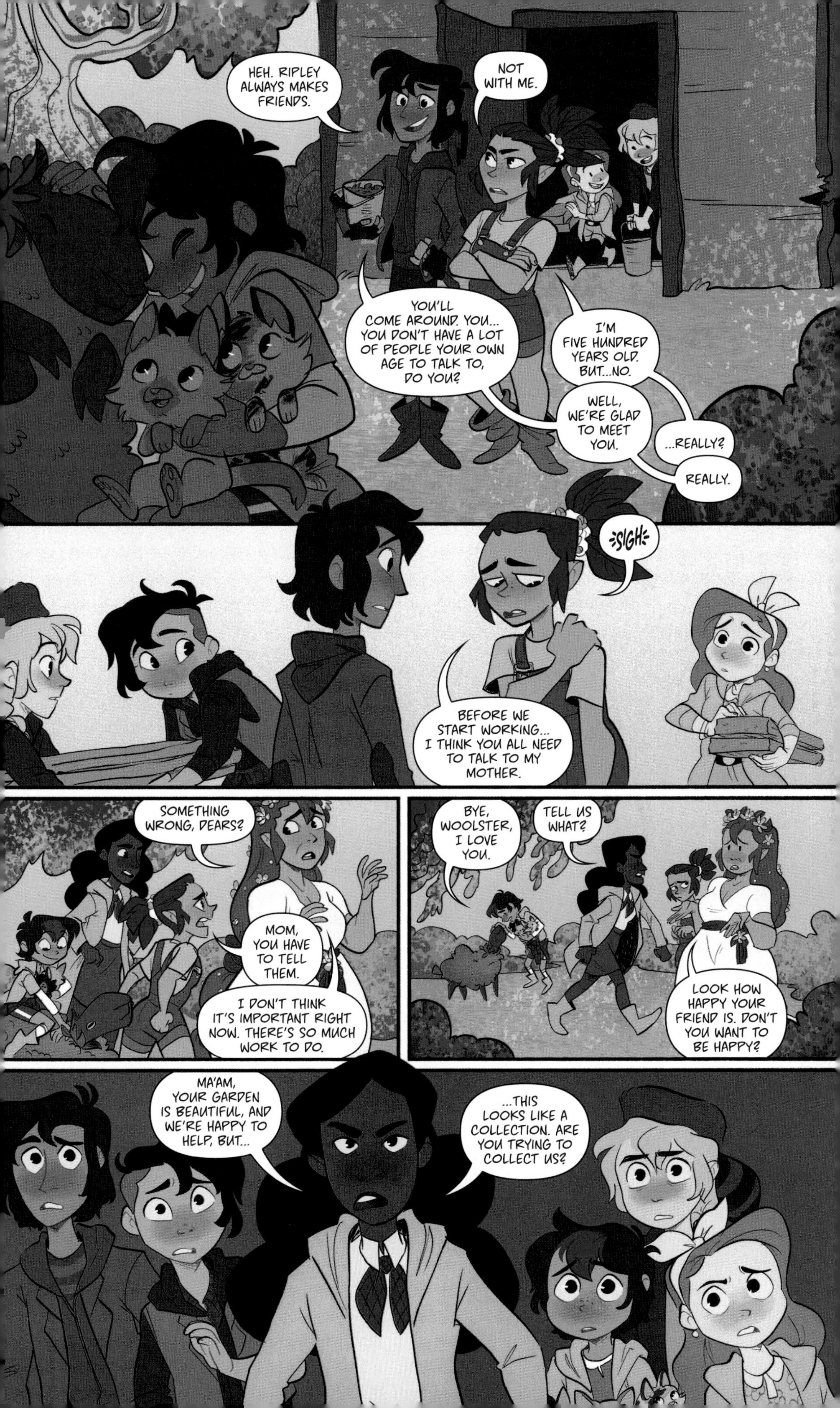
HEH. RIPLEY ALWAYS MAKES FRIENDS.
NOT WITH ME.
YOU'LL COME AROUND. YOU... YOU DON'T HAVE A LOT OF PEOPLE YOUR OWN AGE TO TALK TO, DO YOU?
I'M FIVE HUNDRED YEARS OLD. BUT...NO.
WELL, WE'RE GLAD TO MEET YOU.
...REALLY?
REALLY.
SIGH
BEFORE WE START WORKING... I THINK YOU ALL NEED TO TALK TO MY MOTHER.
SOMETHING WRONG, DEARS?
MOM, YOU HAVE TO TELL THEM.
I DON'T THINK IT'S IMPORTANT RIGHT NOW. THERE'S SO MUCH WORK TO DO.
BYE, WOOLSTER, I LOVE YOU.
TELL US WHAT?
LOOK HOW HAPPY YOUR FRIEND IS. DON'T YOU WANT TO BE HAPPY?
MA'AM, YOUR GARDEN IS BEAUTIFUL, AND WE'RE HAPPY TO HELP, BUT...
...THIS LOOKS LIKE A COLLECTION. ARE YOU TRYING TO COLLECT US?

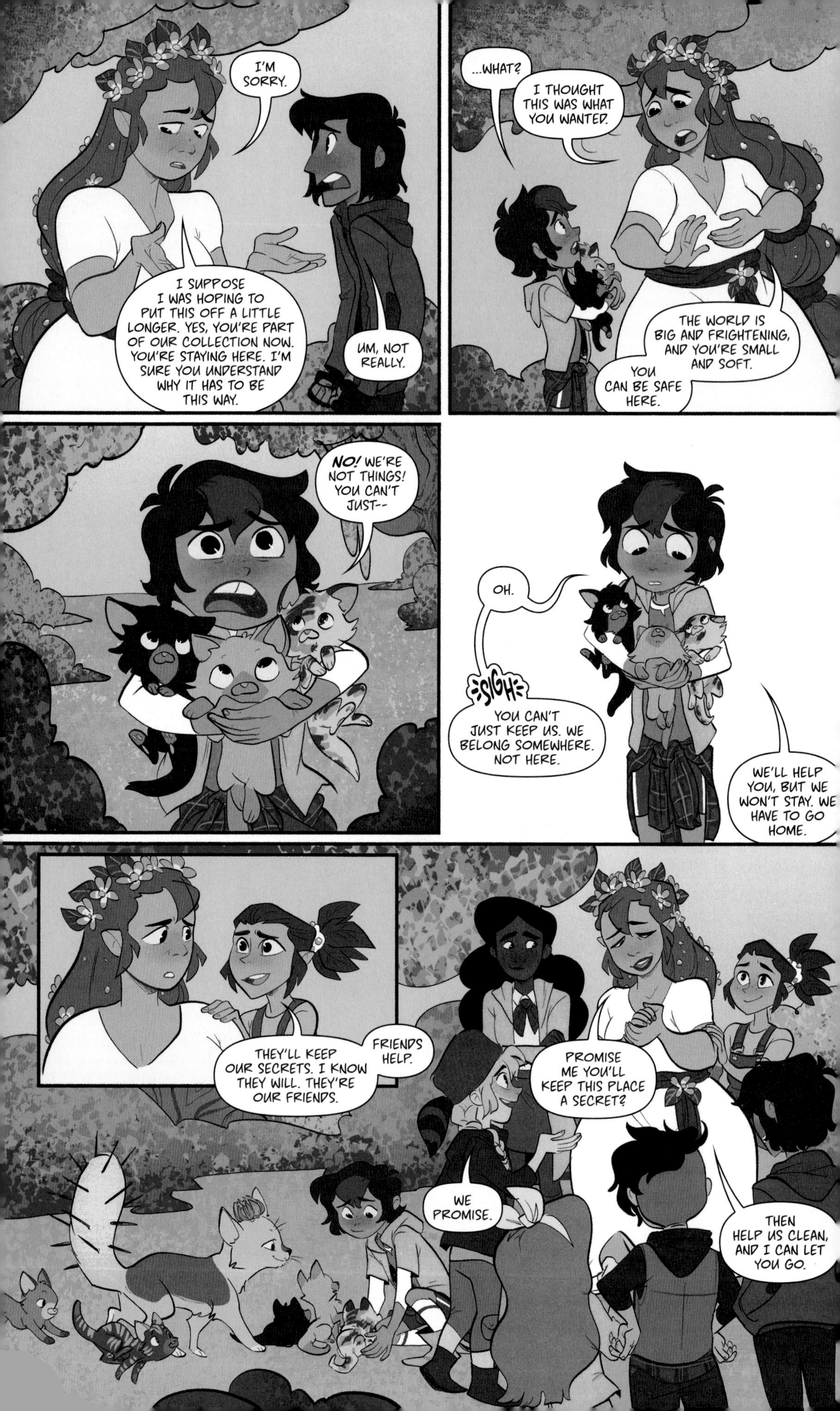
I'M SORRY.
I SUPPOSE I WAS HOPING TO PUT THIS OFF A LITTLE LONGER. YES, YOU'RE PART OF OUR COLLECTION NOW. YOU'RE STAYING HERE. I'M SURE YOU UNDERSTAND WHY IT HAS TO BE THIS WAY.
UM, NOT REALLY.
...WHAT?
I THOUGHT THIS WAS WHAT YOU WANTED.
THE WORLD IS BIG AND FRIGHTENING, AND YOU'RE SMALL AND SOFT.
YOU CAN BE SAFE HERE.
NO! WE'RE NOT THINGS! YOU CAN'T JUST--
OH.
SIGH
YOU CAN'T JUST KEEP US. WE BELONG SOMEWHERE. NOT HERE.
WE'LL HELP YOU, BUT WE WON'T STAY. WE HAVE TO GO HOME.
THEY'LL KEEP OUR SECRETS. I KNOW THEY WILL. THEY'RE OUR FRIENDS.
FRIENDS HELP.
PROMISE ME YOU'LL KEEP THIS PLACE A SECRET?
WE PROMISE.
THEN HELP US CLEAN, AND I CAN LET YOU GO.

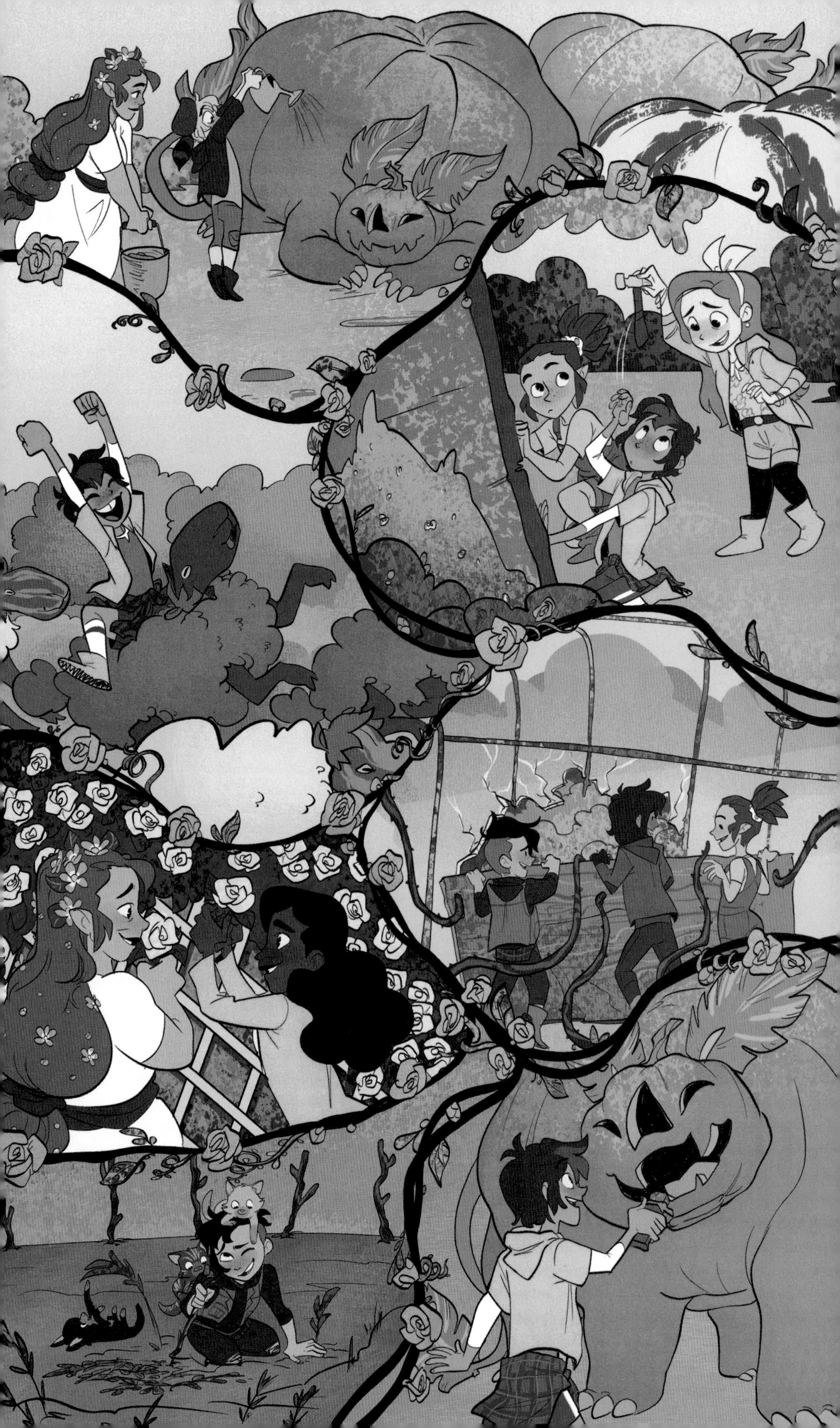

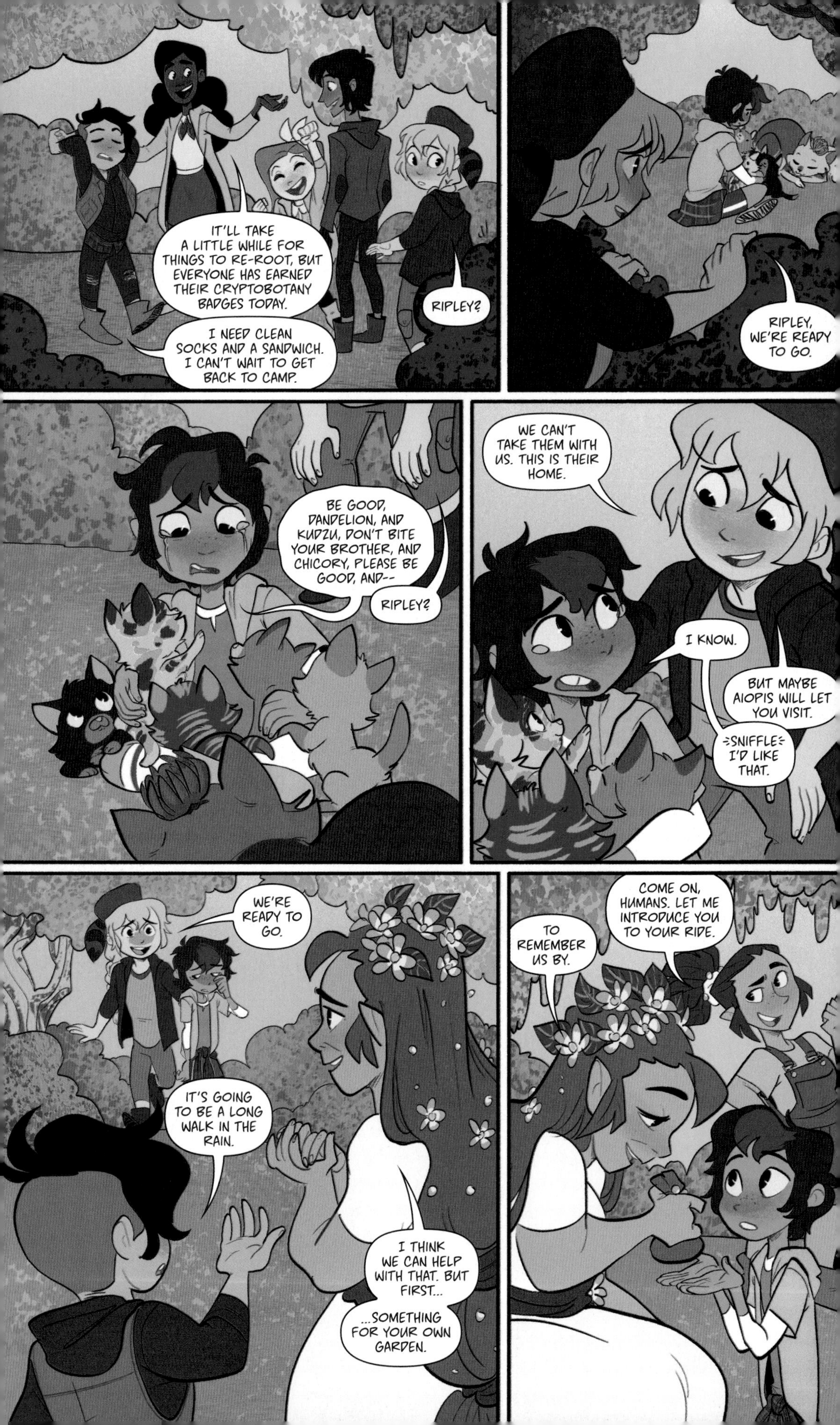
IT'LL TAKE A LITTLE WHILE FOR THINGS TO RE-ROOT, BUT EVERYONE HAS EARNED THEIR CRYPTOBOTANY BADGES TODAY.
I NEED CLEAN SOCKS AND A SANDWICH. I CAN'T WAIT TO GET BACK TO CAMP.
RIPLEY?
RIPLEY, WE'RE READY TO GO.
BE GOOD, DANDELION, AND KUDZU, DON'T BITE YOUR BROTHER, AND CHICORY, PLEASE BE GOOD, AND--
RIPLEY?
WE CAN'T TAKE THEM WITH US. THIS IS THEIR HOME.
I KNOW.
BUT MAYBE AIOPIS WILL LET YOU VISIT.
=SNIFFLE= I'D LIKE THAT.
WE'RE READY TO GO.
IT'S GOING TO BE A LONG WALK IN THE RAIN.
I THINK WE CAN HELP WITH THAT. BUT FIRST...
...SOMETHING FOR YOUR OWN GARDEN.
TO REMEMBER US BY.
COME ON, HUMANS. LET ME INTRODUCE YOU TO YOUR RIDE.

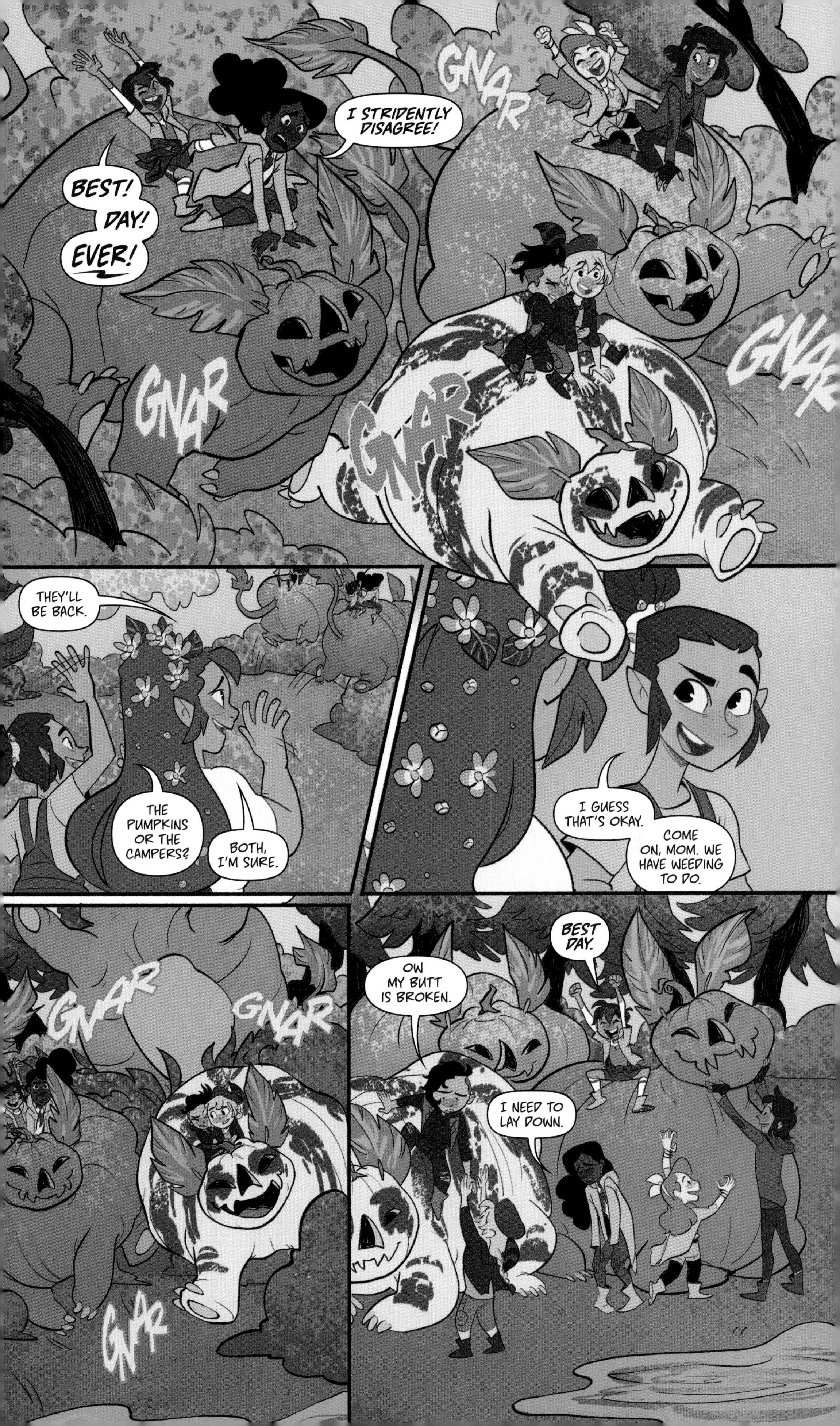
GNAR
I STRIDENTLY DISAGREE!
BEST! DAY! EVER!
GNAR
GNAR
GNAR
THEY'LL BE BACK.
THE PUMPKINS OR THE CAMPERS?
BOTH, I'M SURE.
I GUESS THAT'S OKAY.
COME ON, MOM. WE HAVE WEEDING TO DO.
GNAR
GNAR
GNAR
BEST DAY.
OW MY BUTT IS BROKEN.
I NEED TO LAY DOWN.

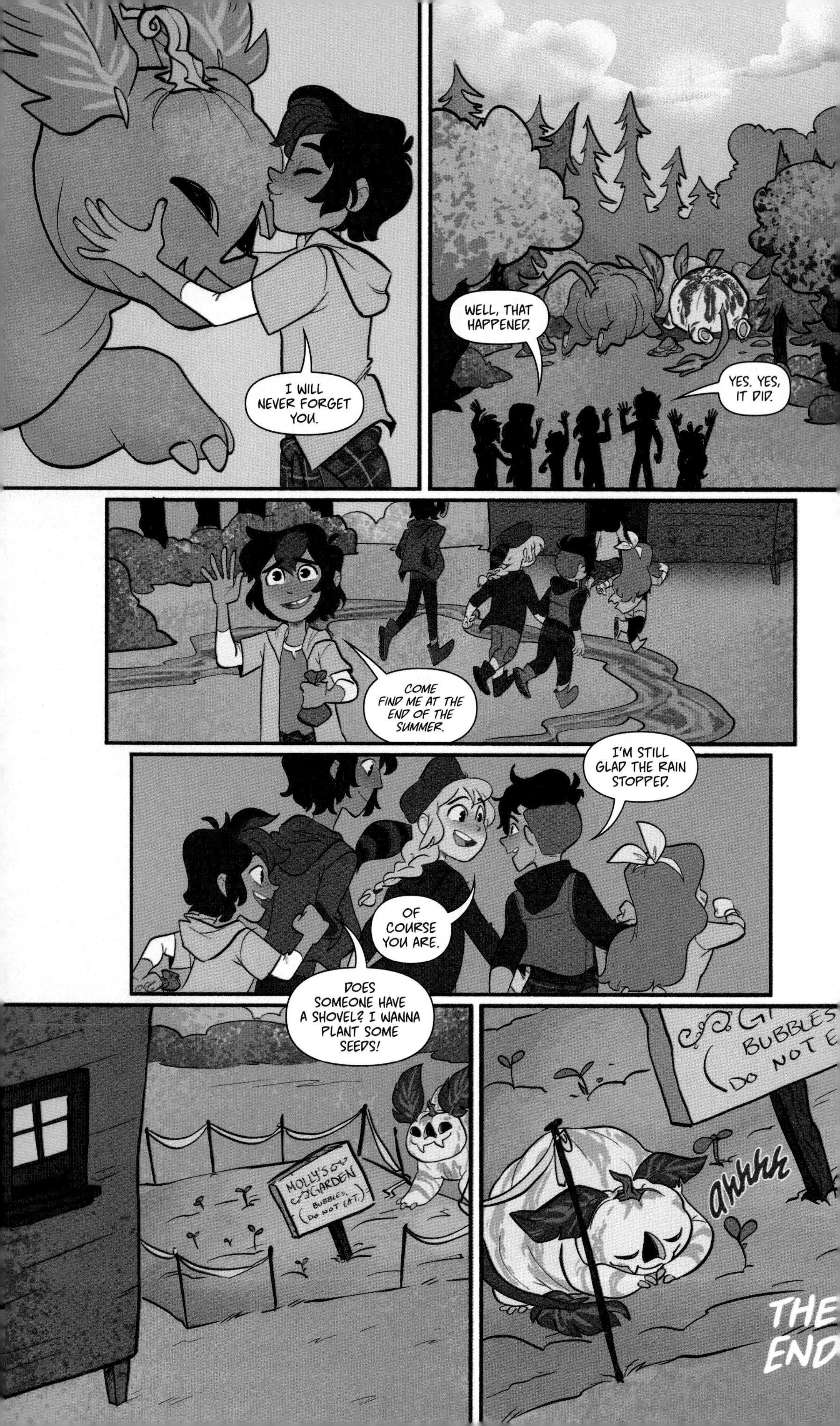
I WILL NEVER FORGET YOU.
WELL, THAT HAPPENED.
YES. YES, IT DID.
COME FIND ME AT THE END OF THE SUMMER.
I'M STILL GLAD THE RAIN STOPPED.
OF COURSE YOU ARE.
DOES SOMEONE HAVE A SHOVEL? I WANNA PLANT SOME SEEDS!
MOLLY'S GARDEN
BUBBLES, (DO NOT EAT.)
AHHHH
THE END

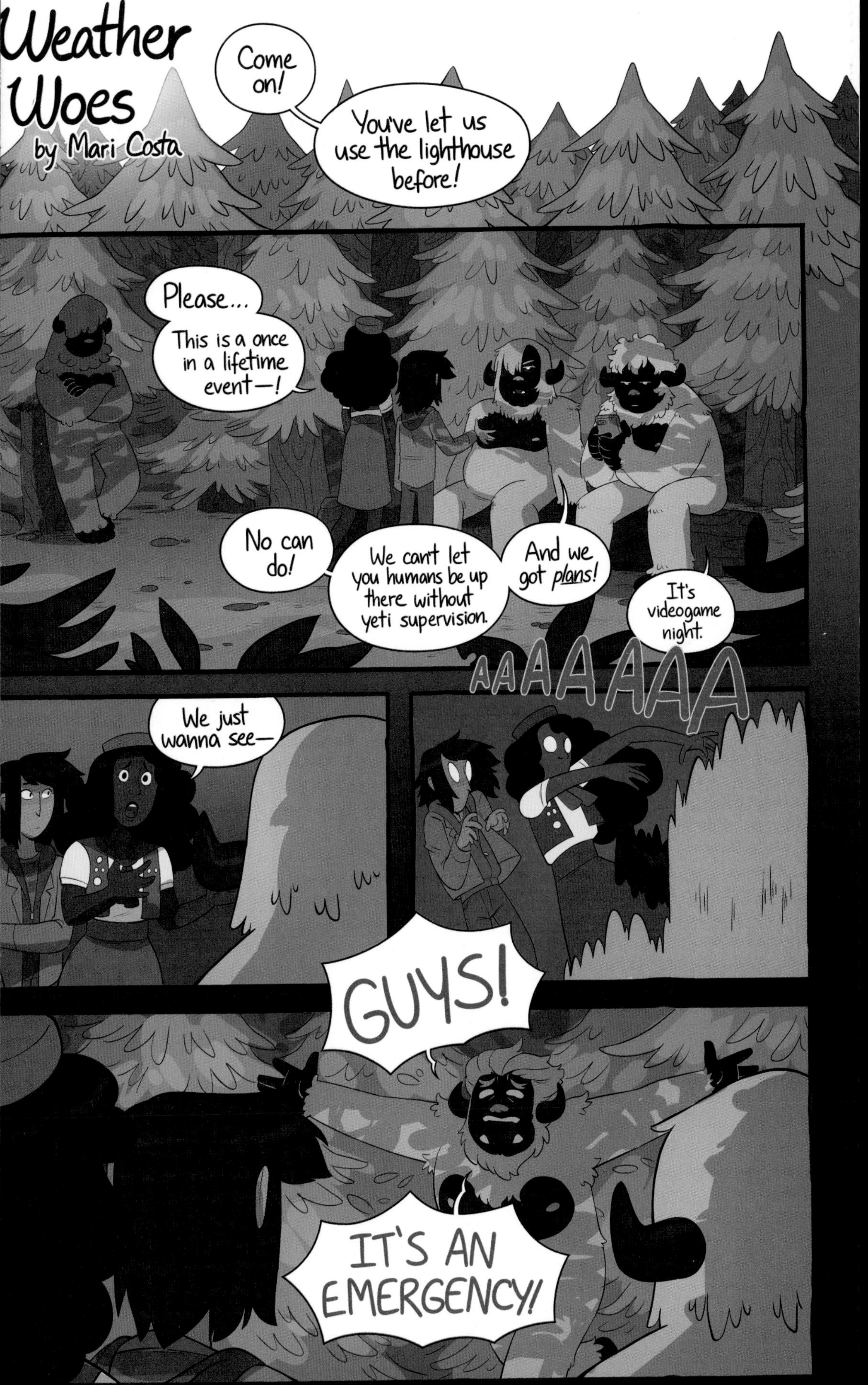

Weather Woes
by Mari Costa
Come on!
You've let us use the lighthouse before!
Please...
This is a once in a lifetime event—!
No can do!
We can't let you humans be up there without yeti supervision.
And we got *plans*!
It's videogame night.
We just wanna see—
AAAAAAAA
GUYS!
IT'S AN EMERGENCY!

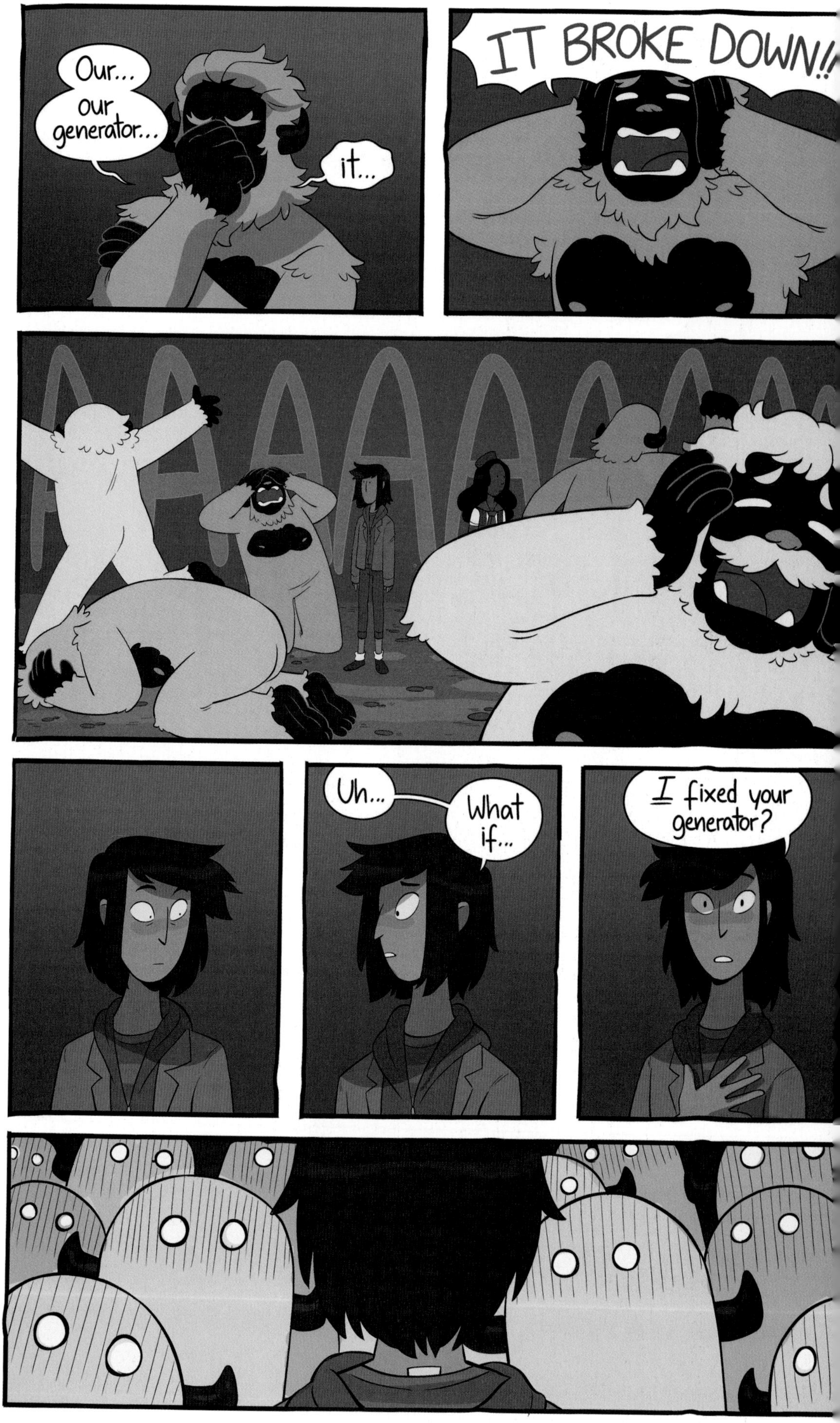
Our...
our generator...
it...
IT BROKE DOWN!!
AAAAAAAAA
Uh...
What if...
I fixed your generator?

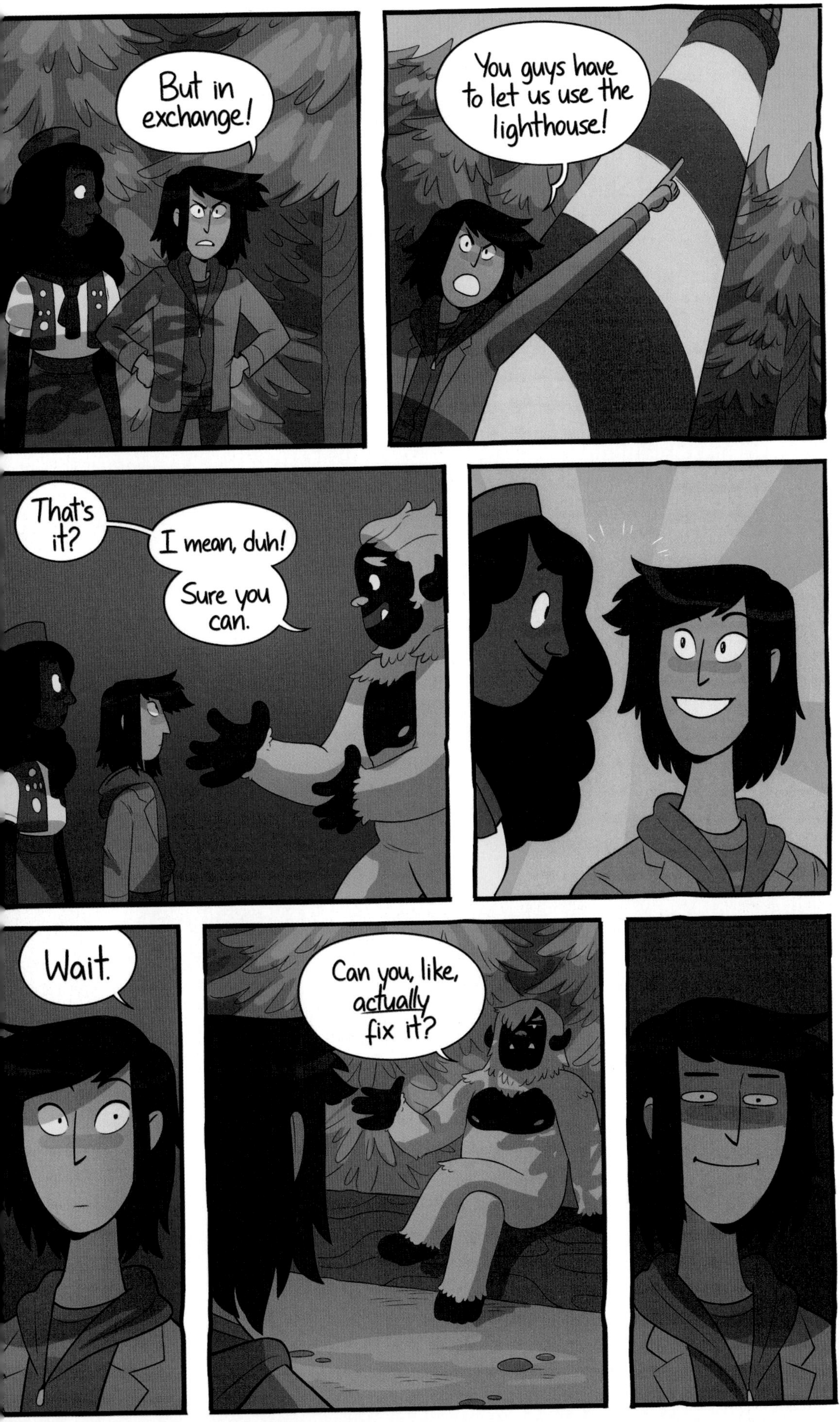
But in exchange!
You guys have to let us use the lighthouse!
That's it?
I mean, duh!
Sure you can.
Wait.
Can you, like, actually fix it?

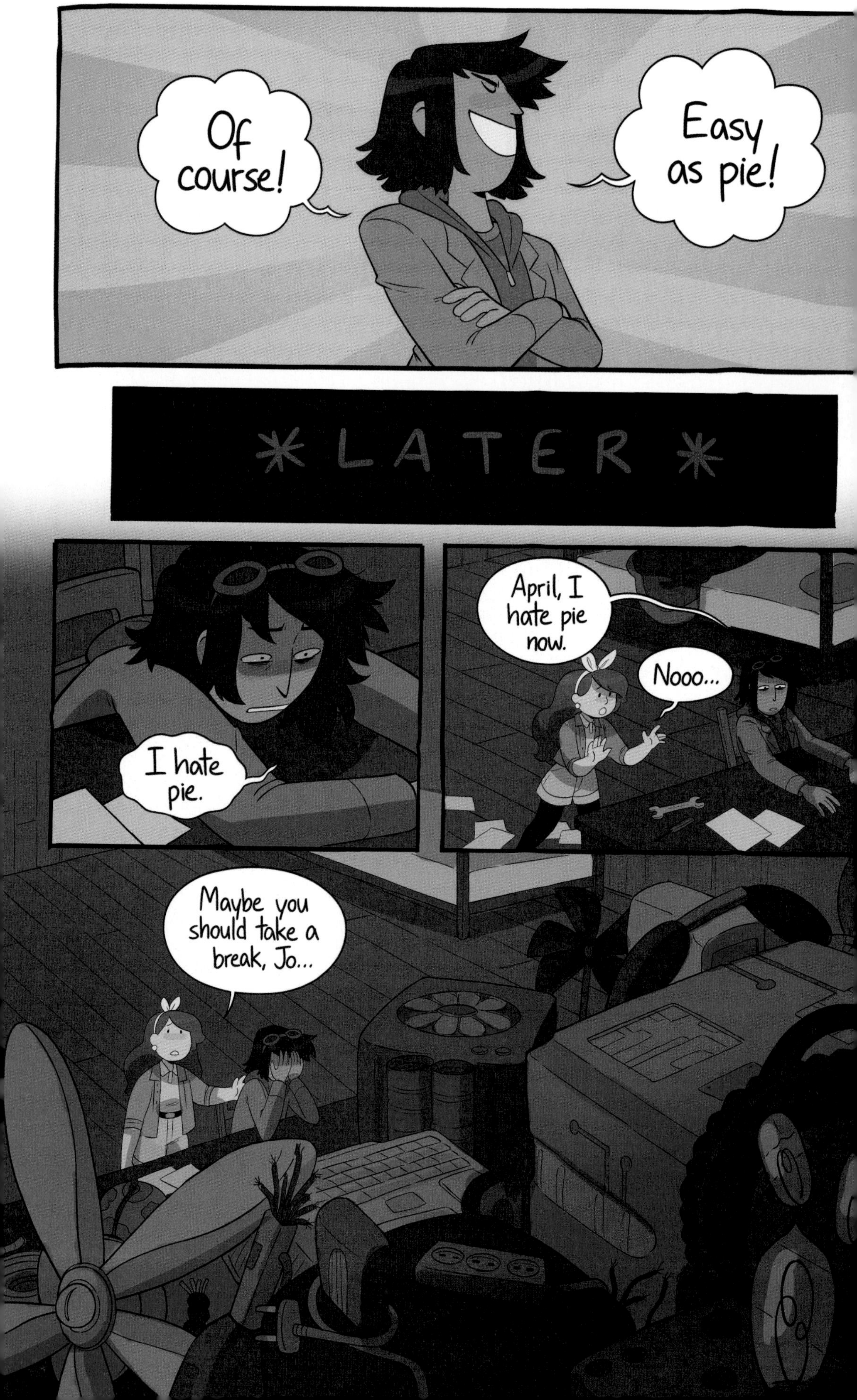
Of course!
Easy as pie!
LATER
I hate pie.
April, I hate pie now.
Nooo...
Maybe you should take a break, Jo...

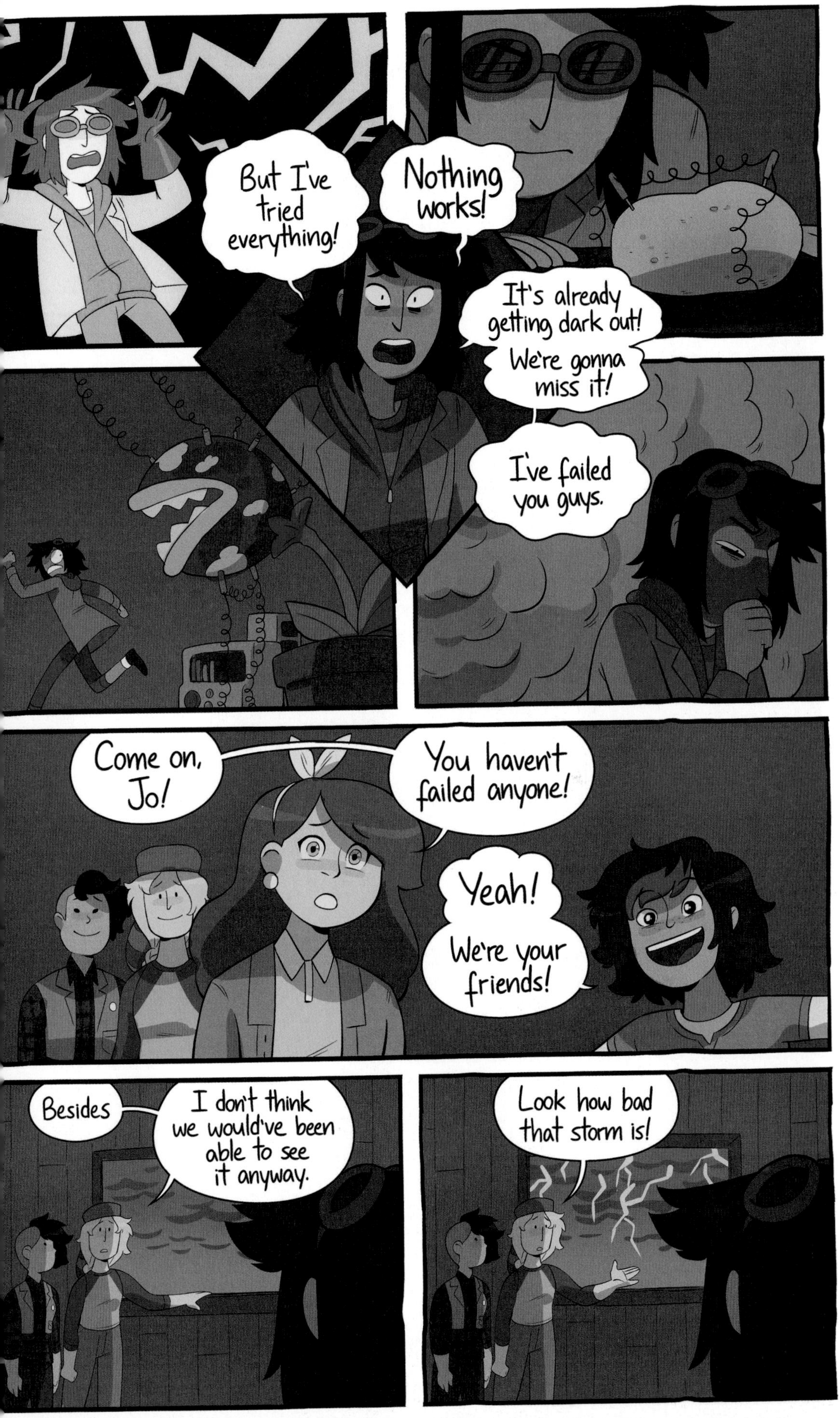
But I've tried everything!
Nothing works!
It's already getting dark out!
We're gonna miss it!
I've failed you guys.
Come on, Jo!
You haven't failed anyone!
Yeah!
We're your friends!
Besides
I don't think we would've been able to see it anyway.
Look how bad that storm is!

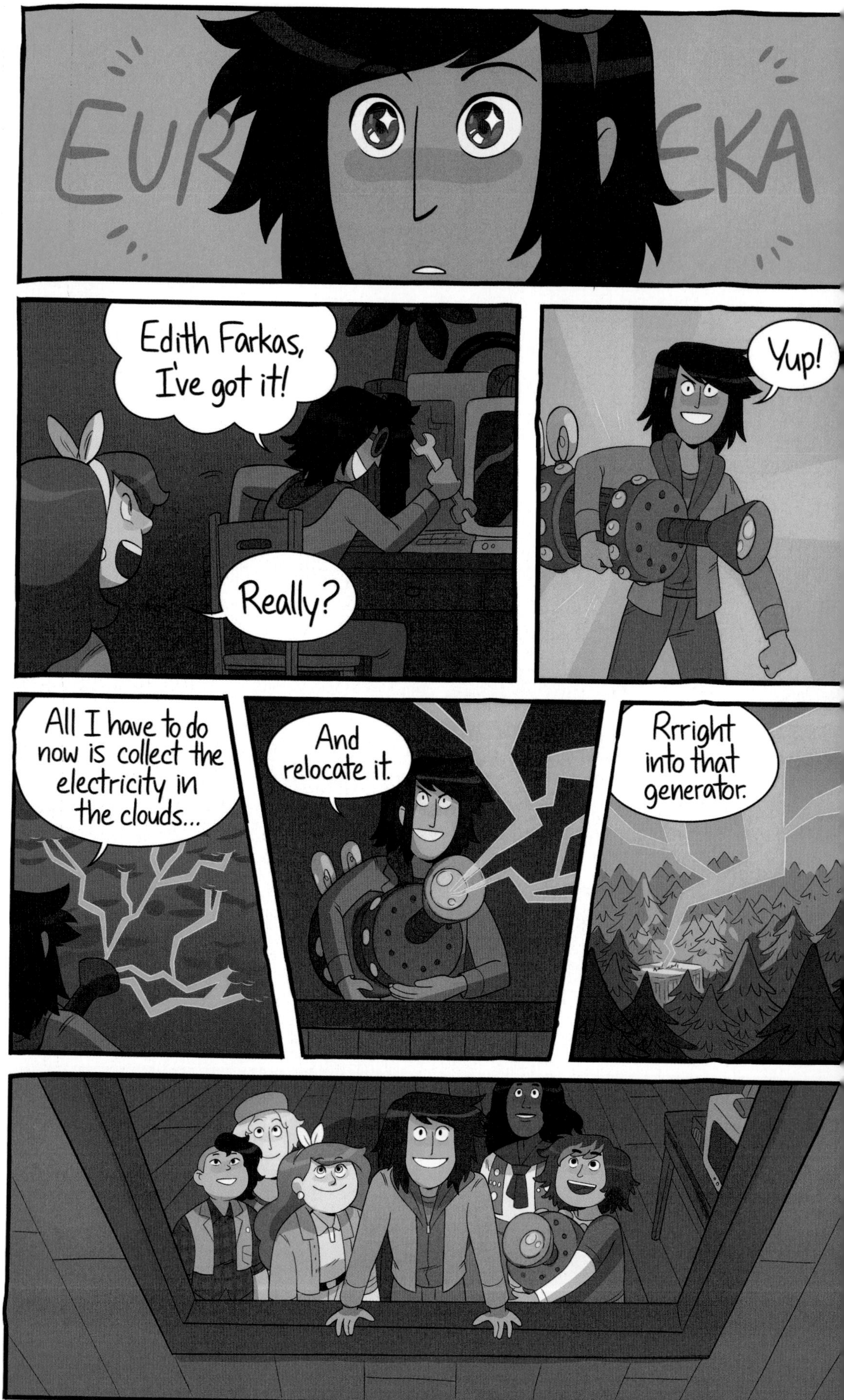
EUREKA
Edith Farkas, I've got it!
Really?
Yup!
All I have to do now is collect the electricity in the clouds...
And relocate it.
Rrright into that generator.

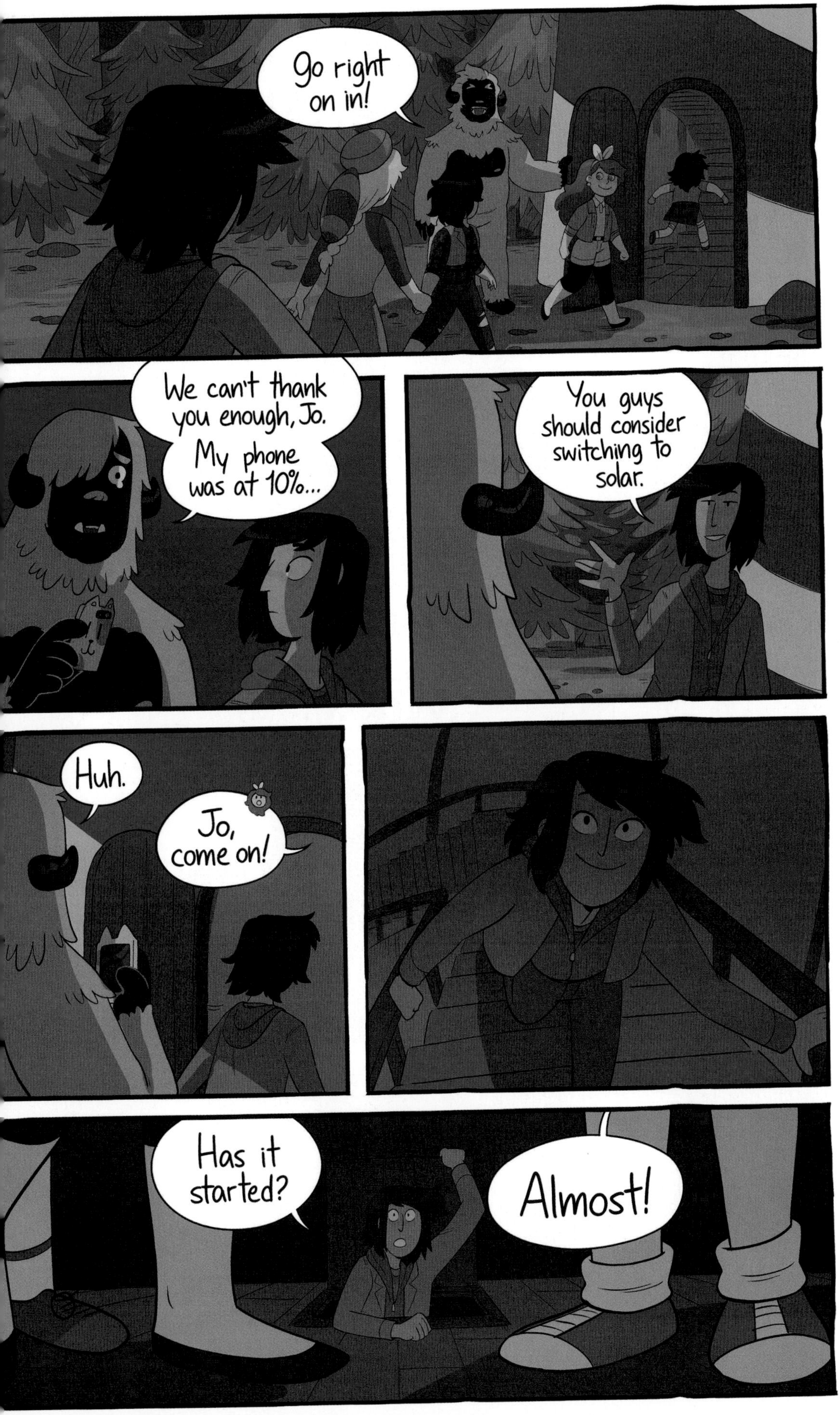

Go right on in!
We can't thank you enough, Jo.
My phone was at 10%...
You guys should consider switching to solar.
Huh.
Jo, come on!
Has it started?
Almost!

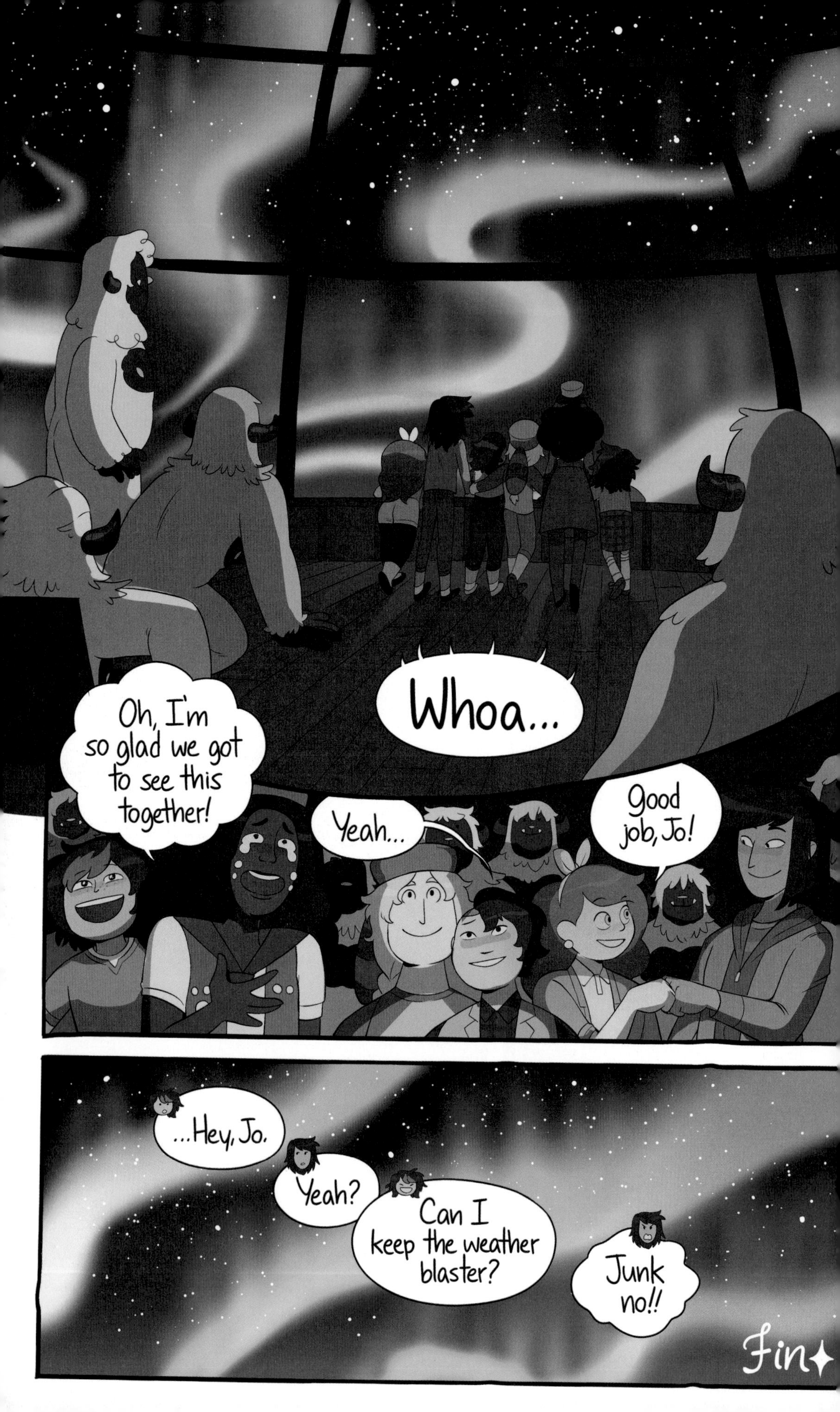
Whoa...
Oh, I'm so glad we got to see this together!
Yeah...
Good job, Jo!
...Hey, Jo.
Yeah?
Can I keep the weather blaster?
Junk no!!
Fin

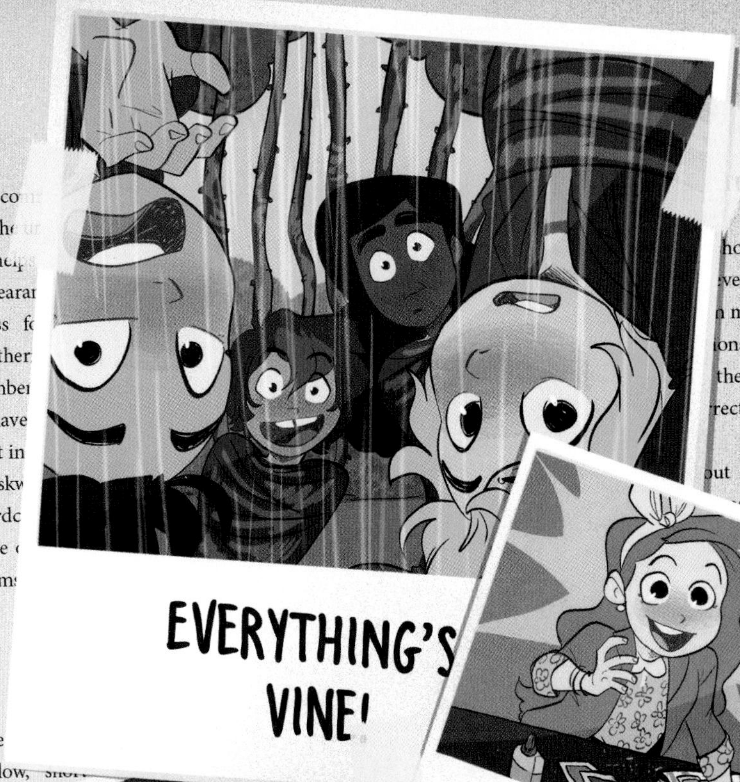
EVERYTHING'S
VINE!

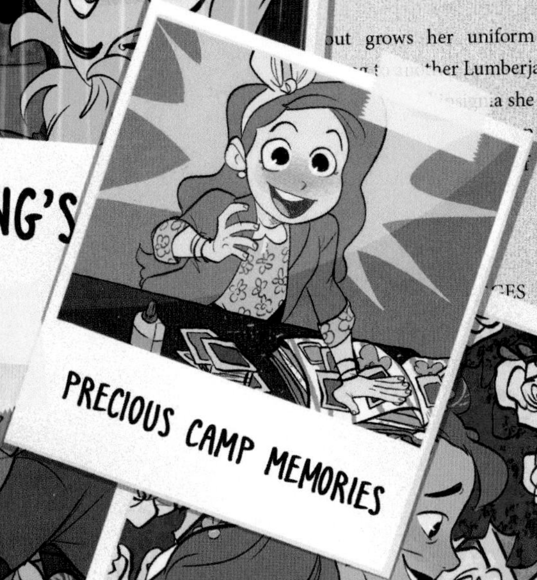
PRECIOUS CAMP MEMORIES

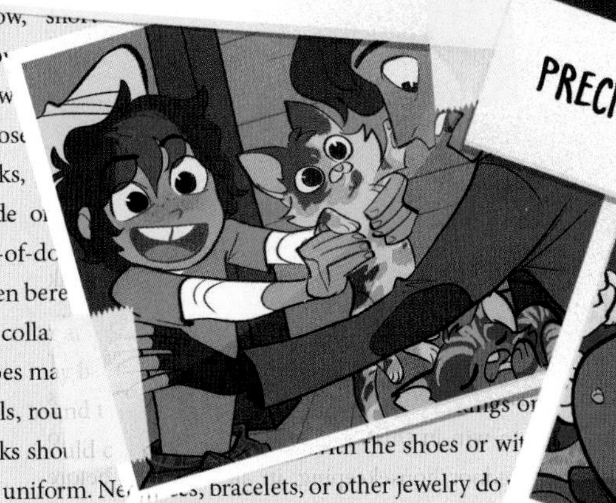

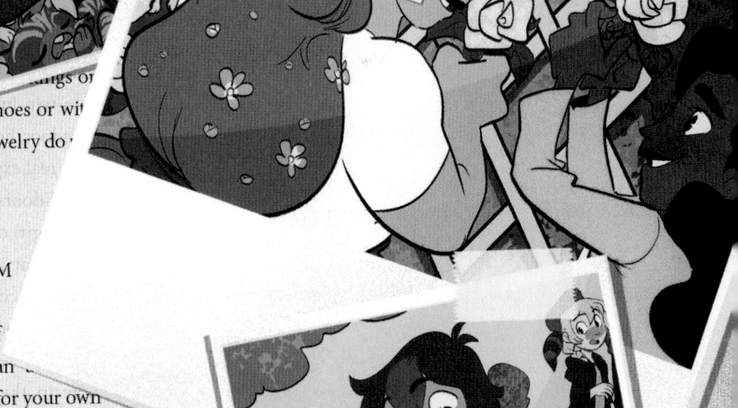

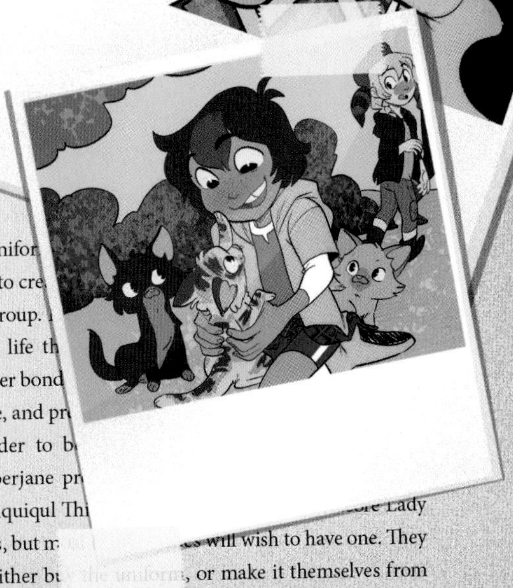

will co
The
It helps
appearan
dress fo
Further
Lumber
to have
part in
Thiskw
Hardc
have
thems

HE UNIFORM

hould be worn at camp
vents when Lumberjanes
n may also be worn at other
ions. It should be worn as a
the uniform dress with
rrect shoes, and stocking or

out grows her uniform or
ther Lumberjane.
a she has
her
her

The
yellow,
emb
the w
choose
slacks,
made o
out-of-do
green bere
the colla
Shoes ma
heels, rou ngs or
socks shou with the shoes or wit
the uniform. Ne es, bracelets, or other jewelry do
belong with a Lumberjane uniform.

HOW TO WEAR THE UNIFORM

To look well in a uniform demands first of
uniform be kept in good condition—clean
pressed. See that the skirt is the right length for your own height and build, that the belt is adjusted to your waist, that your shoes and stockings are in keeping with the uniform, that you watch your posture and carry yourself with dignity and grace. If the beret is removed indoors, be sure that your hair is neat and kept in place with an inconspicuous clip or ribbon. When you wear a Lumberjane uniform you are identified as a member of this organization and you should be doubly careful to conduct yourself in a way that will show everyone that courtesy and thoughtfulness are part of being a Lumberjane. People are likely to judge a whole nation by the selfishness of a few individuals, to criticize a whole family because of the misconduct of one member, and to feel unkindly toward an organization because of the

The unifor
helps to cre
in a group.
active life th
another bond
future, and pr
in order to b
Lumberjane pr
Penniquiqul Thi re Lady
Types, but m s will wish to have one. They
can either bu the uniform, or make it themselves from
materials available at the trading post.

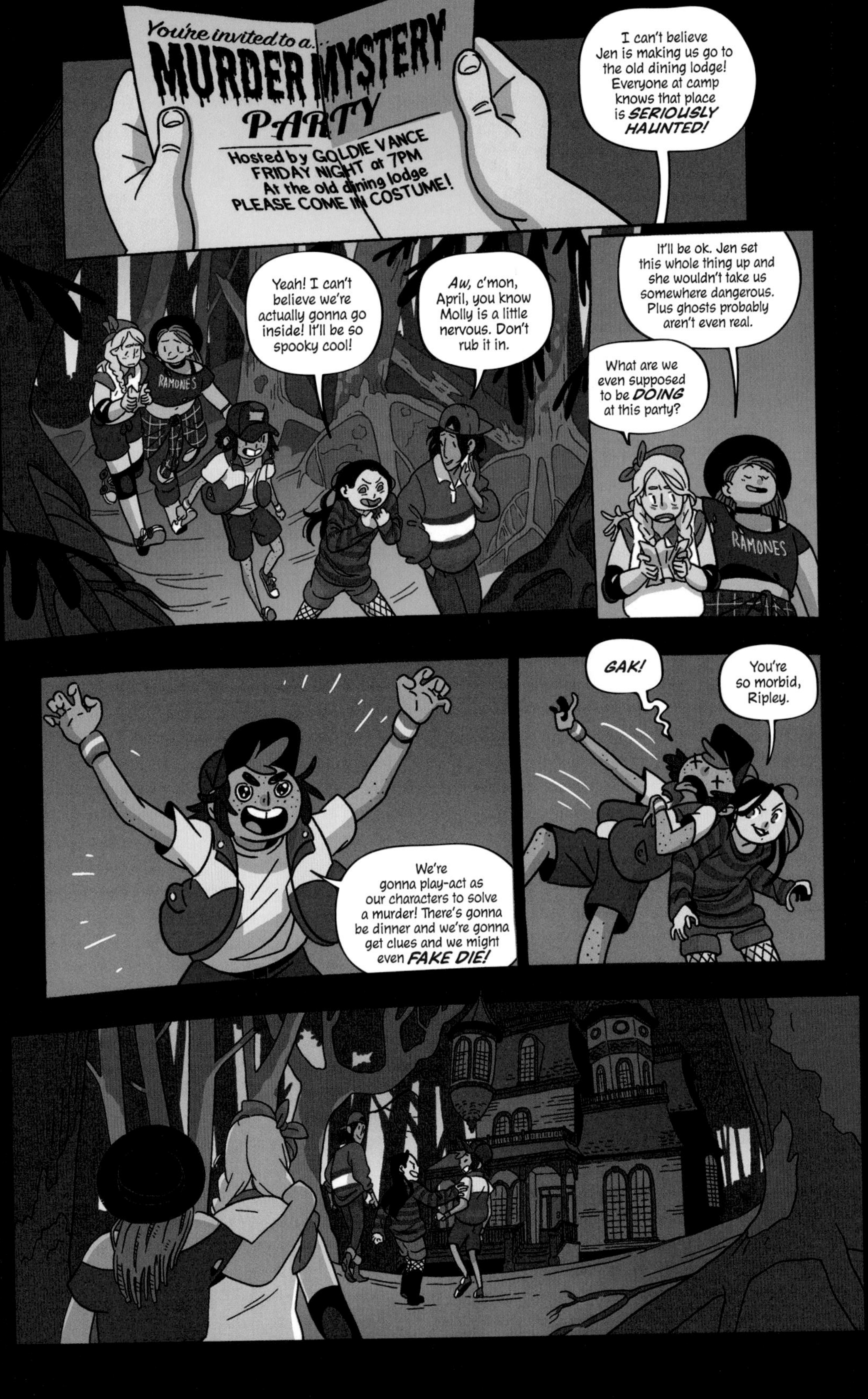
You're invited to a...
MURDER MYSTERY
PARTY
Hosted by GOLDIE VANCE
FRIDAY NIGHT at 7PM
At the old dining lodge
PLEASE COME IN COSTUME!
I can't believe Jen is making us go to the old dining lodge! Everyone at camp knows that place is SERIOUSLY HAUNTED!
Yeah! I can't believe we're actually gonna go inside! It'll be so spooky cool!
Aw, c'mon, April, you know Molly is a little nervous. Don't rub it in.
RAMONES
It'll be ok. Jen set this whole thing up and she wouldn't take us somewhere dangerous. Plus ghosts probably aren't even real.
What are we even supposed to be DOING at this party?
RAMONES
We're gonna play-act as our characters to solve a murder! There's gonna be dinner and we're gonna get clues and we might even FAKE DIE!
GAK!
You're so morbid, Ripley.

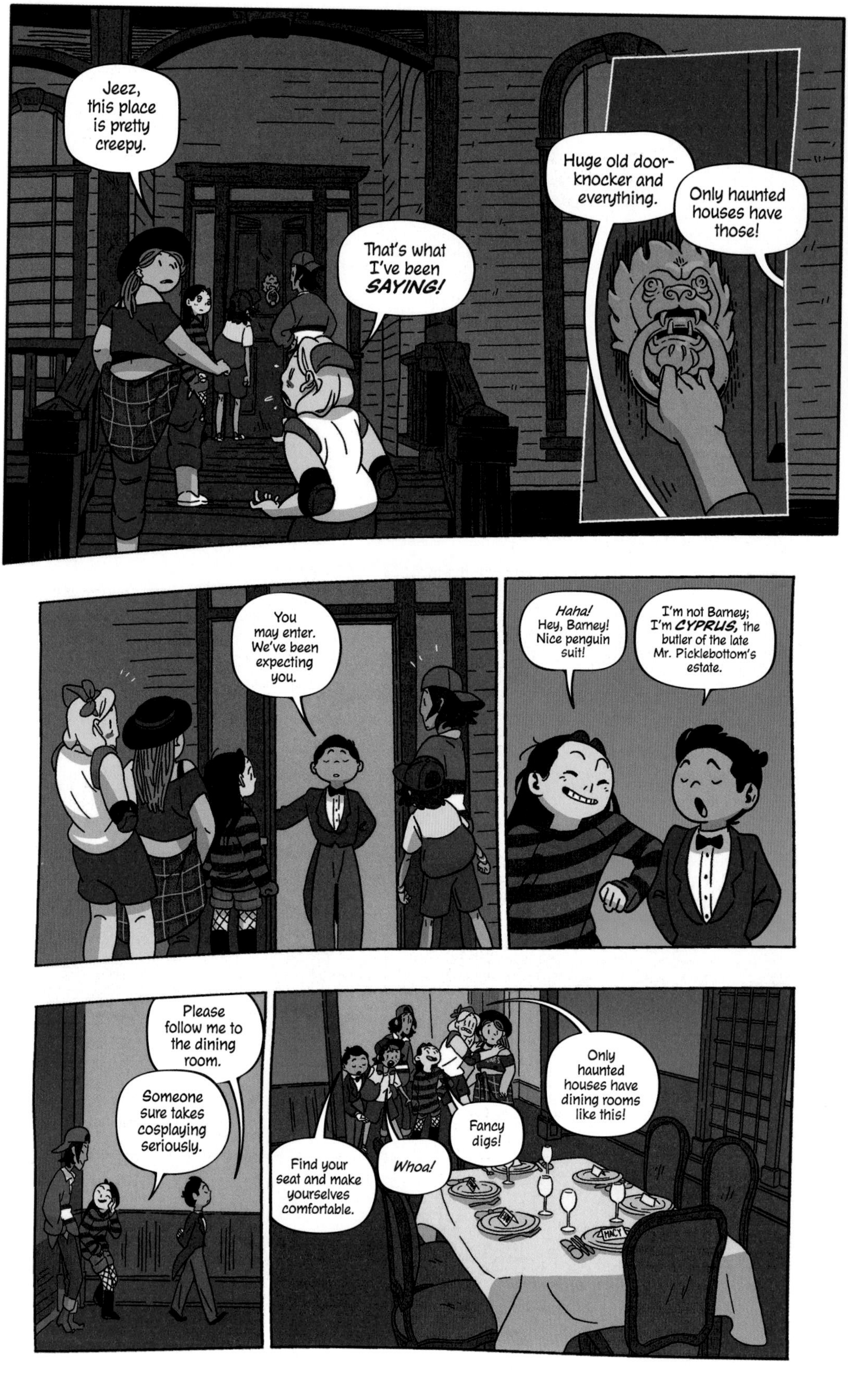

Jeez, this place is pretty creepy.
That's what I've been *SAYING!*
Huge old door-knocker and everything.
Only haunted houses have those!
You may enter. We've been expecting you.
Haha! Hey, Barney! Nice penguin suit!
I'm not Barney; I'm *CYPRUS,* the butler of the late Mr. Picklebottom's estate.
Please follow me to the dining room.
Someone sure takes cosplaying seriously.
Only haunted houses have dining rooms like this!
Fancy digs!
Whoa!
Find your seat and make yourselves comfortable.

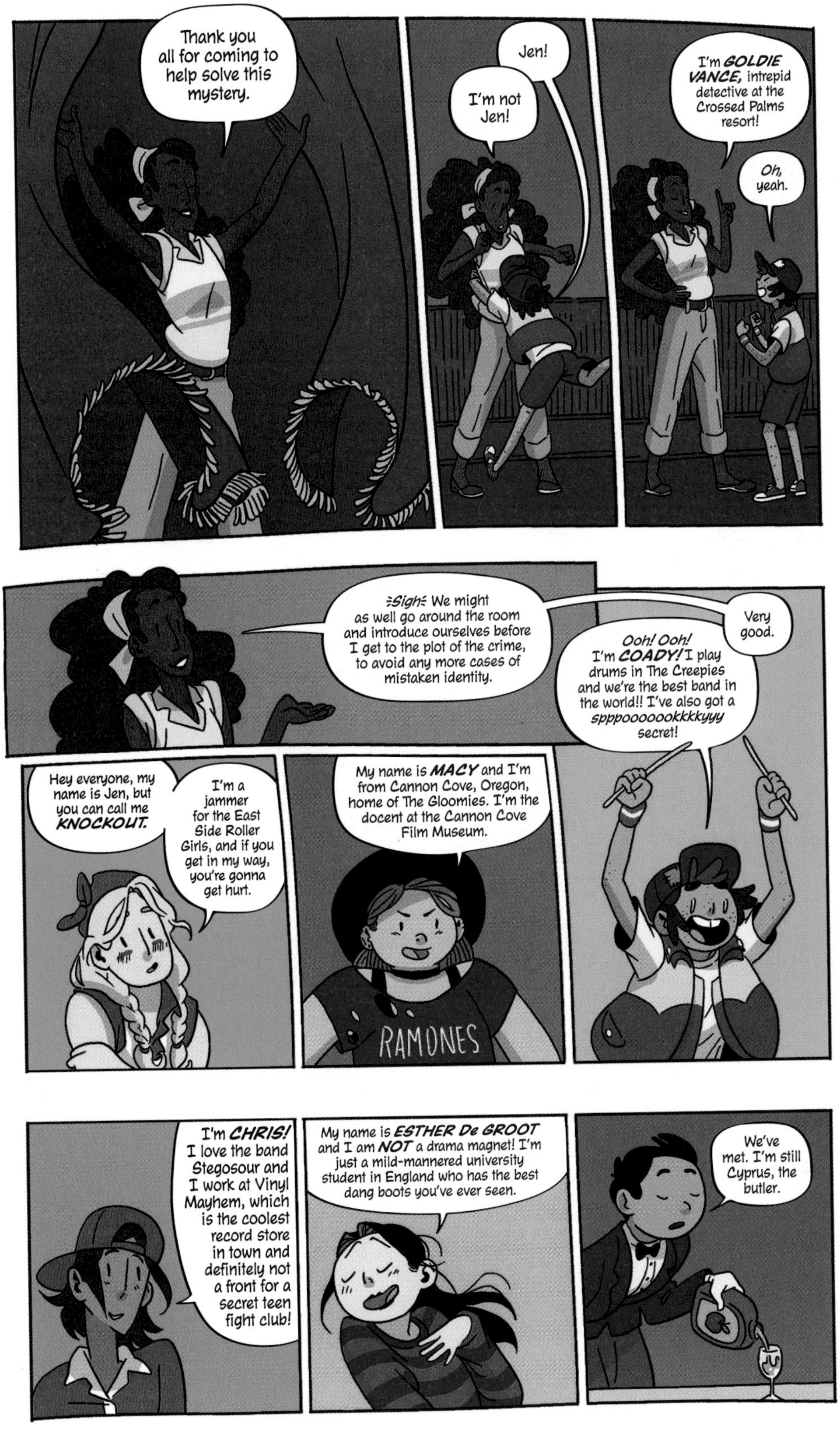
Thank you all for coming to help solve this mystery.
Jen!
I'm not Jen!
I'm GOLDIE VANCE, intrepid detective at the Crossed Palms resort!
Oh, yeah.
≈Sigh≈ We might as well go around the room and introduce ourselves before I get to the plot of the crime, to avoid any more cases of mistaken identity.
Very good.
Ooh! Ooh! I'm COADY! I play drums in The Creepies and we're the best band in the world!! I've also got a spppoooooookkkkyyy secret!
Hey everyone, my name is Jen, but you can call me KNOCKOUT.
I'm a jammer for the East Side Roller Girls, and if you get in my way, you're gonna get hurt.
My name is MACY and I'm from Cannon Cove, Oregon, home of The Gloomies. I'm the docent at the Cannon Cove Film Museum.
RAMONES
I'm CHRIS! I love the band Stegosour and I work at Vinyl Mayhem, which is the coolest record store in town and definitely not a front for a secret teen fight club!
My name is ESTHER De GROOT and I am NOT a drama magnet! I'm just a mild-mannered university student in England who has the best dang boots you've ever seen.
We've met. I'm still Cyprus, the butler.

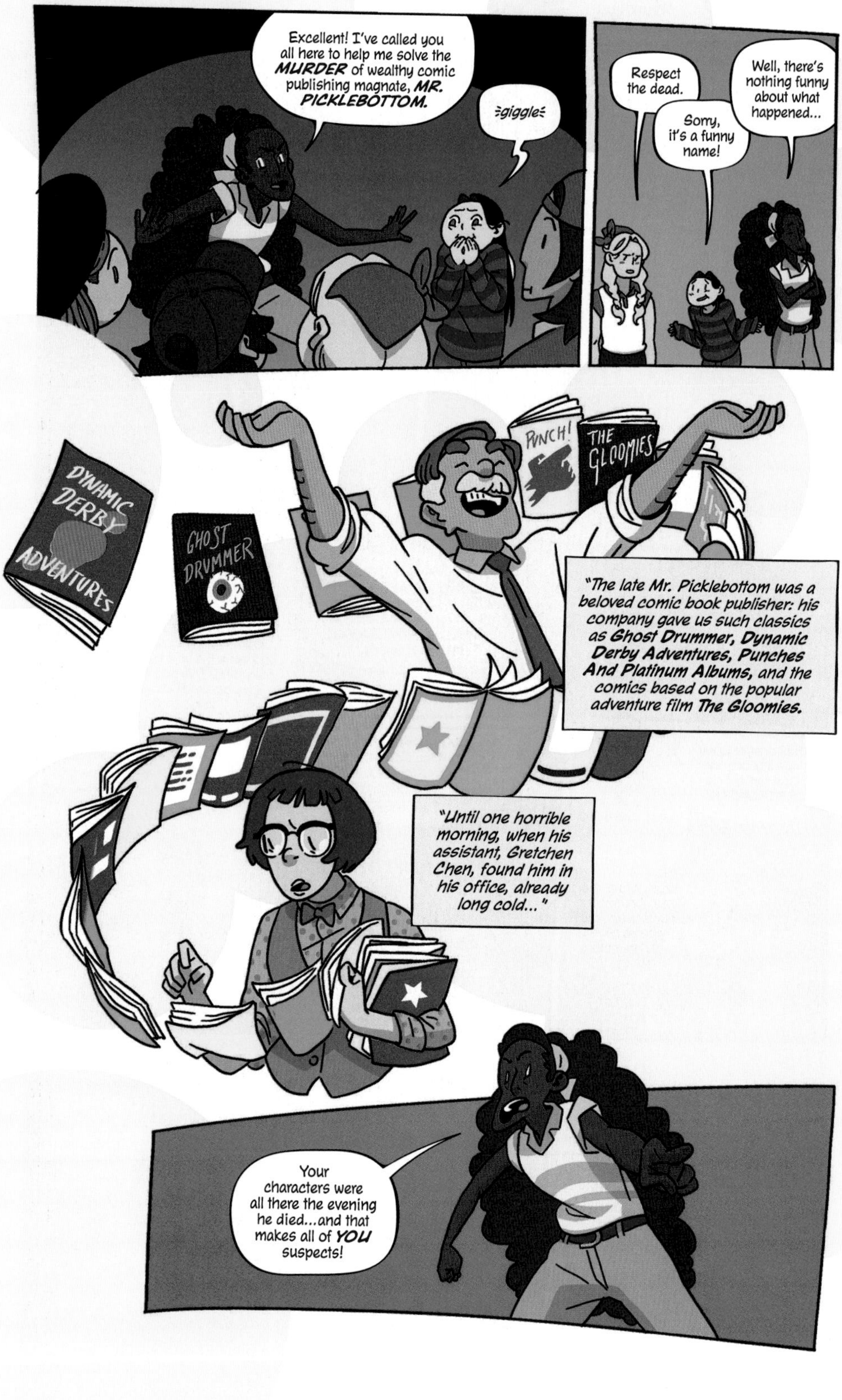

Excellent! I've called you all here to help me solve the MURDER of wealthy comic publishing magnate, MR. PICKLEBOTTOM.
giggle
Respect the dead.
Sorry, it's a funny name!
Well, there's nothing funny about what happened...
DYNAMIC DERBY ADVENTURES
GHOST DRUMMER
PUNCH!
THE GLOOMIES
"The late Mr. Picklebottom was a beloved comic book publisher: his company gave us such classics as Ghost Drummer, Dynamic Derby Adventures, Punches And Platinum Albums, and the comics based on the popular adventure film The Gloomies.
"Until one horrible morning, when his assistant, Gretchen Chen, found him in his office, already long cold..."
Your characters were all there the evening he died...and that makes all of YOU suspects!

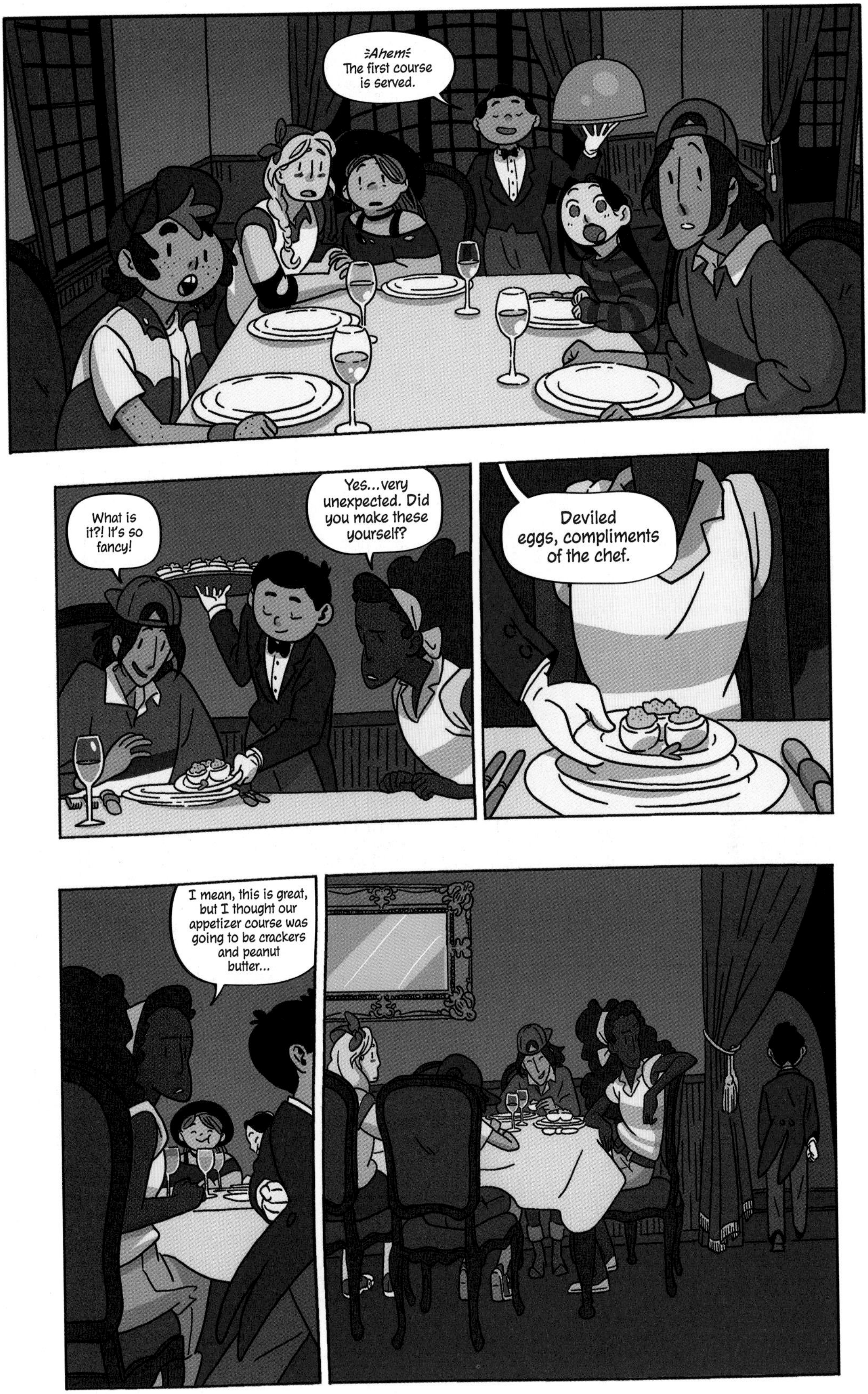
Ahem
The first course is served.
What is it?! It's so fancy!
Yes...very unexpected. Did you make these yourself?
Deviled eggs, compliments of the chef.
I mean, this is great, but I thought our appetizer course was going to be crackers and peanut butter...

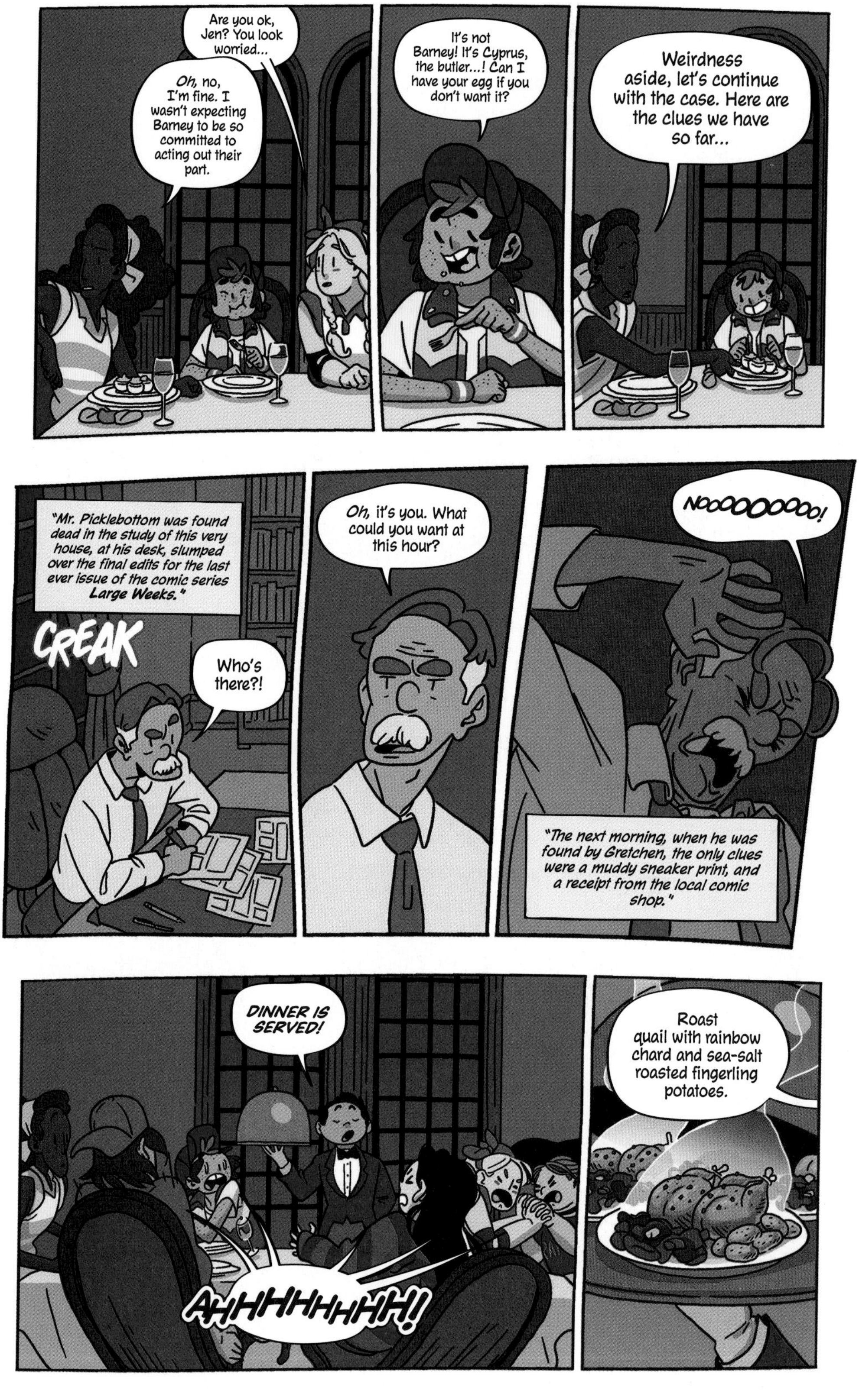
Are you ok, Jen? You look worried...
Oh, no, I'm fine. I wasn't expecting Barney to be so committed to acting out their part.
It's not Barney! It's Cyprus, the butler...! Can I have your egg if you don't want it?
Weirdness aside, let's continue with the case. Here are the clues we have so far...
"Mr. Picklebottom was found dead in the study of this very house, at his desk, slumped over the final edits for the last ever issue of the comic series Large Weeks."
CREAK
Who's there?!
Oh, it's you. What could you want at this hour?
NOOOOOOOOO!
"The next morning, when he was found by Gretchen, the only clues were a muddy sneaker print, and a receipt from the local comic shop."
DINNER IS SERVED!
AHHHHHHHH!
Roast quail with rainbow chard and sea-salt roasted fingerling potatoes.

This is the best thing I've ever eaten at camp--dang, it might be the best thing I've ever eaten...*EVER!*

Yeah, Jen, who'd you hire to cater this shindig? Martha Stewart?

I didn't hire anyone! I brought sandwiches and juice boxes from the Mess Hall...

I knew this place was haunted! We're eating ghost food!

Ghost food?! My favorite!

You know what that means! We've got a *REAL MYSTERY* to solve!

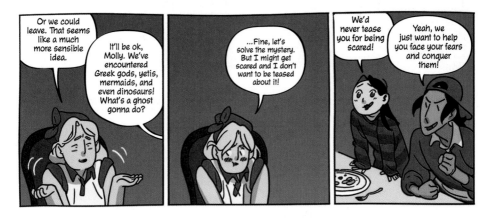

Or we could leave. That seems like a much more sensible idea.

It'll be ok, Molly. We've encountered Greek gods, yetis, mermaids, and even dinosaurs! What's a ghost gonna do?

...Fine, let's solve the mystery. But I might get scared and I don't want to be teased about it!

We'd never tease you for being scared!

Yeah, we just want to help you face your fears and conquer them!

Plus, you're not scared of me, and I'm a ghost!

≥Sigh≥ Thank you for trying, but I think my role-playing game has been abandoned.

Don't be sad, Jen! We're gonna need the help of Goldie Vance to solve this case, too!

Oh, alright.

Whee! Let's go find a ghost!

Why do I always let myself get dragged into this?

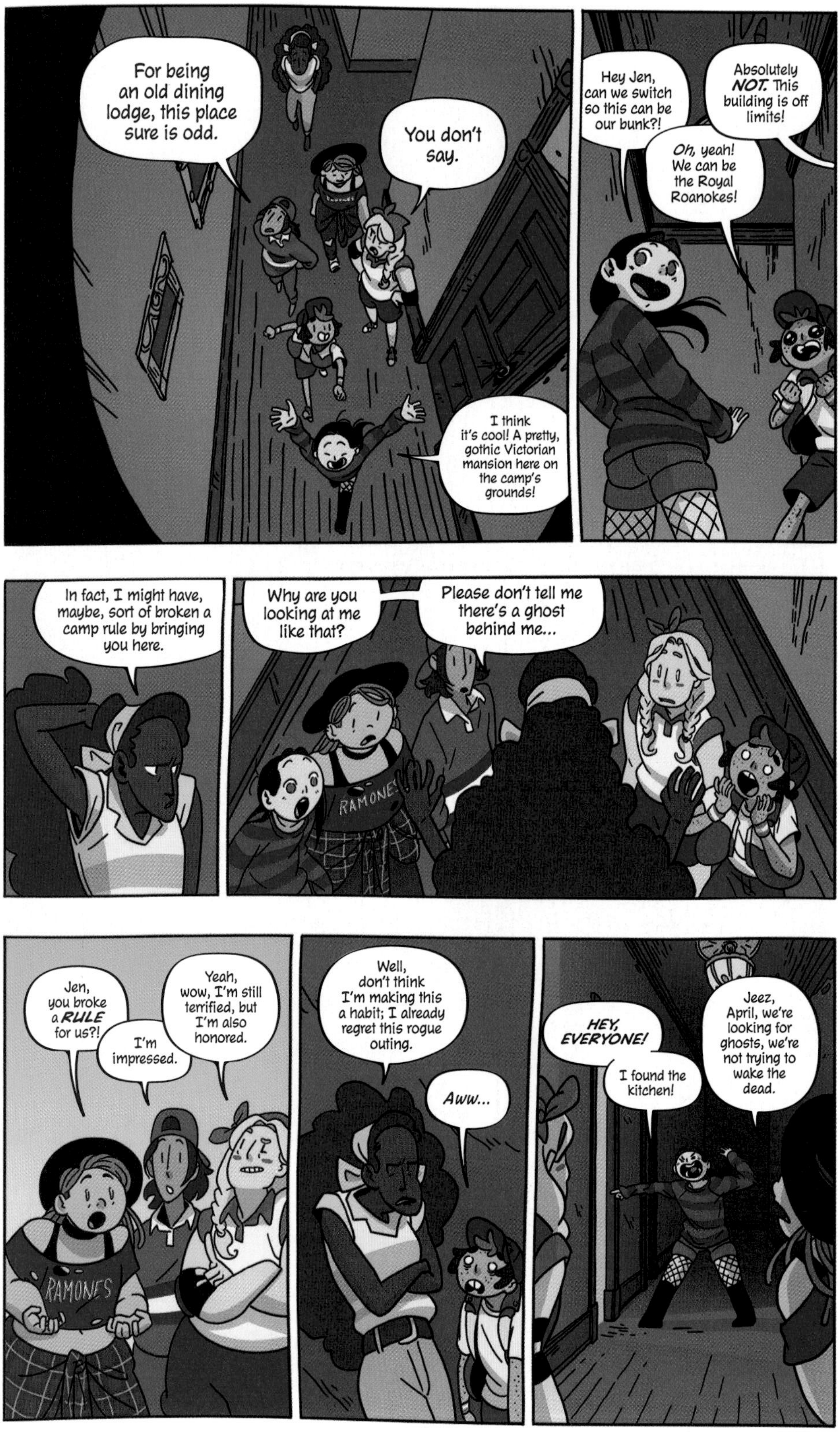
For being an old dining lodge, this place sure is odd.
You don't say.
I think it's cool! A pretty, gothic Victorian mansion here on the camp's grounds!
Hey Jen, can we switch so this can be our bunk?!
Absolutely NOT. This building is off limits!
Oh, yeah! We can be the Royal Roanokes!
In fact, I might have, maybe, sort of broken a camp rule by bringing you here.
Why are you looking at me like that?
Please don't tell me there's a ghost behind me...
RAMONES
Jen, you broke a RULE for us?!
I'm impressed.
Yeah, wow, I'm still terrified, but I'm also honored.
RAMONES
Well, don't think I'm making this a habit; I already regret this rogue outing.
Aww...
HEY, EVERYONE!
I found the kitchen!
Jeez, April, we're looking for ghosts, we're not trying to wake the dead.

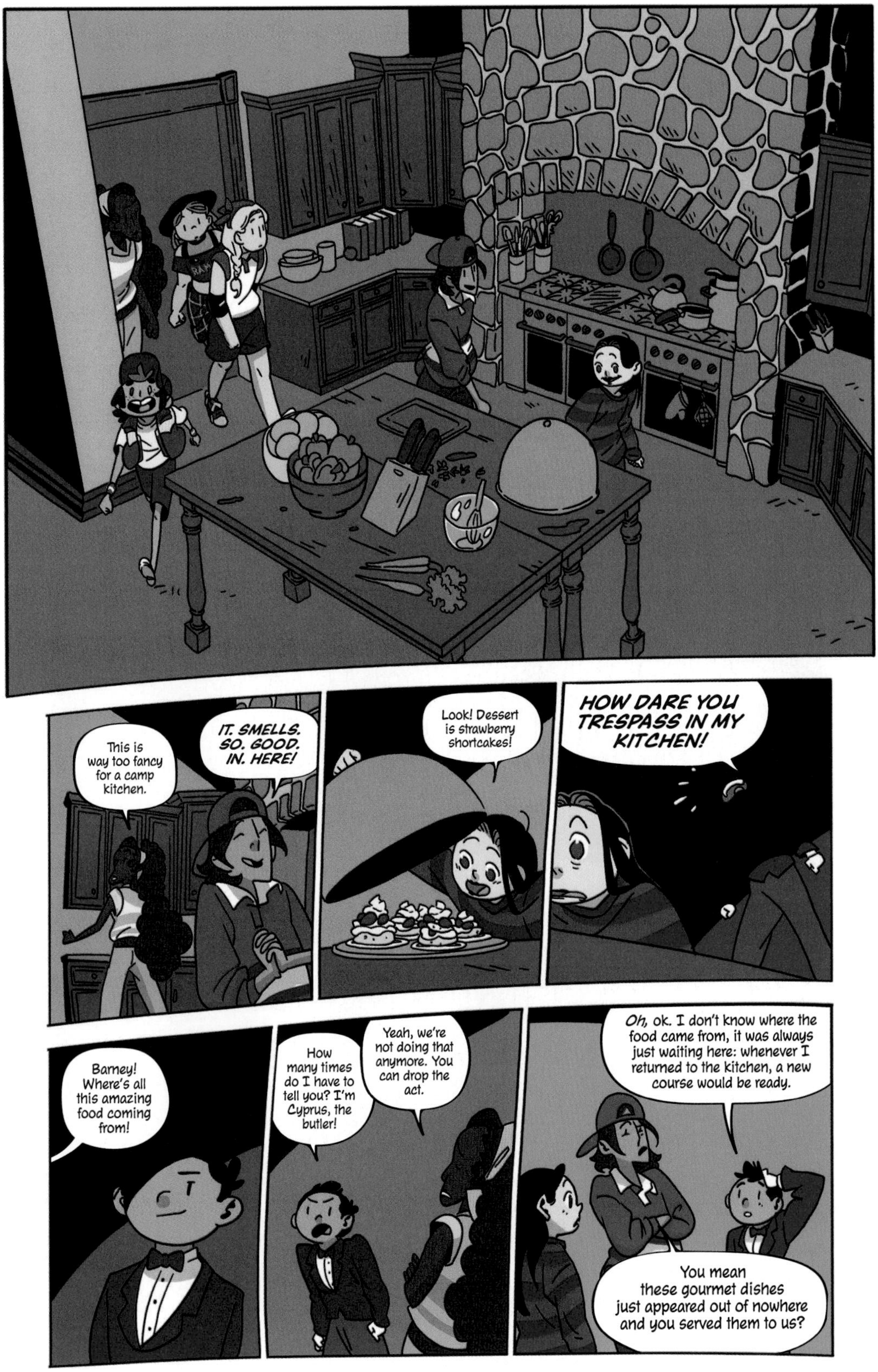
This is way too fancy for a camp kitchen.
IT. SMELLS. SO. GOOD. IN. HERE!
Look! Dessert is strawberry shortcakes!
HOW DARE YOU TRESPASS IN MY KITCHEN!
Barney! Where's all this amazing food coming from!
How many times do I have to tell you? I'm Cyprus, the butler!
Yeah, we're not doing that anymore. You can drop the act.
Oh, ok. I don't know where the food came from, it was always just waiting here: whenever I returned to the kitchen, a new course would be ready.
You mean these gourmet dishes just appeared out of nowhere and you served them to us?

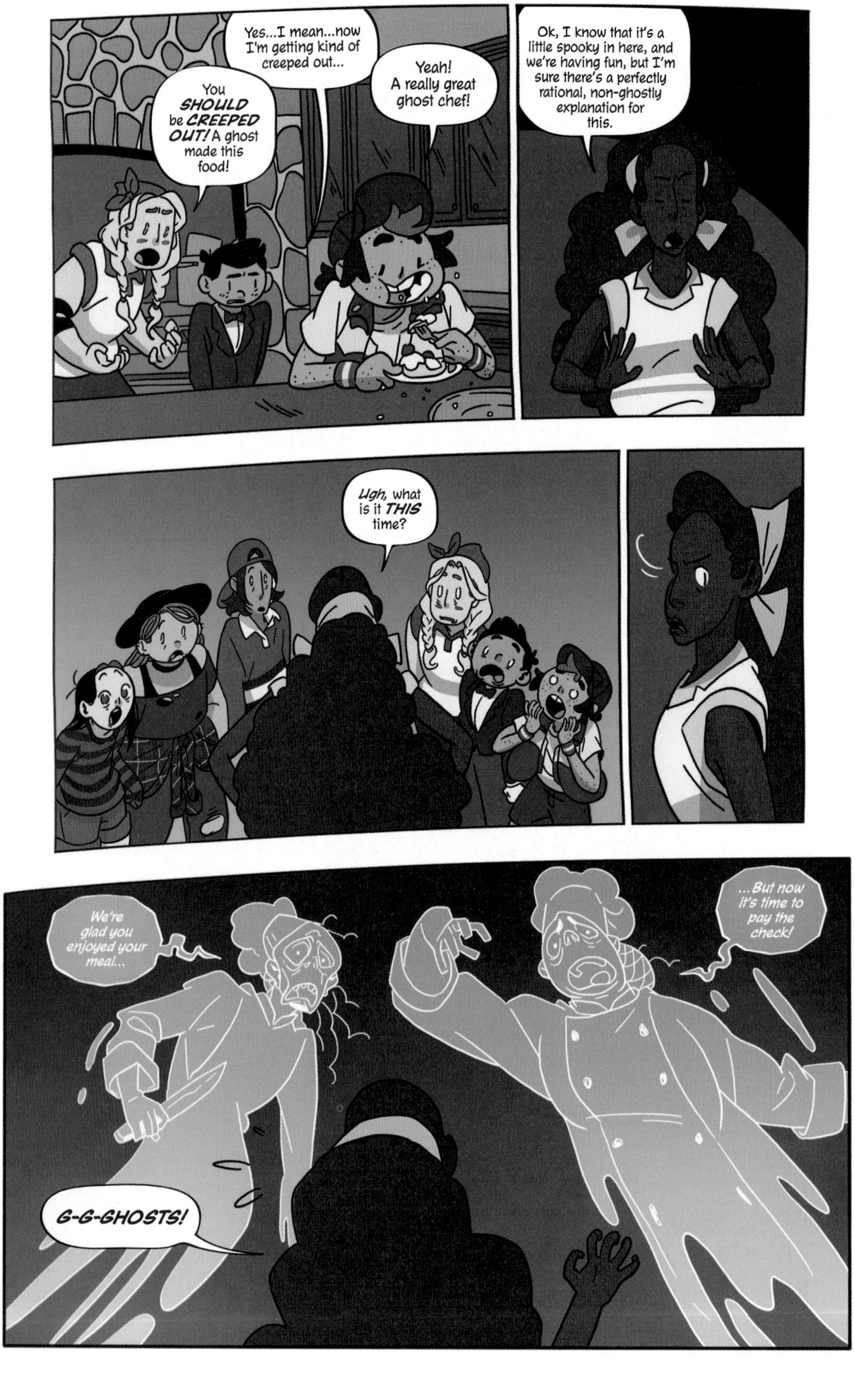
You SHOULD be CREEPED OUT! A ghost made this food!
Yes...I mean...now I'm getting kind of creeped out...
Yeah! A really great ghost chef!
Ok, I know that it's a little spooky in here, and we're having fun, but I'm sure there's a perfectly rational, non-ghostly explanation for this.
Ugh, what is it THIS time?
We're glad you enjoyed your meal...
...But now it's time to pay the check!
G-G-GHOSTS!

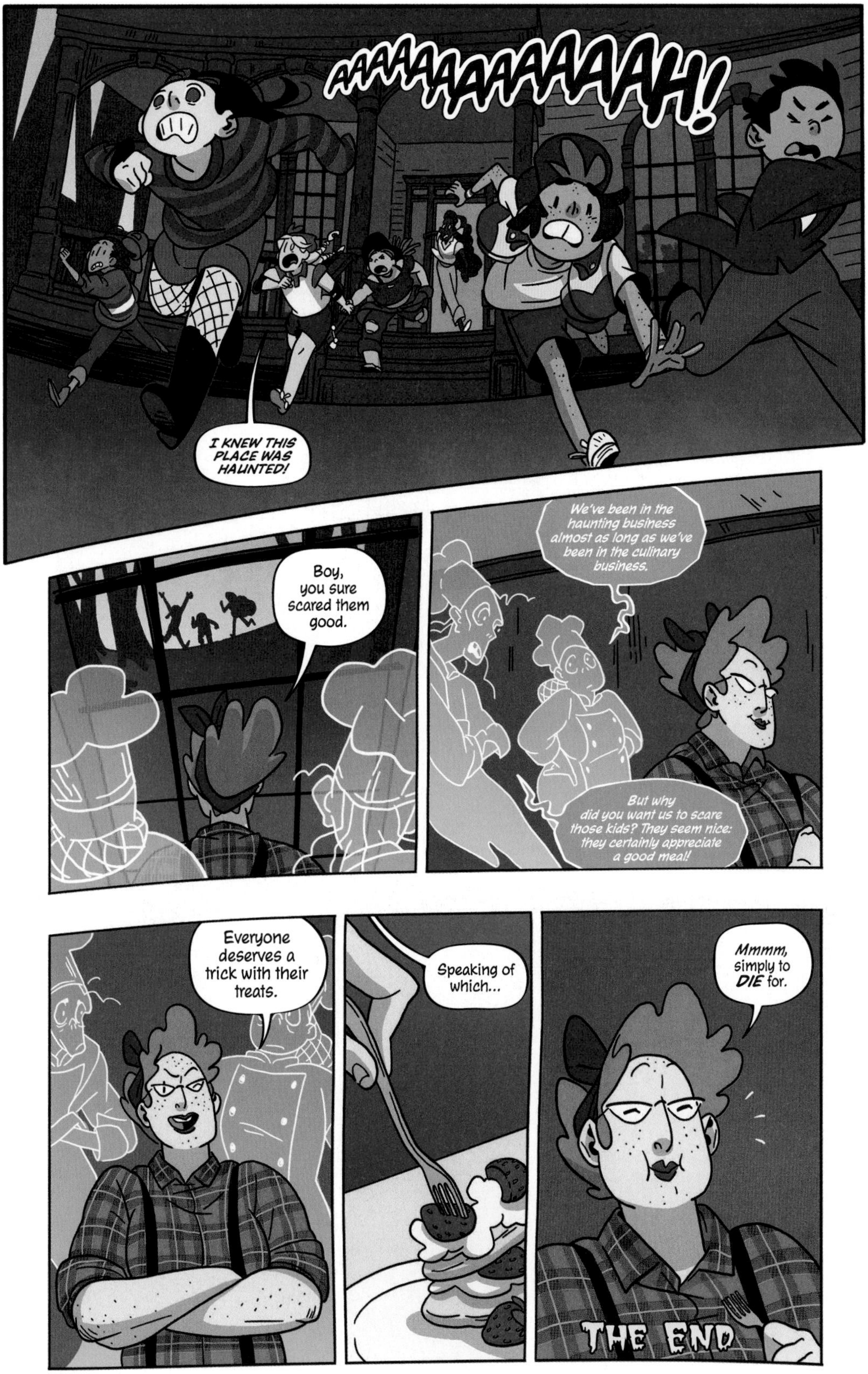
AAAAAAAAAAAAH!
I KNEW THIS PLACE WAS HAUNTED!
Boy, you sure scared them good.
We've been in the haunting business almost as long as we've been in the culinary business.
But why did you want us to scare those kids? They seem nice: they certainly appreciate a good meal!
Everyone deserves a trick with their treats.
Speaking of which...
Mmmm, simply to DIE for.
THE END

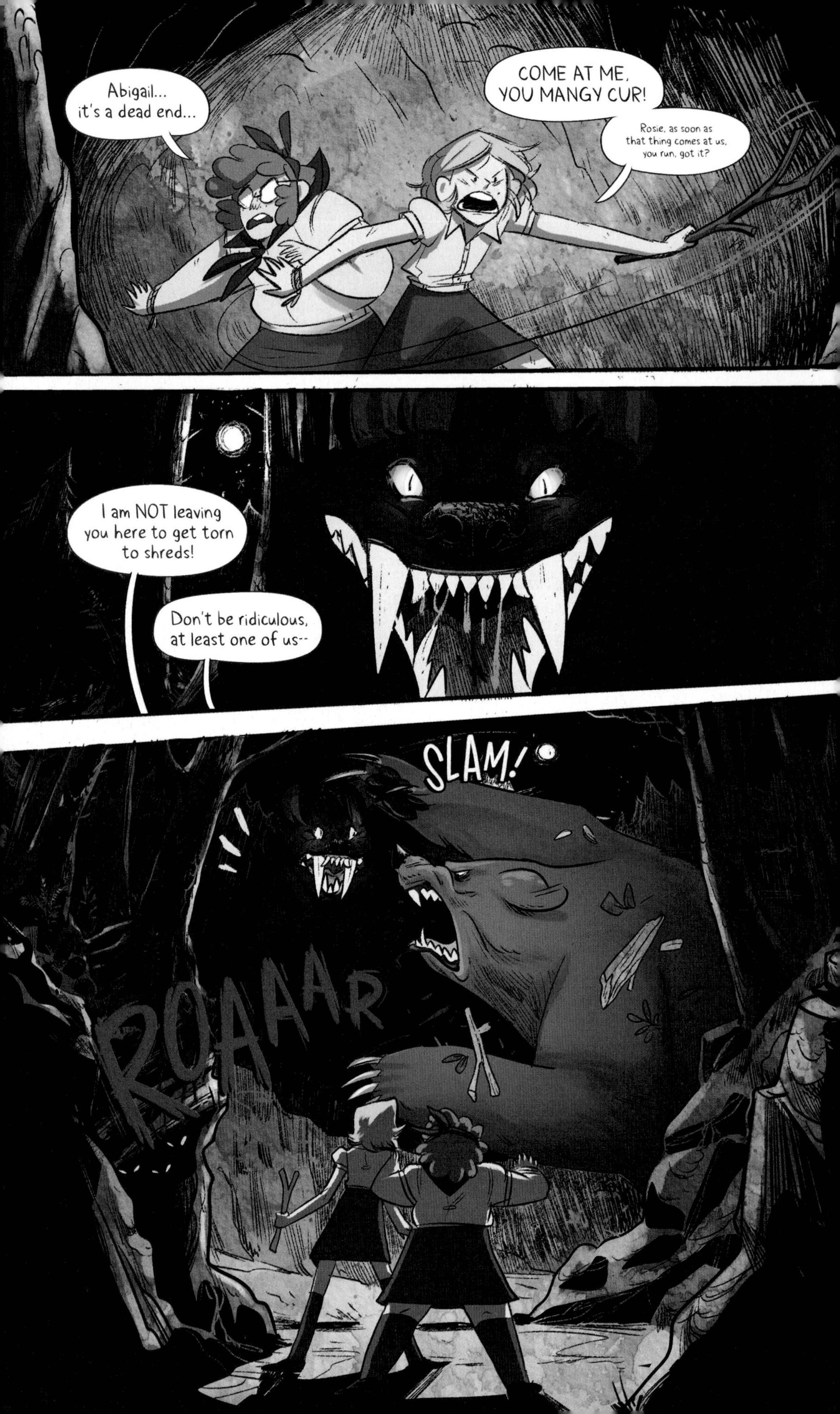
Abigail...
it's a dead end...
COME AT ME,
YOU MANGY CUR!
Rosie, as soon as that thing comes at us, you run, got it?
I am NOT leaving you here to get torn to shreds!
Don't be ridiculous, at least one of us--
SLAM!
ROAAAR

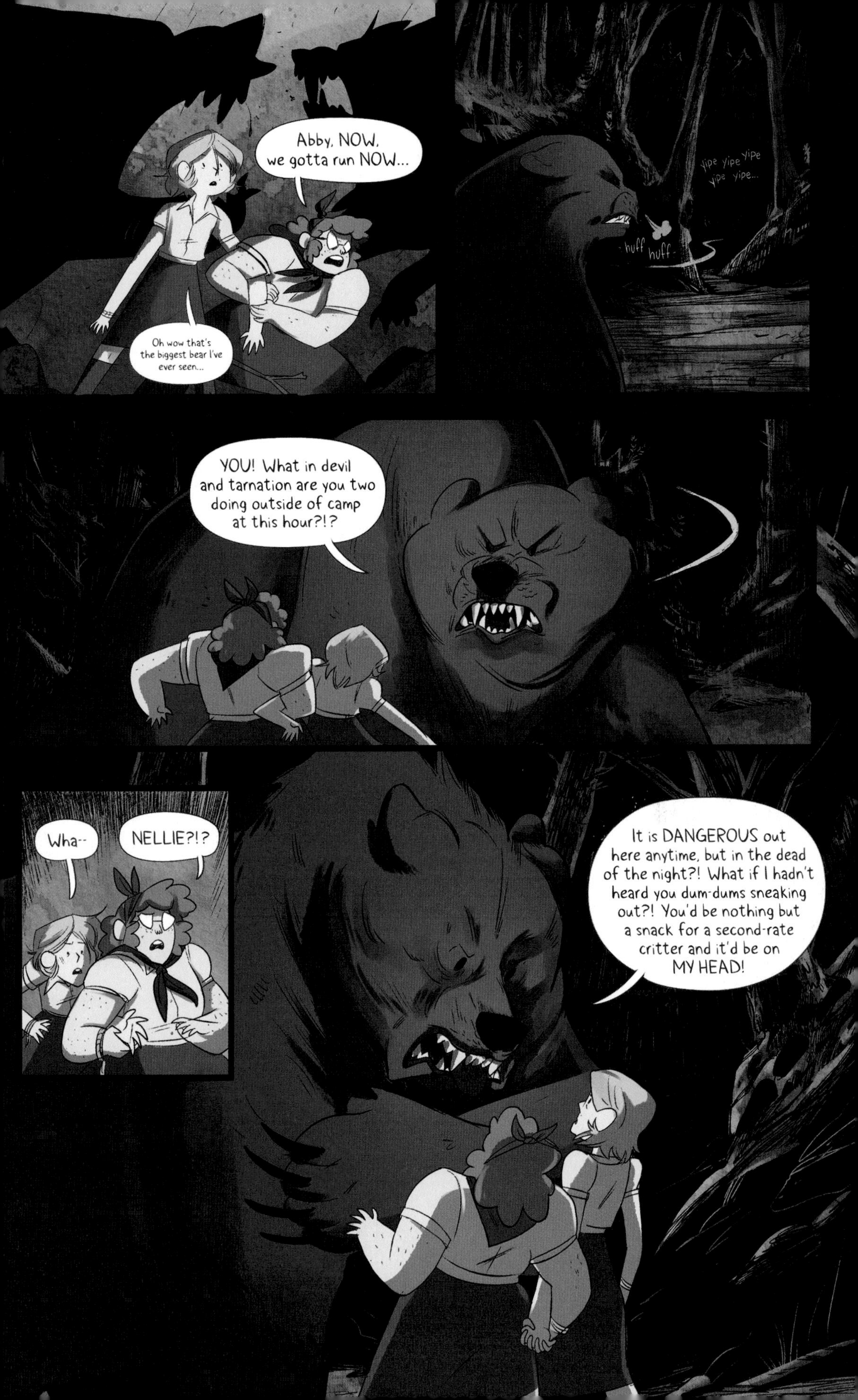
Abby, NOW, we gotta run NOW...
Oh wow that's the biggest bear I've ever seen...
yipe yipe yipe yipe yipe...
huff huff
YOU! What in devil and tarnation are you two doing outside of camp at this hour?!?
Wha--
NELLIE?!?
It is DANGEROUS out here anytime, but in the dead of the night?! What if I hadn't heard you dum-dums sneaking out?! You'd be nothing but a snack for a second-rate critter and it'd be on MY HEAD!

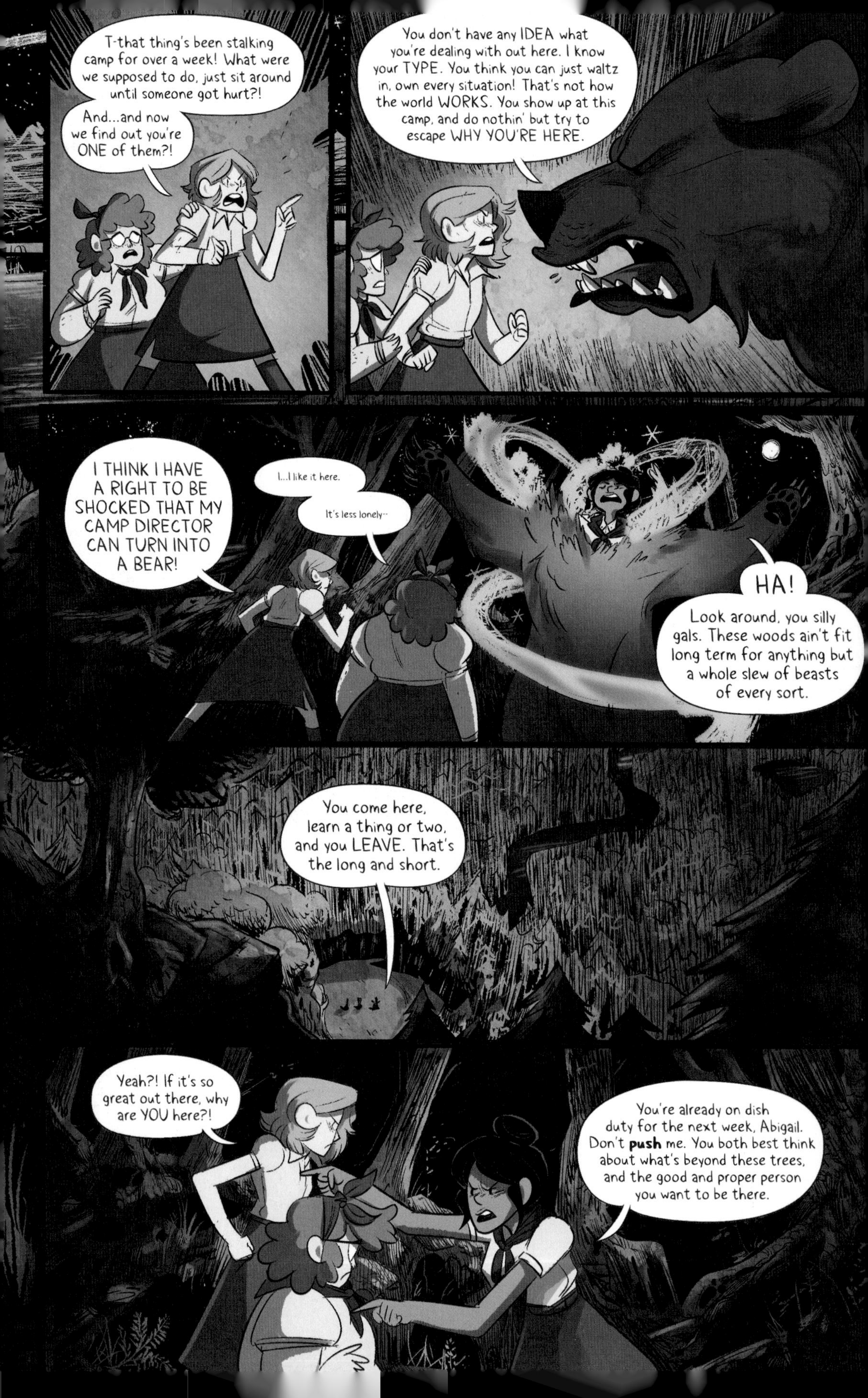
T-that thing's been stalking camp for over a week! What were we supposed to do, just sit around until someone got hurt?!
And...and now we find out you're ONE of them?!
You don't have any IDEA what you're dealing with out here. I know your TYPE. You think you can just waltz in, own every situation! That's not how the world WORKS. You show up at this camp, and do nothin' but try to escape WHY YOU'RE HERE.
I THINK I HAVE A RIGHT TO BE SHOCKED THAT MY CAMP DIRECTOR CAN TURN INTO A BEAR!
I...I like it here.
It's less lonely--
HA!
Look around, you silly gals. These woods ain't fit long term for anything but a whole slew of beasts of every sort.
You come here, learn a thing or two, and you LEAVE. That's the long and short.
Yeah?! If it's so great out there, why are YOU here?!
You're already on dish duty for the next week, Abigail. Don't **push** me. You both best think about what's beyond these trees, and the good and proper person you want to be there.

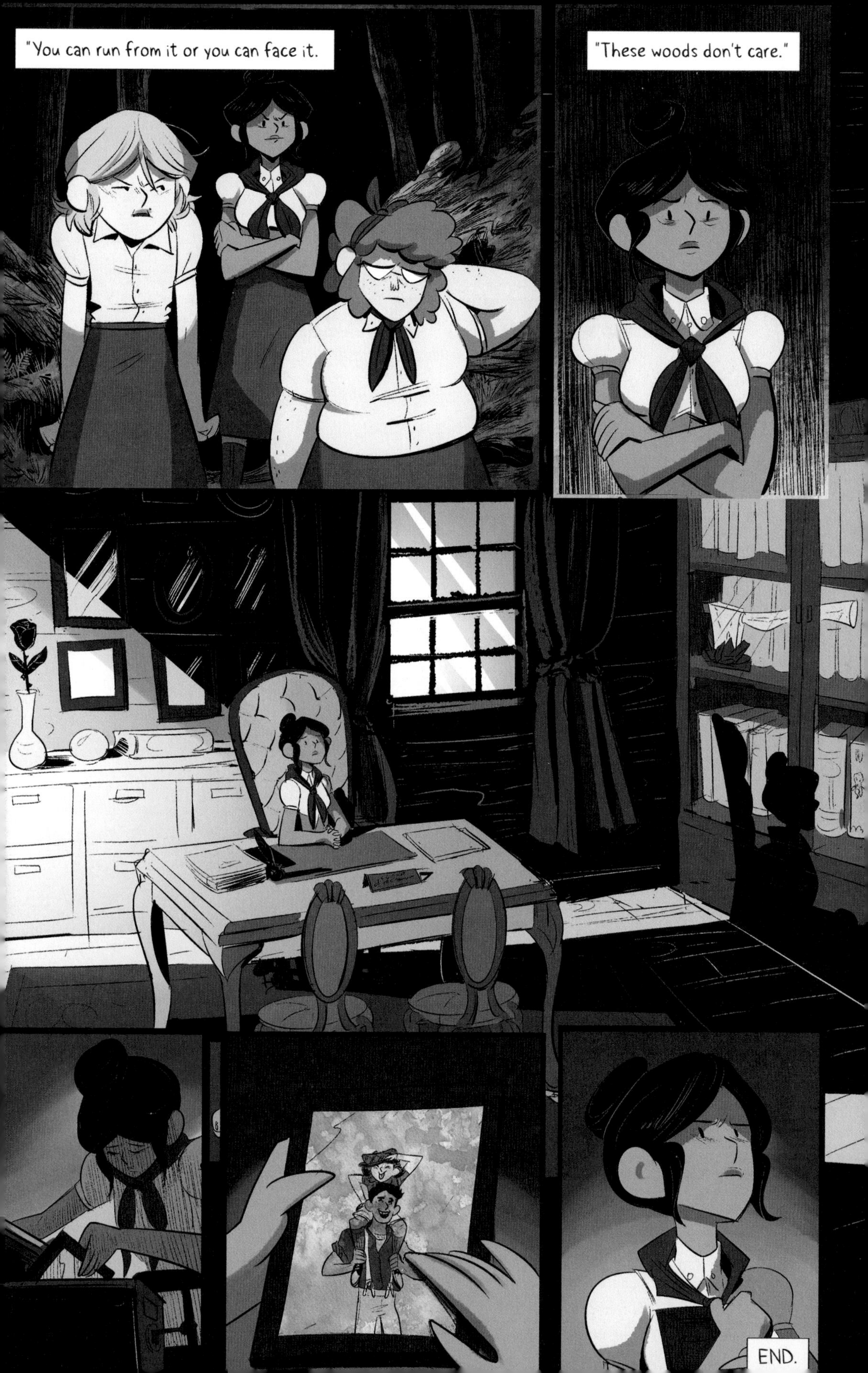

"You can run from it or you can face it.
"These woods don't care."
END.

COVER GALLERY

Lumberjanes "Heart to Heart" Program Field

A MIDSUMMER NIGHT'S SCHEME

"Mask and you shall receive."

At the peak of summer, when the days are as long as they get, and the nights blink past in a morass of mosquitos biting, fireflies alighting, and crickets chirping, there is a special kind of magic in the humid air. A sense of possibility and potentiality, of freedom and frolicsomeness. Perhaps it is just that in these moments, children are free from obligations: free from books and schoolrooms, free to explore and delight in what they will. Or perhaps there really is a particularly exciting energy to the warmer months of the year, which draws a Lumberjane scout toward adventure! There is so much to be done while the sun is still out, and so many avenues to explore while we can.

Actions are important, but plans are, too. Most people find they lean toward one or the other—either acting before they think, or looking before they leap. Whether you're a planner or a dreamer, an improviser or a schemer, you likely have things you want to change in your life and in your world, both big and small. Are there stories you want to tell, things you want to make, games you want to play? What about larger impacts you want to have on your environment, your school, or your family? What can you do to make things happen, or to start a change? How can you work with your friends to create something—to plant a garden, or build a building? To plan for the future, or to put together a project for right now? Right now, while the summer heat is blaring, and you have time to create something together.

A Midsummer Night's Scheme Cover
NATACHA BUSTOS

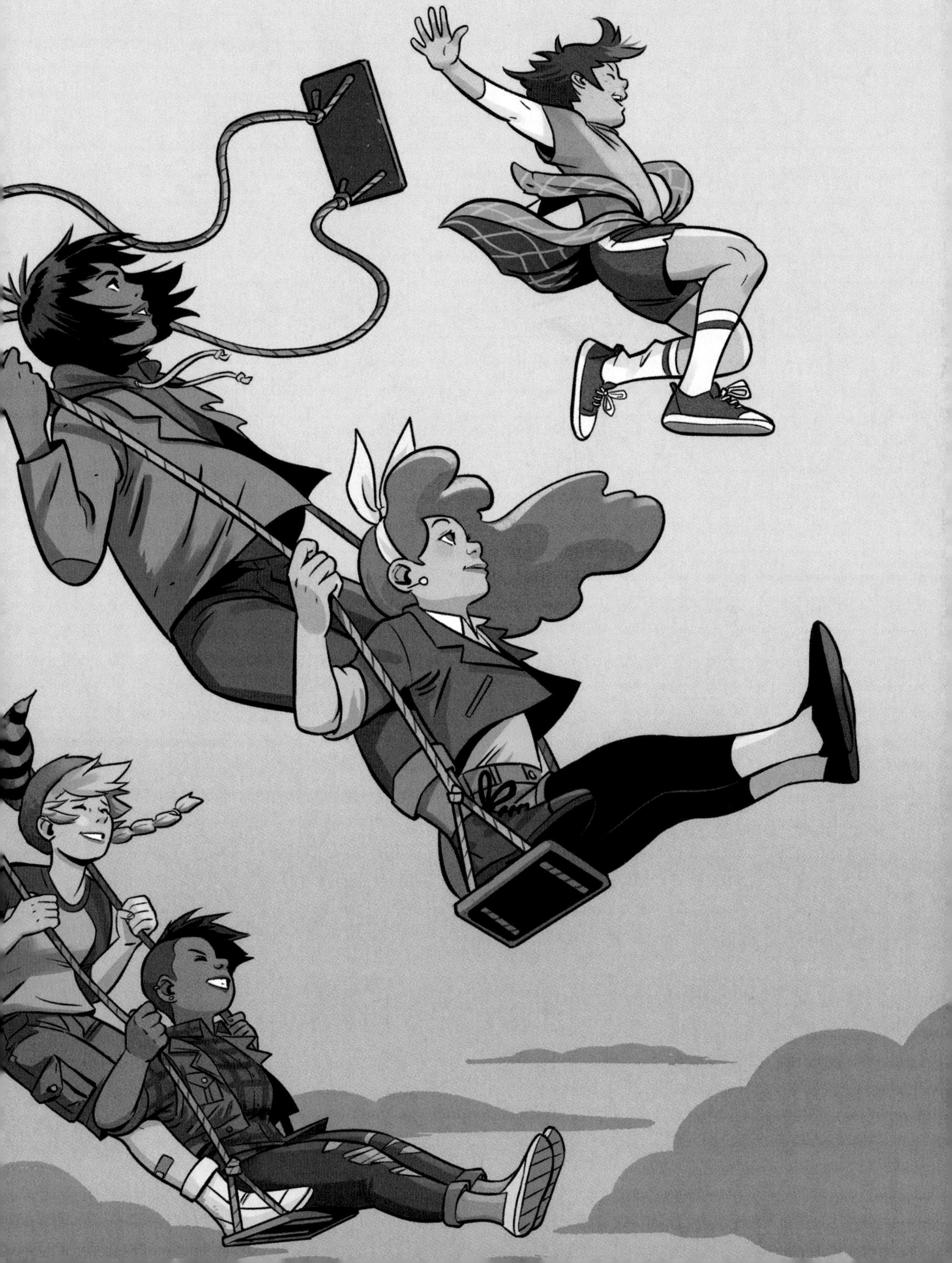

A Midsummer Night's Scheme Preorder Cover
BRITTNEY WILLIAMS

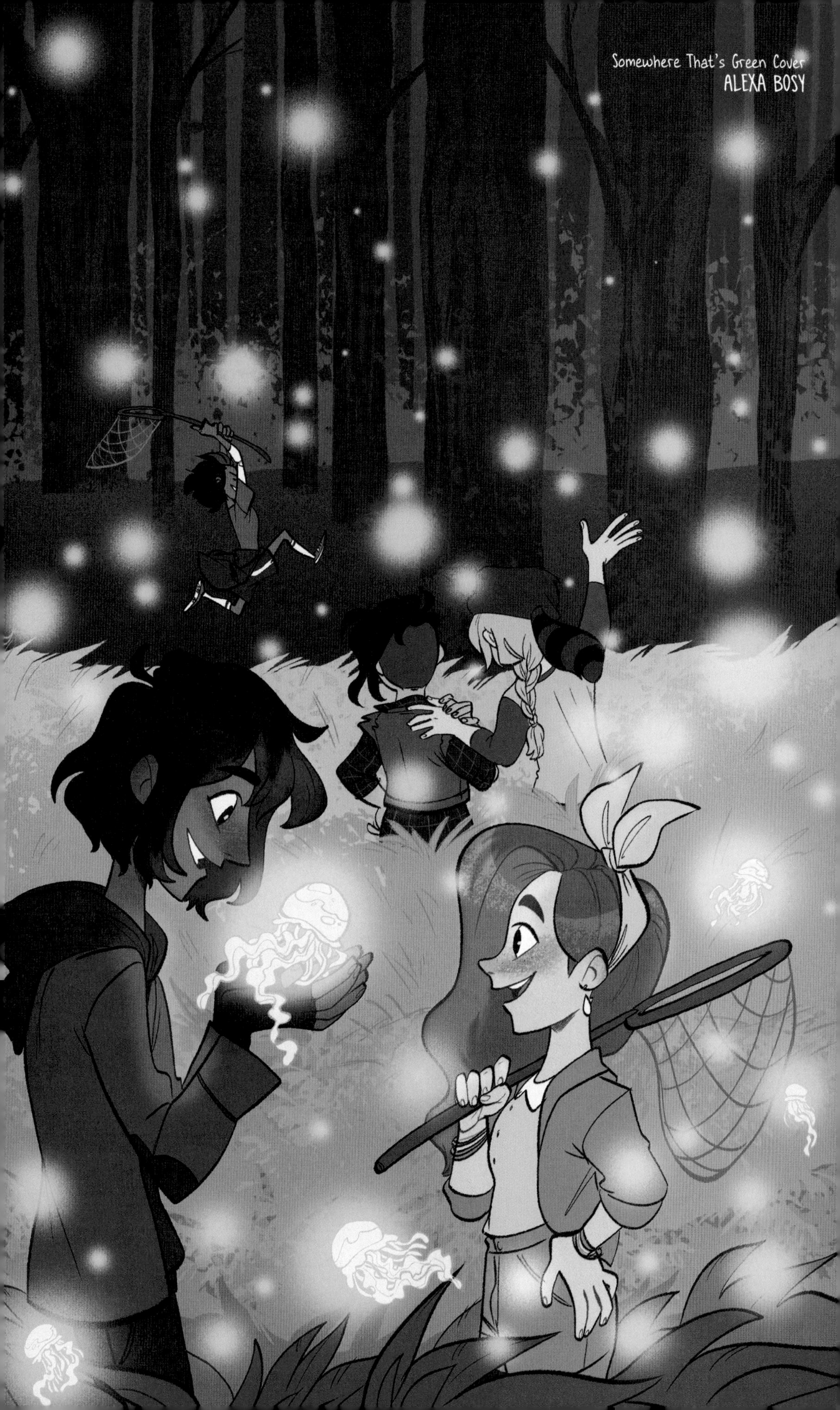

Somewhere That's Green Cover
ALEXA BOSY

Somewhere That's Green Preorder Cover
VERONICA FISH

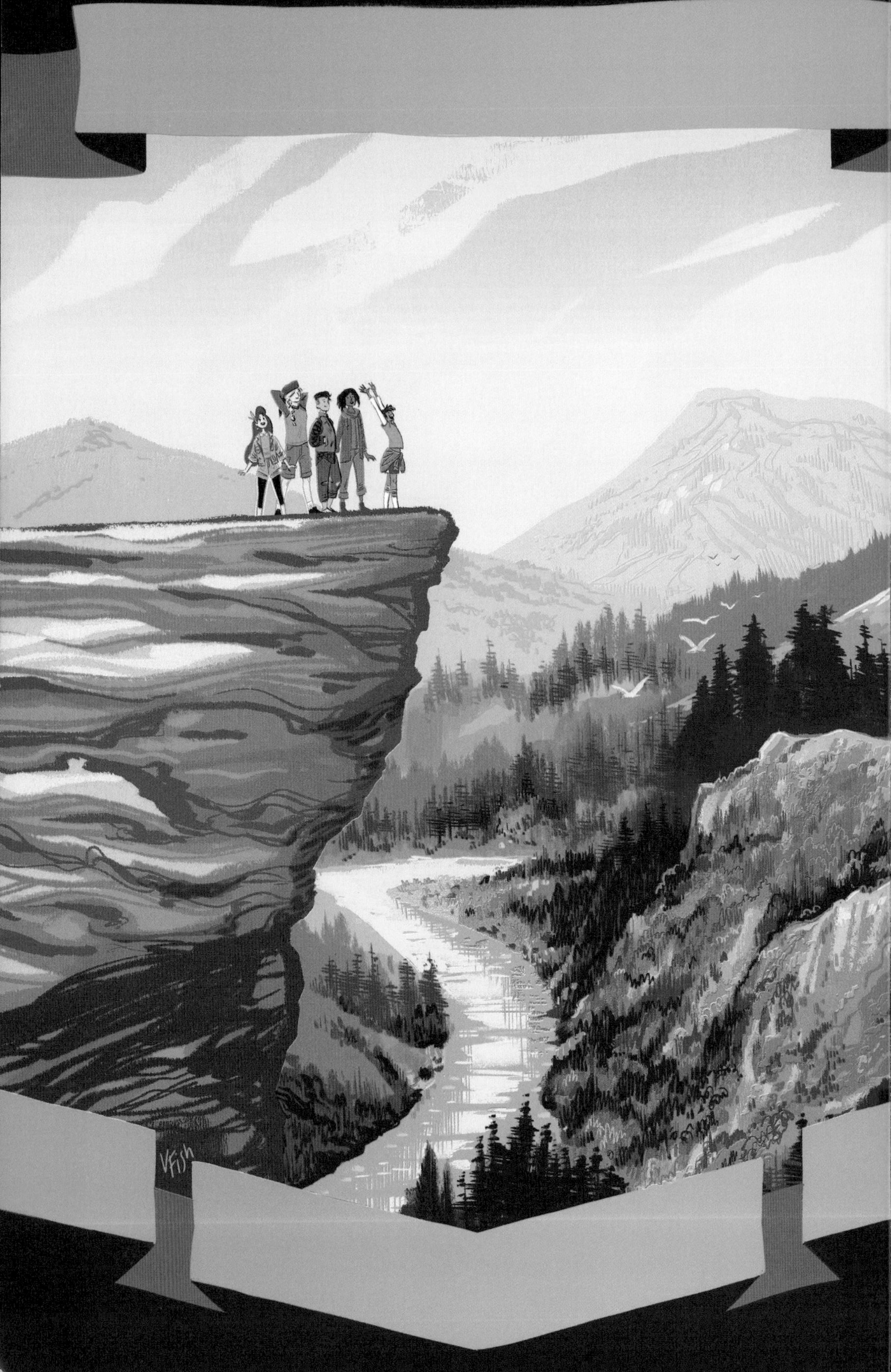
VFish

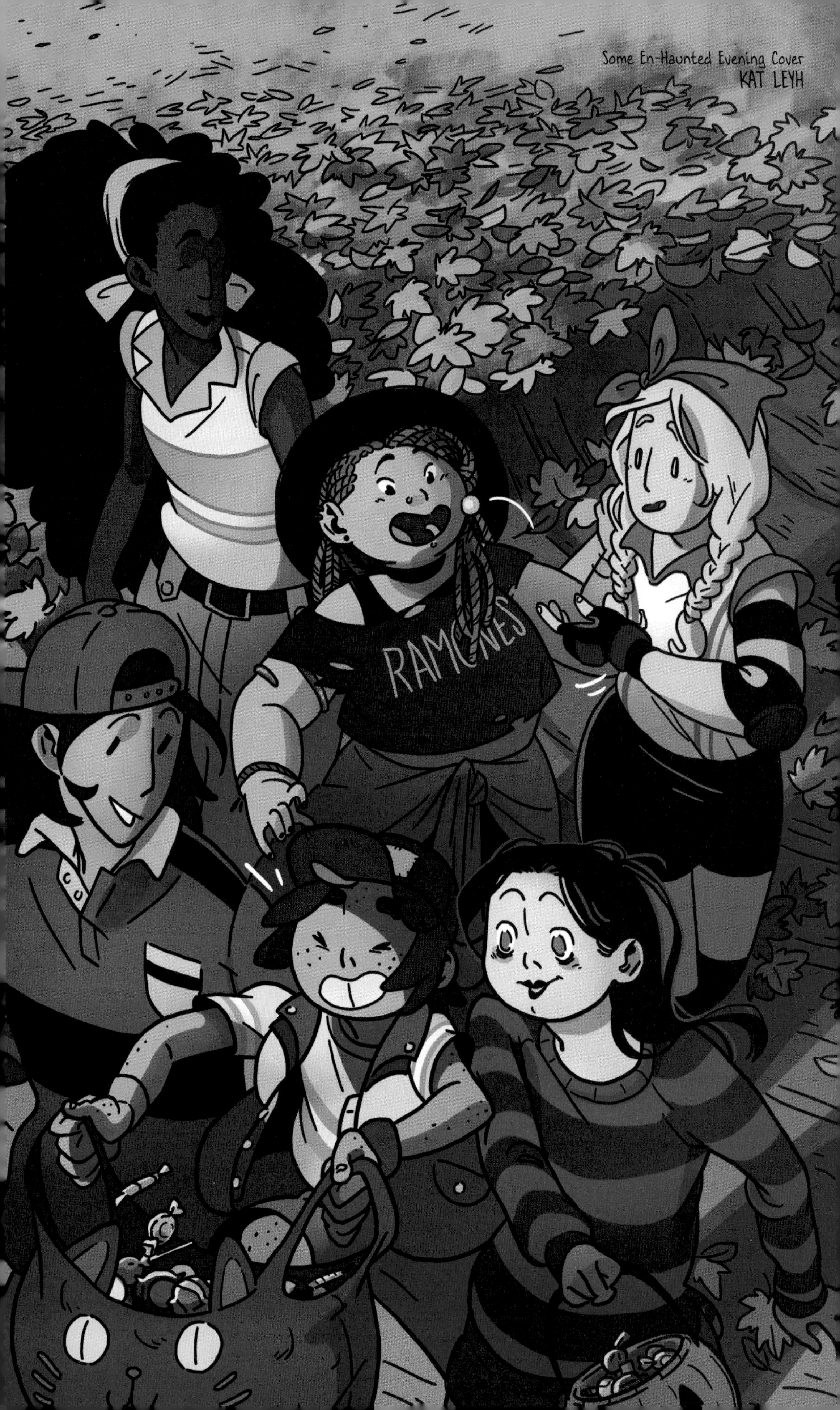
RAMONES

Some En-Haunted Evening Cover
KAT LEYH

DISCOVER
ALL THE HITS

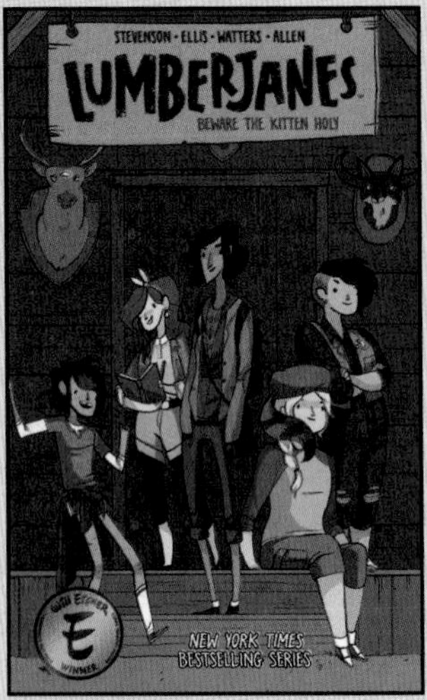
STEVENSON · ELLIS · WATTERS · ALLEN
LUMBERJANES
BEWARE THE KITTEN HOLY
NEW YORK TIMES BESTSELLING SERIES

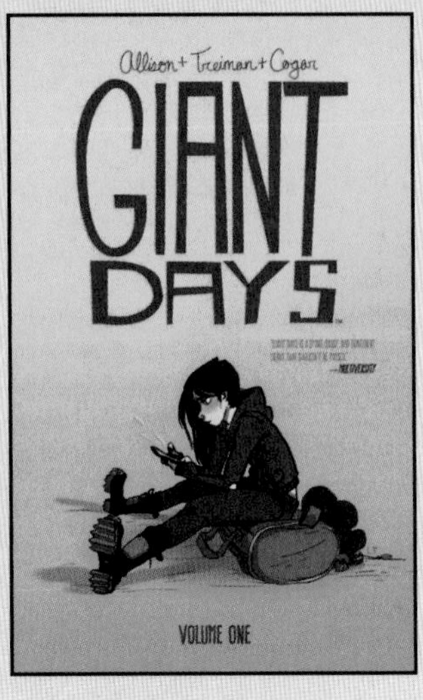
Allison + Treiman + Cogar
GIANT DAYS
VOLUME ONE

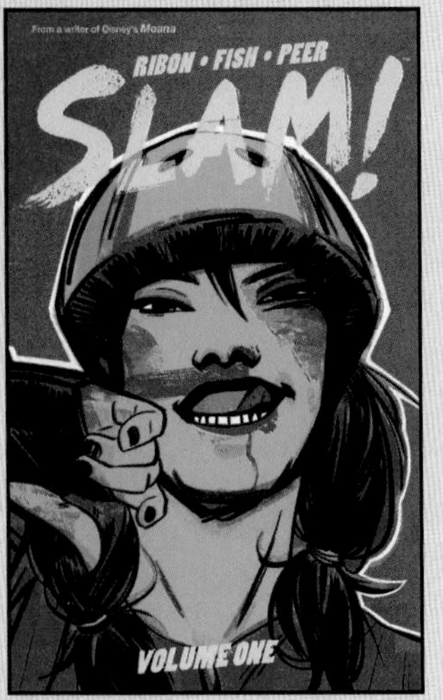
RIBON • FISH • PEER
SLAM!
VOLUME ONE

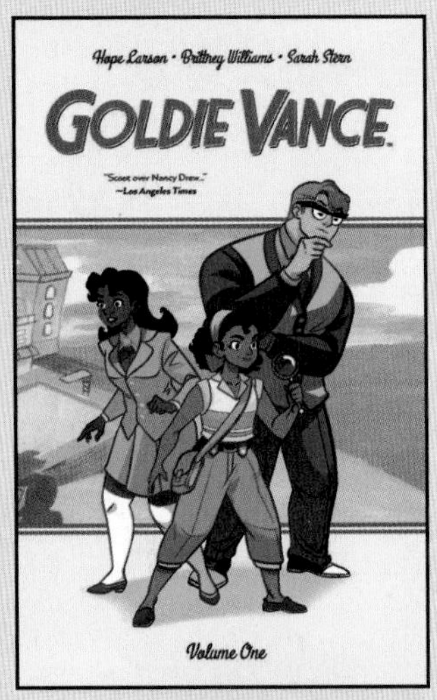
Hope Larson • Brittney Williams • Sarah Stern
GOLDIE VANCE
Volume One

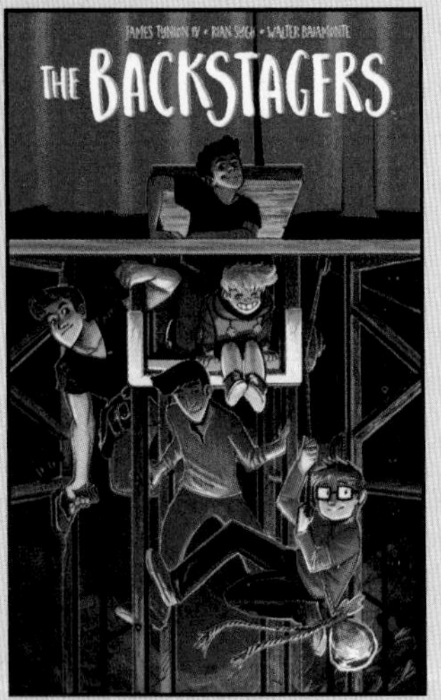
THE BACKSTAGERS

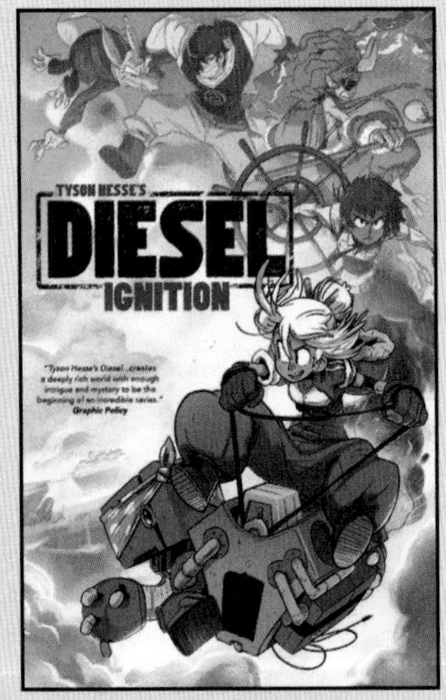
TYSON HESSE'S
DIESEL
IGNITION

BOOM! BOX™

AVAILABLE AT YOUR LOCAL COMICS SHOP AND BOOKSTORE

To find a comics shop in your area, visit www.comicshoplocator.com

WWW.**BOOM-STUDIOS**.COM

Lumberjanes
Noelle Stevenson, Shannon Watters, Grace Ellis, Brooklyn Allen, and Others

Volume 1: Beware the Kitten Holy
ISBN: 978-1-60886-687-8 | $14.99 US
Volume 2: Friendship to the Max
ISBN: 978-1-60886-737-0 | $14.99 US
Volume 3: A Terrible Plan
ISBN: 978-1-60886-803-2 | $14.99 US
Volume 4: Out of Time
ISBN: 978-1-60886-860-5 | $14.99 US
Volume 5: Band Together
ISBN: 978-1-60886-919-0 | $14.99 US

Giant Days
John Allison, Lissa Treiman, Max Sarin

Volume 1
ISBN: 978-1-60886-789-9 | $9.99 US
Volume 2
ISBN: 978-1-60886-804-9 | $14.99 US
Volume 3
ISBN: 978-1-60886-851-3 | $14.99 US

Jonesy
Sam Humphries, Caitlin Rose Boyle

Volume 1
ISBN: 978-1-60886-883-4 | $9.99 US
Volume 2
ISBN: 978-1-60886-999-2 | $14.99 US

Slam!
Pamela Ribon, Veronica Fish, Brittany Peer

Volume 1
ISBN: 978-1-68415-004-5 | $14.99 US

Goldie Vance
Hope Larson, Brittney Williams

Volume 1
ISBN: 978-1-60886-898-8 | $9.99 US
Volume 2
ISBN: 978-1-60886-974-9 | $14.99 US

The Backstagers
James Tynion IV, Rian Sygh

Volume 1
ISBN: 978-1-60886-993-0 | $14.99 US

Tyson Hesse's Diesel: Ignition
Tyson Hesse

ISBN: 978-1-60886-907-7 | $14.99 US

Coady & The Creepies
Liz Prince, Amanda Kirk, Hannah Fisher

ISBN: 978-1-68415-029-8 | $14.99 US